Nobel Quotes

智慧＋詞彙，一本就搞定！

詹森 著

用諾貝爾金句拯救你的破英文！

引言有力、句式漂亮、想法深刻，三個願望一本搞定！

名人金句當範例，諾貝爾大咖幫你開場白！

中英對照超貼心，優雅詞句不再只是考卷裝飾

靈感卡關？翻一頁就有英文神助攻，英文作文不必再苦惱！

目 錄

■ 編譯說明　　　　　　　　　　　　　　　　　　　　　005

■ 1901–1910 啟蒙與創見　　　　　　　　　　　　　　007

■ 1911–1920 動盪中的信念　　　　　　　　　　　　　047

■ 1921–1930 思想的交鋒　　　　　　　　　　　　　　073

■ 1931–1939 黑暗時代的堅持　　　　　　　　　　　　109

■ 1943–1950 重建與省思　　　　　　　　　　　　　　147

■ 1951–1960 科學與人文的對話　　　　　　　　　　　177

■ 1961–1970 革新與抗爭　　　　　　　　　　　　　　245

■ 1971–1980 理性與良知的碰撞　　　　　　　　　　　297

■ 1981–1990 全球視野與道德辯證　　　　　　　　　　383

The Nobel Prizes are much more than awards to scholars; they are a celebration of civilization, of mankind, and of what makes humans unique —— that is their intellect from which springs creativity. (Stanley B. Prusiner)

諾貝爾獎遠非僅為對學者的褒獎,更是對文明、對人類、對人類獨特性來源的頌揚 —— 這來源就是激發創造力的人類智慧。

(史坦利‧布魯希納,1997年諾貝爾生理學或醫學獎得主)

編譯說明

　　阿佛烈·諾貝爾（Alfred Nobel，西元 1833～1896 年），瑞典化學家、工程師和實業家。他獻身科學研究，熱衷技術創新，發明了矽藻土炸藥及其他炸藥。他對人道主義和科學的慈善事業慷慨捐贈，將鉅額財產交付信託，設立了作為國際最高榮譽的諾貝爾獎。

　　諾貝爾獎於 1901 年始，每年由瑞典皇家科學院等 4 個機構頒發。按照諾貝爾遺囑，該獎授予在物理學、化學、生理學或醫學、文學、和平這幾個領域內，「前一年中對人類做出最大貢獻的人」。後又由瑞典央行增設經濟學獎，並於 1969 年起頒發。至 2024 年，不計重複者，共有 976 人及 28 個機構獲獎。

　　此書以有關創新和人生的言論為主題，收集並選譯 962 位獲獎者的 2,800 條語錄，中英對照。它們由近及遠分年度排列，每年又以物理學、化學、生理學或醫學、文學、和平、經濟學諸獎項為序。

　　本書作為語錄集，可以用於雙語閱讀；然而編譯者的本意，是為讀者的學習或研究拓展視野，提供啟迪，從而為科技創新和社會進步一盡綿薄。

編譯說明

1901–1910
啟蒙與創見

1901 年

If the hand be held between the discharge-tube and the screen, the darker shadow of the bones is seen within the slightly dark shadow-image of the hand itself... For brevity's sake I shall use the expression "rays"; and to distinguish them from others of this name I shall call them "X-rays". (Wilhelm Conrad Röntgen)

如果把手放到放電管和螢光幕之間，於手本身的淺色陰影影像中可以看到骨骼的深色陰影。……為了簡便，我將使用「射線」一詞；為了與其他的同名事物區別，我將稱之為「X 射線」。（威廉·倫琴）

A famous name has this peculiarity that it becomes gradually smaller especially in natural sciences where each succeeding discovery invariably overshadows what precedes. (Jacobus Henricus van't Hoff)

顯赫的名字有這種特性：它變得越來越小。尤其在自然科學中，每一項後繼的發現總是掩蓋先前的成就。（雅各布斯·亨里克斯·凡特荷夫）

The fight against cattle tuberculosis only marks a stage on the road which leads finally to the effective protection of human beings against the disease. (Emil Adolf von Behring)

1901-1910 啟蒙與創見

在最終達成有效保護人類免於疾病的征途上,對抗牛型結核病的戰役只是代表了一個階段。(埃米爾·阿道夫·馮·貝林)

The great are only great because we are on our knees. Let us rise up. (Sully Prudhomme)

偉人不過是由於我們跪著而偉大。讓我們站起來。(蘇利·普魯東)

'Tis late; the astronomer in his lonely height

Exploring all the dark, descries from far

Orbs that like distant isles of splendor are,

And mornings whitening in the infinite.…

He summons one disheveled, wandering star, ——

Return ten centuries hence on such a night.

That star will come. It dare not by one hour

Cheat science, or falsify her calculation;

Men will have passed, but watchful in the tower

Man shall remain in sleepless contemplation;

And should all men have perished there in turn,

Truth in their stead would watch that star's return. (Sully Prudhomme)

夜色闌珊,天文學家在大廈上

探望黑暗的空間,辨認遠遠的

星球如眾多閃光的小島一般,

晨光泛白於迢遙的地平線。……

他召喚一顆離群漫遊的星 ——

> 1901 年

一千年後在這樣的夜晚回返。

它會來的。它怎麼敢矇騙科學

一小時，或推翻科學的計算。

眾人會走開，大廈上警覺的人

則只會凝神靜氣而通宵不眠。

即便所有的人從此一睡不醒，

事實也會代為見證這次迴轉。（蘇利·普魯東）

Would it not be possible, in time of peace and quiet, to form relief societies for the purpose of having care given to the wounded in wartime by zealous, devoted and thoroughly qualified volunteers? (Jean Henry Dunant)

莫非在和平年代建立救助團體，由熱心奉獻並訓練有素的志工們來照顧戰爭時期的傷者，是不可能的嗎？（亨利·杜南[01]）

Individual liberty, the sacred character of human life, the inviolability of conscience, respect for work, property, and trade became dogmas for me. (Frédéric Passy)

個人自由、人類生命的神聖性、良知的不可侵犯，以及對工作、財產和貿易的尊重，是為我的信條。（弗雷德里克·帕西）

---

[01] 杜南，紅十字會創始人，與帕西同獲第一屆諾貝爾和平獎。

1901–1910 啟蒙與創見

1902 年

It is comprehensible that a person could not have arrived at such a far-reaching change of view by continuing to follow the old beaten paths, but only by introducing some sort of new idea. (Hendrik Antoon Lorentz)

可以理解，人要達成如此深遠的觀念改變，不可能經由繼續遵循別人走慣的老路，而只能透過引進某種新的想法。（亨德里克‧勞侖茲）

I count myself fortunate to be able to contribute to this work; and the great interest which the Royal Swedish Academy of Sciences has shown in my work and the recognition that it has paid to my past successes, convince me that I am not on the wrong track. (Pieter Zeeman)

能夠為這一項工作做出貢獻，我認為自己十分幸運。瑞典皇家科學院對我的工作所表示的極大興趣，以及對我以往成就所給予的認可，使我相信自己沒有走錯路。（彼得‧塞曼）

You are urgently warned against allowing yourself to be influenced in any way by theories or by other preconceived notions in the observation of phenomena, the performance of analyses and other determinations. (Hermann Emil Fischer)

緊急警告：在觀察現象、著手分析和其他測定時，切勿讓自己以任何方式受到各種理論或其他既有觀念的影響。（赫爾曼‧埃米爾‧費雪）

The work… was… so blinding that I could scarcely see afterwards, and the difficulty was increased by the fact that my microscope was almost worn out, the screws being rusted with sweat from my hands and forehead, and my only remaining eye-piece being cracked… Fortunately invaluable oil-immersion object-glass remained good. (Ronald Ross)

這一項工作……是……如此眩目，事後我簡直喪失了視力。實際情況更是難上加難：顯微鏡幾乎老掉了牙，大小螺絲被我雙手和前額的汗水鏽蝕，僅有的目鏡也破裂了。……幸運的是珍貴的油浸物鏡仍保持良好。（羅納德·羅斯）

Gentlemen, I hope you will permit me to utter a personal note. I cannot help comparing the present moment with that when, seven years ago, I commenced the researches for which you have today given me such great honour. I cannot help remembering the dingy little military hospital, the old cracked microscope, and the medicine bottles which constituted all the laboratory and apparatus which I possessed for the purpose of attacking one of the most redoubtable of scientific problems. Today I have received in this most beautiful capital of the north, the most distinguished of all scientific honours from the hand of your king himself. Gentlemen, I can do no more than thank you. (Ronald Ross)

先生們，請允許我表達個人感想。我不禁將此刻與當初相比。七年前，我開始了列位今天給予我莫大榮譽的研究。我不禁想起那所昏暗狹小的軍用醫院，那架陳舊破損的顯微鏡，以及那些藥瓶，它們就是我擁有的全部實驗室與設備，用於攻克最令人生畏的科學難題之一。今天，我在這個最美麗的北國都城，從你們的國王本人手中接過最著名的科學獎項。先生們，我所能做的只有感謝諸位。（羅納德·羅斯）

Science is the Differential Calculus of the mind. Art the Integral Calculus; they may be beautiful when apart, but are greatest only when combined. (Ronald Ross)

1901-1910 啟蒙與創見

科學是心智的微分學。藝術是積分學。它們在分開時可能是美麗的，然而只有在結合時才是最了不起的。（羅納德・羅斯）

Mankind have infinite difficulty in reaching new creations, and therefore cherish the once developed forms as sacred heirlooms. (Christian Matthias Theodor Mommsen)

人類在獲得創新方面有無限困難，所以將一度成熟的形態視為神聖的傳家寶。（特奧多爾・蒙森）

Fate is mightier than genius. (Christian Matthias Theodor Mommsen)

命運比天才更強大。（特奧多爾・蒙森）

Wars, however frequent and destructive they may be, have never been able to kill entirely the intellectual and moral sense which raises man above the beast. (Élie Ducommun)

戰爭，無論它們可能何等頻繁和凶殘，都不曾得以徹底毀滅使人類超越野獸的理智與道德感。（埃利・迪科門）

I am not one of those who laugh at utopias. The utopia of today can become the reality of tomorrow. Utopias are conceived by optimistic logic which regards constant social and political progress as the ultimate goal of human endeavor; pessimism would plunge a hopeless mankind into a fresh cataclysm. (Charles Albert Gobat)

我不是那些嘲笑烏托邦的人之一。今天的烏托邦可以成為明天的現實。烏托邦由樂觀的邏輯所構想，它將社會和政治的不斷進步視為人類努力的終極目標；悲觀主義會使無望的人類陷入新的災難。（夏爾・阿爾貝・戈巴）

1903 年

I have to keep going, as there are always people on my track. I have to publish my present work as rapidly as possible in order to keep in the race. The best sprinters in this road of investigation are Becquerel and the Curies. (Antoine Henri Becquerel)

我必須繼續前進,因為總有人跟隨我的腳步。我必須盡快發表自己目前的成果,以保持競爭力。在這條研究道路上,最好的短跑者是貝克勒和居禮夫婦。(亨利·貝克勒)

Is it right to probe so deeply into Nature's secrets? The question must here be raised whether it will benefit mankind, or whether the knowledge will be harmful. (Pierre Curie)

如此深入地探究大自然的祕密是否正確?在此必須提出的問題是,它對人類是否有益,或者獲得的知識是否有害。(皮耶·居禮)

I am one of those who believe with Nobel that mankind will derive more good than harm from the new discoveries. (Pierre Curie)

我與這些人一樣相信諾貝爾所言,人類將從新發現中更多得益而非受害。(皮耶·居禮)

All my life through, the new sights of Nature made me rejoice like a child. (Marie Curie)

一生中,大自然的各種新景象使我像個孩子似的興高采烈。(瑪麗·居禮[02])

---

[02] 瑪麗·居禮是第一位獲得諾貝爾獎的女性,第一位兩次獲得諾貝爾獎的人,也是迄今唯一不同學科諾貝爾獎的得主。

1901–1910 啟蒙與創見

We must not forget that when radium was discovered no one knew that it would prove useful in hospitals. The work was one of pure science. And this is a proof that scientific work must not be considered from the point of view of the direct usefulness of it. It must be done for itself, for the beauty of science, and then there is always the chance that a scientific discovery may become like the radium a benefit for humanity. (Marie Curie)

我們不可忘記,發現鐳的時候,沒有人知道它會被證實在醫院裡有用。這一項工作屬於純粹的科學。這是一個證明,即科學工作不能從其直接有用性的角度考量。它必須為其本身、為了科學之美而從事,然後總是有機會,科學發現可能像鐳一樣造福於人類。(瑪麗‧居禮)

I am among those who think that science has great beauty. A scientist in his laboratory is not only a technician: he is also a child placed before natural phenomena which impress him like a fairy tale. We should not allow it to be believed that all scientific progress can be reduced to mechanisms, machines, gearings, even though such machinery also has its beauty. Neither do I believe that the spirit of adventure runs any risk of disappearing in our world. If I see anything vital around me, it is precisely that spirit of adventure, which seems indestructible and is akin to curiosity. (Marie Curie)

我屬於認為科學有非凡之美的人。在實驗室裡,科學家不僅是一名技術人員:他還是個孩子,面對著童話般令他印象深刻的自然現象。我們不可聽任人們誤解,以為所有科學進步都可以簡化為機械裝置、機器、齒輪。儘管這些機械也擁有它的優美。我也不相信冒險精神在我們的世界裡有消失的危險。如果我在自己周圍見到什麼十分重要的東西,那就是冒險精神,它似乎是不可磨滅的,近乎好奇心。(瑪麗‧居禮)

1903 年

I tried out various experiments described in treatises on physics and chemistry, and the results were sometimes unexpected. At times, I would be encouraged by a little unhoped-for success; at others, I would be in the deepest despair because of accidents and failures resulting from my inexperience. (Marie Curie)

我嘗試了物理學和化學論著中描述的各種實驗，結果有時是始料不及的。有些時候，我會獲得些許意外成功的鼓舞；另一些時候，由於缺乏經驗所導致的意外和失敗，使我墜入最深的絕望。（瑪麗・居禮）

During the year 1894, Pierre Curie wrote me letters that seem to me admirable in their form. No one of them was very long, for he had the habit of concise expression, but all were written in a spirit of sincerity and with an evident anxiety to make the one he desired as a companion know him as he was. (Marie Curie)

西元 1894 年間[03]，皮耶・居禮寫信給我，我認為它們的可取之處在於表達方式。沒有一封很長，因為他有行文簡潔的習慣，而句句都寫得情真意切，顯然急於使意中人了解他是何等樣人。（瑪麗・居禮）

Sometimes I had to spend a whole day mixing a boiling mass with a heavy iron rod nearly as large as myself. I would be broken with fatigue at the day's end. Other days, on the contrary, the work would be a most minute and delicate fractional crystallization, in the effort to concentrate the radium. (Marie Curie)

有時我不得不花費一整天，使用一根大小與我本身相當的沉重鐵棍，攪拌一鍋煮沸的物質。一天下來，我會疲憊不堪。與之相反，在另

---

[03] 兩人於西元 1895 年結婚。

1901–1910 啟蒙與創見

外的日子裡的工作則是最細微精密的分級結晶，為了盡量地濃縮鐳。[04]（瑪麗・居禮）

I have no dress except the one I wear every day. If you are going to be kind enough to give me one, please let it be practical and dark so that I can put it on afterwards to go to the laboratory. (Marie Curie)

除了每天身上穿著的那件，我沒有其他連身裙了。如果承蒙你的好意送我一件，就以便於工作和深色的為佳，以便我可以穿著去實驗室。（瑪麗・居禮）

I have frequently been questioned, especially by women, of how I could reconcile family life with a scientific career. Well, it has not been easy. (Marie Curie)

我頻繁受到質疑，尤其來自女性，我如何可能兼顧家庭生活與科學事業。沒錯，這一向是不容易的。（瑪麗・居禮）

For the admirable gift of himself, and for the magnificent service he renders humanity, what reward does our society offer the scientist? Have these servants of an idea the necessary means of work? Have they an assured existence, sheltered from care? The example of Pierre Curie, and of others, shows that they have none of these things; and that more often, before they can secure possible working conditions, they have to exhaust their youth and their powers in daily anxieties. Our society, in which reigns an eager desire for riches and luxury, does not understand the value of science. It does not realize that science is a most precious part of its moral patrimony. Nor does it take

---

[04] 瑪麗・居禮死於再生不良性貧血，這是工作中多年暴露於輻射的後果。她於西元 1899 年至 1902 年的實驗室筆記至今仍有放射性，而且將持續 1,500 年之久。

1903 年

sufficient cognizance of the fact that science is at the base of all the progress that lightens the burden of life and lessens its suffering. Neither public powers nor private generosity actually accord to science and to scientists the support and the subsidies indispensable to fully effective work. (Marie Curie)

對於科學家本身的可貴天賦，對於他給予人類的出色貢獻，我們的社會為科學家提供了什麼回報？這些具備智慧的僕人得到了必要的工作手段嗎？他們享有受到保障的生活，免於憂患了嗎？皮耶‧居禮，以及另一些人的例子表明，他們並沒有這些東西；而更為常見的是，在能夠確保可能的工作條件之前，他們不得不在日復一日的焦慮中耗去青春和精力。我們的社會，充斥對財富與奢華的渴求，不理解科學的價值。它沒有意識到，科學是其精神遺產最珍貴的部分。它也沒有充分理解到這一項事實，即科學屬於全部進步的基礎，而進步減輕了生活的負擔，降低了它的痛苦。事實上，無論公共權力還是私人捐贈，都沒有予以科學、予以科學家充分有效工作所必需的支持和補貼。（瑪麗‧居禮）

Humanity needs practical men, who get the most out of their work, and, without forgetting the general good, safeguard their own interests. But humanity also needs dreamers, for whom the disinterested development of an enterprise is so captivating that it becomes impossible for them to devote their care to their own material profit. Without doubt, these dreamers do not deserve wealth, because they do not desire it. Even so, a well-organized society should assure to such workers the efficient means of accomplishing their task, in a life freed from material care and freely consecrated to research. (Marie Curie)

人類需要務實的人，他們從工作中得到最大的滿足，並且，在不忘公共利益的同時，保障自己的利益。然而人類也需要夢想家，對於他

> 1901–1910 啟蒙與創見

們，事業無私的發展如此迷人，而無須一心關注自己的物質收益。不用說，這些夢想家沒必要擁有財富，因為他們不追求它。即便如此，對這樣的工作者，組織良好的社會也應當確保其具備完成任務的有效手段，使其於物質上無憂無慮，如願獻身於研究的生活中。（瑪麗·居禮）

Humanity stands… before a great problem of finding new raw materials and new sources of energy that shall never become exhausted. In the meantime we must not waste what we have, but must leave as much as possible for coming generations. (Svante August Arrhenius)

人類面臨……尋找永不枯竭的新原料和新能源的巨大難題。與此同時，我們斷不可浪費現有的，而必須為後代留下盡可能多的資源。（斯萬特·阿瑞尼斯）

Chemistry works with an enormous number of substances, but cares only for some few of their properties; it is an extensive science. Physics on the other hand works with rather few substances, such as mercury, water, alcohol, glass, air, but analyses the experimental results very thoroughly; it is an intensive science. Physical chemistry is the child of these two sciences; it has inherited the extensive character from chemistry. Upon this depends its all-embracing feature, which has attracted so great admiration. But on the other hand it has its profound quantitative character from the science of physics. (Svante August Arrhenius)

化學研究數量龐大的物質，但只關心它們的少許屬性；它是一門廣博的科學。另一方面，物理學研究很少的物質，如汞、水、酒精、玻璃、空氣，但非常徹底地分析實驗結果，它是一門精深的科學。物理化學是這兩門科學的產物，它繼承了化學的廣博特性。它包羅一切的特點

即基於此，這引來了極大的讚揚。然而另一方面，它深厚的定量特性則出自於物理科學。（斯萬特‧阿瑞尼斯）

The theoretical side of physical chemistry is and will probably remain the dominant one; it is by this peculiarity that it has exerted such a great influence upon the neighboring sciences, pure and applied, and on this ground physical chemistry may be regarded as an excellent school of exact reasoning for all students of the natural sciences. (Svante August Arrhenius)

物理化學的理論方面現在是，且很可能將一直處於主導地位。就是由於這種特性，它對鄰近學科，純粹的和應用的，產生了巨大的影響。因此，可以將物理化學視為所有自然科學學生學習精確推理的極佳課程。（斯萬特‧阿瑞尼斯）

There is no more elevating spectacle than to contemplate the sky with its thousands of stars on a clear night. When we send our thoughts to those lights glittering in infinite distance, the question forces itself upon us, whether there are not out there planets like our own that will sustain organic life. (Svante August Arrhenius)

沒有比凝望繁星萬點的晴朗夜空更引人遐想的景象了。當我們將思緒送往無盡長空中那些閃爍的光點時，一個問題自然湧上心頭：遠方難道沒有與我們類似的星球，能夠維持有機生命嗎？（斯萬特‧阿瑞尼斯）

Thus we now see that from a theoretical viewpoint there is no obstacle to, on the contrary there is every indication in favour of a use of the light in local, external, bacterial skin diseases. (Niels Ryberg Finsen)

於是現在我們得知，光線可用於治療局部、外部、細菌性的皮膚病，從理論角度看沒有障礙，反而有各種跡象支持。（尼爾斯‧呂貝里‧芬森）

1901–1910 啟蒙與創見

A meaningful life —— this is what we look for in art, in its smallest dewdrops as in its unleashing of the tempest. We are at peace when we have found it and uneasy when we have not. (Bjørnstjerne Martinus Bjørnson)

充滿意義的人生 —— 這就是我們在藝術中尋求的東西，在其最細小的露珠中一如在其暴風雨的肆虐之中。找到時我們就心平氣和，找不到時但覺惴惴不安。（比約恩斯徹納‧比昂松）

Travelers anxious to reach their journey's end, occasionally ask themselves how far they have got and how much farther they have to go before they reach the goal of their hopes. The progress they have made can be easily ascertained, but the remaining distance and possible accidents on the way are more difficult to calculate. (William Randal Cremer)

旅行者急於到達行程的終點，間或自問已經走了多遠，或問在抵達所期望的目的地之前還得走多遠。已經獲得的進展可以很容易確定，然而所餘的距離和可能的意外就難於計算得多了。（蘭德爾‧克里默）

1904 年

One's instinct is at first to try and get rid of a discrepancy, but I believe that experience shows such an endeavour to be a mistake. What one ought to do is to magnify a small discrepancy with a view to finding out the explanation. (John William Strutt)

人的本能是首先盡量消除差異。但我認為，經驗顯示這樣的努力是個錯誤。應該做的是放大微小的差異，以便找出解釋。（約翰‧斯特拉特）

1904 年

Nothing can be more certain than this: that we are just beginning to learn something of the wonders of the world on which we live and move and have our being. (William Ramsay)

確定無疑之事莫過於此：這個我們吃住、走動、存在於其中的世界，關於它的各種神奇，我們只是剛開始有所了解。（威廉·拉姆齊）

We have all heard of the puzzle given to Archimedes… His finding that the crown was of gold was a discovery; but he invented the method of determining the density of solids. Indeed, discoverers must generally be inventors; though inventors are not necessarily discoverers. (William Ramsay)

我們都聽說過阿基米德的難題。……他發現了王冠是由金製成，然而他發明了測定固體密度的方法。的確，發現者通常必定是發明家，雖然發明家未必是發現者。（威廉·拉姆齊）

Progress is made by trial and failure; the failures are generally a hundred times more numerous than the successes; yet they are usually left unchronicled. The reason is that the investigator feels that even though he has failed in achieving an expected result, some other more fortunate experimenter may succeed, and it is unwise to discourage his attempts. (William Ramsay)

進步由嘗試與失敗所成就。失敗的次數一般百倍於成功，然而它們通常失於記載。原因在於，研究者認為，雖然自己未能獲得預期結果，然而其他更幸運的實驗者有可能會成功，而干擾其努力是不明智的。（威廉·拉姆齊）

Chemistry and physics are experimental sciences; and those who are engaged in attempting to enlarge the boundaries of science by experiment are generally unwilling to publish speculations; for they have learned, by long experience,

1901-1910 啟蒙與創見

that it is unsafe to anticipate events. It is true, they must make certain theories and hypotheses. They must form some kind of mental picture of the relations between the phenomena which they are trying to investigate, else their experiments would be made at random, and without connection. (William Ramsay)

化學和物理學是實驗科學。那些著手試圖以實驗擴張科學邊界的人通常不願發表推測,因為他們經由長期經驗得知,預測事件是有風險的。的確,他們必須提出一定的理論和假設。他們必須對力圖探究的現象之間的關係形成某種心像,否則實驗就會是隨意進行而毫無連結的。(威廉‧拉姆齊)

Perfect as the wing of a bird may be, it will never enable the bird to fly if unsupported by the air. Facts are the air of science. Without them a man of science can never rise. (Ivan Petrovich Pavlov)

即便鳥翼堪稱完美,如果沒有空氣托舉,鳥也不可能飛翔。事實就是科學的空氣。沒有它們,科學家無法一飛沖天。(伊凡‧巴夫洛夫)

While you are experimenting, do not remain content with the surface of things. (Ivan Petrovich Pavlov)

做實驗的時候,不要一味滿足於了解事物的表面。(伊凡‧巴夫洛夫)

Don't become a mere recorder of facts, but try to penetrate the mystery of their origin. (Ivan Petrovich Pavlov)

不要僅僅成為事實的記錄者,而要盡力探究它們起源的奧祕。(伊凡‧巴夫洛夫)

Trees with deep roots grow tall. (Frédéric Mistral)

根深則樹高。(腓特烈‧密斯特拉)

Each year, the nightingale dresses with new feathers, but it keeps the same song. (Frédéric Mistral)

每一年,夜鶯都會換上新的羽毛,但牠保持同樣的歌聲。(腓特烈·密斯特拉)

Mathematics forms a sauce that goes well with all the stews of the spirit. Harmonize with music and art. (José Echegaray y Eizaguirre)

數學是一種與所有精神菜餚都搭配得宜的醬汁。它與音樂和美術和諧相得。(荷西·伊克格拉)

1905 年

I am pleased to fulfil my obligation as a Nobel Prize winner to talk to you here on cathode rays. I assume that you would prefer me to tell you what others could not tell you. I shall describe to you the development of the subject —— which also embraces recent theories concerning electricity and matter —— as it has appeared to me, on the basis of my own experience. This will give me a welcome opportunity of showing on the one hand how my work has depended on that of others, and on the other how in one or two points subsequent, or more or less contemporary, work by other investigators is related to mine. Thus —— using the simile which you, my esteemed colleagues of the Academy of Sciences, have used at the head of your member's diploma —— I shall now speak not only of the fruits but also of the trees which have borne them, and of those who planted these trees. This approach is the more suitable in my case, as I have by no means always been numbered among those who pluck the fruit; I have been repeatedly only one of those who planted or cared for the trees, or who helped to do this. (Philipp Eduard Anton von Lenard)

我樂於履行諾貝爾獎得主的義務，在這裡與諸位談論陰極射線。我想，你們應該更希望我告訴你們別人講不了的事。我將根據自身經驗，向各位描述這個主題的發展——也包括近期關於電和物質的理論——如我所看見的那般。這將給我一個很好的機會，一方面表明我的工作如何有賴於他人，另一方面表明，其他研究者的工作，在稍後或約略同時，如何與我的相關。因此——借用諸位尊敬的科學院同事，在你們的院士證書開頭的比喻——我現在不僅要談論果實，還要談論結出它們的樹，以及那些種下這些樹的人。這種方式更適合我的情況，因為我很少屬於採摘果子的那些人；我一直只是種植、照顧樹木，或協助做這些事的人之一。（菲利普・萊納德）

Men who are capable of modifying their first beliefs are very rare. This ability was one of the reasons for the success of Claude Bernard and Pasteur. Out of a very vivid imagination they forged new hypotheses all the time but abandoned them with equal ease as soon as experience contradicted them. (Adolf von Baeyer)

能夠修改自己最初信念的人極為罕見。這種能力是克洛德・貝爾納[05]和巴斯德成功的原因之一。他們憑藉著非常生動的想像力不斷提出新的假設，然而一旦經驗與之相左，他們又同樣自如地拋棄它們。（阿道夫・馮・拜爾）

---

[05] 克洛德・貝爾納，法國著名生理學家。

1905 年

If my efforts have led to greater success than usual, this is due, I believe, to the fact that during my wanderings in the field of medicine, I have strayed onto paths where the gold was still lying by the wayside. It takes a little luck to be able to distinguish gold from dross, but that is all. (Robert Koch)

如果說我的努力已獲得超乎尋常的成功，我認為這是由於我在醫學領域的漫遊中，踏上了路旁還散落著金子的小路。得以披沙揀金需要少許運氣，不過僅此而已。（羅伯・柯霍）

I know from experience that to one who thinks much and feels deeply, it often seems that he has only to put down his thoughts and feelings in order to produce something altogether out of the common; yet as soon as he sets to work he falls into a certain mannerism of style and common phraseology; his thoughts do not come spontaneously, and one might almost say that it is not the mind that directs the pen, but the pen leads the mind into common, empty artificiality. (Henryk Sienkiewicz)

我由經驗得知：一個思考豐富、感受深入的人，常常似乎只須將所思所感記下來，便能產生與眾不同的作品；然而一旦動筆，他就落入既定的寫作風格與習常筆法的框架；他的思想不是出於自發性，而幾乎不妨說，不是心引導筆，而是筆帶著心進入平庸、空洞的人為境地。（亨利克・顯克微支）

After the verb "to Love," "to Help" is the most beautiful verb in the world. (Bertha von Suttner)

僅次於「愛」，「幫助」是世界上最美的動詞。（貝爾塔・馮・蘇特納）

1901–1910 啟蒙與創見

1906 年

As we conquer peak after peak we see in front of us regions full of interest and beauty, but we do not see our goal, we do not see the horizon; in the distance tower still higher peaks, which will yield to those who ascend them still wider prospects, and deepen the feeling, the truth of which is emphasised by every advance in science, that "Great are the Works of the Lord." (Joseph John Thomson)

當我們一座接一座地征服高峰時，但見迎面風光滿眼，景色迷人，然而望不到我們的目標，望不到地平線。遠方矗立著更高的山峰，它們將為那些攀登者提供更加廣闊的前景，更加深刻的感受。每一次科學進步都強調了其中的真諦：「上帝的傑作偉大非凡。」（J·J·湯木生）

If the modern conception of the atom is correct the barrier which separated physics from chemistry has been removed. (Joseph John Thomson)

原子的現代觀念如果正確，將物理學與化學分隔的屏障就去除了。（J·J·湯木生）

A research on the lines of applied science would doubtless have led to improvement and development of the older methods —— the research in pure science has given us an entirely new and much more powerful method. In fact, research in applied science leads to reforms, research in pure science leads to revolutions, and revolutions, whether political or industrial, are exceedingly profitable things if you are on the winning side. (Joseph John Thomson)

從應用科學角度進行的研究無疑會造成原有方法的改進和發展——

1906 年

純科學的研究為我們提供了全新的、更強大的方法。事實上，應用科學的研究引發改革，純科學的研究引發革命，而革命，無論政治的還是產業的，如果你處於獲勝一方，都是極其有益的事。（J‧J‧湯木生）

Will fluorine ever have practical applications? It is very difficult to answer this question. I may, however, say in all sincerity that I gave this subject little thought when I undertook my researches, and I believe that all the chemists whose attempts preceded mine gave it no more consideration. A scientific research is a search after truth, and it is only after discovery that the question of applicability can be usefully considered. (Henri Moissan)

氟會有什麼實際用途嗎？回答這個問題非常困難。不過，我可以非常真誠地說，從事研究時，我幾乎很少考慮這個問題。我相信，所有在我之前致力於此的化學家，也都不曾予以更多考慮。科學研究是對真理的探索，只有在獲得發現之後，適用性問題才能得到有效考慮。（亨利‧莫瓦桑）

When I think how the modern period of scientific research, whose developments I have had the good fortune to witness, has really enlarged, in a surprising way, our knowledge of the organization of the nervous system, I feel irresistably bound to trust in the fine words of Alfred Nobel, whose mind was so widely open to the highest idealism, who said: "Each new discovery leaves in the brains of men seeds which make it possible for an ever-increasing number of minds of new generations to embrace even greater scientific concepts." (Camillo Golgi)

我有幸見證了現代科學研究的突飛猛進。想到其如何以驚人的方式擴大了我們對神經系統組織的了解，我不禁對阿佛烈‧諾貝爾的精闢言論心悅誠服：「每一個新發現都在人們的頭腦中留下種子，它們使越來

> 1901–1910 啟蒙與創見

多的人得以接受更加非凡的科學觀念，新的一代又一代人。」諾貝爾是完全認同極度理想主義的。（卡米洛・高基）

It is fair to say that, in general, no problems have been exhausted; instead, men have been exhausted by the problems. (Santiago Ramón y Cajal)

完全可以說，一般而言，沒有哪些問題業已被探討得窮形盡相；反倒是，這些問題已經把人們折騰得精疲力竭。（桑地牙哥・拉蒙卡哈）

Even granting that the genius subjected to the test of critical inspection emerges free from all error, we should consider that everything he has discovered in a given domain is almost nothing in comparison with what is left to be discovered. (Santiago Ramón y Cajal)

即便天才經過苛刻檢驗的測試全無錯誤，我們也應該認為，他在既定領域的所有發現，比起尚待發現的來，都幾乎不值一提。（桑地牙哥・拉蒙卡哈）

All outstanding work, in art as well as in science, results from immense zeal applied to a great idea. (Santiago Ramón y Cajal)

一切傑出的成就，無論在科學還是藝術方面，都出自於對非凡想法的巨大熱情。（桑地牙哥・拉蒙卡哈）

Like the entomologist in search of colorful butterflies, my attention has chased in the gardens of the grey matter cells with delicate and elegant shapes, the mysterious butterflies of the soul, whose beating of wings may one day reveal to us the secrets of the mind. (Santiago Ramón y Cajal)

就像昆蟲學家尋找鮮豔的蝴蝶一樣，我的注意力在灰質細胞的花園中追尋。這些精神的神祕蝴蝶形態精緻而優雅，它們拍打著的翅膀，也許有一天會向我們揭示心靈的祕密。（桑地牙哥・拉蒙卡哈）

1906 年

If a solution fails to appear... and yet we feel success is just around the corner, try resting for a while... Like the early morning frost, this intellectual refreshment withers the parasitic and nasty vegetation that smothers the good seed. Bursting forth at last is the flower of truth. (Santiago Ramón y Cajal)

如果解決方案未能出現……而依然覺得成功即將來臨，就試著休息一下。……這種腦力的恢復猶如清晨的霜凍，使扼殺優良種子的、寄生的、可惡的雜草凋萎。最終綻放的是真理之花。（桑地牙哥·拉蒙卡哈）

The indescribable pleasure —— which pales the rest of life's joys —— is abundant compensation for the investigator who endures the painful and persevering analytical work that precedes the appearance of the new truth, like the pain of childbirth. It is true to say that nothing for the scientific scholar is comparable to the things that he has discovered. Indeed, it would be difficult to find an investigator willing to exchange the paternity of a scientific conquest for all the gold on earth. And if there are some who look to science as a way of acquiring gold instead of applause from the learned, and the personal satisfaction associated with the very act of discovery, they have chosen the wrong profession. (Santiago Ramón y Cajal)

這種無法形容的快樂 —— 使人生的其他樂趣黯然失色 —— 是對研究者的豐厚補償。在新真相出現以前，他堅持艱苦困難的分析工作，猶如分娩的痛苦。完全可以說，對於科學家而言，沒有任何東西比得上他的發現。的確，要找出一個研究者，願意以其科學成就的創始權換取世上的全部黃金，是很困難的。而如果有人視科學為發財的途徑，而非為了獲得學界喝采以及探索行為本身帶來的個人滿足，他們就選錯了行業。（桑地牙哥·拉蒙卡哈）

Our novice runs the risk of failure without additional traits: a strong inclination toward originality, a taste for research, and a desire to experience the incomparable gratification associated with the act of discovery itself. (Santiago Ramón y Cajal)

我們的新手勇於冒失敗的風險，賦有本質上的特徵：對原創性的強烈偏愛、對研究的喜好，以及體驗探索行為本身帶來的無比滿足的渴望。（桑地牙哥‧拉蒙卡哈）

What a wonderful stimulant it would be for the beginner if his instructor, instead of amazing and dismaying him with the sublimity of great past achievements, would reveal instead the origin of each scientific discovery, the series of errors and missteps that preceded it —— information that, from a human perspective, is essential to an accurate explanation of the discovery. Skillful pedagogical tactics such as this would instill the conviction that the discoverer, along with being an illustrious person of great talent and resolve, was in the final analysis a human being just like everyone else. (Santiago Ramón y Cajal)

對於初學者而言，這將會是多麼美妙的激勵，如果他的導師，不是以往日非凡成就的氣勢使之生畏，而是會揭示每一項科學發現的起源，先前的各種差錯與失誤 —— 這樣的資訊，在人們看來，對於準確解釋這種發現是不可或缺的。如此高明的教學策略會灌輸這樣的信念：發現者既以非凡的才華與決心出類拔萃，說到底也跟一般人沒多大不同。（桑地牙哥‧拉蒙卡哈）

To bring scientific investigation to a happy end once appropriate methods have been determined, we must hold firmly in mind the goal of the project.

1906 年

The object here is to focus the train of thought on more and more complex and accurate associations between images based on observation and ideas slumbering in the unconscious. (Santiago Ramón y Cajal)

為了使科學研究得到滿意的結果，適當的方法一旦確定，我們就必須將項目的目標牢記在心。基於觀察的心像和蟄伏在潛意識中的想法，其關聯越來越複雜、精細，我們的目標就是要將思路集中於二者的關聯。（桑地牙哥·拉蒙卡哈）

Oh comforting solitude, how favorable thou art to original thought! (Santiago Ramón y Cajal)

啊，令人欣慰的孤獨，你對創新思考何其有益！（桑地牙哥·拉蒙卡哈）

Nearly all the great creators were almost recluses. Either one has many ideas and few friends, or many friends and few ideas. (Santiago Ramón y Cajal)

幾乎所有非凡的創造者都近乎隱士。一個人若非想法很多而朋友很少，便是朋友很多而想法很少。（桑地牙哥·拉蒙卡哈）

In my own view, some advice about what should be known, about what technical education should be acquired, about the intense motivation needed to succeed, and about the carelessness and inclination toward bias that must be avoided is far more useful than all the rules and warnings of theoretical logic. (Santiago Ramón y Cajal)

依我個人看來，有的建議，關於應該了解什麼、關於應該獲得什麼技術教育、關於成功所需的強烈動機，以及關於必須避免的粗心大意和偏見傾向，這些遠比理論邏輯的各種規則和警告有用得多。（桑地牙哥·拉蒙卡哈）

1901-1910 啟蒙與創見

Perseverance is a virtue of the less brilliant. (Santiago Ramón y Cajal)

堅持不懈是一種不那麼耀眼的美德。（桑地牙哥・拉蒙卡哈）

In summary, all great work is the fruit of patience and perseverance, combined with tenacious concentration on a subject over a period of months or years. (Santiago Ramón y Cajal)

概言之，一切非凡成就都是耐心和毅力的結果，加上數月或數年時間對一個課題的執著專注。（桑地牙哥・拉蒙卡哈）

Buffon said unreservedly, "Genius is simply patience carried to the extreme." To those who asked how he achieved fame he replied: "By spending forty years of my life bent over my writing desk." (Santiago Ramón y Cajal)

布豐直截了當地說：「天才無非是臻於極致的耐心。」對於詢問其成名之道的人們，他答曰：「此生伏案寫作積 40 年之久。」（桑地牙哥・拉蒙卡哈）

Not under a steel nib that scratches in nasty furrows

its dull thoughts onto dry white paper;

but under the ripe sun, as breezes gust

through wide-open clearings beside a swift stream,

the heart's sighs, dwindling into infinity, are born,

the sweet, wistful flower of melody is born. (Giosuè Carducci)

不是沉悶的思緒犁過蒼白的紙

鋼製的筆尖劃出刺耳的沙沙聲；

而是在溪水奔流的寬敞空地上

明麗的陽光下吹拂著的和風中，

> 1906 年

心的嘆息雲消霧散，轉而化為

美妙的、憧憬的旋律之花誕生。（焦蘇埃・卡爾杜奇）

Far and away the best prize that life has to offer is the chance to work hard at work worth doing. (Theodore Roosevelt)

不言而喻，生活所能給予的最高獎勵，就是有機會為值得做的工作而努力。（狄奧多・羅斯福）

Keep your eyes on the stars, and your feet on the ground. (Theodore Roosevelt)

眼望星空，腳踏實地。（狄奧多・羅斯福）

Do what you can, with what you have, where you are. (Theodore Roosevelt)

盡一己所能，憑既有條件，於原地發力。（狄奧多・羅斯福）

In any moment of decision, the best thing you can do is the right thing, the next best thing is the wrong thing, and the worst thing you can do is nothing. (Theodore Roosevelt)

在任何決定性時刻，你所能做的最好的事情就是對的事情，其次好的事情就是錯的事情，最糟的事情是什麼都不做。（狄奧多・羅斯福）

The only time you really live fully is from thirty to sixty. The young are slaves to dreams; the old servants of regrets. Only the middle-aged have all their five senses in the keeping of their wits. (Theodore Roosevelt)

你唯一真正充實地生活的年齡是 30 至 60 歲。年輕人是夢想的奴隸，老年人是悔恨的僕人。只有中年人五智[06]俱全，具備智慧。（狄奧多・羅斯福）

---

[06] 舊時認為人具有五項智慧：常識、想像、幻想、判斷與記憶。

1901–1910 啟蒙與創見

1907 年

While it is never safe to affirm that the future of Physical Science has no marvels in store even more astonishing than those of the past, it seems probable that most of the grand underlying principles have been firmly established, and that further advances are to be sought chiefly in the rigorous applications of these principles to all the phenomena which come under our notice. It is here that the science of measurement shows its importance —— where the quantitative results are more to be desired than qualitative work. An eminent physicist has remarked that the future truths of Physical Science are to be looked for in the sixth place of decimals. (Albert Abraham Michelson)

認定物理科學的未來再也沒有以往那些更驚人的奇蹟，這絕非可靠；大部分重要基本原則似乎已經牢固樹立，而對深入進展的尋求，主要在於將這些原則嚴格應用於我們注意到的所有現象。就在此處，計量科學顯示了它的重要性 —— 定量結果比定性工作更受期待。一位傑出的物理學家曾說過，物理科學的未來真理，將在小數點後第六位尋找。（阿爾伯特·邁克生）

We are seeing the cells of plants and animals more and more clearly as chemical factories, where the various products are manufactured in separate workshops. (Eduard Buchner)

我們越來越清楚地見到，植物和動物的細胞就像化學工廠，各式各樣的產品在不同工廠裡製造出來。（愛德華·布赫納）

> 1907 年

Science, especially natural and medical science, is always undergoing evolution, and one can never hope to have said the last word upon any branch of it. (Charles Louis Alphonse Laveran)

科學，尤其是自然科學和醫學科學，總是在不斷演進，人永遠無法指望對其任何分支下定論。（夏爾·路易·阿方斯·拉韋朗）

After you've made a mistake —— ye don't make fewer'n a hundred a day —— the next best thing's to own up to it like men. (Rudyard Kipling)

做錯了之後 —— 你每天不少於上百次 —— 下一個最好的行動就是像男人一樣承認。（魯德亞德·吉卜林）

Never look backwards or you'll fall down the stairs. (Rudyard Kipling)

切不可回頭張望，否則會摔下樓梯。（魯德亞德·吉卜林）

Gardens are not made by singing "Oh, how beautiful," and sitting in the shade. (Rudyard Kipling)

花園不是經由唱起「噢，多麼美麗」和坐到陰涼下面建成的。（魯德亞德·吉卜林）

He travels the fastest who travels alone. (Rudyard Kipling)

獨行者走得最快。（魯德亞德·吉卜林）

Everyone is more or less mad on one point. (Rudyard Kipling)

每個人在某一點上都是或多或少瘋狂的。（魯德亞德·吉卜林）

I am a member of the Peace Society because I was a soldier: because I have fought and seen what war is like from personal experience. It was on the battlefield that I pledged myself to the cause of peace. (Ernesto Teodoro Moneta)

1901-1910 啟蒙與創見

我是和平協會的一員，因為我曾經是一名士兵；因為我戰鬥過，由個人經歷見識了戰爭。就是在戰場上，我把自己交給了和平事業。（埃內斯托・泰奧多羅・莫內塔）

Habit is often a poor counselor, encouraging unjustified opposition to measures which would be to the general good. (Louis Renault)

習慣往往是個糟糕的顧問，貿然支持抵制一些本來有益於大眾的措施。（路易・雷諾）

1908 年

Life is short and progress is slow. (Gabriel Lippmann)

人生短暫而進步緩慢。（加布里埃爾・李普曼）

Now I know what the atom looks like. (Ernest Rutherford)

現在我知道原子是什麼樣子了。（歐尼斯特・拉塞福）

An alleged scientific discovery has no merit unless it can be explained to a barmaid. (Ernest Rutherford)

若不能對酒吧女服務生解釋清楚，所謂的科學發現就乏善可陳。（歐尼斯特・拉塞福）

I've just finished reading some of my early papers, and you know, when I'd finished I said to myself, "Rutherford, my boy, you used to be a damned clever fellow." (Ernest Rutherford)

1908 年

我剛讀完自己早期的一些論文，你知道，當我讀完的時候，我對自己說：「拉塞福，你這小子，你曾經是個聰明絕頂的傢伙。」（歐尼斯特·拉塞福）

I think a strong claim can be made that the process of scientific discovery may be regarded as a form of art. This is best seen in the theoretical aspects of Physical Science. The mathematical theorist builds up on certain assumptions and according to well understood logical rules, step by step, a stately edifice, while his imaginative power brings out clearly the hidden relations between its parts. A well constructed theory is in some respects undoubtedly an artistic production. (Ernest Rutherford)

我認為可以強烈主張，不妨將科學發現的過程視為一門藝術。這在物理科學的理論方面最明顯。數學理論家以某些假設為基礎，根據眾所周知的邏輯規則，一步一步地建起宏偉的大廈，其想像力則清楚揭示出各部分之間的隱含關係。精心建構的理論在某些方面無疑即為藝術品。（歐尼斯特·拉塞福）

It is not the nature of things for any one man to make a sudden, violent discovery; science goes step by step and every man depends on the work of his predecessors. When you hear of a sudden unexpected discovery —— a bolt from the blue —— you can always be sure that it has grown up by the influence of one man or another, and it is the mutual influence which makes the enormous possibility of scientific advance. Scientists are not dependent on the ideas of a single man, but on the combined wisdom of thousands of men, all thinking of the same problem and each doing his little bit to add to the great structure of knowledge which is gradually being erected. (Ernest Rutherford)

1901–1910 啟蒙與創見

任何一個人要獲得突然的、轟動的發現，都不合事物的本來性質。科學是循序漸進的，每一個人都有賴於前人的工作。當你得知一個突然的、意外的發現時──晴空一道閃電──你永遠可以確定，它是由某個人的影響促成的，而正是這種互相影響，造成了科學進步的巨大可能性。科學家所依靠的不是單一個人的想法，而是千萬人的綜合智慧，所有人都思考著同一個問題，每一個人都在為逐步建立的知識大廈添磚加瓦。（歐尼斯特・拉塞福）

If your result needs a statistician then you should design a better experiment. (Ernest Rutherford)

如果你的研究結果需要一名統計學家，那麼你應該設計一個更好的實驗。（歐尼斯特・拉塞福）

One day when the whole family had gone to a circus to see some extraordinary performing apes, I remained alone with my microscope, observing the life in the mobile cells of a transparent star-fish larva, when a new thought suddenly flashed across my brain. It struck me that similar cells might serve in the defence of the organism against intruders. Feeling that there was in this something of surpassing interest, I felt so excited that I began striding up and down the room and even went to the seashore in order to collect my thoughts.

I said to myself that, if my supposition was true, a splinter introduced into the body of a star-fish larva, devoid of blood-vessels or of a nervous system, should soon be surrounded by mobile cells as is to be observed in a man who runs a splinter into his finger. This was no sooner said than done.

There was a small garden to our dwelling, in which we had a few days previously organised a "Christmas tree" for the children on a little tangerine

1908 年

tree; I fetched from it a few rose thorns and introduced them at once under the skin of some beautiful star-fish larvae as transparent as water.

I was too excited to sleep that night in the expectation of the result of my experiment, and very early the next morning I ascertained that it had fully succeeded.

That experiment formed the basis of the phagocyte theory, to the development of which I devoted the next twenty-five years of my life. (Ilya Ilyich Mechnikov)

有一天,家人都去馬戲團看精采的猴戲了,我依舊獨自抱著顯微鏡,觀察一個透明的海星幼體,看它移動細胞中的生命活動。這時,一個新想法突然閃過腦海。我猛然想到,類似的細胞也許發揮著保護生物體抵禦入侵者的作用。覺得其中意味深長,我興奮得在房間裡大步來回走,甚至跑到海邊去歸攏思緒。

我對自己說,海星幼體內既無血管亦無神經系統,倘若我的假設正確,那麼一根置入的小刺,應該迅速被移動細胞包圍,就像將一根刺扎入手指時可觀察到的一樣。這是應聲而至的事情。

我們家有個小花園。幾天前,在一株小橘子樹上,我們提前為孩子們裝飾了一棵「聖誕樹」。我從上面摘下幾根玫瑰刺,隨即將其置於一些形態美麗、透明似水的海星幼體皮下。

那天夜裡我興奮得難以入睡,一心期待實驗結果,而第二天一大早我就確定它已完全成功。

這個實驗構成了吞噬細胞理論的基礎。致力於這一項理論的發展,我付出了此生隨後的 25 年。(伊利亞・梅契尼可夫)

1901–1910 啟蒙與創見

The duration of the life of men may be considerably increased. It would be true progress to go back to the simple dishes of our ancestors.⋯ Progress would consist in simplifying many sides of the lives of civilised people. (Ilya Ilyich Mechnikov)

人們的壽命可能大大增加。回到祖先的簡樸飯菜會是真正的進步。……進步會存在於簡化文明大眾生活的許多方面。（伊利亞・梅契尼可夫）

Success in research needs four Gs: Glück, Geduld, Geschick und Geld. Luck, patience, skill and money. (Paul Ehrlich)

研究的成功需要德語的四個 G：Glück、Geduld、Geschick 和 Geld，即運氣、耐心、技能和金錢。（保羅・埃爾利希）

The National Academy of Sciences would be unable to give a unanimous decision if asked whether the sun would rise tomorrow. (Paul Ehrlich)

如果被問到第二天太陽是否會升起，美國國家科學院將無法做出一致的決議。（保羅・埃爾利希）

For the past, rightly understood, is no mere past. (Rudolf Christoph Eucken)

就過去而言，正確理解的過去不僅是過去。（倭鏗）

Without confidence in a cause, there is no action. Ignorance may be enlightened, superstition wiped out; intolerance may become tolerant, and hate be changed into love; ideas may be quickened, intelligence widened, and men's hearts may be ennobled; but from pessimism which can see nothing but gloomy visions nothing is to be expected. (Klas Pontus Arnoldson)

對事業沒有信心，就沒有行動。蒙昧可以啟迪，迷信可以消除；狹隘可以變成寬容，恨可以化為愛；思想可以啟發，智力可以拓展，情感可以昇華；然而落入悲觀，眼前唯有一片昏暗，也就無可期待。（克拉斯・蓬圖斯・阿諾爾德松）

We demand too much of others and too little of ourselves. No one wishes to be the first to take the straight and narrow path. (Klas Pontus Arnoldson)

我們對別人要求太多，對自己要求太少。沒有人願意當第一個走上正道的人。（克拉斯・蓬圖斯・阿諾爾德松）

By a great man, however, we mean a man who, because of his spiritual gifts, his character, and other qualities, deserves to be called great and who as a result earns the power to influence others. (Fredrik Bajer)

然而，所謂偉人，我們指的是一個人由於其精神上的天賦，其品格，以及其他特質，理應稱之偉大，他也從而贏得了影響他人的力量。（腓特烈・巴耶爾）

1909 年

Every day sees humanity more victorious in the struggle with space and time. (Guglielmo Marconi)

每一天都目睹人類在與空間和時間的抗爭中獲得更多的勝利。（古列爾莫・馬可尼）

The field of measurements in relation to practice was beginning to be opened up. From then on, the work spread further and further outwards,

1901-1910 啟蒙與創見

branching into that of the scientific laboratories on the one hand, and the conversion of their results into practice with its complicated conditions and extensive requirements on the other. (Karl Ferdinand Braun)

與實務相關的測量領域開始拓展。此後,這一項工作日益擴大,一方面延伸到科學實驗室的範圍,另一方面涉及將研究成果轉化為實務,以因應複雜的情況和廣泛的要求。(卡爾・布勞恩)

Science is one land, having the ability to accommodate even more people, as more residents gather in it; it is a treasure that is the greater the more it is shared. Because of that, each of us can do his work in his own way, and the common ground does not mean conformity. (Wilhelm Ostwald)

科學是一片土地,聚居者越多其承載能力越強;它是一座寶庫,分享得越多其珍藏越豐。因而,人人都能以自己的方式從事工作,而共存並不意味著一致。(威廉・奧士華)

In our civilization, men are afraid that they will not be men enough and women are afraid that they might be considered only women. (Emil Theodor Kocher)

在我們的文明中,男人唯恐自己不夠男人,而女人唯恐自己只被視為女人。(埃米爾・特奧多爾・科赫爾)

Strange, when you ask anyone's advice you see yourself what is right. Even while you are asking, you discover all at once what you hadn't been able to find out in three whole years. (Selma Ottilia Lovisa Lagerlöf)

奇怪的是,在徵求無論任何人的建議時,你會自己看出正確的意見。甚至就在問的當下,你會猛然發現自己整整三年都未能找到的答案。(塞爾瑪・拉格洛夫)

1909年

I thought of my father and felt a deep sorrow that he should no longer be alive, and that I could not go to him and tell him that I had been awarded the Nobel Prize. I knew that no one would have been happier than he to hear this. (Selma Ottilia Lovisa Lagerlöf)

我想起我的父親,為他竟已過世而深感哀傷,我無法去見他,告訴他自己被授予諾貝爾獎。我知道,沒有人會比他更高興聽到這個消息了。(塞爾瑪·拉格洛夫)

Nothing on earth can make up for the loss of one who has loved you. (Selma Ottilia Lovisa Lagerlöf)

失去愛你的人是世上任何東西都無法彌補的。(塞爾瑪·拉格洛夫)

Have you ever seen a child sitting on its mother's knee listening to fairy stories? As long as the child is told of cruel giants and of the terrible suffering of beautiful princesses, it holds its head up and its eyes open; but if the mother begins to speak of happiness and sunshine, the little one closes its eyes and falls asleep with its head against her breast… I am a child like that, too. Others may like stories of flowers and sunshine; but I choose the dark nights and sad destinies. (Selma Ottilia Lovisa Lagerlöf)

你見過孩子坐在母親膝上聽童話故事嗎?只要講起凶殘的巨人,講起美麗公主的深重苦難,孩子就抬起頭來,睜大眼睛;而母親要是說到幸福和陽光,小傢伙就閉上眼睛,頭靠在她胸前睡著了。⋯⋯我也是個這樣的孩子。別人可能喜歡鮮花和陽光的故事,但我選擇黑暗的夜晚和悲傷的命運。(塞爾瑪·拉格洛夫)

After this horrible war we shall have more reason than ever to believe in the spirit of self-sacrifice, in the benefits of painful creative effort, in the sanc-

1901–1910 啟蒙與創見

tified nature of the resistance that springs from both heart and head, and in the triumph of Reason, Good Will and Justice over the sterile forces of ignorance, pride and violence. (Auguste Beernaert)

經過這場可怕的戰爭[07]，我們將比以往更有理由相信自我犧牲精神，相信艱苦的創造性努力的益處，相信源於情理的抵抗的神聖性，相信理性、善意和正義的勝利，它們擊敗了無知、傲慢和狂暴這些負面勢力。（奧古斯特·貝爾納特）

1910年

The crowning of my studies by the esteemed Royal Swedish Academy affords me satisfaction and fills me with gratitude, a gratitude which I cannot call eternal and in my old age I cannot even promise that it will be of long duration, but perhaps for this very reason my gratitude is all the more intense. (Johannes Diderik van der Waals)

尊敬的瑞典皇家科學院授予我的研究至高榮譽，這使我心滿意足，十分感激。我不能說感激不盡，在我這把年紀甚至無法承諾長久，但也許正由於此，我的感激之情才更加熱烈。（約翰尼斯·凡得瓦）

As soon as science has solved one problem, new ones arise. This is the essence of science. (Otto Wallach)

科學一旦解決了一個問題，各種新的問題隨即出現。這是科學的本質。（奧托·瓦拉赫）

---

[07] 指第一次世界大戰。

1910 年

As soon as we can wrest from Nature the secret of the internal structure of the compounds produced by her, chemical science can then even surpass Nature by producing compounds as variations of the natural ones, which the living cell is unable to construct. (Otto Wallach)

對於大自然產生的化合物，我們一旦獲取其內部結構的祕密，化學科學就能夠超越大自然，產生變種的天然化合物，那是生命細胞所無法構成的。（奧托・瓦拉赫）

When we consider that through the combination of letters an infinitely large number of thoughts may be expressed, we can understand how vast a number of the properties of the organism may be recorded in the small space which is occupied by the protein molecules. It enables us to understand how it is possible for the proteins of the sex-cells to contain, to a certain extent, a complete description of the species and even of the individual. We may also comprehend how great and important the task is to determine the structure of the proteins, and why the biochemist has devoted himself with so much industry to their analysis. (Albrecht Kossel)

當我們考慮到透過字母的組合可以表達數量無限的想法，我們就能理解，在蛋白質分子使用的微小空間之中可以記錄多麼大量的生物體特性。這使我們得以理解，性細胞的蛋白質如何在一定程度上包含對物種乃至個體的完整描述。我們還可以領會，確定蛋白質結構的任務是多麼重大，以及生物化學家何以如此勤勉地致力於對它們的分析。（阿爾布雷希特・科塞爾）

It was so refreshing to be tramping along this path, overgrown with bushes, fifty feet above the torrent, to feel the fine spray of the waterfall dash… to

1901-1910 啟蒙與創見

see the lizards slipping over the stones, and the graceful butterflies chasing the furtive sunligh. (Paul Johann Ludwig Heyse)

　　走在這條小路上令人實在神清氣爽。灌木叢生，山溪在下方 50 英尺處流淌，感受瀑布飛落濺起的水霧……看蜥蜴在石頭上竄過，蹁躚的蝴蝶追逐閃爍的陽光。（保羅・海澤）

1911–1920
動盪中的信念

1911 年

In science, the redeeming idea often comes from an entirely different direction, investigations in an entirely different field often throw unexpected light on the dark aspects of unresolved problems. (Wilhelm Wien)

科學上，變換的思路往往出自完全不同的方向。對於未解難題的晦暗之處，完全不同領域的研究常會帶來意想不到的啟示。（威廉・維因）

Science often draws its impetus from man's practical needs, and if technical optics had not required general laws of image-formation, it seems clear that science would not have found these laws. Such a need was strongly felt in opthalmology and physiological optics. (Allvar Gullstrand)

科學往往從人的實際需求中汲取動力。假如技術光學不需要影像形成的普遍定律，顯然科學也不會發現它們。在眼科學和生理光學領域中可以強烈感受到這種需求。（阿爾瓦・古爾斯特蘭德）

Our reason is only a feeble ray that has issued from Nature. (Maurice Polidore Marie Bernhard Maeterlinck)

我們的理性不過是大自然發出的微光。（莫里斯・梅特林克）

1911–1920 動盪中的信念

An act of goodness is an act of happiness. No reward coming after the event can compare with the sweet reward that went with it. (Maurice Polidore Marie Bernhard Maeterlinck)

善良的行為是幸福的行為。伴隨的快慰沒有任何回報可比。(莫里斯・梅特林克)

War is not, in itself, a condition so much as the symptom of a condition —— that of international anarchy. If we wish to substitute for war the settlement of disputes by justice, we must first substitute for the condition of international anarchy a condition of international order. (Alfred Hermann Fried)

戰爭的本身並非一種狀態，而是國際無政府狀態的徵候。我們若想憑藉正義，以解決爭端取代戰爭，就必須首先以國際秩序的狀態取代國際無政府的狀態。(阿爾弗雷德・赫爾曼・弗里德)

1912 年

On the terrace of the Pepiniere, the 150 pupils of the Institut Chemique talk chemistry as they leave the auditoria and the laboratory. The echoes of the magnificent public garden of the city of Nancy make the words reverberate; coupling, condensation, grignardization. Moreover, their clothes stay impregnated with strong and characteristic odours; we follow the initiates of Hermes by their scent. In such an environment, how is it possible not to be productive? (Victor Grignard)

在校區的臺地上，化學學院的 150 名學生走出講堂和實驗室，談論著化學。言談中的詞語在南錫市寬敞美觀的公共花園中迴響：耦合、縮聚、格氏反應。此外，他們的衣服帶有強烈獨特的氣味，我們循著氣息跟在這群荷米斯[08]的傳人後面。在這樣的環境中，學習怎能不富於成效？（維克多・格林尼亞）

Suffering is the true cement of love. (Paul Sabatier)

艱難困苦是愛的真正黏合劑。（保羅・薩巴捷）

A few observation and much reasoning lead to error; many observations and a little reasoning to truth. (Alexis Carrel)

些許觀察和大量推論導致錯誤，眾多觀察和少量推論引向真理。（亞歷克西・卡雷爾）

Those who desire to rise as high as our human condition allows, must renounce intellectual pride, the omnipotence of clear thinking, belief in the absolute power of logic. (Alexis Carrel)

那些想達到我們人類條件所允許之極致的人，必須放棄知識的驕傲、清晰思考的全能以及對邏輯絕對力量的信念。（亞歷克西・卡雷爾）

Intuition comes very close to clairvoyance; it appears to be the extrasensory perception of reality. (Alexis Carrel)

直覺非常接近千里眼，它似乎就是現實的超感官知覺。（亞歷克西・卡雷爾）

Science has to be understood in its broadest sense, as a method for comprehending all observable reality, and not merely as an instrument for acquiring specialized knowledge. (Alexis Carrel)

---

[08] 荷米斯，希臘神話中的一位神，多才多藝。

1911-1920 動盪中的信念

科學必須在最廣泛的意義上被理解，作為領會所有可見現實的方法，而非僅僅作為獲取專業知識的工具。（亞歷克西·卡雷爾）

The atmosphere of libraries, lecture rooms and laboratories is dangerous to those who shut themselves up in them too long. It separates us from reality like a fog. (Alexis Carrel)

圖書館、教室和實驗室的氛圍，對那些把自己關在裡面太久的人是危險的。它像霧一樣將我們與現實隔離。（亞歷克西·卡雷爾）

The quality of life is more important than life itself. (Alexis Carrel)

生命的品質比生命本身更重要。（亞歷克西·卡雷爾）

Man cannot remake himself without suffering, for he is both the marble and the sculptor. (Alexis Carrel)

人無法不經受痛苦而重塑自我，因為他既是大理石又是雕刻家。（亞歷克西·卡雷爾）

Hard conditions of life are indispensable to bringing out the best in human personality. (Alexis Carrel)

艱難困苦對於激發人類最優秀的品格是不可或缺的。（亞歷克西·卡雷爾）

The most efficient way to live reasonably is every morning to make a plan of one's day and every night to examine the results obtained. (Alexis Carrel)

最有效的合理生活方式是每個早晨制定一天的計畫，每個晚上檢查獲得的結果。（亞歷克西·卡雷爾）

All of us, at certain moments of our lives, need to take advice and to receive help from other people. (Alexis Carrel)

我們所有的人，在一生中的某些時刻，都需要聽取別人的建議和接受別人的幫助。（亞歷克西·卡雷爾）

Life is an unbroken chain of discoveries. (Gerhart Johann Robert Hauptmann)

人生是一連串不間斷的探索。（格哈特·霍普特曼）

Once in solitude I learned to stand on my own feet and have my own thoughts. (Gerhart Johann Robert Hauptmann)

一旦孤身獨處，我學會了獨立自主，具有自己的想法。（格哈特·霍普特曼）

Men do not fail; they give up trying. (Elihu Root)

人們不是失敗，他們是放棄了努力。（伊萊休·魯特）

1913 年

For this happiness, one can only thank in a way that is the one that the Nobel laureates have instructed, having devoted their whole life to science. To do this to the best of my ability is my innermost need. (Heike Kamerlingh Onnes)

對於這種幸福，只能以一種方式感謝，即如諾貝爾獎得主們所言，他們將一生都獻給了科學。盡我所能如此致謝，是我出自內心的需要。（海克·卡末林·昂內斯）

According to my views, aiming at quantitative investigations, that is at

1911–1920 動盪中的信念

establishing relations between measurements of phenomena, should take first place in the experimental practice of physics. By measurement to knowledge (door meten tot weten[09]) I should like to write as a motto above the entrance to every physics laboratory. (Heike Kamerlingh Onnes)

在我看來，以定量研究為目標，即在現象的測量值之間建立關係，在物理學實驗的實務中應該居首要地位。經由測量獲得知識，我很想把它作為箴言，寫在每一個物理實驗室的入口上方。（海克・卡末林・昂內斯）

Chemistry must become the astronomy of the molecular world. (Alfred Werner)

化學必定成為分子世界的天文學。（阿爾弗雷德・維爾納）

Your aim is no better than your knowledge of chemistry. (Alfred Werner)

你的槍法還比不上你的化學知識。[10]（阿爾弗雷德・維爾納）

I never said it was possible. I only said it was true. (Charles Robert Richet)

我從不說這是可能的。我只說這是確實的。（夏爾・羅貝爾・里歇）

I possess every good quality, but the one that distinguishes me above all is modesty. (Charles Robert Richet)

各種優良特質我都擁有，但最使我與眾不同的是謙虛。（夏爾・羅貝爾・里歇）

Age considers; youth ventures. (Rabindranath Tagore)

年長凡事三思，年輕不憚一試。（泰戈爾）

---

[09] 昂內斯是一位荷蘭物理學家，這句話為荷蘭文。
[10] 這話是維爾納對一個槍擊他的學生說的，該生因考試失敗而行為失當。

You can't cross the sea merely by standing and staring at the water. (Rabindranath Tagore)

你無法只站在岸邊凝望而渡過大海。（羅賓德拉納特・泰戈爾）

Fruit is a noble cause, the cause of flower is sweet, but still let me in the obscurity of the shadow of the dedication to do it cause leaf. (Rabindranath Tagore)

果實的工作高貴，花朵的工作美好，不過還是讓我在奉獻的陰影裡默默做葉子的工作吧。（羅賓德拉納特・泰戈爾）

Let your life lightly dance on the edges of Time like dew on the tip of a leaf. (Rabindranath Tagore)

讓你的生命在時間的邊緣輕盈舞動，猶如葉尖的露珠。（羅賓德拉納特・泰戈爾）

Let life be beautiful like summer flowers and death like autumn leaves. (Rabindranath Tagore)

讓生如夏花之絢麗，死如秋葉之華美。（羅賓德拉納特・泰戈爾）

1914 年

Whatever may happen to the latest theory of Dr. Einstein, his treatise represents a mathematical effort of overwhelming proportions. It is the more remarkable since Einstein is primarily a physicist and only incidentally a mathematician. He came to mathematics rather of necessity than by predilection,

1911–1920 動盪中的信念

and yet he has here developed mathematical formulae and calculations springing from a colossal knowledge. (Max von Laue)

無論愛因斯坦博士的最新理論發展如何，他的論述展現出壓倒性的數學力量。更值得注意的是，愛因斯坦首先是位物理學家，他只是附帶作為數學家。他訴諸數學，與其說由於嗜好莫如說屬於必然，而他就此又憑藉著淵博的知識發展出數學公式和運算。（馬克斯・馮・勞厄）

Every student of science, even if he cannot start his journey where his predecessors left off, can at least travel their beaten track more quickly than they could while they were clearing the way：and so before his race is run, he comes to virgin forest and becomes himself a pioneer. (Theodore William Richards)

每一位科學研究者，即便不能在先行者止步之處出發，他走在前人開闢的路上，至少能比他們披荊斬棘時做得到的更迅速。如此，在踏上自己的路之前，他抵達原始森林，自己又成為開拓者。（西奧多・威廉・理查茲）

The incorrectness and weaknesses of a theory cause other minds to formulate the problems more exactly and in this way scientific progress is made. (Robert Bárány)

一種理論的不正確和薄弱之處，引起其他頭腦更準確地提出問題，遂以此方式帶來科學進步。（羅伯特・巴拉尼）

1915 年

The important thing in science is not so much to obtain new facts as to discover new ways of thinking about them. (William Lawrence Bragg)

在科學中,重要的與其說是獲得新事實,莫如說是發現思考它們的新方式。(威廉・勞倫斯・布拉格)

I feel very strongly indeed that a Cambridge education for our scientists should include some contact with the humanistic side. The gift of expression is important to them as scientists; the best research is wasted when it is extremely difficult to discover what it is all about. (William Lawrence Bragg)

我的確非常強烈地感到,劍橋對於科學工作者的教育應該包括一些與人文學科的接觸。作為科學工作者,表達能力對於他們很重要;一旦晦澀難解、不知所云,最好的研究亦屬白費。(威廉・勞倫斯・布拉格)

Presently, science undergraduates do not learn to write clearly and briefly, marshalling their points in due and aesthetically satisfying order, and eliminating inessentials. They are inept at those turns of phrase or happy analogy which throw a flying bridge across a chasm of misunderstanding and make contact between mind and mind. (William Lawrence Bragg)

目前,理科的大學生仍未學會如何清晰、簡潔地寫作,如何以適當的、令人愉悅的秩序組織觀點,並刪除無關緊要的部分。他們不善於運用措辭或巧妙的類比以跨越誤解的鴻溝,在思想之間建立連繫。(威廉・勞倫斯・布拉格)

Light brings us the news of the Universe. (William Henry Bragg)

光帶給我們宇宙的消息。(威廉・亨利・布拉格)

1911-1920 動盪中的信念

I watched Baeyer activating magnesium with iodine for a difficult Grignard reaction; it was done in a test tube, which he watched carefully as he moved it gently by hand over a flame for three quarters of an hour. The test tube was the apparatus to Baeyer. (Richard Martin Willstätter)

我看著拜爾[11]用碘使鎂活化,以取得困難的格氏反應。實驗是在一隻試管中完成的,拜爾拿著它緩緩地在火苗上移動了45分鐘,細心地觀察。這一隻試管就是拜爾的設備。(里夏德・維爾施泰特)

We should misjudge this scientist (Fritz Haber) seriously if we were to judge him only by his harvest. The stimulation of research and the advancement of younger scholars become ever more important to him than his own achievements. (Richard Martin Willstätter)

如果僅以成果評價,我們就嚴重誤判了這位科學家(佛列茲・哈伯[12])。對於他,激發研究熱情和年輕學者們的進步,比自己的成就還要重要。(里夏德・維爾施泰特)

Fritz Haber's greatness lies in his scientific ideas and in the depth of his searching. The thought, the plan, and the process are more important to him than the completion. The creative process gives him more pleasure than the yield, the finished piece. Success is immaterial. "Doing it was wonderful." (Richard Martin Willstätter)

佛列茲・哈伯的偉大之處在於其科學理念,在於其探索的深度。對於他,想法、計畫和過程比完成更重要。創造的過程比獲得成果給予他更多的快樂。成功是非物質的。「做這件事太棒了。」(里夏德・維爾施泰特)

---

[11] 阿道夫・馮・拜爾(Adolf von Baeyer),1905年諾貝爾化學獎得主。
[12] 佛列茲・哈伯,1918年諾貝爾化學獎得主。

1915 年

There is only one heroism in the world: to see the world as it is, and to love it. (Romain Rolland)

世間只有一種大無畏精神：看清生活的真相，而依然熱愛生活。（羅曼·羅蘭）

A hero is a man who does what he can. (Romain Rolland)

英雄就是做自己能做之事的人。（羅曼·羅蘭）

It is not peace that I seek, but life. (Romain Rolland)

我尋求的不是安寧，而是人生。（羅曼·羅蘭）

Each man must learn his own ideal and try to accomplish it: that is a surer way of progress than to take the ideas of another. (Romain Rolland)

每個人都必須了解自己的理想，並努力實現它：與接受別人的想法相比，這是更可靠的進步方式。（羅曼·羅蘭）

Every man who is truly a man must learn to be alone in the midst of all others, and if need be against all others. (Romain Rolland)

每個真正的人，都必須學會在眾人之中孤獨一人，必要的話與所有人對抗。（羅曼·羅蘭）

Be reverent towards each day. Love it, respect it, do not sully it, do not hinder it from coming to flower. (Romain Rolland)

敬畏每一天。熱愛它，尊重它，不要玷汙它，不要妨礙它開出花朵。（羅曼·羅蘭）

As he could be free only for an hour or two a day, his strength flowed into that space of time like a river between walls of rock. It is a good discipline for art for a man to confine his efforts between unshakable bounds. In that sense it may be said that misery is a master, not only of thought, but of style; it teaches sobriety to the mind as to the body. When time is doled out and thoughts measured, a man says no word too much, and grows accustomed to thinking only what is essential; so he lives at double pressure, having less time for living. (Romain Rolland)

由於每天只有一、兩個小時的空閒時間，他的力量猶如峭壁間的河流一般注入這條時間的水道。將一個人的努力局限於不可動搖的界限之間，對於藝術而言是很好的訓練。在這個意義上，可以說痛苦是位大師，不僅是思想的，還是風格的。它教導人節制，身心皆是。當時間被分配、想法被衡量時，人所言不多，並且習慣於只思考必要的事物；於是他生活在雙重壓力下，用於生活的時間更少。（羅曼‧羅蘭）

If a man is to shed the light of the sun upon other men, he must first of all have it within himself. (Romain Rolland)

要把陽光灑到別人身上，人必須首先自己心中存有陽光。（羅曼‧羅蘭）

No one ever reads a book. He reads himself through books, either to discover or to control himself. (Romain Rolland)

沒有一個人是在讀書。他透過讀書閱讀自己，以發現或掌握自己。（羅曼‧羅蘭）

1916 年

There is a spark dwells deep within my soul.

To get it out into the daylight's glow

Is my life's aim both first and last, the whole.

It slips away, it burns and tortures me.

That little spark is all the wealth I know;

That little spark is my life's misery. (Carl Gustaf Verner von Heidenstam)

我的內心深處有個火花。

把它帶到明亮的陽光下

是我一生始終的目標，捨此無他。

它溜走了，它燃燒並折磨著我。

這小火花是我所知的全部財富，

這小火花是我糾纏一生的痛苦。（維爾納‧馮‧海登斯坦）

1917 年

It seems to me that the Swedish Academy of Science may be qualifying for the Nobel Peace Prize. It recognises no nationality; it discourages unworthy national feeling and prejudice. (Charles Glover Barkla)

在我看來，瑞典科學院可以有資格獲得諾貝爾和平獎。它無視國籍，它排斥無謂的民族感情和偏見。（查爾斯‧巴克拉）

We are all dwellers on this one small earth; we live one life, die one death; we have the same difficulties to contend with; we ought in common to fight the foes of ignorance and wrong. (Charles Glover Barkla)

1911-1920 動盪中的信念

我們都是這一個小小地球的居民；我們生一世，死一回；我們有同樣的困難要應對；我們理當共同迎戰無知與錯誤之敵。（查爾斯・巴克拉）

When my first book appeared forty years earlier, it had been influenced by German idealism. Just three years later (in the thesis awarded the gold medal) I was a follower of English naturalism, after which I returned to a position under those elevated signs of the zodiac which constitute my rightful habitat, only this time the guiding star was not Hegel as in En idealist, but Kant and Schopenhauer. (Karl Adolph Gjellerup)

40年前我的第一本書[13]出版時，它受到了德國唯心主義的影響。僅僅三年後（在獲得金獎的論文中），我是英國自然主義的追隨者。隨後，我回到那些巨星照耀下的地方，它成為我的宜居之處，只是這次的指路明燈不是寫《一個唯心主義者》時的黑格爾，而是康德和叔本華。（卡爾・阿道夫・蓋勒魯普）

This thought has been ascribed to Voltaire: If God did not exist, mankind would have invented Him. I find more truth in the reverse: If there really is a God, then we should seek to forget Him, to raise up men who will to do good for goodness' sake, not out of fear of punishment for their bad deeds. How can someone give alms to a poor man with a clean heart when he believes, and has an interest in believing, that there is a God who keeps score in heaven, who looks down and nods in approval? (Henrik Pontoppidan)

這種想法出自於伏爾泰：如果上帝不存在，人類就會把祂創造出來。我發現相反的想法更具真理：如果真的有上帝，我們應該盡量忘記祂，

---

[13] 書名為《一個唯心主義者》（En Idealist）。

以培養為了善的緣故而行善的人，而非害怕因自己不良行為遭受懲罰的人。當一個人相信、並且有興趣相信，天堂中有個上帝，俯瞰著一切並一邊評分一邊點頭認可的時候，他如何能心無雜念地對窮人施捨？（亨利克・蓬托皮丹）

1918 年

We have no right to aassume that any physical laws exist, or if they have existed up to now, that they will continue to exist in a similar manner in the future. (Max Karl Ernst Ludwig Planck)

我們沒有權利假設任何物理定律存在，或者它們如果現在已存在，將來就還會以類似的方式繼續存在。（馬克斯・普朗克）

New scientific ideas never spring from a communal body however organized, but rather from the head of an individually inspired researcher who struggles with his problems in lonely thought and unites all his thought on one single point which is his whole world for the moment. (Max Karl Ernst Ludwig Planck)

新的科學思想從不出自於集體，無論其怎樣組織，而是誕生於受到個人啟發的研究者的頭腦。他在獨自思考中與難題纏鬥，將所有想法整合起來，而這就是他當時的整個世界。（馬克斯・普朗克）

Science… means unresting endeavor and continually progressing development toward an aim which the poetic intuition may apprehend, but the intellect can never fully grasp. (Max Karl Ernst Ludwig Planck)

1911-1920 動盪中的信念

科學……意味著不息的努力和不斷進步的發展，朝向詩意的直覺可以領會、但智力永遠無法充分掌握的目標邁進。（馬克斯‧普朗克）

Science sets out confidently on the endeavor finally to know the thing in itself, and even though we realize that this ideal goal can never be completely reached, still we struggle on towards it untiringly. And we know that at every step of the way each effort will be richly rewarded. (Max Karl Ernst Ludwig Planck)

科學滿懷信心地開始努力，最終理解事物本身。即使意識到這個理想目標永遠無法完全實現，我們仍然為它不懈地奮鬥。我們知道，在前進的每一個階段，每一項努力都將獲得豐厚的回報。（馬克斯‧普朗克）

We cannot rest and sit down lest we rust and decay. Health is maintained only through work. And as it is with all life so it is with science. We are always struggling from the relative to the absolute. (Max Karl Ernst Ludwig Planck)

我們不能坐下來歇息，以免生鏽腐敗。只有透過工作才能保持健康。所有生命如此，科學也不例外。我們總是奮力從相對走向絕對。（馬克斯‧普朗克）

The whole strenuous intellectual work of an industrious research worker would appear after all, in vain and hopeless, if he were not occasionally through some striking facts to find that he had, at the end of all his criss-cross journeys, at last accomplished at least one step which was conclusively nearer the truth. (Max Karl Ernst Ludwig Planck)

一位勤奮的研究人員全部艱苦的腦力勞動，最終很可能顯得徒勞而絕望；所幸他偶然獲得一些顯著的事實發現，經過一番上下求索之後，

至少終於完成了決定性地更接近真相的一步。（馬克斯‧普朗克）

An important scientific innovation rarely makes its way by gradually winning over and converting its opponents. What does happen is that its opponents gradually die out, and that the growing generation is familiarized with the ideas from the beginning. (Max Karl Ernst Ludwig Planck)

重大的科學創新很少以逐漸勝過和轉變舊觀念的方式成功。真實情況是，舊有的逐漸消亡，而成長中的一代從一開始就熟悉新觀念。（馬克斯‧普朗克）

A scientist is happy, not in resting on his attainments but in the steady acquisition of fresh knowledge. (Max Karl Ernst Ludwig Planck)

科學家的快樂，不在於享受成就，而在於穩定地獲取新知。（馬克斯‧普朗克）

It is not the possession of truth, but the success which attends the seeking after it, that enriches the seeker and brings happiness to him. (Max Karl Ernst Ludwig Planck)

不是對真理的占有，而是對真理的尋求帶來的成功，豐富了尋求者並給予他快樂。（馬克斯‧普朗克）

Scientific discovery and scientific knowledge have been achieved only by those who have gone in pursuit of them without any practical purpose whatsoever in view. (Max Karl Ernst Ludwig Planck)

科學發現和科學知識只由這些人獲得：他們一心追求它們，而眼中全無任何實用目的。（馬克斯‧普朗克）

Modern physics has taught us that the nature of any system cannot be discovered by dividing it into its component parts and studying each part by itself... We must keep our attention fixed on the whole and on the interconnection between the parts. The same is true of our intellectual life. It is impossible to make a clear cut between science, religion, and art. The whole is never equal simply to the sum of its various parts. (Max Karl Ernst Ludwig Planck)

現代物理學教導我們，任何系統的本質都不能透過將之分解為各個組成部分並單獨研究每一個部分來發現。……我們必須將注意力集中在整體性，以及各部分的相互關係。我們的智性生活也是這樣。在科學、宗教和藝術之間劃清界限是不可能的。整體絕非簡單地等於各個部分之和。（馬克斯‧普朗克）

The entire world we apprehend through our senses is no more than a tiny fragment in the vastness of Nature. (Max Karl Ernst Ludwig Planck)

我們經由各種感官理解的整個世界，不過是大自然廣闊天地中的一小塊碎片。（馬克斯‧普朗克）

Experimenters are the shock troops of science. (Max Karl Ernst Ludwig Planck)

實驗者是科學的突擊隊。（馬克斯‧普朗克）

Experiments are the only means of knowledge at our disposal. The rest is poetry, imagination. (Max Karl Ernst Ludwig Planck)

實驗是我們所掌握的唯一理解方法。餘者為詩歌，想像。（馬克斯‧普朗克）

An experiment is a question which science poses to Nature, and a measurement is the recording of Nature's answer. But before an experiment can be performed, it must be planned──the question to nature must be formulated before being posed. Before the result of a measurement can be used, it must be interpreted —— Nature's answer must be understood properly. These two tasks are those of theorists, who find himself always more and more dependent on the tools of abstract mathematics. (Max Karl Ernst Ludwig Planck)

實驗是科學向大自然提出的問題，測量則是大自然回答的紀錄。但是在實驗可以進行之前，它必須經過規劃 —— 對大自然的問題必須在提出之前加以闡釋。在測量結果可以使用之前，它必須經過說明 —— 大自然的回答必須正確理解。這兩項任務是理論家的任務，他們發現自己總是越來越依靠抽象數學的工具。（馬克斯‧普朗克）

The field of scientific abstraction encompasses independent kingdoms of ideas and of experiments and within these, rulers whose fame outlasts the centuries. But they are not the only kings in science. He also is a king who guides the spirit of his contemporaries by knowledge and creative work, by teaching and research in the field of applied science, and who conquers for science provinces which have only been raided by craftsmen. (Fritz Haber)

科學的抽象領域包括獨立的思想王國和實驗王國，其統治者的聲望在王國中歷數世紀而不衰。然而他們不僅是科學之王，也是以知識和創造性工作、以應用科學領域的教學和研究引導同時代人精神的王者，也是為科學拓土開疆的征服者，那裡本為工匠橫行的地方。（佛列茲‧哈伯）

> 1911-1920 動盪中的信念

1919 年

Research into these phenomena can do no more than contribute a little to the solution of the great problem of the structure of the atom. It will still need the work of many generations to reach that solution. Our advance from the speculative hypothesis of the atom formed by the Greek mind to the discovery of the electric nature of the structure of the atom through the Germanic research of the past century should be an encouragement and a lesson for the century to come. (Johannes Stark)

針對這些現象的研究，僅對原子結構的巨大難題稍有貢獻。仍將需要許多代人的努力才能解決。從希臘人形成的推測性原子假說，到 19 世紀德國人的研究所得出的原子結構帶電性質的發現，我們的進展應將帶給新世紀激勵和經驗。（約翰尼斯・史塔克）

As for the study of the constitution of the matter and the energy, and the physical and chemical properties beyond our planet, it requires prior knowledge that is rather thorough⋯ Current science can not answer it since it touches only the outline of things. But she does not despair of ever being able to penetrate the secret, for her progress never stops. Conscious of her power, she has faith in her destinies. This is expressed in the motto inscribed on the medal of one of our universities and which must be ours: "Science defeats darkness". (Jules Bordet)

至於地球以外的物質與能量結構、物理和化學性質，此種研究需要相當透澈的既有知識。⋯⋯目前的科學只觸及事情的概要，無法回答這些問題。然而科學並不因無法洞察祕密而絕望，因為她的進步從不停止。她意識到自己的力量，對自己的命運具備信心。這展現在一所大學徽章的箴言上，它也必然是我們的箴言：「科學戰勝蒙昧。」（朱爾・博爾代）

The ship went its steady course,

The sea was far, the day was long.

I lay in the dull doors,

A dream came to me. (Carl Friedrich Georg Spitteler)

乘船登海路，

途遠日亦長。

閉門且高臥，

悠然入夢鄉。（卡爾・施皮特勒）

It is not men that interest or disturb me primarily; it is ideas. Ideas live; men die. (Thomas Woodrow Wilson)

吸引或擾動我的主要不是人，是想法。思想活躍，人們消亡。（伍德羅・威爾遜）

Life does not consist in thinking, it consists in acting. (Thomas Woodrow Wilson)

生活不在於思索，在於行動。（伍德羅・威爾遜）

The only use of an obstacle is to be overcome. All that an obstacle does with brave men is, not to frighten them, but to challenge them. (Thomas Woodrow Wilson)

障礙的唯一用途是供人克服。對於勇敢的人，障礙所產生的全部作用並非恐嚇，而是挑戰。（伍德羅・威爾遜）

1911-1920 動盪中的信念

A man's rootage is more important than his leafage. (Thomas Woodrow Wilson)

人的根比葉更重要。（伍德羅‧威爾遜）

Character is a by-product; it is produced in the great manufacture of daily duty. (Thomas Woodrow Wilson)

性格是副產品，出自日常本分的大規模生產。（伍德羅‧威爾遜）

I am not sure that it is of the first importance that you should be happy. Many an unhappy man has been of deep service to himself and to the world. (Thomas Woodrow Wilson)

我不確定人應該快樂是否為最重要的。許多不快樂的人為自己和世界都做出了意義深刻的事情。（伍德羅‧威爾遜）

I would rather lose in a cause that will someday win, than win in a cause that will someday lose. (Thomas Woodrow Wilson)

我寧願在有一天會勝利的事業中失敗，也不願在有一天會失敗的事業中勝利。（伍德羅‧威爾遜）

There is no higher religion than human service. To work for the common good is the greatest creed. (Thomas Woodrow Wilson)

沒有比為人類服務更高尚的宗教。致力於共同利益是最偉大的信條。（伍德羅‧威爾遜）

You cannot, in human experience, rush into the light. You have to go through the twilight into the broadening day before the noon comes and the full sun is upon the landscape. (Thomas Woodrow Wilson)

> 1920 年

依照人們的經驗，你無法一下子就沐浴到天光。在麗日高懸、豔陽普照的正午來臨前，你必須經歷黃昏與逐漸展開的晨曦。（伍德羅‧威爾遜）

1920 年

To begin with, kindly contradict the vexatiously erroneous opinion, held not only by hoi polloi but even by many of the learned with respect to the achievements of the metrologist. It is true enogh that he is commonly conceded to have trained hands and eyes, to be a faithful observer, and to possess the inexhaustible perseverance required to make calculations involving the 10-millionth part of a millimeter, but it is too frequent a mistake to deny him the possession of creative imagination. Why, it was only the other day that some dull and tedious occupant of a profesor's chair solemnly remarked that the metrologist must be compared to the plow-horse patiently digging his furrow while the man of new and original ideas is the race-horse swiftly covering space to the plaudits of an admiring crowd! However, the metaphor is not entirely displeasing to me —— for when once the race is over what is there to show for it but a little dust and a little noise, while in the furrow traced by the steady plow-horse the coming harvest will tomorrow lift its head. Is it not a patent fact, indeed, that the great discoveries of scince bear a close relation to the methodical labors of the metrologist? (Charles Edouard Guillaume)

關於計量學家的成就，我首先要溫和地否定一種惱人的錯誤看法，

1911–1920 動盪中的信念

這種看法不僅一般人，甚至許多學者都持有。人們的確普遍承認計量學家具備訓練有素的手與眼，堪稱可靠的觀察者，還擁有計算直至一公釐的 10 萬分之一所需的無窮耐心，卻又否認他具有創造性想像力。這是極其常見的錯誤。譬如說，就在前些日子，有一個身居教授職位的乏味之人，一本正經地提出，須將計量學家比作悶頭翻地的耕馬，而具有新穎、原創想法的人就是賽馬，飛快地掠過場地，引得支持者一片喝采！不過，這個比方並未使我全然不快——因為一旦比賽結束，除了些許塵土、三兩雜音，還有什麼可資炫耀的？而在務實的耕馬翻出的犁溝裡，未來的收穫次日即將抬起頭來。科學的偉大發現與計量學家嚴謹的工作的確具有密切的關係，這難道不是明顯的事實嗎？（夏爾·紀堯姆）

Knowledge is the death of research. (Walther Hermann Nernst)

知識是研究的死亡。（瓦爾特·能斯特）

One should avoid carrying out an experiment requiring more than 10 per cent accuracy. (Walther Hermann Nernst)

應該避免從事準確率要求超過百分之十的實驗。（瓦爾特·能斯特）

We may fondly imagine that we are impartial seekers after truth, but with a few exceptions, to which I know that I do not belong, we are influenced —— and sometimes strongly —— by our personal bias; and we give our best thoughts to those ideas which we have to defend. (Schack August Steenberg Krogh)

我們可以天真設想自己是真理的公正追尋者，然而除了少數例外（我知道自己不在其中），我們——有時強烈地——受到個人偏見的影響。我們一心傾向於那些我們須捍衛的思想。（克羅伊）

1920 年

Personally, I bow my head under the weight of such great distinctions, but I am also proud that your Academy should have judged my shoulders strong enough to bear them. (Knut Pedersen Hamsun)

就個人而言，我為如此巨大的榮譽低下頭，不過也為貴學院[14]居然認為我的肩膀堅強得足以承受它們而自豪。（克努特·漢森）

In old age we are like a batch of letters that someone has sent. We are no longer in the past, we have arrived. (Knut Pedersen Hamsun)

人到老年，我們就像某人寄來的一批信件。我們不再處於過去，我們已經抵達。（漢克努特·漢森）

Human passions, like the forces of nature, are eternal; it is not a matter of denying their existence, but of assessing them and understanding them. Like the forces of nature, they can be subjected to man's deliberate act of will and be made to work in harmony with reason. (Léon Victor Auguste Bourgeois)

人類的熱情，猶如自然的力量，是永恆的。這並不是忽視它們的存在，而是對它們的評估和理解。猶如自然的力量，人類審慎的意志行為能夠影響它們，並使之與理性和諧地合作。（萊昂·布儒瓦）

---

[14] 即瑞典皇家科學院。

1911–1920 動盪中的信念

1921–1930
思想的交鋒

1921 年

Innovation is not the product of logical thought, even though the final product is tied to a logical structure. (Albert Einstein)

創新並非邏輯思考的產物，儘管最終結果受邏輯結構制約。（阿爾伯特·愛因斯坦）

If at first an idea isn't absurd, there's no hope for it. (Albert Einstein)

想法起初若不荒唐，它就沒有希望。（阿爾伯特·愛因斯坦）

A person who never made a mistake never tried anything new. (Albert Einstein)

從沒出過錯的人從沒嘗試過新東西。（阿爾伯特·愛因斯坦）

Imagination is more important than knowledge. For knowledge is limited, whereas imagination embraces the entire world, stimulating progress, giving birth to evolution. It is, strictly speaking, a real factor in scientific research. (Albert Einstein)

1921–1930 思想的交鋒

想像力比知識更重要。因為知識是有限的，而想像力涵蓋整個世界，刺激著進步，催生著演化。嚴格地說，它是科學研究的一個真正因素。（阿爾伯特·愛因斯坦）

Logic will get you from A to B. Imagination will take you everywhere. (Albert Einstein)

邏輯會把你從 A 引向 B。想像力會帶你到任何地方。（阿爾伯特·愛因斯坦）

The important thing is to not stop questioning. Curiosity has its own reason for existing. (Albert Einstein)

重要的是不停止提問。好奇心自有其存在的理由。（阿爾伯特·愛因斯坦）

I have no special talent. I am only passionately curious. (Albert Einstein)

我沒有特別的天分。我只是強烈地好奇。（阿爾伯特·愛因斯坦）

The only real valuable thing is intuition. The intellect has little to do on the road to discovery. (Albert Einstein)

唯一真正可貴的是直覺。智力在探索之路上用處不大。（阿爾伯特·愛因斯坦）

I think and think for months and years, ninety-nine times, the conclusion is false. The hundredth time I am right. (Albert Einstein)

我想來想去，成年累月，九十九次的結論都是錯誤的。第一百次我對了。（阿爾伯特·愛因斯坦）

Never give up on what you really want to do. The person with big dreams is more powerful than the one with all the facts. (Albert Einstein)

1921 年

永遠不要放棄真正想做的事。具有遠大夢想的人比掌握所有事實的人更強大。（阿爾伯特・愛因斯坦）

There are only two ways to live your life. One is as though nothing is a miracle. The other is as though everything is a miracle. (Albert Einstein)

你的生活只有兩種方式。一種為好像沒有一件事是奇蹟。另一種為好像每件事都是奇蹟。（阿爾伯特・愛因斯坦）

The mere formulation of a problem is far more essential than its solution, which may be merely a matter of mathematical or experimental skills. To raise new questions, new possibilities, to regard old problems from a new angle requires creative imagination and marks real advances in science. (Albert Einstein)

問題的構想本身遠比其解決重要得多，解決也許只牽涉數學或實驗技能。提出新的問題、新的可能性，從新的角度看待舊問題，需要創造性想像，代表著科學的真正進步。（阿爾伯特・愛因斯坦）

If we knew what we were doing, it wouldn't be called research, would it? (Albert Einstein)

如果我們知道自己在做什麼，這就不叫研究了。對吧？（阿爾伯特・愛因斯坦）

Creativity is contagious. Pass it on. (Albert Einstein)

創造性可以感染。傳遞下去。（阿爾伯特・愛因斯坦）

Man like every other animal is by nature indolent. If nothing spurs him on, then he will hardly think, and will behave from habit like an automation. (Albert Einstein)

人跟其他所有動物一樣，天性懶散。如果沒有刺激，他就難得動腦，只會如自動化系統般循例行事。（阿爾伯特・愛因斯坦）

1921–1930 思想的交鋒

The real value of science is in the getting, and those who have tasted the pleasure of discovery alone know what science is. A problem solved is dead. A world without problems to be solved would be devoid of science. (Frederick Soddy)

科學的真正價值在於了解，只有那些體驗過探索之樂的人才知道科學是什麼。已經解決的問題是死的。一個沒有問題需要解決的世界也會缺乏科學。（弗雷德里克‧索迪）

One thing above all gives charm to men's thoughts, and this is unrest. A mind that is not uneasy irritates and bores me. (Anatole France)

有一樣東西最使人們的思想增色，即不安分。四平八穩的頭腦令我不快而生厭。（安那托爾‧佛朗士）

It is by acts and not by ideas that people live. (Anatole France)

人皆以行動而非想法為生。（安那托爾‧佛朗士）

To accomplish great things, we must not only act, but also dream; not only plan, but also believe. (Anatole France)

欲成就非凡之事，我們不僅須行動，還須夢想；不僅須籌劃，還須相信。（安那托爾‧佛朗士）

Existence would be intolerable if we were never to dream. (Anatole France)

我們若從不夢想，生活會無法忍受。（安那托爾‧佛朗士）

It is well for the heart to be naive and the mind not to be. (Anatole France)

心性天真而頭腦未必幼稚，如此甚好。[15]（安那托爾‧佛朗士）

---

[15] 對照：大人者，不失其赤子之心者也。（孟子）

I thank fate for having made me born poor. Poverty taught me the true value of the gifts useful to life. (Anatole France)

我感謝命運使我生於寒門。貧困使我了解到實用謀生技能的真正價值。（安那托爾‧佛朗士）

Technology is a useful servant but a dangerous master. (Christian Lous Lange)

技術是得力的僕人，卻是危險的主人。（克里斯蒂安‧勞斯‧朗格）

1922 年

Every valuable human being must be a radical and a rebel for what he must aim at is to make things better than they are. (Niels Henrik David Bohr)

每一個有價值的人都必定是激進的人、叛逆的人，因為他力求使事物變得更好。（尼爾斯‧波耳）

We are all agreed that your theory is crazy. The question that divides us is whether it is crazy enough to have a chance of being correct. (Niels Henrik David Bohr)

我們都同意你的理論是瘋狂的。造成我們分歧的問題為，它是否瘋狂到有可能是正確的。（尼爾斯‧波耳）

How wonderful that we have met with a paradox. Now we have some hope of making progress. (Niels Henrik David Bohr)

多好啊，我們遇上了一個悖論。現在我們有了獲得進展的某種希望。（尼爾斯‧波耳）

1921-1930 思想的交鋒

Truth is something that we can attempt to doubt, and then perhaps, after much exertion, discover that part of the doubt is not justified. (Niels Henrik David Bohr)

真理是我們可以嘗試懷疑的東西,然後也許,在百般努力之後,發現部分懷疑並不合理。(尼爾斯·波耳)

The opposite of a correct statement is a false statement. The opposite of a profound truth may well be another profound truth. (Niels Henrik David Bohr)

正確說法的對立面是錯誤說法。深刻真理的對立面很可能是另一項深刻真理。(尼爾斯·波耳)

Two sorts of truth: profound truths recognized by the fact that the opposite is also a profound truth, in contrast to trivialities where opposites are obviously absurd. (Niels Henrik David Bohr)

兩種真理:深刻的真理,由對立面也是深刻真理的事實而獲得認同;相形之下為淺顯的道理,其對立面是明顯的荒謬。(尼爾斯·波耳)

Every sentence I utter must be understood not as an affirmation, but as a question. (Niels Henrik David Bohr)

我說的每一句話都不應被理解為肯定,而應理解為疑問。(尼爾斯·波耳)

An expert is a person who has found out by his own painful experience all the mistakes that one can make in a very narrow field. (Niels Henrik David Bohr)

專家就是這樣的人,經由自己的痛苦經驗,他找出了一個人在一個很小的領域中所能犯下的所有錯誤。(尼爾斯·波耳)

1922 年

It is wrong to think that the task of physics is to find out how nature is. Physics concerns what we can say about nature. (Niels Henrik David Bohr)

認為物理學的任務是揭示自然,這是錯誤的。物理學關注我們對自然的見解。(尼爾斯・波耳)

Physics is to be regarded not so much as the study of something a priori given, but rather as the development of methods of ordering and surveying human experience. In this respect our task must be to account for such experience in a manner independent of individual subjective judgement and therefore objective in the sense that it can be unambiguously communicated in ordinary human language. (Niels Henrik David Bohr)

與其將物理學看作對先驗結論的研究,不如視之為對整理與考察人類經驗的方法的發展。就此而言,我們的任務必須是,不依賴個人主觀判斷,從而可以用一般的人類語言明確交流的意義上屬於客觀的方式,解釋這種經驗。(尼爾斯・波耳)

The word "reality" is also a word, a word which we must learn to use correctly. (Niels Henrik David Bohr)

「真實」一詞也是個詞,一個我們必須學會正確使用的詞。(尼爾斯・波耳)

We must be clear that when it comes to atoms, language can be used only as in poetry. The poet, too, is not nearly so concerned with describing facts as with creating images and establishing mental connections. (Niels Henrik David Bohr)

我們必須清楚,談到原子時,語言只能像在詩歌中那樣運用。詩人也不那麼關心描述事實,而是關心創造意象和建立心理連結。(尼爾斯・波耳)

1921-1930 思想的交鋒

Nowadays, the individual seems to be able to choose the spiritual framework of his thoughts and actions quite freely, and this freedom reflects the fact that the boundaries between the various cultures and societies are beginning to become more fluid. But even when an individual tries to attain the greatest possible degree of independence, he will still be swayed by the existing spiritual structures —— consciously or unconsciously. (Niels Henrik David Bohr)

如今，個人似乎能夠相當自由地選擇自己思想和行動的精神框架，這種自由反映了各種文化和社會之間的界限開始變得不那麼固定的事實。但是，即便個人力圖獲得最大可能程度的獨立，他仍然會被現有的精神結構所左右 —— 有意識或無意識地。（尼爾斯·波耳）

It is a great pity that human beings cannot find all of their satisfaction in scientific contemplativeness. (Niels Henrik David Bohr)

人類無法在科學沉思中找到全部滿足，這是極大的遺憾。（尼爾斯·波耳）

Some subjects are so serious that one can only joke about them. (Niels Henrik David Bohr)

有些話題如此嚴肅，人們只能拿它們開玩笑。（尼爾斯·波耳）

Make more, more, and yet more measurements. (Francis William Aston)

做更多、更多、還要更多的測量。（弗朗西斯·阿斯頓）

Perhaps the most impressive illustration of all is to suppose that you could label the molecules in a tumbler of water... threw it anywhere you please on the earth, and went away from the earth for a few million years while all the water on the earth, the oceans, rivers, lakes and clouds had had time to mix up perfectly. Now supposing that perfect mixing had taken place, you come back to earth and draw a similar tumbler of water from the nearest tap, how many of those marked molecules would you expect to find in it? Well, the answer is 2,000. There are 2,000 times more molecules in a tumbler of water than there are tumblers of water in the whole earth. (Francis William Aston)

也許最令人印象深刻的例子是,假設你能夠將一杯水中的分子加以標記。……把水任意倒在地球上隨便什麼地方,然後離開地球幾百萬年,而地球上全部的水,海洋、河流、湖泊和雲,都有時間完全混合。現在假設完全混合已畢,你返回地球,在最近的水龍頭取類似的一杯水。你預計在杯中會找到多少個這些帶標記的分子?嗯,答案是 2,000。一杯水裡的分子數量,超過整個地球上水的杯數 2,000 倍。(弗朗西斯・阿斯頓)

The pursuit of natural knowledge, the investigation of the world —— mental and material —— in which we live, is not a dull and spiritless affair; rather is it a voyage of adventure of the human mind, a holiday for reckless and imaginative souls. (Archibald Vivian Hill)

對自然知識的追求,對我們生活於其中的世界 —— 精神和物質的 —— 的研究,不是枯燥乏味的事務,而是人類精神的冒險之旅,是隨意率性、富於想像的心靈假期。(阿奇博爾德・希爾)

Those whose lives are so filled with the romance of discovery, whose years are a holiday of exploration, do not need, do not deserve, payment for their toil. Their work itself is adequate reward, they have more happiness already than their share. (Archibald Vivian Hill)

那些一生都充滿發現之浪漫的人,他們的歲月是探索的假期,對他們的辛勞無須也不應補償。他們的工作本身即為足夠的回報,他們的快樂已經超過了自己應得的份額。(阿奇博爾德・希爾)

1921-1930 思想的交鋒

Perhaps the spirit of adventure, be it mental or material adventure, is a factor so essential in human progress, that no emphasis of it is undue. (Archibald Vivian Hill)

無論精神的還是物質的冒險，冒險精神也許是人類進步如此不可或缺的因素，怎樣強調都不為過。（阿奇博爾德·希爾）

Many luckless people imagine that romance is dead; some, over civilised, fondly suppose that there never was romance; a poet tells us that romance is unrecognised though really present; but scientists can meet him daily, walking at large and undisguised in the world. (Archibald Vivian Hill)

許多不走運的人認為浪漫已死；有些人過於文明，天真地認為從來沒有浪漫；一個詩人告訴我們，浪漫儘管確實存在但不為人知；然而科學家們每天都能遇見他，率性隨意、不遮不掩地在世上行走。（阿奇博爾德·希爾）

Biochemistry has an important bearing on the progress of medicine. But because of this, it must itself remain a pure science, whose initiates are inspired by a craving for understanding and by nothing else. (Otto Fritz Meyerhof)

生物化學對醫學進步具有重要作用。正因為如此，它本身必須始終是一門純科學，其研究者的動力出自對理解的渴望而非其他。（奧托·邁爾霍夫）

The joy of doing well is in the planting, not the harvesting. (Jacinto Benavente)

把事情做得好的快樂在於播種，而非收穫。（哈辛托·貝納文特）

If people could hear our thoughts, very few of us would escape from being locked away as mad men. (Jacinto Benavente)

1922 年

假如人們聽得到我們的思想，我們極少有人能免於被當作瘋子而被關起來。（哈辛托・貝納文特）

Everyone thinks that having a talent is a matter of luck; no one thinks that luck could be a matter of talent. (Jacinto Benavente)

人人都認為擁有天賦是運氣問題，沒有人認為運氣可能是天賦問題。（哈辛托・貝納文特）

The difficult is what takes a little time; the impossible is what takes a little longer. (Fridtjof Nansen)

困難就是需要一點時間，不可能就是需要更長的時間。（弗里喬夫・南森）

Have you not succeeded? Continue! Have you succeeded? Continue! (Fridtjof Nansen)

你還沒成功？繼續！你成功了？繼續！（弗里喬夫・南森）

Is it not in the struggle to obtain knowledge that happiness exists? I am very ignorant, consequently the conditions of happiness are mine. (Fridtjof Nansen)

幸福難道不是存在於獲得知識的奮鬥中嗎？我非常缺乏知識，所以幸福的先決條件是我的。（弗里喬夫・南森）

Happiness is the struggle towards a summit and, when it is attained, it is happiness to glimpse new summits on the other side. (Fridtjof Nansen)

幸福就是朝向頂峰奮力攀登。當登上頂峰時，幸福則是瞥見對面新的頂峰。（弗里喬夫・南森）

1921–1930 思想的交鋒

I demolish my bridges behind me —— then there is no choice but forward. (Fridtjof Nansen)

我拆掉了身後的橋——如此便別無選擇，唯有前行。（弗里喬夫·南森）

1923 年

The fact that Science walks forward on two feet, namely theory and experiment, is nowhere better illustrated than in the two fields for slight contributions to which you have done me the great honour of awarding the the Nobel Prize in Physics for the year 1923. Sometimes it is one foot that is put forward first, sometimes the other, but continuous progress is only made by the use of both —— by theorizing and then testing, or by finding new relations in the process of experimenting and then bringing the theoretical foot up and pushing it on beyond, and so on in unending alterations. (Robert Andrews Millikan)

科學依靠理論和實驗這兩隻腳而前進的事實，沒有比在 1923 年你們授予我諾貝爾物理學獎的這兩個領域展現得更鮮明的了。這雙腳有時一隻先邁出，有時是另一隻，但實現持續進步只能靠兩足並用——理論化，然後測試；或者在實驗過程中發現新的關係，從而帶動理論之足並推動其前行，如此交替而無止無休。（羅伯特·密立坎）

I therefore am very hopeful that in the future quantitative organic microanalysis will find many more fields of application and expansion, and that it will make possible much insight and discernment. (Fritz Pregl)

1923 年

我因而非常希望，在未來的定量有機微分析中將發現更多的應用和擴展領域，而它將帶來許多洞察力與辨別力。（弗里茨·普雷格爾）

One has to exceed the limit to know where the limit is. (Frederick Grant Banting)

人必須越過極限以了解極限何在。（弗雷德里克·班廷）

No one has ever had an idea in a dress suit. (Frederick Grant Banting)

從來沒有人身著正裝而產生想法。（弗雷德里克·班廷）

The greatest joy of life is to accomplish. It is the getting, not the having. It is the giving, not the keeping. I am a firm believer in the theory that you can do or be anything that you wish in this world, within reason, if you are prepared to make the sacrifices, think and work hard enough and long enough. (Frederick Grant Banting)

人生最大的快樂是有所成就。是獲得，而非擁有。是給予，而非保留。我堅信這一項理論：在這個世界上，只要準備好做出犧牲，足夠努力、足夠長久地思考和工作，在合理的範圍內，你就能如願做到任何事，成為任何人。（弗雷德里克·班廷）

I have attempted to review but a small part of the work relating to insulin and have only cursorily referred to the perplexing problem of the mechanism of its action in the animal body. Facts of importance in this regard come almost daily to light and it is to be anticipated that, as these accumulate, a great advance will become possible in our knowledge of the history of carbohydrates in the animal body. (John James Rickard Macleod)

我試著回顧了一下與胰島素有關的一小部分工作，只粗略涉及它在動物體內作用機制的複雜問題。在這方面，重要的事實幾乎天天出現。

可以預期，隨著這些事實的累積，我們對動物體內碳水化合物歷史的了解將可能獲得重大進展。（約翰・麥克勞德）

What is literature but the expression of moods by the vehicle of symbol and incident? And are there not moods which need heaven, hell, purgatory, and fairyland for their expression, no less than this dilapidated earth? Nay, are there not moods which shall find no expression unless there be men who dare to mix heaven, hell, purgatory, and fairyland together, or even to set the heads of beasts to the bodies of men, or to thrust the souls of men into the heart of rocks? Let us go forth, the tellers of tales, and seize whatever prey the heart long for, and have no fear. (William Butler Yeats)

文學不就是藉助象徵和事件以表達心境嗎？難道沒有除了凋敝的人世，還需要天堂、地獄、煉獄和仙界來表達的心境嗎？甚而，要由大膽的人將天堂、地獄、煉獄和仙界合成一處，乃至把獸首安到人身上，把人的靈魂注入岩石中——難道沒有非如此即無從表達的心境嗎？講故事的人們，讓我們放縱想像，隨心所欲地獵異逐奇，而無須顧忌。（威廉・巴特勒・葉慈）

The intellect of man is forced to choose Perfection of the life, or of the work. (William Butler Yeats)

人的理智被迫選擇生活的完美或工作的完美。（威廉・巴特勒・葉慈）

What can be explained is not poetry. (William Butler Yeats)

能夠解釋的就不是詩。[16]（威廉・巴特勒・葉慈）

There are things it is well not to ponder over too much, things that bare words are the best suited for. (William Butler Yeats)

---

[16] 對照：詩無達詁。（董仲舒）

有些事最好不要過於推敲思索，採用直白的話語就極其合適。（威廉·巴特勒·葉慈）

One loses, as one grows older, something of the lightness of one's dreams; one begins to take life up in both hands, and to care more for the fruit than the flower. (William Butler Yeats)

隨著年歲增加，人會日益務實，開始珍視人生，更看重果實而非花朵。（威廉·巴特勒·葉慈）

1924 年

All the information on what goes on in this field of physical phenomena is, so to speak, transmitted in the language of the X-rays; it is a language which we must master if we are to be able to understand and interpret this information properly. (Karl Manne Georg Siegbahn)

可以說，關於這個物理現象領域的所有資訊都是以 X 射線的語言傳送的。想要正確地理解和解釋這種資訊，我們就必須掌握這門語言。（曼內·西格巴恩）

A new chapter has been opened in the study of heart diseases, not by the work of a single investigator, but by that of many talented men. (Willem Einthoven)

心臟病研究翻開了新篇章，不是由於單一研究者的工作，而是由於許多富於才華的人的共同努力。（威廉·埃因托芬）

I dreamed of great actions, of voyages —— rovings across the oceans of a free and independent life. (Wladyslaw Stanislaw Reymont)

1921-1930 思想的交鋒

我夢想偉業，夢想遠航——漫遊四海，憧憬自由而獨立的人生。（瓦迪斯瓦夫·雷蒙特）

Everything must go its own way. One has to plow in order to sow, one has to sow in order to harvest, and what is disturbing has to be weeded out, like a bad weed. (Wladyslaw Stanislaw Reymont)

萬物均須循自己的途徑發展。農人必須耕地才能播種，必須播種才能收穫，是干擾就必須排除，猶如剷去雜草。（瓦迪斯瓦夫·雷蒙特）

1925 年

The only way I can tell that a new idea is really important is the feeling of terror that seizes me. (James Franck)

我能確定一個新想法的確重要的唯一途徑，是突如其來的恐懼感。（詹姆斯·法蘭克）

Actually, I became interested in physics much earlier than I knew the word physics. I remember that I was always astonished about everything that I saw around me. (James Franck)

實際上，我對物理產生興趣遠遠早於知道物理這個詞。我記得自己總是驚奇於眼中的周圍每一樣東西。（詹姆斯·法蘭克）

My whole life has showed me that it is very difficult to change one's mind, but that if one wants to be a scientist one has always to be willing to change one's mind and forget. (James Franck)

1925 年

畢生經驗告訴我，改變一個人的想法難乎其難；但想當科學家，就必須願意改變自己的想法並將其忘卻。（詹姆斯・法蘭克）

You see things; you say, "Why?" But I dream things that never were; and I say "Why not?" (George Bernard Shaw)

你看見事物，你說：「為什麼？」然而我夢想從來沒有的事物，並說「為什麼沒有？」（蕭伯納）

Imagination is the beginning of creation. You imagine what you desire, you will what you imagine and at last you create what you will. (George Bernard Shaw)

想像是創造的開始。你想像所渴望的，你追求所想像的，最後你創造所追求的。（蕭伯納）

Those who cannot change their minds cannot change anything. (George Bernard Shaw)

不能改變想法的人，什麼都改變不了。（蕭伯納）

Life isn't about finding yourself. Life is about creating yourself. (George Bernard Shaw)

人生不在於尋找你自己。人生在於創造你自己。（蕭伯納）

People are always blaming circumstances for what they are. I don't believe in circumstances. The people who get on in this world are the people who get up and look for the circumstances they want, and, if they can't find them, make them. (George Bernard Shaw)

人們總是將自己的狀況歸咎於環境。我不相信環境。世間出類拔萃之輩皆為起而尋求如意環境之人，並且，倘若找不到它們，就創造它們。（蕭伯納）

1921-1930 思想的交鋒

The reasonable man adapts himself to the world; the unreasonable one persists in trying to adapt the world to himself. Therefore all progress depends upon the unreasonable man. (George Bernard Shaw)

明事理的人使自己適應世界,不明事理的人堅持使世界適應自己。所以一切進步全靠不明事理的人。(蕭伯納)

Remember that you are a human being with a soul and the divine gift of articulate speech: that your native language is the language of Shakespeare and Milton and The Bible; and don't sit there crooning like a bilious pigeon. (George Bernard Shaw)

記住你是擁有靈魂和非凡口才之人:你的母語是莎士比亞、米爾頓和《聖經》的語言,不要坐在那裡像一隻令人不快的鴿子一樣咕咕噥噥。(蕭伯納)

A life spent making mistakes is not only more honorable, but more useful than a life spent doing nothing. (George Bernard Shaw)

與無所事事的一生相比,屢屢犯錯的一生不僅更可敬,而且更有用。(蕭伯納)

After all, the wrong road always leads somewhere. (George Bernard Shaw)

畢竟,錯誤的路總會帶你去某個地方。(蕭伯納)

When I was young I observed that nine out of every ten things I did were failures, so I did ten times more work. (George Bernard Shaw)

年輕的時候,我注意到自己每做十件事有九件失敗,於是我就做十倍的工作。(蕭伯納)

Success does not consist in never making mistakes but in never making the same one a second time. (George Bernard Shaw)

成功不在於永不犯錯,而在於永不再犯同樣的錯誤。(蕭伯納)

A little learning is a dangerous thing; Drink deep or taste not the Pierian spring. (George Bernard Shaw)

學習淺嘗輒止是危險的;熟讀深思,否則喝不到知識之泉。(蕭伯納)

Science is always wrong: it never solves a problem without creating ten more. (George Bernard Shaw)

科學總是不對勁:它每解決一個問題都必定再造出十個來。(蕭伯納)

If you have an apple and I have an apple and we exchange these apples then you and I will still each have one apple. But if you have an idea and I have an idea and we exchange these ideas, then each of us will have two ideas. (George Bernard Shaw)

如果你有一個蘋果,我有一個蘋果,我們交換這些蘋果,那麼你我仍然各有一個蘋果。但如果你有一個想法,我有一個想法,我們交換這些想法,那麼每個人都會有兩個想法。(蕭伯納)

You don't stop laughing when you grow old, you grow old when you stop laughing. (George Bernard Shaw)

年老時你別停止笑,停止笑時你就老了。(蕭伯納)

We move from one crisis to another. We suffer one disturbance and shock after another. (Austen Chamberlain)

1921–1930 思想的交鋒

我們從一個危機轉到另一個危機。我們一次又一次擔驚受怕。（奧斯丁·張伯倫）

Hope is a willing slave; despair is free. (Charles Gates Dawes)

希望畢恭畢敬聽憑調遣，絕望無需費用不請自來。（查爾斯·蓋茲·道威斯）

How majestic is naturalness. I have never met a man whom I really considered a great man who was not always natural and simple. Affectation is inevitably the mark of one not sure of himself. (Charles Gates Dawes)

本色天然何等高貴。我見過並真正認為非凡的人，無一不總是自然樸實的。矯揉造作必定是缺乏自信之人的象徵。（查爾斯·蓋茲·道威斯）

1926 年

Particularly at the end of the last century, certain scholars considered that since the appearances on our scale were finally the only important ones for us, there was no point in seeking what might exist in an inaccessible domain. I find it very difficult to understand this point of view since what is inaccessible today may become accessible tomorrow (as has happened by the invention of the microscope), and also because coherent assumptions on what is still invisible may increase our understanding of the visible. (Jean Baptiste Perrin)

尤其在上世紀末，有些學者認為，既然天平上稱得出來的東西最終才是對我們唯一重要的，在無法進入的領域中尋找也許存在之物就沒有意義。我覺得這種觀點很難理解，因為今天不可接近之物可能明天變得

可以接近（就像顯微鏡的發明），而且對尚不可見事物的連貫假設可能增加對可見事物的理解。（尚·佩蘭）

A glance at the history of science and technics shows that it is precisely the search for truth without any preconceived ideas, research for the sake of knowledge alone, that in the long run has most benefited humanity. The investigations which have seemingly been the most purely abstract have often formed the foundation of the most important changes or improvements in the conditions of human life. (Theodor Svedberg)

瀏覽科學技術史，從長遠看來，正是對真理沒有任何預設觀念的尋求，僅僅為了知識而進行的研究，方才最有益於人類。看似最純粹抽象的研究，往往形成人類生活條件中最重要的變化或改善的基礎。（特奧多爾·斯韋德貝里）

The study of the manifold problems presented by cancer has, in recent years, seemed to offer many more riddles than were previously thought to exist; but the history of medicine has never known a period in which problems could be attacked in so many different ways as those made accessible today by the working methods now at our command. (Johannes Andreas Grib Fibiger)

近年來，對癌症帶來的各種問題的研究，似乎提出了比先前認為的更多的謎團；然而，醫學史也從未見過一個時期，其中的難題可以經由眾多的不同途徑突破瓶頸，就像如今我們掌握的工作方法所能採取的一樣。（約翰尼斯·菲比格）

It is the supreme art of the teacher to awaken joy in creative expression and knowledge. (Grazia Deledda)

1921–1930 思想的交鋒

喚醒學生對於創造性表達和知識的喜悅是教師的最高藝術。（格拉齊亞・黛萊達）

I have come to believe that a great teacher is a great artist and that there are as few as there are any other great artists. Teaching might even be the greatest of the arts since the medium is the human mind and spirit. (Grazia Deledda)

我於是相信，偉大的教師是偉大的藝術家，而且其數量之少一如其他偉大的藝術家。教學甚至可能是最偉大的藝術，因為媒介是人類的思想與精神。（格拉齊亞・黛萊達）

Success is not the key to happiness. Happiness is the key to success. If you love what you are doing, you will be successful. (Aristide Briand)

成功不是快樂的關鍵。快樂是成功的關鍵。熱愛正在做的事情，你就會成功。（阿里斯蒂德・白里安）

People think too historically. They are always living half in a cemetery. (Aristide Briand)

人們的思考過於拘泥歷史了。他們總是一半活在墓地裡。（阿里斯蒂德・白里安）

The life of the individual is a continuous combat with errors and obstacles, and no victory is more satisfying than the one achieved against opposition. (Gustav Stresemann)

人生是一場與錯誤與障礙的持續戰鬥，而迎難而上所獲得的勝利最為酣暢淋漓。（古斯塔夫・施特雷澤曼）

To walk behind others on a road you are traveling together, to give precedence to others without envy —— this is painful for an individual and painful for a nation. (Gustav Stresemann)

一路同行而落後於他人，讓出領先位置而無妒意 —— 這對於個人是痛苦的，對於國家也一樣。（古斯塔夫・施特雷澤曼曼）

1927 年

Several years ago I was reading Marco Polo's account of his experiences in the employ of the great Emperor of China, Kublai Khan. He was telling his incredulous Venetian friends of the daily life of the Chinese. "They take two baths daily", he wrote, "one in the morning and another in the evening. Not only this, but the baths are in warm water". The idea of daily baths was itself sufficiently difficult for the Venetians to believe, but that water could be warmed twice daily seemed to them to present an insurmountable difficulty.

Polo replied that it would indeed have been impossible to heat the water for millions of Chinese if they had relied on wood for fuel. They had however solved the difficulty by finding a kind of black rock which would burn. This rock had the advantage over wood that it would hold its fire overnight and have the water warm for the morning bath. Then Polo described in accurate detail how this black rock occurred in veins in the mountains, and the manner in which it was quarried. If the idea of baths twice daily was marvelous, the story of the burning rocks was beyond the realm of possibility.

Marco Polo's stories read like the tales of a man who after visiting a highly civilized country returns to his semi-barbaric home to tell of the wonders he has seen. At that time, hardly seven centuries ago, China was far in advance of Italy, a land whose culture was the pride of our Western civilization.

Last year I had the privilege of visiting China, and I saw what, gauged by Western standards, was a primitive country. In seven short centuries the leadership has passed from the East to the West, until now we are as far ahead of the Orient as in Polo's day China was ahead of Italy.

Why this rapid change? Differences in native ability will not explain it. It was only a few centuries ago that a Mongolian ruler, Jenghis Khan, held sway over the greatest empire, with regard to both area and population, which has ever been united under one government. Nor have the Chinese been lacking in feats of engineering. The Great Wall of China, a massive pile of masonry extending over mountainous country for fifteen hundred miles[17], takes a high place among the wonders of the world. Is it doubtful whether either in individual ability or in aptitude for organization the European has any real advantage over the Mongolian.

Shortly after the days of Polo, however, there arose in various parts of Europe the scientific spirit —— the eagerness to learn from Nature her truths, and to put these truths to the use of mankind. The rapid change in our mode of living since that time can certainly be traced to the consequences of the development of this spirit of science. When we seek the reason for the present preeminence of the European peoples, we find that it lies in the great power given

---

[17]　原文如此。

to us by the search for truth and its application to our daily lives.

I verily believe that in the advancement of science lies the hope of our civilization. (Arthur Holly Compton)

幾年前，我讀到馬可·波羅作為大帝忽必烈汗朝臣的自述。他向半信半疑的威尼斯朋友們講述中國人的日常生活。「他們每天洗兩次澡，」他寫道，「早上一次，晚上一次。不僅如此，還是泡熱水澡。」對於威尼斯人，每天洗澡的說法本身就很難置信；而每天能燒兩次水，在他們看來更是難乎其難。

波羅答曰，他們若是靠木柴，的確不可能讓千百萬中國人燒熱水。然而，他們憑著找到一種可燃的黑色石頭，解決了這個困難。這種石頭優越於木柴之處，在於它的火會整夜不熄，維持用於早晨沐浴的水溫。然後，波羅細緻地描述了這種黑色石頭是如何在山間形成礦脈，以及怎樣開採。如果每天洗兩次澡的想法不可思議，燃燒石頭的故事就超出了可能性的範圍。

馬可·波羅的故事，讀起來就像有人訪問一個高度文明的國家後，回到半野蠻的家，講述所見的各種奇觀。那時候，不過7個世紀之前，中國還遠遠領先於義大利，而義大利這片土地的文化是西方文明的驕傲。

1926年我有機會訪問中國，見到的是以西方標準衡量的一個原始國家。在短短7個世紀裡，領導地位已經從東方轉移到西方。直到現在，我們遙遙領先於東方，就像在波羅的時代裡中國領先於義大利。

如此急遽的變化原因何在？國人能力的差異是解釋不了的。就在幾個世紀前，蒙古統治者，成吉思汗，控制著有史以來最大的帝國，面積與人口皆如此，統一於一個統治政權。中國人也從不缺乏工程技藝。中國長城，一道巨大的石牆，綿延山野數千英里，在世界奇觀中占據了很

> 1921–1930 思想的交鋒

高的地位。無論個人能力還是組織天分，與蒙古人相比，歐洲人是否有任何真正優勢，值得懷疑。

然而，在波羅的時代之後不久，歐洲各地都湧現出科學精神——向大自然學習她的真理，並付諸人類運用的渴望。我們生活模式從那時起的迅速變化，當然可以追溯至這種科學精神的發展結果。尋找歐洲人民當今卓越的原因時，我們發現，它就在於對真理及其日常應用的索求所賦予的偉大力量。

我堅信，科學的進步承載著我們文明的希望。（阿瑟·康普頓）

My choice of a subject to work upon was not due to any forethought on my own part nor to any good advice received, but just to the fact that in the autumn of 1894 I spent a few weeks on a cloudy Scottish hill-top —— the top of Ben Nevis. Morning after morning I saw the sun rise above a sea of clouds and the shadow of the hill on the clouds below surrounded by gorgeous coloured rings. The beauty of what I saw made me fall in love with clouds and I made up my mind to make experiments to learn more about them. Working in J. J. Thomson's laboratory during the years when X-rays and radio-activity were discovered, I could not help being interested in ions —— and with ions and clouds I have worked ever since. (Charles Thomson Rees Wilson)

我對研究課題的選擇，既非出於自己的什麼先見之明，也非得自任何卓越建議，而只是由於西元1894年秋，我在蘇格蘭的一座山——本尼維斯山多雲的峰頂盤桓了幾個星期。每天清晨，我都眺望一輪朝陽從雲海中升起，下方雲上的山影周遭輝映著絢麗的五彩光環。滿目華美使我愛上了雲，於是決意以實驗更多地了解它們。在人們發現X射線和放

1927 年

射性的那些年,我在 J·J·湯木生[18]的實驗室裡工作,不禁對離子產生了興趣——從那時起,我就從事離子和雲的研究了。(C·T·R·威爾遜)

However learned or eloquent, man knows nothing truly that he has not learned from experience. (Heinrich Otto Wieland)

無論何等博學或雄辯,只要不曾從經驗中學習,人即無真知。(海因里希·奧托·威蘭)

For, as the ambition of the Napoleonic soldiers was aroused by the saying that everyone wears the Marshal's Staff in his knapsack, so that all who work in the said peaceful areas should hold the entitlement to the Nobel Prize, so that they take the beautiful Homeric verse as a guideline:"Always to be the first and to stand out from others". (Julius Wagner-Jauregg)

每一個士兵都在背包裡裝著元帥的權杖,這句名言激發了拿破崙部下的雄心。同樣地,所有在所謂和平區域工作的人都應該秉持獲得諾貝爾獎的資格,從而將荷馬優美的詩句作為指南:「出類拔萃,永遠爭先。」(朱利葉斯·瓦格納－堯雷格)

The more deeply we study the nature of time, the better we understand that duration means invention, creation of forms, continuous elaboration of the absolutely new. (Henri Bergson)

越深入研究時間的本質,就越充分理解時間的持續意味著發明、形式的創造、對全新事物的不斷詮釋。(亨利·柏格森)

To exist is to change, to change is to mature, to mature is to go on creating oneself endlessly. (Henri Bergson)

---

[18] J·J·湯木生,1906 年諾貝爾物理學獎得主。

1921-1930 思想的交鋒

生存就是改變，改變就是成熟，成熟就是持續不斷地自我創造。（亨利・柏格森）

A Prague superintendent of instruction, Mr. Franta, has asked his pupils to adopt the habit of asking themselves the following question: Who benefited mankind more, the conqueror of Cannes —— or the poor unknown man who first forged an iron plough? (Ferdinand Buisson)

布拉格有位督學，弗朗塔先生，曾要求學生養成問自己如下問題的習慣：誰更造福於人類，是坎城的征服者，還是最先鍛造出鐵犁的那位貧窮的無名氏？（費迪南・比松）

In life, particularly in public life, psychology is more powerful than logic. (Ludwig Quidde)

在生活中，尤其在公共生活中，心理學比邏輯更強大。（路德維希・克維德）

1928 年

I willingly admit that Stockholm is one of the finest cities of the world. Indeed I am not prepared to quarrel with the assertion that it is the world's finest city. I also hope that, as one of the fortunate beneficiaries under his magnificent bequest, I am prepared to pay a fitting tribute to the genius and magnanimity of Alfred Nobel. I will not, however, pursue these matters further. The same theme has been admirably covered by my colleague Sir Frederick Hopkins. If I were to succeed in doing it better, I might be in danger of acquiring his perpetual enmity. If on the other hand I succeeded in doing it much worse, I might be equally in danger of losing, what I value much, your continued friendship. (Owen Willans Richardson)

我欣然承認，斯德哥爾摩是世界上最美好的城市之一。即便說它就是世界上最美好的城市，我也全無異議。作為阿佛烈·諾貝爾高尚遺贈的幸運接受者，我還希望，對他的天才與慷慨致以得當的敬意。不過，這些話我就不再說下去了。同樣的話題已被我的同事弗雷德里克·霍普金斯先生精采談及。我要是說得更好，恐怕招致他的永久敵意。另一方面，我要是講得遠遠不如，又同樣怕失去自己異常珍視的，你們的持久友誼。[19]（歐文·理查森）

To have to look at injustice and not to be able to help is difficult to bear. (Adolf Otto Reinhold Windaus)

不得不目睹不公正而無能為力，這令人難以承受。（阿道夫·溫道斯）

If in 1914 we had been unaware of the mode of transmission of typhus, and if infected lice had been imported into Europe, the war would not have ended by a bloody victory. It would have ended in an unparalleled catastrophe, the most terrible in human history. Soldiers at the front, reserves, prisoners, civilians, neutrals even, the whole of humanity would have collapsed. (Charles Jules Henri Nicolle)

假如1914年我們不知道斑疹傷寒的傳播模式[20]，假如感染的蝨子傳入歐洲，第一次世界大戰就不會以慘勝結束。它會在空前的災難中結

---

[19] 這是理查森在諾貝爾獎宴會上的發言。弗雷德里克·霍普金斯，1929年諾貝爾生理學或醫學獎得主。
[20] 尼科勒發現了蝨子是傳播斑疹傷寒的媒介。由於對斑疹傷寒的研究，他於1928年獲得諾貝爾生理學或醫學獎。

1921-1930 思想的交鋒

束，人類史上最可怕的一場。前線士兵、後備部隊、囚犯、平民，甚至中立者，整個人類都會崩潰。（夏爾·尼科勒）

All my days I have longed equally to travel the right road and to take my own errant path. (Sigrid Undset)

我畢生都渴望既循規蹈矩又特立獨行。（西格麗德·溫塞特）

It's a good thing when you don't dare do something if you don't think it's right. But it's not good when you think something's not right because you don't dare do it. (Sigrid Undset)

認為某事不對而不敢做，這是好事。然而由於不敢做而認為某事不對，這個不好。（西格麗德·溫塞特）

1929 年

Vulnerable, like all men, to the temptations of arrogance, of which intellectual pride is the worst, the scientist must nevertheless remain sincere and modest, if only because his studies constantly bring home to him that, compared with the gigantic aims of science, his own contribution, no matter how important, is only a drop in the ocean of truth. (Louis-Victor Pierre Raymond de Broglie)

科學家與常人無異，難免流於自高自大，其中以知識為傲最為糟糕，科學家還是必須保持誠懇和謙虛，因為其研究不斷提醒他，與科學的巨大目標相比，自己的貢獻無論多麼重要，不過是真理的滄海一粟。（路易·德布羅意）

> 1929 年

Two seemingly incompatible conceptions can each represent an aspect of the truth… They may serve in turn to represent the facts without ever entering into direct conflict. (Louis-Victor Pierre Raymond de Broglie)

兩種貌似不相容的觀念能夠各自表現真理的一個方面。……它們可以輪流表現事實,而永不直接衝突。(路易·德布羅意)

Biochemistry, one of the youngest of the Sciences, has gradually arisen as an independent branch of learning and research during the last fifty years. This science continues the line of study which was at first that of organic chemistry, which, as its name indicates, was devoted to the chemistry of organised matter. (Arthur Harden)

生物化學,最年輕的學科之一,作為學習和研究的獨立分支,在過去 50 年中逐漸興起。這一門學科延續了起先屬於有機化學的研究路線,而有機化學,如其名稱所示,致力於有機物質的化學研究。(阿瑟·哈登)

If I may for a moment yield to the Scandinavian atmosphere of Saga and fairy tale, Biochemistry was for long the Cinderella of the Sciences, lorded over by her elder —— though I will not say ugly —— sisters, Chemistry and Physiology. But now the secret visit to the ball has been paid, the fur slipper has been found and brought home (no doubt to the Nobel Institute) by the Prince, and Biochemistry, raised to a position of proud independence, knocks boldly at the door of the Palace of Life itself. (Arthur Harden)

我若可暫且採取北歐傳說和童話故事的斯堪地那維亞風格,生物化學就長期相當於科學的灰姑娘,屈居於她的 —— 雖然我不會說醜陋的 —— 姊姊,化學和生理學之下。不過現在,秘密參加舞會之舉已經獲得回報，舞鞋[21]已由王子發現並帶回家（不用說就是諾貝爾協會），而生物化學被提升至自豪的獨立地位，大膽地叩響了生命的宮殿大門。（阿瑟・哈登）

Any scientific problem must be attacked by research into detail; the natural scientist did not win his victories until he left meditation on the great riddles of the world and began a careful study of special problems; our knowledge —— of more general associations and of far-reaching laws —— has grown out of the results of such research. (Hans Karl August Simon von Euler-Chelpin)

任何科學問題都必須經由細緻深入的探究解決。在放棄對世界重大謎團的冥想，而著手對特定問題的認真研究之前，自然科學家的勝利無從談起。我們的知識 —— 關於更普遍的關聯、關於影響深遠的法則 —— 就是從這些探究的成果中得出。（漢斯・馮・奧伊勒—切爾平）

The world is my country, science is my religion. (Christiaan Eijkman)

世界是我的國家，科學是我的宗教。（克里斯蒂安・艾克曼）

Simplicity is no sign of truth. (Christiaan Eijkman)

簡單並不是真理的符號。（克里斯蒂安・艾克曼）

Are honours and rewards the more desirable in the days of full vigour or after most of one's work is done? I am not sure that the more obvious answer is the right one. Youth, it is true, needs sustenance, but should need no tonic. The pulse of age may be quickened by the recognition of past efforts and unsuspected capacity for further effort thus revealed. (Frederick Gowland Hopkins)

---

[21] 在灰姑娘故事的最初版本中，她穿的是毛皮便鞋。水晶鞋是在後來的版本中出現並取而代之的。

1929 年

榮譽和獎勵是在一個人生龍活虎的日子裡比較值得擁有，還是在大多數工作完成之後？我不確定更明顯的答案就是正確的。年輕，的確需要營養，但不需要進補。對於以往成就，以及從而顯示其獲得進一步成就的潛力的認可，可能會加快年齡的脈搏。（弗雷德里克·霍普金斯）

Solitude begets originality, bold and disconcerting beauty, poetry. But solitude can also beget perversity, disparity, the absurd and the forbidden. (Thomas Mann)

孤獨產生創意、大膽而令人不安的美感與詩歌。但孤獨也能導致反常、另類、荒誕和禁忌。（湯瑪斯·曼）

Thought that can merge wholly into feeling, feeling that can merge wholly into thought, these are the artist's highest joy. (Thomas Mann)

能夠完全融入感覺的思想、能夠完全融入思想的感覺，這些是藝術家的至高樂趣。（湯瑪斯·曼）

A writer is someone for whom writing is more difficult than it is for other people. (Thomas Mann)

作家是那些比其他人覺得寫作更困難的人。（湯瑪斯·曼）

We are not born, my dear daughter, to pursue our own small personal happiness, for we are not separate, independent, self-subsisting individuals, but links in a chain; and it is inconceivable that we would be what we are without those who have preceded us and shown us the path that they themselves have scrupulously trod. (Thomas Mann)

親愛的女兒，我們不是生來追求自身小小個人幸福的，因為我們不是分別的、獨立的、自力生存的個體，而是鏈條上的環節。如果沒有那

1921-1930 思想的交鋒

些先行者，他們把自己謹慎前行的路指給我們看，我們不可能獲得今天的成就。（湯瑪斯·曼）

It is not to be expected that human nature will change in a day. (Frank Billings Kellogg)

不要指望人類本性一朝一夕就會改變。（弗蘭克·B·凱洛格）

1930 年

The essence of science is independent thinking, hard work, and not equipment. When I got my Nobel Prize, I had spent hardly 200 rupees on my equipment. (Chandrasekhara Venkata Raman)

科學的要素是獨立思考、努力工作，而不是設備。我獲得諾貝爾獎時，花在設備上的錢幾乎不到 200 盧比。（錢德拉塞卡拉·拉曼）

Owing to the difficulty of dealing with substances of high molecular weight we are still a long way from having determined the chemical characteristics and the constitution of proteins, which are regarded as the principal constituents of living organisms. (Karl Landsteiner)

由於處理高分子量物質的困難，要確定蛋白質的化學特性和構成，我們還有很長的路要走，而蛋白質被認為是生物體的主要成分。（卡爾·蘭德施泰納）

He is the only real revolutionary the authentic scientist because he alone knows how little he knows. (Sinclair Lewis)

> 1930 年

他是唯一真正革命性的、實實在在的科學家,因為唯有他清楚自己所知何等有限。(辛克萊・路易斯)

In the study of the profession to which he had looked forward all his life he found irritation and vacuity as well as serene wisdom; he saw no one clear path to Truth but a thousand paths to a thousand truths far-off and doubtful. (Sinclair Lewis)

在一生都放不下的專業研究中,他既發現了澄明的智慧,也發現了氣惱與虛空。他看不出一條直達真理的路,而只見上千條通往上千種真實的路,路途遙遠,疑慮重重。(辛克萊・路易斯)

He insisted that there is no Truth, but only many truths; that Truth is not a colored bird to be chased among the rocks and captured by it's tail, but a skeptical attitude on life. (Sinclair Lewis)

他堅持並不存在真理,只有許多事實;所謂真理並非一隻色彩斑斕的鳥,在山石間由人追逐,揪住尾巴捕獲,而是一種對生活的懷疑態度。(辛克萊・路易斯)

We must struggle to win peace, struggle against schism, against the mad measures of fear, against the ruthlessness of Mammon, against hatred and injustice. (Lars Olof Jonathan Söderblom)

我們必須奮力贏得和平,奮力反對分裂,反對恐懼的瘋狂手段,反對貪婪的無情,反對仇恨和不公正。(納坦・瑟德布盧姆)

1921–1930 思想的交鋒

1931–1939
黑暗時代的堅持

1931 年

Schools cannot shut their door and expect a safe "castle" where outside influences don't enter. (Carl Bosch)

學校不能關閉大門並指望成為隔絕外界影響的安全「城堡」。（卡爾·博施）

The house in which I received my first training as a chemist, the laboratory of the University of Breslau, carried in its entrance hall the motto "Seek the truth and do not ask what it benefits". I have followed this doctrine only a few years and have then set myself the goal of seeking insights that should benefit mankind. (Friedrich Bergius)

我接受最初化學培訓的處所是布雷斯勞大學的實驗室。入口大廳牆上有一句格言：「尋求真理而不問益處」。我遵從這一項信條幾年之後，就一心尋求有益於人類的見解。（弗里德里希·貝吉烏斯）

And should any poem of mine recall

The surge of the storm, the cataract's fall,

1931-1939 黑暗時代的堅持

Some thought with a manly ring,

A lark's note, the glow of the heath, somehow,

Or the sigh of the woodland vast ——

You sang in silence through ages past

That song by your cart and your plough. (Erik Axel Karlfeldt)

我的每首詩作都應當喚起

飛瀑的轟鳴,暴風雨的激盪,

某種籠罩強烈光環的思想,

乃至雲雀的啼聲,荒野的熱浪,

或者廣袤林地的唏噓感嘆 ——

你在靜靜流逝的歲月中歌唱,

趕著你的馬車,扶著你的犁杖。(艾瑞克‧阿克塞爾‧卡爾費爾特)

It was very important not to pretend to understand what you didn't understand and that you must always be honest with yourself inside, whatever happened. (Jane Addams)

非常重要的是,不懂的事情不要裝懂,對自己內心必須永遠誠實,無論任何事情。(珍‧亞當斯)

You do not know what life means when all the difficulties are removed! I am simply smothered and sickened with advantages. It is like eating a sweet dessert the first thing in the morning. (Jane Addams)

一旦所有的困難都被消除,你就不知道生命的意義何在了!我只會感到煩悶,對無往不利生厭。猶如早餐先吃甜點一樣。(珍‧亞當斯)

1931 年

All the problems of the world could be settled easily if men were only willing to think. The trouble is that men very often resort to all sorts of devices in order not to think, because thinking is such hard work. (Nicholas Murray Butler)

只要人們願意思考，世界上所有的問題都可以輕易解決。麻煩在於，人們一再地經由各種手段以避免思考，因為思考實在辛苦。（尼古拉斯·默里·巴特勒）

Optimism is essential to achievement and it is also the foundation of courage and true progress. (Nicholas Murray Butler)

樂觀對成就不可或缺，也是勇氣和真正進步的基礎。（尼古拉斯·默里·巴特勒）

Cherish yesterday, dream tomorrow, live like crazy today! (Nicholas Murray Butler)

珍愛昨天，夢想明天，瘋狂般地過好今天！（尼古拉斯·默里·巴特勒）

I divide the world into three Classes —— The few who make things happen, the many who watch things happen, the overwhelming majority who have no notion of what happens. (Nicholas Murray Butler)

我把世人分成三大類 —— 少數使事情發生的人、多數看著事情發生的人、絕大多數不明白發生了什麼的人。（尼古拉斯·默里·巴特勒）

Education is in no small measure preparing the way for the intellectual life and pointing to it. Those who cannot enter in at its gates are doomed, in Leonardo da Vinci's words, to "possess neither the profit nor the beauty of the world." For them life must be short, however many its years, and barren, how-

1931-1939 黑暗時代的堅持

ever plentiful its acts. Their ears are deaf to the call of the indwelling Reason, and their eyes are blind to all the meaning and the values of human experience. (Nicholas Murray Butler)

在不小的程度上，教育為智性的生活鋪平了道路並指明了方向。那些不得其門而入的人，用李奧納多·達文西的話說，注定「無法擁有世上的利益與美好」。對於他們，生命必定短暫，無論壽命多麼長久；必定貧乏，無論表現多麼豐富。他們對內在理性的呼喚聽而不聞，對人類經驗的全部意義與價值視而不見。（尼古拉斯·默里·巴特勒）

The maxim, "An unexamined life is not worth living," is the priceless legacy of Socrates to the generations of men who have followed him upon this earth. The beings who have stood on humanity's summit are those, and only those, who have heard the voice of Socrates across the centuries. The others are a superior kind of cattle. (Nicholas Murray Butler)

「未經權衡的生活不值得度過」，這句箴言是蘇格拉底對世上一代代後人的無價遺訓。歷來登峰造極者，僅有古往今來聞知蘇格拉底此言之人。餘者高等動物而已。（尼古拉斯·默里·巴特勒）

The epitaphs on tombstones of a great many people should read: Died at thirty, and buried at sixty. (Nicholas Murray Butler)

許多人的碑文應該標明：30歲去世，60歲入土。（尼古拉斯·默里·巴特勒）

An expert is one who knows more and more about less and less. (Nicholas Murray Butler)

專家就是對越來越少之事所知越來越多之人。（尼古拉斯·默里·巴特勒）

1932 年

In general, scientific progress calls for no more than the absorption and elaboration of new ideas —— and this is a call most scientists are happy to heed. (Werner Karl Heisenberg)

一般而言,科學進步所要求的,不過是對新思想的領會和發揮——而這是大部分科學家所樂於關注的。(維爾納·海森堡)

The existing scientific concepts cover always only a very limited part of reality, and the other part that has not yet been understood is infinite. (Werner Karl Heisenberg)

現有的科學觀念總是只涵蓋現實非常有限的一部分,而另外尚未了解的部分是無窮的。(維爾納·海森堡)

Every experiment destroys some of the knowledge of the system which was obtained by previous experiments. (Werner Karl Heisenberg)

每一項實驗都打破了先前實驗所獲得的某種系統知識。(維爾納·海森堡)

Nature is made in such a way as to be able to be understood. Or perhaps I should put it —— more correctly —— the other way around, and say that we are made in such a way as to be able to understand Nature. (Werner Karl Heisenberg)

自然是以能夠理解的方式創造出來的。或許我應該——更準確地——說,換言之,我們生來就是能夠理解自然的。(維爾納·海森堡)

1931-1939 黑暗時代的堅持

Not only is the universe stranger than we think, it is stranger than we can think. (Werner Karl Heisenberg)

宇宙不僅比我們所想的奇特,而且比我們能想的奇特。(維爾納・海森堡)

The world thus appears as a complicated tissue of events, in which connections of different kinds alternate or overlap or combine and thereby determine the texture of the whole. (Werner Karl Heisenberg)

因此,世界看起來就像一個複雜的事件組織,其中各種不同的連結交替、重疊或結合,從而決定了整體的結構。(維爾納・海森堡)

There is a fundamental error in separating the parts from the whole, the mistake of atomizing what should not be atomized. Unity and complementarity constitute reality. (Werner Karl Heisenberg)

將部分從整體剝離有個根本性錯誤,即把不應分割的事物分割的過失。統一與互補構成真實。(維爾納・海森堡)

What we observe is not nature itself but nature exposed to our method of questioning. Our scientific work in physics consists in asking questions about nature in the language that we possess and trying to get an answer from experiment by the means that are at our disposal. (Werner Karl Heisenberg)

我們所觀察到的並非自然本身,而是經由我們的探究方法而呈現的自然。我們在物理學方面的科學工作,在於以所擁有的語言提出有關自然的問題,並力圖用所掌握的方法從實驗中獲得答案。(維爾納・海森堡)

If nature leads us to mathematical forms of great simplicity and beauty —— by forms, I am referring to coherent systems of hypotheses, axioms, etc. —— to forms that no one has previously encountered, we cannot help thinking that they are true, that they reveal a genuine feature of nature. (Werner Karl Heisenberg)

如果大自然把我們引向極為簡單和優美的數學形式──所謂形式，我指的是連貫的假設、公理等系統──引向沒人遇到過的形式，我們就不由得認為它們是正確的，它們揭示了大自然的真正特徵。（維爾納・海森堡）

I frankly admit that I am strongly attracted by the simplicity and beauty of mathematical schemes which nature presents us. You must have felt this too: the almost frightening simplicity and wholeness of the relationship, which nature suddenly spreads out before us. (Werner Karl Heisenberg)

我坦率承認，自己被大自然所呈現的數學體系之簡單與優美強烈吸引了。你一定也曾體會到：大自然忽然在我們面前展現出令人震撼的樸素和完整的關係。（維爾納・海森堡）

An expert is someone who knows some of the worst mistakes that can be made in his subject, and how to avoid them. (Werner Karl Heisenberg)

專家就是清楚在其專業中可能犯的一些最嚴重的錯，以及如何避免它們的人。（維爾納・海森堡）

The reality we can put into words is never reality itself. (Werner Karl Heisenberg)

我們能以語言表達的現實從來不是現實本身。（維爾納・海森堡）

Whenever we proceed from the known into the unknown we may hope to understand, but we may have to learn at the same time a new meaning of the word "understanding." (Werner Karl Heisenberg)

1931-1939 黑暗時代的堅持

每當由已知進入未知，我們可能希望了解，然而我們可能必須同時領會「了解」一詞的新含義。（維爾納·海森堡）

It will never be possible by pure reason to arrive at some absolute truth. (Werner Karl Heisenberg)

純粹的理性永遠不可能得出某種絕對的真理。（維爾納·海森堡）

I think that the discovery of antimatter was perhaps the biggest jump of all the big jumps in physics in our century. (Werner Karl Heisenberg)

我認為，反物質的發現，也許是20世紀物理學所有巨大突破之中最大的突破。（維爾納·海森堡）

To my mind, the most important aspect of the Nobel Awards is that they bring home to the masses of the peoples of all nations, a realization of their common interests. They carry to those who have no direct contact with science the international spirit. (Irving Langmuir)

在我看來，諾貝爾獎最重要的意義在於使所有國家的人民大眾認清共同利益。各個獎項把國際精神帶給那些與科學沒有直接接觸的人。（歐文·朗繆爾）

In the case of research director, Willis R. Whitney, whose style was to give talented investigators as much freedom as possible, you may define "serendipity" as the art of profiting from unexpected occurrences. When you do things in that way you get unexpected results. Then you do something else and you get unexpected results in another line, and you do that on a third line and then all of a sudden you see that one of these lines has something to do with the other. Then you make a discovery that you never could have made by going on a direct road. (Irving Langmuir)

> 1932 年

對於研究主任威利斯·R·惠特尼而言，他的做法是對有才華的研究者盡量放手。你可以把「意外發現」定義為得益於意想不到的情況的藝術。以這種方式做研究時，你會獲得意想不到的結果。然後你進行別的研究，在另一條線上獲得意想不到的結果。你又在第三條線上做研究，這時突然看出其中一條線和另一條線有所關聯。於是你獲得了一項發現，而它是絕不可能由直接途徑得出的。（歐文·朗繆爾）

Scientist is a... learned child. Others must outgrow it. Scientists can stay that way all their life. (Charles Scott Sherrington)

科學家是個⋯⋯博學的孩子。其他人必須長成大人。科學家們可以畢生如此。（查爾斯·斯科特·謝靈頓）

A scientist lives with all of reality. There is nothing better. To know reality is to accept it and eventually to love it. (Charles Scott Sherrington)

科學家與所有現實朝夕與共。沒有更好的安排了。了解現實就是接受它並終於熱愛它。（查爾斯·斯科特·謝靈頓）

Each waking day is a stage dominated for good or ill, comedy, farce, or tragedy, by a dramatis personae, the "self", and so it will be until the curtain drops. (Charles Scott Sherrington)

每一個醒著的日子都是「自我」的舞臺。好也罷、壞也罷，喜劇、鬧劇或悲劇，天天上演，直至落幕。（查爾斯·斯科特·謝靈頓）

Unless social sciences can be as creative as natural science, our new tools are not likely to be of much use to us. (Edgar Douglas Adrian)

除非社會科學能夠像自然科學一樣具有創造性，否則這些新工具對我們恐怕沒多大用處。（埃德加·阿德里安）

1931-1939 黑暗時代的堅持

Men are in fact, quite unable to control their own inventions; they at best develop adaptability to the new conditions those inventions create. (John Galsworthy)

事實上,人幾乎無法控制自己的發明,他們至多是逐漸適應這些發明所創造的新條件。(約翰・高爾斯華綏)

Life calls the tune, we dance. (John Galsworthy)

生命呼喚曲調,我們舞蹈。(約翰・高爾斯華綏)

Dreaming is the poetry of Life, and we must be forgiven if we indulge in it a little. (John Galsworthy)

夢想是生命的詩,我們稍為沉湎其中亦必獲得諒解。(約翰・高爾斯華綏)

1933 年

The task is... not so much to see what no one has yet seen; but to think what nobody has yet thought, about that which everybody sees. (Erwin Schrödinger)

我們的任務⋯⋯未必是看到還沒人看到過的東西,而是對人人都看到的東西加以還沒人思考過的思考。(埃爾溫・薛丁格)

The scientist only imposes two things, namely truth and sincerity, imposes them upon himself and upon other scientists. (Erwin Schrödinger)

1933 年

科學家只以兩樣東西要求自己和其他科學家，即真理與真誠。[22]（埃爾溫・薛丁格）

We must not wait for things to come, believing that they are decided by irrescindable destiny. If we want it, we must do something about it. (Erwin Schrödinger)

我們不能坐等事情到來，相信它們取決於不可避免的命運。想要的話，就必須有所作為。（埃爾溫・薛丁格）

Scientific education is fabulously neglected⋯ This is an evil that is inherited, passed on from generation to generation. The majority of educated persons are not interested in science, and are not aware that scientific knowledge forms part of the idealistic background of human life. Many believe —— in their complete ignorance of what science really is —— that it has mainly the ancillary task of inventing new machinery, or helping to invent it, for improving our conditions of life. They are prepared to leave this task to the specialists, as they leave the repairing of their pipes to the plumber. If persons with this outlook decide upon the curriculum of our children, the result is necessarily such as I have just described it. (Erwin Schrödinger)

科學教育被嚴重忽視了。……這是一大不幸，代代相傳。大多數受過教育的人對科學不感興趣，也沒意識到科學知識構成人類生活理想背景的一部分。許多人以為 —— 對科學的本質一無所知地 —— 科學的主要任務是輔助性的，發明新機器，或幫助發明它，以改善我們的生活條件。他們打算把這項任務留給專家，就像把管道維修留給水管工人一樣。如果持這種看法的人制定我們孩子的課程，後果必然一如我方才所描述。（埃爾溫・薛丁格）

---

[22] 對照：實事求是。（《漢書》）

1931–1939 黑暗時代的堅持

If you cannot, in the long run, tell everyone what you have been doing, your doing has been worthless. (Erwin Schrödinger)

從長遠來看，你若不能告訴每個人自己一直在做什麼，你的研究就始終沒有價值。（埃爾溫・薛丁格）

Science cannot tell us a word about why music delights us, of why and how an old song can move us to tears. (Erwin Schrödinger)

科學無法告訴我們音樂何以讓我們愉悅，一首老歌何以及如何令我們感動得流淚。（埃爾溫・薛丁格）

I found the best ideas usually came, not when one was actively striving for them, but when one was in a more relaxed state… I used to take long solitary walks on Sunday during which I tended to review the current situation in a leisurely way. Such occasion often proved fruitful, even though (or perhaps, because) the primary purpose of the walk was relaxation and not research. (Paul Adrien Maurice Dirac)

我發現，一個人最好的想法，通常並非出於冥思苦想之際，而是來自更加放鬆的狀態中。……我常在星期日獨行很遠，途中往往漫不經心地回顧近況。事實證明，這種時候經常收穫頗豐，即便（或者也許，由於）散步的主要目的是放鬆而非研究。（保羅・狄拉克）

I think it is the general rule that the originator of a new idea is not the most suitable person to develop it, because his fears of something going wrong are really too strong. (Paul Adrien Maurice Dirac)

我認為，一種新思想的提出者並不是最適合發展它的人，這是普遍規律，因為前者唯恐出錯的顧慮實在過於強烈。（保羅・狄拉克）

1933 年

The beauty of a fundamental theory in physics has several characteristics in common with a great work of art: fundamental simplicity, inevitability, power and grandeur. Like every great work of art, a beautiful theory in physics is always ambitious, never trifling. (Paul Adrien Maurice Dirac)

物理學基礎理論之美,與偉大的藝術作品有若干共同之處:根本上的質樸、必然性、力量和壯麗。跟所有偉大的藝術作品一樣,物理學中美的理論總是充滿張力,絕不瑣碎。(保羅‧狄拉克)

The measure of greatness in a scientific idea is the extent to which it stimulates thought and opens up new lines of research. (Paul Adrien Maurice Dirac)

衡量一種科學思想之偉大,在於其激發思考和開闢新研究領域的程度。(保羅‧狄拉克)

Scientific progress is measured in units of courage, not intelligence. (Paul Adrien Maurice Dirac)

科學進步的衡量單位是勇氣,而不是智力。(保羅‧狄拉克)

Living is worthwhile if one can contribute in some small way to this endless chain of progress. (Paul Adrien Maurice Dirac)

一個人若能以某種微小的方式為這無盡的進步做出貢獻,活著就是有價值的。(保羅‧狄拉克)

Mathematics is the tool specially suited for dealing with abstract concepts of any kind and there is no limit to its power in this field. (Paul Adrien Maurice Dirac)

數學是特別適合處理任何種類抽象觀念的工具,它在這個領域的力量是無限的。(保羅‧狄拉克)

1931-1939 黑暗時代的堅持

I want to emphasize the necessity for a sound mathematical basis for any fundamental physical theory. Any philosophical ideas that one may have play only a subordinate role. Unless such ideas have a mathematical basis they will be ineffective. (Paul Adrien Maurice Dirac)

我想強調堅實的數學基礎對所有基本物理理論的必要性。一個人可能擁有的任何哲學思想只能發揮從屬作用。除非這樣的思想有數學基礎，否則它們將是無效的。（保羅・狄拉克）

It seems to be one of the fundamental features of nature that fundamental physical laws are described in terms of a mathematical theory of great beauty and power, needing quite a high standard of mathematics for one to understand it. You may wonder: Why is nature constructed along these lines? One can only answer that our present knowledge seems to show that nature is so constructed. We simply have to accept it. One could perhaps describe the situation by saying that God is a mathematician of a very high order, and He used very advanced mathematics in constructing the universe. Our feeble attempts at mathematics enable us to understand a bit of the universe, and as we proceed to develop higher and higher mathematics we can hope to understand the universe better. (Paul Adrien Maurice Dirac)

自然的一個基本特徵似乎是以極其美麗和強大的數學理論來描述基本物理定律，需要相當高的數學水準才能理解。你可能驚奇：大自然何以如此建構？回答只能是，我們現有的知識似乎顯示自然就是這般建構的。我們只能接受。或許可以這樣描述此種狀況：上帝是一位非常高階的數學家，他運用非常先進的數學建構宇宙。對於數學上的微薄嘗試使我們得以對宇宙略有所知，隨著繼續發展漸次高等的數學，我們有望更容易理解宇宙。（保羅・狄拉克）

1933 年

It is quite clear that beauty does depend on one's culture and upbringing for certain kinds of beauty, pictures, literature, poetry and so on... But mathematical beauty is of a rather different kind. I should say perhaps it is of a completely different kind and transcends these personal factors. It is the same in all countries and at all periods of time. (Paul Adrien Maurice Dirac)

顯而易見,對於某些類型的美,繪畫、文學、詩歌等等,美的確取決於一個人的文化和教養。⋯⋯但數學之美屬於相當不同的類型。應該說,也許它屬於完全不同的類型,超越了這些個人因素。這在所有國家和所有時期都是一樣的。(保羅・狄拉克)

What makes the theory of relativity so acceptable to physicists in spite of its going against the principle of siplicity is its great mathematical beauty. This is a quality which cannot be defined, any more than beauty in art can be defined, but which people who study mathematics usually have no difficulty in appreciating. (Paul Adrien Maurice Dirac)

儘管違背簡明易解的原則,相對論卻如此得以為物理學家所接受,原因即在於其非凡的數學之美。這是一種無法定義的特質,與藝術之美不同,不過研究數學的人通常不難欣賞。(保羅・狄拉克)

I think it's a peculiarity of myself that I like to play about with equations, just looking for beautiful mathematical relations which maybe don't have any physical meaning at all. Sometimes they do. (Paul Adrien Maurice Dirac)

我想這是我個人的一種特別癖好。我喜歡玩方程式,只是尋求美妙的數學關係。它們也許完全沒有物理學意義,有些時候有。(保羅・狄拉克)

If there is not complete agreement between the results of one's work and experiment, one should not allow oneself to be too discouraged, because the discrepancy may well be due to minor features that are not properly taken into account and that will get cleared up with further development of the theory. (Paul Adrien Maurice Dirac)

如果一個人的工作和實驗兩者的結果不吻合，他不應該放任自己氣餒，因為這種差異很可能出於考慮不周的次要特徵，而這些特徵將隨著理論的進一步發展而獲得解決。（保羅・狄拉克）

I was taught at school never to start a sentence without knowing the end of it. (Paul Adrien Maurice Dirac)

我在學校學到，不可以在不知道句子結尾的情況下開始句子。（保羅・狄拉克）

If everyone in the world spent twelve hours a day placing individual atoms into a thimble, a century would elapse before it was filled. (Paul Adrien Maurice Dirac)

假如世界上每個人每天都花 12 個小時把單一原子放進頂針之中，填滿它得在一個世紀之後。（保羅・狄拉克）

Two years work wasted, I have been breeding those flies for all that time and I've got nothing out of it. (Thomas Hunt Morgan)

兩年的工作白費了，我一直在培育這些蒼蠅而從中一無所獲。[23]（托馬斯・亨特・摩爾根）

You should not have idle hands, you should always be working. All your life. (Ivan Alekseyevich Bunin)

你不應該讓手閒著，你應該總是工作。畢生如此。（伊凡・蒲寧）

---

[23] 摩爾根以實蠅研究而建立遺傳的染色體學說，並因此獲得 1933 年諾貝爾生理學或醫學獎。

A man is made happy by three things: love, interesting work and the opportunity to travel. (Ivan Alekseyevich Bunin)

三件事令人快樂：愛、有趣的工作和旅行的機會。（伊凡・蒲寧）

The greatest service we can do the common man is to abolish him and make all men uncommon. (Norman Angell)

對於普通人，我們所能做的最了不起的事就是消除其平凡，而讓所有的人都非同尋常。（諾曼・安吉爾）

The economic difficulty of the modern world is not shortage of materials but the organization of their exchange and distribution; distress arises, not from scarcity but from dislocation and maladjustment. (Norman Angell)

現代世界的經濟困難不在於物質短缺，而在於物質交換和分配的組織；痛苦的產生不是由於匱乏，而是由於混亂與失調。（諾曼・安吉爾）

1934 年

I looked for it (heavy hydrogen, deuterium) because I thought it should exist. I didn't know it would have industrial applications or be the basic for the most powerful weapon ever known (the nuclear bomb)... I thought maybe my discovery might have the practical value of, say, neon in neon signs. (Harold Clayton Urey)

我尋找它（重氫，氘），因為認為它應該存在。我不清楚它會有工業用途或者成為已知最強大武器（核彈）的基礎……我想，也許我的發現可

能具有實用價值，譬如說，霓虹燈中的氖。[24]（哈羅德・尤里）

Pure research is worth every penny it costs. (Harold Clayton Urey)

純研究所花的每一分錢都是值得的。（哈羅德・尤里）

I come to this assembly in a very humble spirit but in time I hope to justify the confidence of the Nobel Committee by continuance of my work with hope for future accomplishments. Any investigator is indeed fortunate who can contribute a tiny stone to the great edifice which we call scientific truth. (George Hoyt Whipple)

我懷著非常謙恭的心情來到這個集會，同時願意繼續工作以獲得進一步成就，以不辜負諾貝爾委員會的信任。能夠為我們稱為科學真理的大廈添磚加瓦，這樣的研究者就是真正幸運的。（喬治・惠普爾）

As each bit of information is added to the sum of human knowledge it is evident that it is the little things that count; that give all the fertility and character; that give all the hope and happiness to human affairs. The concept of bigness is apt to be a delusion, and standardizing processes must not supplant creative impulses. (George Richards Minot)

隨著每一點資訊新增到人類知識的總和中，顯而易見，微小的事物非常重要，它賦予全部的豐饒與特質，為人類事務帶來一切希望和幸福。「大」的概念往往是錯覺，而標準化過程必定無法取代創造性衝動。（喬治・邁諾特）

In clinical investigation the sick individual is at the centre of the picture.

---

[24] 尤里因發現氘而獲得 1931 年諾貝爾化學獎。

1934 年

The physician must have a deep interest in his patient's economic and social structure as well as in his physical and psychic state. If attention is not paid to the diagnosis of the person the clinical investigator is apt to fail in studies of the patient's disease. (George Richards Minot)

在臨床研究中，病人處於觀察的中心。醫生必須對患者的身體與精神狀態及其經濟和社會情況均具深厚興趣。臨床研究者的診斷如果不專注，對疾病的研究就易於失敗。（喬治・邁諾特）

It gives me the greatest joy to have the privilege, as a recipient of a Nobel Prize Award, of participating actively in this ceremony of homage to Alfred Nobel. My joy is intensified by the belief that the work for which this award has been made typifies the Nobel ideal. (William Parry Murphy)

作為諾貝爾獎得主，我很榮幸參加這個向阿佛烈・諾貝爾致敬的典禮，這給予我最大的喜悅。由於相信這一獎項所授予的工作代表了諾貝爾的理想，更加深了我的喜悅。（威廉・莫菲）

Every true man, sir, who is a little above the level of the beasts and plants does not live for the sake of living, without knowing how to live; but he lives so as to give a meaning and a value of his own to life. (Luigi Pirandello)

先生，每一個真正的人，略高於獸類和植物一籌的，都不是為了活著而活著，不懂得如何生活；他之所以活著，是為了賦予個人生命意義與價值。（路伊吉・皮藍德羅）

Anyone can be heroic from time to time, but a gentleman is something which you have to be all the time. Which isn't easy. (Luigi Pirandello)

任何人都能夠不時地宛如英雄，然而紳士風度是你必須始終具備的特質。這並不容易。（路伊吉・皮藍德羅）

1931-1939 黑暗時代的堅持

Thoughts are most fruitful in action. (Arthur Henderson)

思想在行動中最有成效。（阿瑟‧亨德森）

This is our world, and we must make the best of it. (Arthur Henderson)

這是我們的世界，我們必須珍重它。（阿瑟‧亨德森）

1935 年

I thingk we shall have to make a real search for the neutron. (James Chadwick)

我認為，我們應該對中子展開真正的探究。（詹姆斯‧查兒克）

The farther the experiment is from theory the closer it is to the Nobel Prize. (Frédéric Joliot-Curie)

實驗離理論越遠，離諾貝爾獎越近。（弗雷德里克‧約里奧—居禮）

I have always attached great importance to the manner in which an experiment is set up and conducted... the experiment should be set up to open as many windows as possible on the unforeseen. (Frédéric Joliot-Curie)

我一向非常重視實驗的立意和實施方式。⋯⋯實驗應該立足於對未預見情況打開盡可能多的視窗。（弗雷德里克‧約里奧—居禮）

That one must do some work seriously and must be independent and not merely amuse oneself in life —— this our mother has told us always, but never that science was the only career worth following. (Irène Joliot-Curie)

一個人必須認真地做某種工作，必須自立，而不可一味尋歡作樂——母親[25]總是這麼教導我們；但她從來沒說科學是唯一值得追隨的事業。（伊雷娜·約里奧－居里）

We stand in the presence of riddles, but not without the hope of solving them. And riddles with the hope of solution —— what more can a scientist desire? (Hans Spemann)

我們面臨一道道謎題，但並非沒有解決它們的希望。還有解決希望的謎題——科學家還能渴求更多嗎？（漢斯·斯佩曼）

We cannot look to the conscience of the world when our own conscience is asleep. (Carl von Ossietzky)

在自己的良心沉睡時，我們不能指望世人的良心。（卡爾·馮·奧西茨基）

1936 年

The atom can't be seen, yet its existence can be proved. And it is simple to prove that it can't ever be seen. It has to be studied by indirect evidence —— and the technical difficulty has been compared to asking a man who has never seen a piano to describe a piano from the sound it would make falling downstairs in the dark. (Carl David Anderson)

原子看不見，但是其存在可以被證明。並且很容易證明它是不可能被看見的。必須經由間接證據研究——而其技術之困難曾被比作讓從未

---

[25] 即瑪麗·居禮。

1931-1939 黑暗時代的堅持

見過鋼琴的人依據夜裡樓上傳來的琴聲來描述鋼琴。(卡爾・戴維・安德森)

From a consideration of the immense volume of newly discovered facts in the field of physics, especially atomic physics, in recent years it might well appear to the layman that the main problems were already solved and that only more detailed work was necessary. This is far from the truth, as will be shown by one of the biggest and most important newly opened fields of research, with which I am closely associated, that of cosmic rays. (Victor Franz Hess)

考慮到物理學，尤其是原子物理學領域大量新發現的事實，近年來，在外行人眼中似乎主要問題業已解決，只有更細緻的工作是必要的。這與事實相去甚遠，猶如我與之關係密切的宇宙射線領域將顯示的一樣，它是新開闢的最大、最重要的研究領域之一。(維克托・赫斯)

If a problem is clearly stated, it has no further interest to the physicist. (Petrus Josephus Wilhelmus Debye)

一個難題如果被清楚地闡述，物理學家對它也就失去了進一步的興趣。(彼得・德拜)

If the principle of chemical transmission is ultimately to find a further extension to the interneuronal transmission in the brain itself, it is by patient testing of the groundwork of experimental fact, at each new step, that a safe and steady advance will be achieved. The possible importance of such an extension, even for practical medicine and therapeutics, could hardly be overestimated. (Henry Hallett Dale)

如果化學傳遞的原理最終得以進而擴展到腦部本身的神經元間傳遞，經由對實驗事實基礎的耐心測試，步步推進，便可望獲得可靠穩定

> 1936 年

的進展。這種擴展可能具有的重要性,甚至對於實用醫學和治療學而言,都很難被高估。[26]（亨利・哈利特・戴爾）

The night before Easter Sunday of that year (1920) I awoke, turned on the light, and jotted down a few notes on a tiny slip of thin paper. Then I fell asleep again. It occurred to me at six o'clock in the morning that during the night I had written down something most important, but I was unable to decipher the scrawl. The next night, at three o'clock, the idea returned. It was the design of an experiment to determine whether the hypothesis of chemical transmission that I had uttered seventeen years ago was correct. I got up immediately, went to the laboratory, and performed a simple experiment on a frog heart according to the nocturnal design. I have to describe this experiment briefly since its results became the foundation of the theory of chemical transmission of the nervous impulse. The hearts of two frogs were isolated, the first with its nerves, the second without. Both hearts were attached to Straub cannulas filled with a little Ringer solution. The vagus nerve of the first heart was stimulated for a few minutes. Then the Ringer solution that had been in the first heart during the stimulation of the vagus was transferred to the second heart. It slowed and its beats diminished just as if its vagus had been stimulated. Similarly, when the accelerator nerve was stimulated and the Ringer from this period transferred, the second heart speeded up and its beats increased. These results unequivocally proved that the nerves do not influence the heart directly but liberate from their terminals specific chemical substances which, in their turn, cause the well-known modifications of the function of the

---

[26] 戴爾和勒維由於他們關於神經衝動的化學傳遞的發現,同獲 1936 年諾貝爾生理學或醫學獎。

1931-1939 黑暗時代的堅持

heart characteristic of the stimulation of its nerves. (Otto Loewi)

那年（1920年）復活節前一天，夜裡我醒來，打開燈，在一張薄薄的紙條上記下幾句話。隨後又睡著了。早上6點鐘想起來，夜間自己寫下了什麼非常重要的東西，可是筆跡潦草，無從辨認。第二天夜裡，3點鐘，先前的想法回來了。這是一個實驗的設計，以確定我17年前所提出的化學傳遞假設是否正確。我馬上爬起來，跑到實驗室去，按照夜間的設計，在青蛙心臟上做了個簡單的實驗。我得簡短地描述一下這個實驗，因為它的結果成了神經衝動的化學傳遞理論的基礎。取出兩隻青蛙的心臟，第一個帶有神經，第二個沒有。兩個都接到施特勞布套管上，套管裡裝有少量林格氏溶液。刺激第一個蛙心的迷走神經幾分鐘。隨後，將刺激期間第一個蛙心裡的林格氏溶液注入第二個蛙心。它的搏動放慢並且減弱，一如其迷走神經受過刺激。同樣，當加速神經受到刺激，並將此過程中的林格氏溶液注入第二個蛙心時，它的搏動加速並且增強。這些結果明確證實，神經並不直接影響心臟，而是從末梢釋放特定的化學物質，它們繼而引起眾所周知的心臟功能改變，其特徵是刺激心臟神經。（奧托‧勒維）

Why am I afraid to dance, I who love music and rhythm and grace and song and laughter? Why am I afraid to live, I who love life and the beauty of flesh and the living colors of the earth and sky and sea? Why am I afraid to love, I who love love? (Eugene Gladstone O'Neill)

為什麼鍾情於音樂、節奏、優雅、歌曲和歡笑的我畏懼跳舞？為什麼鍾情於生命、肉體之美、大地、天空與海洋鮮活色彩的我畏懼生活？為什麼鍾情於愛的我畏懼愛？（尤金‧歐尼爾）

Man's loneliness is but his fear of life. (Eugene Gladstone O'Neill)

人的孤獨感不過是對生活的恐懼。（尤金·歐尼爾）

The world longs for peace; it needs it as the fertilizing rain is desired by the earth. (Carlos Saavedra Lamas)

世界渴望和平。它需要和平，猶如大地企盼滋養萬物的雨水。（卡洛斯·薩維德拉·拉馬斯）

1937 年

Discoveries in physics are made when the time for making them is ripe, and not before; the stage is set, the time is ripe, and the event occurs —— more often than not at widely separated places at almost the same moment. (Clinton Joseph Davisson)

物理學上的發現是在時機成熟時做出的，而不是在時機成熟之前；舞臺已經搭好，時機已經成熟，於是事件發生 —— 通常是在相距甚遠的地方幾乎同時發生。（柯林頓·戴維孫）

The recipient is transformed overnight from, in my case, an exceedingly private citizen to something in the nature of a semi-public institution. (Clinton Joseph Davisson)

就我而言，一夜之間，獲獎者從極其個人的公民變成了半公共性質的機構。（柯林頓·戴維孫）

The goddess of learning is fabled to have sprung full-grown from the brain of Zeus, but it is seldom that a scientific conception is born in its final form, or owns a single parent. More often it is the product of a series of minds, each in turn modifying the ideas of those that came before, and providing material for those that come after. The electron is no exception. (George Paget Thomson)

在傳說中,學問女神是成長完全之後從宙斯大腦中跳出來的。然而,科學概念很少以其最終形式誕生,或者只有單一父母。它更經常是一系列思想的產物,每一種想法都轉而修改先前的想法,並為後來者提供材料。電子也不例外。(喬治・湯木生)

The influence of science on men's lives comes in two rather different ways, one through the ideas themselves, and the other through their material consequences. (George Paget Thomson)

科學對人們生活產生影響經由兩條頗為不同的途徑,一條透過思想本身,另一條透過其物質結果。(喬治・湯木生)

It is in keeping with the universal character of physical science that this single small branch of it should touch on the one hand on the fundamentals of scientific philosophy and on the other, questions of everyday life. (George Paget Thomson)

它符合物理科學的普遍特性,即它的這個小分支應該一方面涉及科學哲學的基本原理,另一方面涉及日常生活的各種問題。(喬治・湯木生)

By popular assent the Nobel Prize is the most coveted honour in the world. Whereas the orders of chivalry may hold higher official rank yet, as is abundantly evident, in the minds of the common people the Nobel award is a thing apart, an international assent, a recognition of proved worth from an unpolluted fount of honour. Thus does it make its appeal to the devotees of learning and more widely to the popular imagination. (Walter Norman Haworth)

> 1937 年

諾貝爾獎是世人公認最嚮往的榮譽。儘管騎士勳位可能具有更高的官方等級，但顯然在一般民眾心目中，諾貝爾獎是另一回事，是一種國際認可，一種清明的榮譽之源對確切價值的表彰。它因而吸引學者，也更廣泛地激發大眾想像。（華特·霍沃思）

It has often been said that it is only the first discovery which is difficult and that the ensuing discoveries are usually only the continuations of the first. (Paul Karrer)

人們常說，最初的發現是最困難的，隨後的一些發現通常只是最初發現的延續。（保羅·卡勒）

A discovery is said to be an accident meeting a prepared mind. (Albert von Szent-Györgyi Nagyrápolt)

據說一項發現是一場意外，與一個準備好的頭腦相逢。（阿爾伯特·聖捷爾吉）

Discovery consists of looking at the same thing as everyone else and thinking something different. (Albert von Szent-Györgyi Nagyrápolt)

發現就是像其他人那樣看待同樣的事物，而思考不同的東西。（阿爾伯特·聖捷爾吉）

What I want to stress is that the pre-condition of scientific discovery is a society which does not demand "usefulness" from the scientist, but grants him the liberty which he needs for concentration and for the conscientious detailed work without which creation is impossible. (Albert von Szent-Györgyi Nagyrápolt)

我要強調的是，科學發現的前提條件，是社會不要求科學家「有

用」，而是給予他專心致志和認真細緻工作所需要的自由，沒有這種自由就無法論及創造。（阿爾伯特・聖捷爾吉）

Research is four things: brains with which to think, eyes with which to see, machines with which to measure, and fourth, money. (Albert von Szent-Györgyi Nagyrápolt)

研究就是四件事：思考的頭腦、觀察的眼睛、測量的機器，以及第四，錢。（阿爾伯特・聖捷爾吉）

A discovery must be, by definition, at variance with existing knowledge. During my lifetime, I made two. Both were rejected offhand by the popes of the field. (Albert von Szent-Györgyi Nagyrápolt)

不言自明，發現必須與已有知識不一致。此生中，我做出了兩個發現。兩個都被該領域的大人物們輕率否定了。（阿爾伯特・聖捷爾吉）

If I go out into nature, into the unknown, to the fringes of knowledge, everything seems mixed up and contradictory, illogical, and incoherent. This is what research does; it smooths out contradictions and makes things simple, logical, and coherent. (Albert von Szent-Györgyi Nagyrápolt)

如果我走入自然，進入未知領域，到達知識的邊緣，事事似乎都是混亂的、矛盾的、不合邏輯、沒有條理。這就是研究所做的，它消除矛盾，使事情簡單明瞭、合乎邏輯、條理清晰。（阿爾伯特・聖捷爾吉）

Think boldly. Don't be afraid of making mistakes. Don't miss small details, keep your eyes open and be modest in everything except your aims. (Albert von Szent-Györgyi Nagyrápolt)

大膽思考。不要怕犯錯。不要錯過細枝末節，睜大眼睛，事事謙虛，除了你的目標。（阿爾伯特・聖捷爾吉）

1937 年

Knowledge is a sacred cow, and my problem will be how we can milk her while keeping clear of her horns. (Albert von Szent-Györgyi Nagyrápolt)

知識是一頭聖牛。我的難題在於,怎樣在避開犄角的同時擠牛奶。(阿爾伯特·聖捷爾吉)

If any student comes to me and says he wants to be useful to mankind and go into research to alleviate human suffering, I advise him to go into charity instead. Research wants real egotists who seek their own pleasure and satisfaction, but find it in solving the puzzles of nature. (Albert von Szent-Györgyi Nagyrápolt)

要是有哪一位學生到我這裡來,說他想對人類有所貢獻,要做研究工作以減輕人的痛苦,我建議他還是去做慈善事業。研究需要真正的自我主義者,他們尋求個人的快樂與滿足,不過是在解決自然難題時找到。(阿爾伯特·聖捷爾吉)

I am not religious, but I am a pious man... A religious man has a definite religion. He says "God is there" or "God is there," "God is there." "Your god is not my god, and that's all." But the pious man, he just looks out with awe, and says, "where is God?" And "well, I don't understand it and I would like to know what this creation really means." That is a pious man, who is really touched by the greatness of nature and of the creation. (Albert von Szent-Györgyi Nagyrápolt)

我不信教,但我是一個虔誠的人。⋯⋯信教的人有明確的宗教信仰。他反覆說「上帝在那裡」,說「你的上帝不是我的上帝,就是這樣」。而虔誠的人,他只是懷著敬畏張望,說:「上帝在哪裡?」以及「哦,我不理解它,我想弄懂這個世界究竟意義何在。」那是一個虔誠的人,他

1931-1939 黑暗時代的堅持

被自然的、萬物的偉大深深感動。（阿爾伯特・聖捷爾吉）

It is impossible to encircle the hips of a girl with my right arm and hold her smile in my left hand, then proceed to study the two items separately. Similarly, we can not separate life from living matter, in order to study only living matter and its reactions. Inevitably, studying living matter and its reactions, we study life itself. (Albert von Szent-Györgyi Nagyrápolt)

我不可能用右臂摟著一個女郎的臀部，左手抓住她的微笑，再分別研究這兩者。同樣地，我們無法將生命與生命的物質分開，而只研究生命的物質和它的反應。不可避免地，研究生命的物質及其反應，我們就是在研究生命本身。（阿爾伯特・聖捷爾吉）

The real scientist … is ready to bear privation and if need be starvation rather than let anyone dictate to him which direction his work must take. (Albert von Szent-Györgyi Nagyrápolt)

真正的科學家……寧肯準備承受貧困，必要的話忍饑挨餓，也不願讓任何人就他的工作方向指手畫腳。（阿爾伯特・聖捷爾吉）

I always tried to live up to Leo Szilard's commandment, "don't lie if you don't have to." I had to. I filled up pages with words and plans I knew I would not follow. When I go home from my laboratory in the late afternoon, I often do not know what I am going to do the next day. I expect to think that up during the night. How could I tell them what I would do a year hence? (Albert von Szent-Györgyi Nagyrápolt)

我一直努力遵守利奧・西拉德的戒律：「除非不得已不要說謊。」我不得不說謊。我以明知不會實行的說法和計畫填滿了一頁頁紙。傍晚從實驗室回家時，我經常不知道第二天要做什麼。我指望在夜裡想出來。

> 1937 年

我該如何告訴他們一年後我會做什麼？（阿爾伯特・聖捷爾吉）

Basic research may seem very expensive. I am a well-paid scientist. My hourly wage is equal to that of a plumber, but sometimes my research remains barren of results for weeks, months or years and my conscience begins to bother me for wasting the taxpayer's money. But in reviewing my life's work, I have to think that the expense was not wasted. (Albert von Szent-Györgyi Nagyrápolt)

基礎研究可能顯得非常昂貴。我是一名待遇優厚的科學家。我的時薪跟水管工人的相當，但有時我的研究數週、數月或數年都一直沒有結果，我的良心開始由於浪費納稅人的錢而感到不安。不過在回顧此生的工作時，我不得不認為，這筆費用沒有浪費。（阿爾伯特・聖捷爾吉）

Basic research, to which we owe everything, is relatively very cheap when compared with other outlays of modern society. The other day I made a rough calculation which led me to the conclusion that if one were to add up all the money ever spent by man on basic research, one would find it to be just about equal to the money spent by the Pentagon this past year. (Albert von Szent-Györgyi Nagyrápolt)

與現代社會的其他支出相比，基礎研究——我們的一切都應歸功於它——相對而言是非常便宜的。不久前我做了一次粗略的計算，從而得出結論：如果把人類曾經花在基礎研究上的錢全部加起來，就會發現，總數不過大致等於五角大廈去年所花的錢。（阿爾伯特・聖捷爾吉）

I always have a pad of paper and a pencil within reach, to catch on the wing this turn of phrase which strikes me as felicitous, that idea which I hope to be able to examine more closely in the light of day. (Roger Martin du Gard)

1931–1939 黑暗時代的堅持

我手邊總是備有一疊紙和一支鉛筆，以捕捉這種覺得精妙而稍縱即逝的措辭，我希望能在白天更仔細地思索這個想法。（羅傑・馬丁・杜・加爾）

You can always do more than you thought you can do. (Roger Martin du Gard)

你總是可以做得比你所設想的多。（羅傑・馬丁・杜・加爾）

The character and the prosperity of the nation depend on the character of the individuals that compose it, the form of government which best promotes individual development is the best for the people as a whole. (Edgar Algernon Robert Gascoyne Cecil)

國家的特性和繁榮取決於組成它的個人的特性。對於作為整體的人民，最能促進個人發展的政府形式就是最好的。（羅伯特・塞西爾）

1938 年

There are two possible outcomes: if the result confirms the hypothesis, then you've made a measurement. If the result is contrary to the hypothesis, then you've made a discovery. (Enrico Fermi)

可能的結局有兩種：如果結果證實假設，你就完成了一項測量。如果結果與假設相反，你就完成了一項發現。（恩里科・費米）

Whatever Nature has in store for mankind, unpleasant as it may be, men must accept, for ignorance is never better than knowledge. (Enrico Fermi)

1938 年

　　無論大自然為人類準備了什麼，儘管可能不愉快，人們都必須接受，因為無知絕對不如知識。（恩里科·費米）

　　In recent years several new particles have been discovered which are currently assumed to be "elementary", that is, essentially structureless. The probability that all such particles should be really elementary becomes less and less as their number increases. It is by no means certain that nucleons, mesons, electrons, neutrinos are all elementary particles. (Enrico Fermi)

　　近年來發現了幾種新粒子，這些粒子目前被認為是「基本的」，也就是說，本質上沒有結構。所有這些粒子都是真正的基本粒子的機率，隨著其數量的增加而變得越來越小。核子、介子、電子、中微子都是基本粒子的看法絕非定論。（恩里科·費米）

　　Young man, if I could remember the names of these particles, I would have been a botanist. (Enrico Fermi)

　　年輕人，我要是能記住這些粒子的名稱，就會當上植物學家了。（恩里科·費米）

　　When you have made a new discovery, people begin by saying that it is not true, then when the truth of what you have proposed becomes absolutely evident, they say that it is not you who discovered it. (Corneille Jean François Heymans)

　　當你得出新發現，人們起初說它不是真的；然後當你見解的真實性變得無可置疑時，他們說發現它的不是你。（柯奈爾·海門斯）

　　The truly creative mind in any field is no more than this: A human creature born abnormally, inhumanly sensitive. To him... a touch is a blow, a sound is a noise, a misfortune is a tragedy, a joy is an ecstasy, a friend is a

1931-1939 黑暗時代的堅持

lover, a lover is a god, and failure is death. Add to this cruelly delicate organism the overpowering necessity to create, create, create —— so that without the creating of music or poetry or books or buildings or something of meaning, his very breath is cut off from him. He must create, must pour out creation. By some strange, unknown, inward urgency he is not really alive unless he is creating. (Pearl Buck)

在任何領域，真正的創造性頭腦不過如此：一個天生異常、非凡敏感的人。對於他……觸碰就是打擊，聲音就是嘈雜，不幸就是悲劇，快樂就是狂喜，朋友就是戀人，戀人就是神祇，而失敗就是滅亡。對於這種感受入微的人物，若加以非常的重負，使之創造、創造、創造 —— 如果沒有音樂、詩歌、書籍、建築等富於意義之物的創造，他就連氣都喘不過來。他必須創造，必須釋放創造力。由於某種奇異的、未知的、內在的緊迫感，除非處於創造中，他就不算真正活著。（賽珍珠）

All things are possible until they are proved impossible and even the impossible may only be so, as of now. (Pearl Buck)

萬事皆有可能，直到被證明不可能，甚至所謂不可能也許截至目前也不過爾爾。（賽珍珠）

Talent fulfilled brings the deepest content that an individual can know. (Pearl Buck)

天賦的實現帶給個人可知最深切的滿足。（賽珍珠）

I don't wait for moods. You accomplish nothing if you do that. Your mind must know it has got to get down to work. (Pearl Buck)

我不等待情緒。那樣做你就會一事無成。你的頭腦必須明白它得開始工作。（賽珍珠）

1938 年

The secret of joy in work is contained in one word —— excellence. To know how to do something well is to enjoy it. (Pearl Buck)

工作快樂的祕密寓於一個詞 —— 卓越。懂得怎麼把事情做好就是享受它。（賽珍珠）

To serve is beautiful, but only if it is done with joy and a whole heart and a free mind. (Pearl Buck)

服務是美好的，但從事時須感到快樂，全心全意，自由自在。（賽珍珠）

Every mistake has a halfway moment, a split second when it can be recalled and perhaps remedied. (Pearl Buck)

每一個錯誤都有一個中途時刻，在那一瞬間，此時錯誤可以被取消或補救。（賽珍珠）

I should not be truly myself if I did not, in my own wholly unofficial way, speak also of the people of China, whose life has for so many years been my life also, whose life, indeed, must always be a part of my life. The minds of my own country and of China, my foster country, are alike in many ways, but above all, alike in our common love of freedom. And today more than ever, this is true, now when China's whole being is engaged in the greatest of all struggles, the struggle for freedom. I have never admired China more than I do now, when I see her uniting as she has never before, against the enemy who threatens her freedom. With this determination for freedom, which is in so profound a sense the essential quality in her nature, I know that she is unconquerable. (Pearl Buck)

假如不以自己完全無拘無束的方式談論中國人民，我就不算是真實的自己了。這麼多年來，他們的生活也是我的生活，他們的生活，確實，必然永遠是我的生活的一部分。我自己的國家和養育我的中國，其人民的心靈在許多方面類似，首先就是對自由的共同熱愛。今天確實比往日更甚，現在正當中國全民投入最偉大的抗爭，爭取自由的抗爭之際。目睹中國空前地團結起來，反對威脅其自由的敵人，我從未如此欽佩她。憑著這種爭取自由的決心 —— 在如此深刻的意義上為其天性的本質，我知道她是不可征服的。[27]（賽珍珠）

1939 年

I am mindful that scientific achievement is rooted in the past, is cultivated to full stature by many contemporaries and flourishes only in favorable environment. No individual is alone responsible for a single stepping stone along the path of progress, and where the path is smooth progress is most rapid. In my own work this has been particularly true. (Ernest Orlando Lawrence)

我留意到，科學成就植根於過去，經由許多同時代人培育而旺盛生長，並且只在適宜的環境中枝繁葉茂。在進步的路途上，沒有人能獨自充當一塊墊腳石，而使路面平坦、進步神速。在我自己的工作中尤其如此。（歐內斯特・勞倫斯）

This lecture should have been delivered in December 1939, but owing to a postponement of 6 years forced by the intervention of war, I have been able to use some results obtained in the meantime to round off the overall picture. (Leopold Ruzicka)

---

[27] 1938 年，賽珍珠「由於其對中國農民生活豐富的、真正史詩般的描寫，以及傳記傑作」而獲得諾貝爾文學獎。這段話摘自她在獲獎宴會上的發言。

1939 年

　　這次演講原本應在 1939 年 12 月發表[28]，但迫於戰爭的阻礙而推遲了 6 年。我得以利用在此期間獲得的一些成果來完善整體描述。（拉沃斯拉夫·魯日奇卡）

　　Whatever contributes to the preservation of life is good; all that destroys life is evil. (Gerhard Domagk)

　　任何有助於保護生命的都是善的，所有破壞生命的都是惡的。（格哈德·多馬克）

　　There is almost no summer night in the north; only a lingering evening, darkening slightly as it lingers, but even this darkening has its ineffable clarity. It is the approaching presentiment of the summer morning. When the music of late evening has sunk to a violet, dusky pianissimo, so delicate that it lenghtens into a brief rest, then the first violin awakens with a soft, high cadence in which the cello soon joins, and this inwardly perceived tone picture is supported outwardly by a thousand-tongued accompaniment twittering from a myriad of branches and from the heights of the air. It is already morning, yet a moment ago it was still evening. (Frans Eemil Sillanpää)

　　北方幾乎沒有夏夜。只有遲遲不去的夜晚，在流連的時候稍微黯淡，然而即便這種黯淡也有難以言喻的清晰。它是夏日早晨來臨的預兆。隨著夜晚的推移，它的音樂已經降為紫色的、深沉而聲音極輕的樂章，如此微妙，延伸至短暫的休止。然後第一小提琴以柔和的高音悠然醒來，大提琴隨即加入。這一幅由內心感知的音調畫面由畫外的百鳥啁啾烘托，伴奏來自千叢萬樹，大地長天。時間已是早晨，然而剛才還是夜晚。（弗蘭斯·埃米爾·西蘭帕）

---

[28] 魯日奇卡是 1939 年諾貝爾化學獎得主。

1931–1939 黑暗時代的堅持

1943–1950
重建與省思

1943 年

Being a young man, I was an optimist and felt sure that I should succeed in my task. (George de Hevesy)

作為年輕人，我是樂天派，確信自己能夠完成任務。（喬治·德海韋西）

I decided to dissolve it. While the invading forces marched in the streets of Copenhagen, I was busy dissolving Laue's and also James Franck's medals. (George de Hevesy)

我決定溶解它。當侵略軍進入哥本哈根的街道時，我在忙於溶解勞厄和詹姆斯·法蘭克的獎牌。[29]（喬治·德海韋西）

---

[29] 德海韋西這是在講述一段舊事，類似完璧歸趙的故事。1940 年，他正在波耳設立於哥本哈根的理論物理研究所工作，尚未獲得諾貝爾獎。當時，諾貝爾獎得主馬克斯·馮·勞厄和詹姆斯·法蘭克抗拒德國人禁令，冒死將自己的獎牌送到這裡藏匿，不料納粹入侵丹麥，波耳措手不及。德海韋西建議把它們埋起來，波耳覺得欠妥，因為德國人知道研究所保護猶太科學家，必定搜查大樓，還可能在花園裡翻找。德海韋西急中生智，提出用王水溶解獎牌。儘管過程緩慢，好在納粹闖入時，獎牌已經在一只燒瓶中液化完畢，擱在實驗室的架子上。敵人洗劫研究所，但忽略了它。戰後德海韋西歸來，發現燒瓶完好無損。於是他逆轉化學過程，使黃金沉澱析出，並送回瑞典，1952 年，諾貝爾基金會以之重鑄獎牌，再次頒給了勞厄和法蘭克。
順帶一提，波耳也有一塊諾貝爾獎牌。不過為了替芬蘭救濟基金會籌款，他於 1940 年將其拍賣了。好在後來，有匿名者把它送進丹麥歷史博物館。至今在那裡還看得到它。可見俠肝義

1943-1950 重建與省思

The letter K was the first one in the alphabet which had not, with more or less justification, been used to designate other vitamins, and it also happened to be the first letter in the word "koagulation" according to the Scandinavian and German spelling. (Henrik Carl Peter Dam)

在字母表中，或多或少有些理由，K 是第一個尚未用於指稱其他維生素的字母；而且按照斯堪地那維亞語和德語的拼寫，它也恰好是 koagulation（凝結）一詞的首字母。[30]（亨里克·達姆）

I hope the memory of Ed will be a source of inspiration for men and women to pursue scientific knowledge for many years into the future at Saint Louis University School of Medicine. Nothing would have made Ed happier. (Margaret M. Doisy)

我希望，未來多年在聖路易斯大學醫學院，對埃德[31]的記憶會成為激勵師生尋求科學知識的動力。沒有什麼能讓埃德更高興了。（瑪格麗特·M·多伊西）

1944 年

To me, science is an expression of the human spirit, which reaches every sphere of human culture. It gives an aim and meaning to existence as well as a knowledge, understanding, love, and admiration for the world. It gives a

---

膽，古今中外原本無異。
[30] 維生素 K 亦稱凝血維生素。達姆由於發現維生素 K 而與多伊西同獲 1943 年諾貝爾生理學或醫學獎。
[31] 埃德，愛德華的暱稱。愛德華·阿德爾伯特·多伊西 (Edward Adelbert Doisy)，1943 年諾貝爾生理學或醫學獎得主。編譯者一時查不到他的言論，只找到了其夫人的這段話。

deeper meaning to morality and another dimension to esthetics. (Isidor Isaac Rabi)

在我看來，科學是人文精神的一種表達，它涉及人類文化的各方面。它為世人帶來知識、理解、愛和讚賞，也賦予生存目標和意義。它給予道德更深刻的意義，為美學提供另一個維度。（伊西多·拉比）

Usually, a discovery is not made in the easiest but on a complicated way; the simple cases show up only later. (Otto Hahn)

通常，一項發現並非以最簡單的方式呈現，而是以複雜的方式進行；簡單的例子後來才出現。（奧托·哈恩）

As we sat upon a ledge high up in the Rocky Mountains⋯ viewing the panorama of lofty peaks spread out before us, our conversation turned to problems of nerve physiology. (Joseph Erlanger)

當我們坐在洛磯山脈高處的一處岩石上⋯⋯眺望著崇山峻嶺在面前展開的壯闊景象，我們的談話轉向神經生理學的各種難題。[32]（約瑟夫·厄爾蘭格）

The opportunity which the Institute has above all else is to concentrate on the production of scientific capital⋯ The production cannot be planned. No one knows how. But the conditions for it can be maintained, as they are now and always have been. That means fostering individuals and allowing them freedom. (Herbert Spencer Gasser)

研究機構最重要的機會是專注於科學資本的產出。⋯⋯科學產出無法計劃。沒有人知道該怎麼做。但可以維持它的條件，就像現在和以往

---

[32] 厄爾蘭格與同獲 1944 年諾貝爾生理學與醫學獎的加塞曾合著演講集《神經活動的電訊號》（Electrical Signs of Nervous Activity）。這段話摘自該書前言。

1943-1950 重建與省思

一直做到的。這意味著培養個人,給予他們自由。(赫伯特・斯潘塞・加塞)

Forget the times of your distress, but never forget what they taught you. (Herbert Spencer Gasser)

忘掉各種艱難困苦,但不可忘掉它們教給你的東西。(赫伯特・斯潘塞・加塞)

During half a century of literary work, I have endeavoured to introduce the philosophy of evolution into the sphere of literature, and to inspire my readers to think in evolutionary terms. (Johannes Vilhelm Jensen)

在半個世紀的文學創作中,我一直致力於將演化哲學引入文學領域,啟發讀者以演化的觀點思考。(約翰尼斯・威廉・延森)

1945 年

I don't mind your thinking slowly; I mind your publishing faster than you think. (Wolfgang Pauli)

我不在意你慢慢思考,我在意你發表得比思考快。(沃夫岡・包立)

A colleague who met me strolling rather aimlessly in the beautiful streets of Copenhagen said to me in a friendly manner, "You look very unhappy"; whereupon I answered fiercely, "How can one look happy when he is thinking about the anomalous Zeeman effect?" (Wolfgang Pauli)

在哥本哈根美麗的街道上,一位同事見我六神無主地亂走,就善意

地說:「你看起來很不開心。」我卻氣呼呼地頂嘴:「滿腦袋想著反常塞曼效應[33]，怎麼能看起來開心？」(沃夫岡・包立)

The scientific research seeks to treat phenomena as objectively as possible. (Artturi Ilmari Virtanen)

科學研究力求盡可能客觀地對待現象。(阿爾圖里・伊爾馬里・維爾塔寧)

When I woke up just after dawn on September 28, 1928, I certainly didn't plan to revolutionise all medicine by discovering the world's first antibiotic, or bacteria killer. (Alexander Fleming)

1928 年 9 月 28 日天剛亮醒來時，我當然未曾打算以發現世界上第一種抗生素或殺菌劑來徹底改變整個醫學。(亞歷山大・弗萊明)

It has been demonstrated that a species of penicillium produces in culture a very powerful antibacterial substance which affects different bacteria in different degrees. Generally speaking it may be said that the least sensitive bacteria are the Gram-negative bacilli, and the most susceptible are the pyogenic cocci... In addition to its possible use in the treatment of bacterial infections penicillin is certainly useful... for its power of inhibiting unwanted microbes in bacterial cultures so that penicillin insensitive bacteria can readily be isolated. (Alexander Fleming)

研究顯示，一種青黴菌在培養中會產生一種非常強大的抗菌物質，在不同程度上影響不同的細菌。一般而言，最不敏感的細菌是革蘭氏陰性桿菌，最易受影響的是化膿球菌。……除了可能用於治療細菌感染，青黴

---

[33] 原子的光譜線在外磁場中出現分裂的現象稱作塞曼效應。最初觀測到並獲得理論解釋的現象是一分為三，後來發現了更加複雜難解的情況，稱為反常塞曼效應。

1943-1950 重建與省思

素當然還有許多用途……在細菌培養中，由於青黴素具有抑制不需要的微生物的能力，因此很容易分離對它不敏感的細菌。（亞歷山大·弗萊明）

Science, as long as it limits itself to the descriptive study of the laws of nature, has no moral or ethical quality and this applies to the physical as well as the biological sciences. (Ernst Boris Chain)

科學，只要它僅限於對自然法則的描述性研究，就沒有道德或倫理的性質。這適用於生物科學也適用於物理學。（恩斯特·伯利斯·柴恩）

I feel we must all exert ourselves to the utmost to see that the ideals and hopes held by Alfred Nobel, whom we commemorate today, do not fail from lack of purpose on the part of scientists. (Howard Walter Florey)

我覺得，我們都必須盡力而為，以見證我們今天所紀念的阿佛烈·諾貝爾的理想和希望，不致由於科學家缺乏目標而落空。（霍華德·弗洛里）

You shall create beauty not to excite the senses but to give sustenance to the soul. (Gabriela Mistral)

你應該創造美，不是為了刺激感官，而是為了滋養心靈。（加夫列拉·米斯特拉爾）

To be sure, no piece of social machinery, however well constructed, can be effective unless there is back of it a will and a determination to make it work. (Cordell Hull)

可以肯定，任何社會機制無論建構得多麼好，背後若無意志與決心使之運作，都不可能發揮作用。（科德爾·赫爾）

In all my fifty years of public service I have never seen a document that was more crowded with infamous falsehoods and distortions —— infamous falsehoods and distortions on a scale so huge that I never imagined until today that any government on this planet was capable of uttering them. (Cordell Hull)

在我 50 年的全部公職生涯裡，我從未見過一份文件，更加充斥無恥的謊言與扭曲 —— 無恥的謊言與扭曲的程度如此之大，此前我從未想像世間任何政府能夠說得出來。[34]（科德爾・赫爾）

1946 年

The first business of a man of science is to proclaim the truth as he finds it, and let the world adjust itself as best it can to the new knowledge. (Percy Williams Bridgman)

科學家的首要任務是宣揚他所發現的真理，並讓世界盡其所能適應新知識。（珀西・布里奇曼）

The attitude which the man in the street unconsciously adopts towards science is capricious and varied. At one moment he scorns the scientist for a highbrow, at another anathematizes him for blasphemously undermining his religion; but at the mention of a name like Edison he falls into a coma of veneration. When he stops to think, he does recognize, however, that the whole atmosphere of the world in which he lives is tinged by science, as is shown

---

[34] 1941 年 12 月 7 日，日軍不宣而戰偷襲珍珠港後，日本大使照會時任美國國務卿的赫爾，赫爾如此痛斥。

most immediately and strikingly by our modern conveniences and material resources. A little deeper thinking shows him that the influence of science goes much farther and colors the entire mental outlook of modern civilised man on the world about him. (Percy Williams Bridgman)

大眾對科學所不自覺採取的態度反覆無常，五花八門。他一時嘲笑科學家的自視高雅，一時又痛斥科學家不敬地動搖了他的宗教；而在提到愛迪生這樣的名字時，他又陷入崇拜而不能自拔。然而，當他停下來思考時，他確實意識到，自己所生活的世界的整個氛圍都受到科學的影響，如同我們的現代便利和物質資源所直接明顯展現的一樣。稍許深入思考便能發現，科學的影響非常深遠，改變了現代文明人周遭世界的整個精神面貌。（珀西·布里奇曼）

I wish to tell next why I decided in 1917 to attempt to isolate an enzyme. At that time I had little time for research, not much apparatus, research money, or assistance. I desired to accomplish something of real importance. In other words, I decided to take a "long shot". A number of persons advised me that my attempt to isolate an enzyme was foolish, but this advice made me feel all the more certain that if successful the quest would be worthwile. (James Batcheller Sumner)

接下來我想談談1917年自己何以決定嘗試分離酶。那時我幾乎沒有時間做研究，沒有多少設備、研究經費或援助。我渴望完成某種真正重要的事情。換句話說，我決心進行一次「遠征」。許多人勸告我，嘗試分離酶是愚蠢的，然而這一些勸告使我更加確信，如果成功，這種追求是值得的。（詹姆斯·B·薩姆納）

As the result of discoveries in the field or enzyme chemistry some questions have been answered and many new questions have arisen. We live in an expanding universe in more senses than that of the astronomers. (James Batcheller Sumner)

由於在酶化學領域的發現，一些問題得到解答，許多新的問題又出現了。我們生活在一個不斷膨脹的宇宙中，這比天文學家的理解更深刻。（詹姆斯·B·薩姆納）

I am a plain man, just out of the laboratory, leaving my test tubes behind me. (James Batcheller Sumner)

我是個平凡的人，剛走出實驗室，試管留在身後。（詹姆斯·B·薩姆納）

While the study of enzyme reactions made rapid progress all attempts to isolate an enzyme and so determine its chemical nature were unsuccessful until recently. (John Howard Northrop)

雖然對酶反應的研究獲得了迅速進展，但直到最近，所有分離酶以確定其化學性質的嘗試都沒有成功。（約翰·霍華德·諾思羅普）

The new field of virus research is really in its infancy and much remains to be accomplished. Certain basic and fundamental problems relating to the mode of virus reproduction and mutation have taken definite form. Solution of these problems should yield information of great value to biology, chemistry, genetics and medicine. This new field of research has been laid upon a very broad foundation, for the present status of virus research has been achieved by contributions from almost every branch of science. (Wendell Meredith Stanley)

病毒研究的新領域實際上仍處於初始階段，大量工作有待完成。關於病毒繁殖和變異模式的某些基礎的、根本的問題已經明確成形。這些問題的解決將會產生對生物學、化學、遺傳學和醫學具有重大價值的資訊。這個新的研究領域已經建立在非常廣泛的基礎上,因為病毒研究的現狀幾乎是所有科學分支的共同努力成果。(溫德爾‧梅雷迪思‧斯坦利)

As science is more and more subject to grave misuse as well as to use for human benefit it has also become the scientist's responsibility to become aware of the social relations and applications of his subject, and to exert his influence in such a direction as will result in the best applications of the findings in his own and related fields. Thus he must help in educating the public, in the broad sense, and this means first educating himself, not only in science but in regard to the great issues confronting mankind today. (Hermann Joseph Muller)

隨著科學使人類受益的同時被越來越嚴重地誤用,科學家也負有責任,須關注其研究對象的社會關係和應用,並發揮影響力,以在其本身及相關領域最妥善地應用其研究成果。因此,他必須在廣義上幫助教育大眾,而這意味著首先要教育自己,不僅在科學上,並且包含了當今人類所面臨的重大問題。(赫爾曼‧約瑟夫‧馬勒)

"When someone is searching," said Siddhartha, "then it might easily happen that the only thing his eyes still see is that what he searches for, that he is unable to find anything, to let anything enter his mind, because he always thinks of nothing but the object of his search, because he has a goal, because he is obsessed by the goal. Searching means: having a goal. But finding means: being free, being open, having no goal. You, oh venerable one, are perhaps indeed a searcher because, striving for your goal, there are many things you don't see, which are directly in front of your eyes." (Hermann Hesse)

「人在尋求時,」悉達多[35]說,「很可能他見到的唯一事物是他所尋求

---

[35] 悉達多,即釋迦牟尼。

的東西,他找不到任何東西,無法讓任何東西進入頭腦,因為除了所尋求的對象他總是別無他想,因為他有一個目標,因為他執著於目標。尋求意味著:有一個目標。而找到意味著:自由,開放,沒有目標。你,哦,可敬的人,也許確實是位尋求者,因為,極力追求目標時,有很多東西你見不到,而它們就在眼前。」(赫曼‧赫塞)

Most of all, he learned from it to listen, to pay close attention with a quiet heart, with a waiting, opened soul, without passion, without a wish, without judgement, without an opinion. (Hermann Hesse)

最重要的是,他從中學會了傾聽,密切關注而抱持平靜的心態與等待、開放的精神,不帶熱情,不帶期許,不帶判斷,不帶主張。(赫曼‧赫塞)

What I always hated and detested and cursed above all things was this contentment, this healthiness and comfort, this carefully preserved optimism of the middle classes, this fat and prosperous brood of mediocrity. (Hermann Hesse)

我一直憎恨、厭惡和詛咒之至的就是這種滿足,這種健康與舒適,這種中產階級小心翼翼地保持的樂觀,這種志得意滿而大行其道的平庸沉思。(赫曼‧赫塞)

May diversity in all shapes and colours live long on this dear earth of ours. What a wonderful thing is the existence of many races, many peoples, many languages, and many varieties of attitude and outlook! (Hermann Hesse)

願所有形狀和色彩的多樣性在我們這個可愛的地球上常在。眾多人種、眾多民族、眾多語言、眾多態度和觀點共存,這是何等奇妙的事情!(赫曼‧赫塞)

1943-1950 重建與省思

Those who are rooted in the depths that are eternal and unchangeable and who rely on unshakeable principles, face change full of courage, courage based on faith. (Emily Greene Balch)

那些扎根於永恆不變的深處、依靠不可動搖的原則的人，面對變化時充滿了勇氣，基於信念的勇氣。（愛米莉·巴爾奇）

The future will be determined in part by happenings that it is impossible to foresee; it will also be influenced by trends that are now existent and observable. (Emily Greene Balch)

未來在某種程度上取決於無法預見的事件，並將受到現存的可見的趨勢影響。（愛米莉·巴爾奇）

It is as good as going to one's funeral without having to die first. (Emily Greene Balch)

這跟參加一個人的葬禮而不用先死去差不多。[36]（愛米莉·巴爾奇）

Words… present a picture of the inward man. (John Raleigh Mott)

言語……畫出了人的內在。（約翰·穆德）

1947 年

Your kindness has made me discover a new characteristic of human beings, and that is that it is possible for a person to feel both humble and proud at the same time! I feel humble because I know how much my scientific work

---

[36] 得悉自己獲得諾貝爾獎提名的過程時，巴爾奇如是說。

1947 年

has been dependent on the cooperation and assistance of so many people and organisations, of which I am, tonight, the fortunate representative. (Edward Victor Appleton)

你們的好意使我發現了人類的一個新特性，那就是，一個人有可能同時感到謙卑與自豪！我感到謙卑，因為知道我的科學工作一直多麼依賴如此眾多的人和組織的合作和幫助，今晚，我有幸充當他們的代表。（愛德華・阿普爾頓）

I am only a physicist with nothing material to show for my labours. I have never even seen the ionosphere, although I have worked on the subject for thirty years. That does show how lucky people can be. If there had been no ionosphere I would not have been standing here this morning. (Edward Victor Appleton)

我只是個物理學家，沒有任何物質的東西可以展示我的工作。我甚至從未見過電離層，儘管致力於這一項主題已有 30 年。這真的顯示了人能有多幸運。假如沒有電離層，今天早上我就不會站在這裡了。（愛德華・阿普爾頓）

The history of science has proved that fundamental research is the life-blood of individual progress and that the ideas that lead to spectacular advances spring from it. (Edward Victor Appleton)

科學史業已證明，基礎研究是個體進步的命脈，帶來驚人進展的創意想法也源自於它。（愛德華・阿普爾頓）

I rate enthusiasm even above professional skill. (Edward Victor Appleton)

我認為熱情甚至比專業技能更重要。（愛德華・阿普爾頓）

1943-1950 重建與省思

The older I grow the more I assess the importance of the simple uncomplicated qualities of loyalty and devotion to a cause or to an enterprise. (Edward Victor Appleton)

年紀越大,我越看重對事業或工作的忠誠和奉獻這種簡單樸素特質的重要性。(愛德華・阿普爾頓)

If you want something done, choose a busy man: the other kind has no time. (Edward Victor Appleton)

你要是想做成某件事,就挑個忙碌的人:另一種人沒時間。(愛德華・阿普爾頓)

It is well known that the Nobel Committees bring world opinion to a focus, and that fact still further enhances the prestige attaching to the Prizes. (Robert Robinson)

眾所周知,諾貝爾委員會聚焦世界輿論,而這一項事實進一步提高了諾貝爾獎的聲望。(羅伯特・魯賓遜)

The winners of Nobel Prizes must be assumed to possess at least a modicum of imagination and sensibility, and it is therefore incredible that any of us should not experience at this time a veritable surge of emotion. (Robert Robinson)

諾貝爾獎得主必定被認為至少有幾分想像力和敏感性。因此,我們之中的任何人此時若竟然無動於衷,是難以置信的。(羅伯特・魯賓遜)

To have thus been singled out among so many worthy scientists must evoke a feeling of humility and at the same time renew the determination to go on with the work. (Carl F. Cori)

1947 年

能夠在眾多優秀科學家之中脫穎而出，必然會喚起謙卑之感，並加強繼續工作的決心。（卡爾·斐迪南·科里）

For a research worker the unforgotten moments of his life are those rare ones which come after years of plodding work, when the veil over nature's secret seems suddenly to lift & when what was dark & chaotic appears in a clear and beautiful light and pattern. (Gerty T. Cori)

對於研究工作者，其終生難忘的時刻是經過多年辛苦工作之後的那些珍貴片刻，當遮掩大自然奧祕的面紗似乎突然被揭開，曾經晦暗和混亂的事物以鮮明美好的形態和模式呈現。（格蒂·科里）

The love for and dedication to one's work seems to me to be the basis for happiness. (Gerty T. Cori)

在我看來，對工作的熱愛和奉獻是幸福的基礎。（格蒂·科里）

What another would have done as well as you, do not do it. What another would have said as well as you, do not say it. What another would have written as well as you, do not write it. (André Paul Guillaume Gide)

別人會做得跟你一樣好的，不要做。別人會說得跟你一樣好的，不要說。別人會寫得跟你一樣好的，不要寫。（安德烈·紀德）

Only those things are beautiful which are inspired by madness and written by reason. (André Paul Guillaume Gide)

只有那些由瘋狂啟發、由理性書寫的作品才是美麗的。（安德烈·紀德）

The sole art that suits me is that which, rising from unrest, tends toward serenity. (André Paul Guillaume Gide)

1943-1950 重建與省思

唯一適合我的藝術發自於不安,趨於寧靜。(安德烈‧紀德)

It is only in adventure that some people succeed in knowing themselves —— in finding themselves. (André Paul Guillaume Gide)

只有在冒險中,一些人成功地認識了自己 —— 發現了自己。(安德烈‧紀德)

Man is more interesting than men. God made him and not them in his image. Each one is more precious than all. (André Paul Guillaume Gide)

個人比眾人更有趣。上帝以祂的形象創造了他而非他們。每一個人都比所有的人更珍貴。(安德烈‧紀德)

Believe those who are seeking the truth. Doubt those who find it. (André Paul Guillaume Gide)

相信那些尋求真理的人。懷疑那些找到它的人。(安德烈‧紀德)

1948 年

It's tough watching a good idea lose because its backers are less eloquent or have less clout than its opponents. (Patrick Maynard Stuart Blackett)

眼見一個好主意,由於支持者與反對者相較之下不夠雄辯或影響較小而失敗,實在遺憾。(帕特里克‧布萊克特)

It is a common fallacy to suppose that the demolition of an opponent's argument automatically establishes one's own. (Patrick Maynard Stuart Blackett)

> 1948 年

以為對手的論點被推翻就能自動建立自己的論點,是一個常見的謬誤。(帕特里克・布萊克特)

May every young scientist remember... and not fail to keep his eyes open for the possibility that an irritating failure of his apparatus to give consistent results may once or twice in a lifetime conceal an important discovery. (Patrick Maynard Stuart Blackett)

但願每個年輕科學家都牢記⋯⋯並對這種可能始終保持警惕:一生之中,他的儀器也許偶爾會出現惱人的故障而無法呈現一致的結果,因而掩蓋了重大的發現。(帕特里克・布萊克特)

People who've had happy childhoods are wonderful, but they're bland... An unhappy childhood compels you to use your imagination to create a world in which you can be happy. Use your old grief. That's the gift you're given. (Patrick Maynard Stuart Blackett)

童年快樂的人固然幸運,但也乏味。⋯⋯不快樂的童年迫使你以想像力創造一個你可以快樂的世界。利用往昔的悲傷。這是你的天賦。(帕特里克・布萊克特)

We live in a world where unfortunately the distinction between true and false appears to become increasingly blurred by manipulation of facts, by exploitation of uncritical minds, and by the pollution of the language. (Arne Wilhelm Kaurin Tiselius)

由於對事實的操弄、對無批判能力者的利用以及對語言的毒害,在我們生活的世界上,真實和虛假之間的區別不幸顯得日益模糊。(阿爾內・蒂塞利烏斯)

The field of pest control is immense, and many problems impatiently

1943-1950 重建與省思

await a solution. A new territory has opened up for the synthetics chemist, territory which is still unexplored and difficult, but which holds out the hope that in time further progress will be made. (Paul Hermann Müller)

病蟲害防治範圍龐大，許多問題急待解決。對於合成化學家，一個新的領域已經開放。這個領域尚未被探索，困難充斥，但它帶來希望，隨著時間的推移，未來可望將獲得各種進步。（保羅‧赫爾曼‧穆勒）

I am grateful and glad that I have been permitted to lay a first foundation stone in this puzzling and apparently endless domain. (Paul Hermann Müller)

我滿懷感激，也很高興承蒙允許，在這個令人困惑不已、顯然無邊無垠的領域安放第一塊基石。（保羅‧赫爾曼‧穆勒）

Only those who will risk going too far can possibly find out how far one can go. (Thomas Stearns Eliot)

只有那些會冒險走得太遠的人，才有可能得知自己能夠走多遠。（T‧S‧艾略特）

The experience of a poem is the experience both of a moment and of a lifetime. (Thomas Stearns Eliot)

一首詩的體驗既是瞬時的，也是一生的。（T‧S‧艾略特）

To do the useful thing, to say the courageous thing, to contemplate the beautiful thing: that is enough for one man's life. (Thomas Stearns Eliot)

做有用的事，說勇敢的話，思考美好的事物：這對一個人的生命來說已經足夠了。（T‧S‧艾略特）

The years between fifty and seventy are the hardest. You are always being asked to do things, and yet you are not decrepit enough to turn them down. (Thomas Stearns Eliot)

五十至七十的年紀最難堪。你總是被要求做各種事情，而你還沒衰老到足以拒絕。（T·S·艾略特）

The Nobel is a ticket to one's own funeral. No one has ever done anything after he got it. (Thomas Stearns Eliot)

諾貝爾獎是自己葬禮的門票。沒有人獲獎之後仍有所作為。（T·S·艾略特）

1949 年

(Once I had published my seminal 1934 paper on particle interaction) I felt like a traveler who rests himself at a small tea shop at the top of a mountain slope. At that time I was not thinking about whether there were any more mountains ahead. (Hideki Yukawa)

（1934 年發表開創性的粒子交互作用論文時）我覺得自己像個旅行者，在山坡頂上一個小茶鋪歇腳。那時我並未曾考慮前方還有沒有山。（湯川秀樹）

Suppose there is something which a person cannot understand. He happens to notice the similarity of this something to some other thing which he understands quite well. By comparing them he may come to understand the thing which he could not understand up to that moment. If his understanding turns out to be appropriate and nobody else has ever come to such an understanding, he can claim that his thinking was really creative. (Hideki Yukawa)

假設有一種事物是一個人無法理解的。他碰巧注意到該事物與另一

1943-1950 重建與省思

項他所充分理解的事物的相似性。經由比較，他可能會理解之前無法理解的事情。如果理解證明得當，而其他人從未得出這般理解，他就可以宣稱，自己的思考確實具有創造性。（湯川秀樹）

Reality is complicated. There is no justification for all of the hasty conclusions. (Hideki Yukawa)

現實是複雜的。一切倉促的結論都是沒有道理的。（湯川秀樹）

This is our first visit here, but I have long had a special consciousness for Sweden, and I would like to mention the reason for this.

When I was ready for college, it was on the recommendation of Dr. John Woods Beckman, a native of Sweden, that I left the eastern part of America to enter the University of California. There I found opportunity to do the scientific work which has brought me to Stockholm. During our long friendship with Dr. and Mrs. Beckman they have often told us of Sweden, but with characteristic Swedish modesty, they have not prepared us for what we have seen here.

Stockholm is a beautiful city, it stands as evidence of the energy, and good taste, of Sweden.

Although I am supposed to be well along in the educational process, there has been a serious omission, the study of Swedish. However, your efficient Foreign Office has started, to teach me, and I can at least say – Tack så mycket. (William Francis Giauque)

這是我們第一次來到貴地，不過長期以來，我對瑞典懷有特別的感覺，我想說說其中的原委。

我準備上大學時，是在原籍瑞典的約翰·伍茲·貝克曼博士推薦下，

1949年

離開美國東部進入加州大學。在那裡，我找到了從事科學工作的機會，它把我帶到了斯德哥爾摩。在與貝克曼夫婦長期的親切交往中，他們經常告訴我們瑞典的情況；不過由於典型的瑞典式謙遜，他們不曾使我們為在此的見聞做好準備。

斯德哥爾摩是一座美麗的城市。它證明了瑞典的活力和優異品味。

雖然我在受教育過程中還算順利，但還是存在一個嚴重的遺漏：對瑞典的研究。好在，貴國高效的外交部已經行動了，開始教我，而我至少能夠說：Tack så mycket.[37]（威廉·吉奧克）

It is easy for a chemist to write an equation for a desired reaction, but this does not mean that the reaction will actually take place. (William Francis Giauque)

對於化學家，為所期待的反應寫個方程式很容易，但這並不意味著反應會實際發生。（威廉·吉奧克）

A recognized fact which goes back to the earliest times is that every living organism is not the sum of a multitude of unitary processes, but is, by virtue of interrelationships and of higher and lower levels of control, an unbroken unity. When research, in the efforts of bringing understanding, as a rule examines isolated processes and studies them, these must of necessity be removed from their context. In general, viewed biologically, this experimental separation involves a sacrifice. In fact, quantitative findings of any material and energy changes preserve their full context only through their being seen and understood as parts of a natural order. (Walter Rudolf Hess)

一個很早就得到公認的事實為，每一個生物體都不是大量單一過程

---

[37] 瑞典語：非常感謝。

1943-1950 重建與省思

之總和,而是憑藉各種相互關係及較高與較低控制層級所形成的一個不可分割的統一體。當研究為了便於理解,照例審視單獨的過程並深究它們時,必須將過程從所處環境剝離。總之,從生物學的角度來看,這種實驗性的分離需要一些犧牲。實際上,任何物質和能量變化的定量研究結果,只有經由被視作並理解為自然秩序的組成部分,才能保留其完整環境。(瓦爾特‧魯道夫‧赫斯)

Prefrontal leukotomy is a simple operation, always safe, which may prove to be an effective surgical treatment in certain cases of mental disorder. (Antonio Caetano de Abreu Freire Egas Moniz)

前額葉腦白質切除術是簡單的手術,總是安全的,在某些精神病例中可以證明是有效的手術治療。(安東尼奧‧埃加斯‧莫尼斯)

You cannot swim for new horizons until you have courage to lose sight of the shore. (William Faulkner)

除非你有勇氣看不見海岸,否則你不可能游向新的地平線。(威廉‧福克納)

Don't do what you can do —— try what you can't do. (William Faulkner)

不要做你能做的事 —— 嘗試你不能做的。(威廉‧福克納)

Always dream and shoot higher than you know you can do. Don't bother just to be better than your contemporaries or predecessors. Try to be better than yourself. (William Faulkner)

總是夢想和追求得高於自知所能。不要只想著超越同輩或前人。力求超越自己。(威廉‧福克納)

I feel that this award was not made to me as a man, but to my work ——

1949 年

a life's work in the agony and sweat of the human spirit, not for glory and least of all for profit, but to create out of the materials of the human spirit something which did not exist before. (William Faulkner)

我覺得這個獎項不是授予我這個人，而是授予我的工作──在人類精神的痛苦和辛勞中的一生工作，不是為了名，更不是為了利，而是要以人類精神的材料創造出前所未有的東西。（威廉·福克納）

Read, read, read. Read everything ── trash, classics, good and bad, and see how they do it. Just like a carpenter who works as an apprentice and studies the master. Read! You'll absorb it. Then write. If it's good, you'll find out. If it's not, throw it out of the window. (William Faulkner)

讀，讀，讀。讀所有的東西──垃圾，經典，無論好壞，看他們是怎麼做的。就像當學徒的木匠，跟著師傅學習。讀！你會吸收它。然後寫。如果它是好的，你會知道。如果不好，就扔出窗外。（威廉·福克納）

Why, that's a hundred miles away. That's a long way to go just to eat. (William Faulkner)

哦，那是在一百英里外了。不過是吃頓飯，何必去那麼遠。[38]（威廉·福克納）

In the last fifty years science has advanced more than in the 2,000 previous years and given mankind greater powers over the forces of nature than the ancients ascribed to their gods. (John Boyd Orr)

過去 50 年，科學進步的速度快於先前兩千年。所賦予人類的超乎自然的力量，大於古人心目中的神力。（約翰·博伊德·奧爾）

---

[38] 甘迺迪總統邀請 50 位諾貝爾獎得主共進晚餐，福克納解釋自己何以謝絕。

1943-1950 重建與省思

1950 年

All of us, of course, feel with Newton, that we are like boys who have picked up a few bright pebbles on the beach, whilst the great ocean of truth opens out before us. (Cecil Frank Powell)

自不待言,我們全都與牛頓同感。我們就像在海灘上拾起幾顆光亮鵝卵石的孩子,而真理浩瀚的海洋在面前展開。(塞西爾·鮑威爾)

Any device in science is a window on to nature, and each new window contributes to the breadth of our view. (Cecil Frank Powell)

任何科學設備都是面對自然的窗口,每一個新窗口都有助於拓展我們的視野。(塞西爾·鮑威爾)

Let me wish you good fortune and persistence. Good fortune, for chance plays some role in the lives of scientists as in all human affairs, and opportunity does not knock with equal insistence on every man's door. And persistence in order that you may take advantage of opportunity when it comes. (Cecil Frank Powell)

讓我祝你們好運和堅持。好運,因為機遇在科學家的生活中扮演重要角色,就像在所有的人類事務中一樣;機會也並非以同樣的堅持敲響每個人的門。堅持不懈,以便機會一旦到來時你們可以利用。(塞西爾·鮑威爾)

The time has not yet come when we can give an answer to questions so fundamental and so important to an understanding of the workings of Nature. But I am firmly convinced that this problem —— like all others —— will eventually be solved. (Otto Paul Hermann Diels)

> 1950 年

對於理解大自然運作如此根本、如此重大的問題，我們能夠給出答案的時機尚未到來。但我堅信，這個困難——與其他所有困難一樣——終將得以解決。（奧托·迪爾斯）

Tradition is what you resort to when you don't have the time or the money to do it right. (Kurt Alder)

傳統，就是你沒有時間或金錢正確從事時所訴諸之物。（庫爾特·阿爾德）

The award is for investigations carried out in the fields of both organic chemistry and clinical medicine. This fact illustrates the complex nature of the problem, for without the work of the chemist, the clinician could not advance beyond the stage of hypothesis, and without the clinician the contributions of the organic chemist could not come to fruition. (Edward Calvin Kendall)

這個獎項所獎勵的，是在有機化學和臨床醫學領域一併進行的研究。這個事實表明了問題的複雜性，因為如果沒有化學家的工作，臨床醫生就不能超越假設的階段，而如果沒有臨床醫生，有機化學家的貢獻也無法獲得成果。（愛德華·卡爾文·肯德爾）

You have done me the great honour of awarding me a share of the Nobel Prize for Medicine, together with Dr. Hench and Dr. Kendall, although I possess no more than a layman's knowledge of either medicine or physiology. I hope, therefore, that you will not take it amiss if, in the following remarks, I have to make use of a number of chemical formulae that possibly not all of you understand. It is in this case the only adequate language. (Tadeus Reichstein)

你們讓我、亨奇博士和肯德爾博士分享諾貝爾醫學獎，給予了我巨大榮譽，儘管我對醫學和生理學的所知均無異於門外漢。所以，在接下來的發言中，如果我不得不使用一些可能並非你們所有人都理解的化學公式，希望你們不要認為有何不當。在這種情況下，它是唯一勝任的語言。（塔德烏什・賴希施泰因）

I, a physician, am delighted to stand here with two distinguished chemists, Drs. Reichstein and Kendall. Perhaps the ratio of one physician to two chemists is symbolic, since medicine is so firmly linked to chemistry by a double bond. For medicine, especially during the past twenty-five years, has been receiving its finest weapons from the hands of the chemists, and the chemist finds his richest reward as the fruits of his labor rescue countless thousands from the long shadows of the sickroom. (Philip Showalter Hench)

我，作為一名醫生，很高興能和兩位卓越的化學家，賴希施泰因博士和肯德爾博士一起站在這裡。或許一個醫生與兩個化學家的比例具有象徵意義，因為醫學與化學以雙鍵[39]如此牢固地連結。須知醫學，尤其在過去25年間，從化學家手中得到了最好的武器；化學家也獲得了最豐厚的回報，就是他的勞動成果從病房漫長的陰影中拯救了成千上萬不可勝數的患者。（菲利普・肖瓦特・亨奇）

So infinite is the wisdom of nature, so profound are her secrets that even with these powerful new weapons we cannot finish the job. We can only make a modest and imperfect beginning. (Philip Showalter Hench)

大自然的智慧如此無限，她的祕密如此深奧，以至於即使擁有這些強大的新武器，我們也無法完成這項工作。我們只能造就一個謙虛而不完美的開始。（菲利普・肖瓦特・亨奇）

As a rule, the man who first thinks of a new idea is so much ahead of his

---

[39] 雙鍵，化合物分子中兩個原子以共用兩對電子形成的共價鍵。

time that everyone thinks him silly, so that he remains obscure and is soon forgotten. Then, gradually, the world becomes ready for his idea, and the man who proclaims it at the fortunate moment gets all the credit. (Bertrand Arthur William Russell)

一般來說,首先產生新想法的人是如此遙遙領先於他的時代,以至於人人都認為他愚蠢,所以他仍然默默無聞,很快遭到遺忘。然後,逐漸地,世人準備好了接受他的想法,而在幸運的時刻宣布它的人獲得全部聲譽。(伯特蘭‧羅素)

Some part of life —— perhaps the most important part —— must be left to the spontaneous action of individual impulse, for where all is system there will be mental and spiritual death. (Bertrand Arthur William Russell)

生命的某些部分 —— 也許最重要的部分 —— 必須留給個人衝動的自發性行動,因為在全部都是系統的地方,就會有心智和精神上的死亡。(伯特蘭‧羅素)

We know too much and feel too little. At least we feel too little of those creative emotions from which a good life springs. (Bertrand Arthur William Russell)

我們了解太多而感受太少。至少我們對那些產生美好生活的創造性熱情感受太少。(伯特蘭‧羅素)

Do not fear to be eccentric in opinion, for every opinion now accepted was once eccentric. (Bertrand Arthur William Russell)

不要害怕見解怪異,因為如今被接受的每一種見解一度均屬怪異。(伯特蘭‧羅素)

1943-1950 重建與省思

This seems plainly absurd; but whoever wishes to become a philosopher must learn not to be frightened by absurdities. (Bertrand Arthur William Russell)

這似乎明顯荒謬；然而，任何想成為哲學家的人，都必須學會不要被荒謬的東西嚇住。（伯特蘭・羅素）

The fact that an opinion has been widely held is no evidence whatever that it is not utterly absurd. (Bertrand Arthur William Russell)

一種見解已被許多人所持有的事實完全證明不了這種見解並非全然荒謬。（伯特蘭・羅素）

In all affairs it's a healthy thing now and then to hang a question mark on the things you have long taken for granted. (Bertrand Arthur William Russell)

在所有事務中，不時對你長期認為理所當然的事情打個問號，這是有益健康的。（伯特蘭・羅素）

Science may set limits to knowledge, but should not set limits to imagination. (Bertrand Arthur William Russell)

科學可以限制知識，但不應限制想像力。（伯特蘭・羅素）

Science is what you know, philosophy is what you don't know. (Bertrand Arthur William Russell)

科學是你所知道的，哲學是你所不知道的。（伯特蘭・羅素）

Mathematics possesses not only truth, but supreme beauty —— a beauty cold and austere, like that of sculpture. (Bertrand Arthur William Russell)

數學不僅擁有真理，而且擁有至上的美 —— 冷靜簡樸、雕塑一般的美。（伯特蘭・羅素）

1950 年

The opinions that are held with passion are always those for which no good ground exists; indeed the passion is the measure of the holder's lack of rational conviction. (Bertrand Arthur William Russell)

滿懷熱情地持有的意見，總是那些並無根據的意見。的確，熱情是持有者缺乏理性信念的衡量標準。（伯特蘭‧羅素）

We know very little, and yet it is astonishing that we know so much, and still more astonishing that so little knowledge can give us so much power. (Bertrand Arthur William Russell)

我們知道的太少，但令人驚訝的是我們知道的如此多，更令人驚訝的是如此少的知識卻能給我們如此大的力量。（伯特蘭‧羅素）

Truth is a shining goddess, always veiled, always distant, never wholly approachable, but worthy of all the devotion of which the human spirit is capable. (Bertrand Arthur William Russell)

真理是一位光輝的女神，總是戴著面紗，總是保持距離，永遠無法完全接近，但是值得人類精神所能奉獻的一切。（伯特蘭‧羅素）

Three passions, simple but overwhelmingly strong, have governed my life: the longing for love, the search for knowledge, and unbearable pity for the suffering of mankind. These passions, like great winds, have blown me hither and thither, in a wayward course, over a great ocean of anguish, reaching to the very verge of despair. (Bertrand Arthur William Russell)

有三種單純而又無比強烈的熱情，左右了我的一生：對愛的渴望、對知識的尋求，以及對人類苦難的無法承受的悲憫。這些熱情有如狂風，飄忽不定，將我吹往四處，越過茫茫苦海，直抵萬劫不復之境。（伯特蘭‧羅素）

1943–1950 重建與省思

I would never die for my beliefs because I might be wrong. (Bertrand Arthur William Russell)

我永遠不會為自己的信念而死,因為我也許是錯的。(伯特蘭・羅素)

In rearing my children I have passed on the philosophy that Nana taught me as a youngster.... The right to be treated as an equal by all other men, she said, is man's birthright. Never permit anyone to treat you otherwise. (Ralph Bunche)

撫養孩子時,我把娜娜[40]在我年輕時教給我的理念傳給了他們。……她說:被其他所有人平等對待的權利是與生俱來的。絕對不能允許任何人以其他方式對待你。(拉爾夫・本奇)

There are no warlike people —— just warlike leaders. (Ralph Bunche)

不存在好戰的人民 —— 只有好戰的領導者。(拉爾夫・本奇)

---

[40] 娜娜,本奇的祖母。

1951–1960
科學與人文的對話

1951 年

On one side of the Nobel Medal you can see the genie of Science lifting the veil which obscures the Goddess of Nature. (John Douglas Cockcroft)

在諾貝爾獎章的一面，你可以看到科學精靈在揭開掩蓋自然女神的面紗。（約翰・考克饒夫）

It is an honour so great that even yet it is difficult for me to believe that it is true. (Ernest Thomas Sinton Walton)

這是如此巨大的榮譽，甚至到現在我還難以相信這是真的。（歐尼斯特・沃爾頓）

One way to learn the mind of the Creator is to study His creation. (Ernest Thomas Sinton Walton)

理解造物者思想的一種方式是研究他的創造。（歐尼斯特・沃爾頓）

There has never been in the history of the world any other prize or honor with the international recognition accorded to the Nobel Prize. One reason for this is that it is truly an international honor, given with regard to achievement only. (Edwin Mattison McMillan)

1951-1960 科學與人文的對話

在世界歷史上，從未有任何國際認可的其他獎項或榮譽與諾貝爾獎相當。一個原因為，這是真正只依據成就授予的國際榮譽。（埃德溫·麥克米倫）

It seems to me that this is another case of a phenomenon that has occurred before in science —— the nearly simultaneous appearance of an idea in several parts of the world, when the development of the science concerned has reached such a point that the idea is needed for its further progress. (Edwin Mattison McMillan)

在我看來，這是科學上發生過的一種現象的又一例子——當有關科學的發展已經達到如此地步，一個想法需要進一步發展之際，這個想法幾乎同時出現在世界不同地方。（埃德溫·麥克米倫）

I believe that one of the characteristics of the human race, possibly the one that is primarily responsible for its course of evolution, is that it has grown by creatively responding to failure. (Glenn Theodore Seaborg)

我認為人類的一個特點，可能屬於主要負責其演化過程的一個，是它以創造性地回應失敗而成長。（格倫·西奧多·西博格）

All my life I've been surrounded by people who are smarter than I am, but I found I could always keep up by working hard. (Glenn Theodore Seaborg)

我一生周圍都是比我聰明的人，不過我發現，自己總是可以由努力工作來跟上他們。（格倫·西奧多·西博格）

Surrounded by dazzlingly bright students, I was uncertain I could make the grade. But taking heart in Edison's dictum that genius is 99 percent perspiration, I discovered a pedestrian secret of success. I could work harder than most of them. (Glenn Theodore Seaborg)

> 1951 年

同學個個聰明,光彩照人,我不確定自己是否能達到要求。不過愛迪生的格言說,天才是 99% 的汗水,我從中受到鼓勵,發現了一個說來平淡的成功祕訣。我不妨比他們大多數人更努力地工作。(格倫・西奧多・西博格)

The education of young people in science is at least as important, maybe more so, than the research itself. (Glenn Theodore Seaborg)

在科學領域,年輕人的教育至少跟研究本身一樣重要,也許更重要。(格倫・西奧多・西博格)

Most of my scientific work has been basic research. There were no immediate uses for my discoveries, but today the radioisotopes are the workhorses of nuclear medicine, an isotope of plutonium is a major energy source in the space program, and the element americium is critical to the smoke detectors in every house in the country. (Glenn Theodore Seaborg)

我的科學工作大部分屬於基礎研究。我的發現不具備直接的用途;可是如今,放射性同位素是核子醫學的主力,鈽的同位素是太空計畫的主要能源來源,而元素鋂對美國每所房子裡的煙霧探測器都是十分重要的。(格倫・西奧多・西博格)

By asking questions and quickly reading some books, Melvin Calvin felt comfortable in many fields of endeavor. (Glenn Theodore Seaborg)

透過提問和瀏覽一些書籍,梅爾文・卡爾文[41]在所致力的許多領域都遊刃有餘。(格倫・西奧多・西博格)

Melvin Calvin's marvellous technique for delivering a scientific lecture was unique. His mind must have roamed constantly, especially in planning

---

[41] 梅爾文・卡爾文,1961 年諾貝爾化學獎得主。

lectures. His remarkable memory enabled him to formulate a lecture or manuscript with no breaks in the sequence of his thoughts. His lectures usually began hesitatingly, as if he had little idea of how to begin or what to say. This completely disarmed his audiences, who would try to guess what he might have to say. Soon enough, however, his ideas would coalesce, to be delivered like an approaching freight train, reaching a crescendo of information at breakneck speed and leaving his rapt audience nearly overwhelmed. (Glenn Theodore Seaborg)

梅爾文・卡爾文發表科學演講的絕妙技巧是獨一無二的。他的頭腦似乎不斷地漫遊，尤其在規劃演講內容時。卓越的記憶力使他能夠思路連貫地構思演講稿或腹稿。他的演講開頭通常有些躊躇，似乎不清楚怎樣開始或說些什麼。這完全解除了聽眾的武裝，他們會試著猜測他將要說什麼。然而，很快速地，他的想法會凝聚起來，猶如一列駛近的貨物列車，以極快的速度發出漸強的訊息，使入迷的觀眾近乎應接不暇。(格倫・西奧多・西博格)

I like to feel that in honoring me you are honoring all the workers in the laboratory, field, and jungle who have contributed so much, often under conditions of hardship and danger, to our understanding of this disease. I would also like to feel that you are honoring the memory of those who gave their lives in gaining knowledge which was of inestimable value. They were truly martyrs of science, who died that others might live. (Max Theiler)

我希望感受到，你們在授予我榮耀時，是在向實驗室、田野和叢林裡的所有工作人員致敬。他們經常處於艱苦和危險的條件下，為我們了解這種疾病[42]貢獻良多。我也想感受到，你們是在紀念那些以生命換取無價知識的人，向他們致敬。他們是真正的科學殉道者，他們為了別人的生命而犧牲。（馬克斯·泰累爾）

I wish to express my warm thanks to the Swedish Academy for awarding me the Nobel Prize in Literature. This is so great an honour that one may be excused for asking oneself —— have I really deserved it? Speaking for myself, I dare not even pose the question! Having taken no part in making this decision, however, I can enjoy it with a free conscience. The responsibility rests with my esteemed colleagues and for this, too, I am truly thankful! (Pär Fabian Lagerkvist)

我謹對瑞典科學院授予我諾貝爾文學獎表示誠摯的感謝。這是如此非凡的榮譽，以至人們可以原諒我自問——我真的應得嗎？就我個人而言，我甚至不敢提出這個問題！然而，我不曾參與做出這一項決定，也就不妨坦然地接受。責任在於我尊敬的同事們，而為此，我也真心感謝！（佩爾·拉格奎斯特）

I have never ceased to do my utmost to be the faithful interpreter and devoted servant of the ideals of peace and justice upheld by out trade-union organizations, and at such a solemn moment it was natural for me to regard myself simply as their representative. (Léon Jouhaux)

我從未停止竭盡全力，成為工會以外各組織所信奉的和平與正義理想的忠實詮釋者和忠誠僕人。在這樣一個莊嚴的時刻，自然而然地，我直接將自己視為他們的代表。（萊昂·儒奧）

---

[42] 指黃熱病。

1951–1960 科學與人文的對話

1952 年

I am sure my fellow-scientists will agree with me if I say that whatever we were able to achieve in our later years had its origin in the experiences of our youth and in the hopes and wishes which were formed before and during our time as students. (Felix Bloch)

我相信,與我共事的科學家們會同意我的說法:無論我們在以後的歲月裡能獲得什麼成就,皆源自年輕時的經歷,以及作為學生之前和期間形成的希望和意願。(費利克斯·布洛赫)

It is inevitable that many ideas of the young mind will later have to give way to the hard realities of life. (Felix Bloch)

年輕人的許多想法,隨後不得不屈服於艱難的生活現實,這在所難免。(費利克斯·布洛赫)

I have not yet lost a feeling of wonder, and of delight, that this delicate motion should reside in all the things around us, revealing itself only to him who looks for it. I remember, in the winter of our first experiments, just seven years ago, looking on snow with new eyes. There the snow lay around my doorstep —— great heaps of protons quietly precessing in the earth's magnetic field. To see the world for a moment as something rich and strange is the private reward of many a discovery. (Edward Mills Purcell)

我始終沒有喪失一種驚奇感,喜悅之感,這種微妙的表現應該存在於我們周圍一切事物中,只向尋覓者顯露。我記得,就在七年前我們初次實驗的冬天,我們以新的視角看雪。白雪在我的門前階下鋪開——大

1952 年

量質子靜謐地進入地球磁場。一剎那間看見世界之豐富奇異，這是許多發現帶來的私人回報。（愛德華‧珀塞爾）

The Nobel Prize, so long regarded in our science as the highest reward a man's work can earn, must bring to its recipient a most solemn sense of his debt to his fellow scientists and those of the past. (Edward Mills Purcell)

在我們的科學事業中，諾貝爾獎長期被視為一個人的工作所能得到的最高榮譽，必然使受獎者深刻感受到對科學家同行和前輩負有的恩情。（愛德華‧珀塞爾）

If every conceivable precaution is taken at first, one is often too discouraged to proceed at all. (Archer John Porter Martin)

如果起初就採取一切想得到的預防措施，人們就往往過於氣餒而根本無法進行。（阿徹‧約翰‧波特‧馬丁）

Much can often be learned by the repetition under different conditions, even if the desired result is not obtained. (Archer John Porter Martin)

在不同條件下重複常常能夠學到很多，即便沒有獲得想要的結果也罷。（阿徹‧約翰‧波特‧馬丁）

When the effects with small molecules are better understood we shall be much better able to understand from the structure of the larger molecules what is their function in terms of such intermolecular forces. Then chemistry really will begin to merge with biology as closely as it has already merged with physics. Partition chromatography may well be remembered for this contribution long after it is quite obsolete as an analytical method. (Richard Laurence Millington Synge)

1951-1960 科學與人文的對話

在小分子的效用得到較好的理解時，我們應能更完善地從大分子的結構中，了解它們在這種分子間作用方面的功能。屆時，化學將真正開始與生物學緊密融合，如同它已與物理學融合那樣。儘管分配色譜法作為分析方法久已過時，但它的貢獻仍可能被人們長久銘記。（理察·勞倫斯·米林頓·辛格）

From the moment he is born to the moment he dies, man is subject to the activities of numerous microbes. Some attack his body, his crops, and his domesticated animals, as well as all forms of wild life; some destroy his clothing and his habitations, and assail virtually everything else that civilized man has come to depend upon in his daily life, —— these are the injurious microbes, comprising both saprophytes and parasites. On the other hand, many microbes, notably those inhabiting the earth under our feet and the rivers, lakes, and seas around us, make possible the continuation of higher forms of life by returning the essential nutrient elements to circulation and through innumerable other processes; many microbes are utilized in the preparation of beverages and foodstuffs, in the retting of textiles, and in a variety of essential industrial processes, —— these are the beneficial microbes. In recent years we have learned to domesticate new types of microbes, notably those that produce chemical substances, known as antibiotics, which have the capacity of destroying disease-producing microbes without injuring the host. (Selman Abraham Waksman)

從剛出生到死亡之時，人受到眾多微生物活動的影響。有的攻擊他的身體、他的農作物、他的家畜，以及各式各樣的野生動物；有的破壞他的衣物和住所，幾乎攻擊文明人類日常生活所依賴的其他一切——這

1952 年

些是有害微生物，包括腐生生物和寄生生物。另一方面，許多微生物，尤其是那些棲息於我們腳下土地和周圍江河湖海的微生物，經由將基本營養要素送回循環和透過無數其他過程，使更高的生命形式得以延續；許多微生物用於飲料和食品的製造，織物的浸泡，以及各種基本工業過程——這些是有益微生物。近年來，我們學會了馴化新類型的微生物，尤其是那些產生化學物質的，名為抗生素，它們有能力不傷害宿主而消滅致病微生物。（賽爾曼·瓦克斯曼）

It is usually not recognized that for every injurious or parasitic microbe there are dozens of beneficial ones. Without the latter, there would be no bread to eat nor wine to drink, no fertile soils and no potable waters, no clothing and no sanitation. One can visualize no form of higher life without the existence of the microbes. They are the universal scavengers. They keep in constant circulation the chemical elements which are so essential to the continuation of plant and animal life. (Selman Abraham Waksman)

人們通常不知道，每種有害或寄生的微生物都有數十種有益的微生物相對應。沒有後者，就不會有麵包可吃也無酒可喝，沒有肥沃的土壤也沒有飲用水，沒有衣服也沒有衛生設施。沒有微生物的存在，就無法設想更高的生命形式。它們是無處不在的清道夫。它們維持化學元素不斷循環，這些元素對植物和動物生命的延續十分重要。（賽爾曼·瓦克斯曼）

With the removal of the danger lurking in infectious diseases and epidemics, society can face a better future, can prepare for a time when other diseases not now subject to therapy will be brought under control. Let us hope that in contributing the antibiotics, the microbes will have done their part to make the world a better place to live in. (Selman Abraham Waksman)

隨著傳染病和流行病的潛在危險被消除，社會得以面臨更加美好的未來，得以迎接其他疑難疾病將受到控制的時代。讓我們期待，在提供抗生素的過程中，微生物將發揮作用，使世界成為更適合生存的地方。（賽爾曼・瓦克斯曼）

If you would tell me the heart of a man, tell me not what he reads, but what he rereads. (François Mauriac)

若想告訴我一個人的心，別告訴我他讀什麼，告訴我他重讀什麼。（法蘭索瓦・莫里亞克）

Old age is wonderful⋯A pity it ends so badly. (François Mauriac)

老年是精采的⋯⋯可惜結束得如此糟糕。[43]（法蘭索瓦・莫里亞克）

A great secret of success is to go through life as a man who never gets used up. (Albert Schweitzer)

成功的一大祕訣是作為永遠不會被消耗殆盡的人而度過一生。（亞伯特・史懷哲）

Success is not the key to happiness. Happiness is the key to success. If you love what you are doing, you will be successful. (Albert Schweitzer)

成功不是快樂的關鍵。快樂是成功的關鍵。如果你熱愛正在做的事情，你就會成功。（亞伯特・史懷哲）

An optimist is a person who sees a green light everywhere, while a pessimist sees only the red stoplight... the truly wise person is colorblind. (Albert Schweitzer)

樂天派是處處看到綠燈的人，而悲觀者只看到紅燈⋯⋯真正的智者是色盲。（亞伯特・史懷哲）

---

[43] 對照：夕陽無限好，只是近黃昏。（李商隱）

1952 年

The tragedy of life is what dies inside a man while he lives. (Albert Schweitzer)

生命的悲劇在於人活著的時候內心卻已死去。[44]（亞伯特・史懷哲）

Happiness is nothing more than good health and a bad memory. (Albert Schweitzer)

幸福不過是好身體和壞記性。（亞伯特・史懷哲）

Do something for somebody everyday for which you do not get paid. (Albert Schweitzer)

每天為別人無償地做點什麼。（亞伯特・史懷哲）

Life becomes harder for us when we live for others, but it also becomes richer and happier. (Albert Schweitzer)

當我們為他人而活時，人生變得更加艱苦，但它也變得更加豐富快樂。（亞伯特・史懷哲）

Sometimes our light goes out but is blown into flame by another human being. Each of us owes deepest thanks to those who have rekindled this light. (Albert Schweitzer)

有時我們的燈會熄滅，但被另一個人吹起了火苗。我們每個人都應深深感謝那些重新燃起這盞燈的人。（亞伯特・史懷哲）

---

[44]　對照：哀莫大於心死。（莊子）

1951–1960 科學與人文的對話

1953年

I am impressed by the great limitations of the human mind. How quick are we to learn, that is, to imitate what others have done or thought before. And how slow to understand, that is, to see the deeper connections. Slowest of all, however, are we in inventing new connections or even in applying old ideas in a new field. (Frits Zernike)

人類思想的巨大局限性令我印象深刻。我們仿效別人以前做過或想過的事情，可以學得很快；我們要理解、看出更深層次的連結，卻十分緩慢。而當我們要創造新的連結，甚至在新領域應用舊想法，更是緩慢之至。（弗里茨·澤爾尼克）

Macromolecular chemistry appears today to fit between low molecular organic chemistry and cytology. It is the connecting link between them, growing systematically out of low molecular chemistry but, with the incomparably larger wealth of its chemical scope, forming living matter. In addition, over and above the quantitative laws of pure chemistry, macromolecular chemistry makes use of a number of qualitative correlations: those of shape and of the associated configurational scope, up to the level of the "atomos" of living substance, on which the game of Life ensues. In the light of this new knowledge of macromolecular chemistry, the wonder of Life in its chemical aspect is revealed in the astounding abundance and masterly macromolecular architecture of living matter. (Hermann Staudinger)

現在看來，大分子化學處於低分子有機化學和細胞學之間。它是連接二者的環節，由低分子化學系統地發展起來，然而，由於其化學作用

1953 年

大到無與倫比的豐富,形成了生命物質。此外,在純化學的定量定律之外,大分子化學運用許多定性的相互關係:關於形狀和相關組態作用,直至生命物質的「原子」層面,生命的遊戲就是在此基礎上進行的。依據大分子化學的這種新知,揭示了生命奇蹟的化學層面,即生命物質的驚人豐富性和高超的大分子結構。(赫爾曼·施陶丁格)

The research I have been doing —— studying how foodstuffs yield energy in living cells —— does not lead to the kind of knowledge that can be expected to give immediate practical benefits to mankind. If I have chosen this field of study, it was because I believed in its importance in spite of its theoretical character. My reason for this belief was that all living things must be continuously fed with energy and I am convinced that an understanding of the process of energy production will eventually help us in solving some of the practical problems of medicine. (Hans Adolf Krebs)

我一直在做的研究 —— 探索食物如何在活細胞中產生能量 —— 並不能帶來一種可以指望給予人類直接實際益處的知識。如果我選擇了這個研究領域,那是由於我相信它重要,而不管它的理論特性。這個信念的理由在於,所有生物都必須不斷被賦予能量,我確信,對能量產生過程的理解,最終將幫助我們解決醫學上的一些實際問題。(漢斯·阿道夫·克雷布斯)

About 100 years ago Michael Faraday, when asked by Mr. Gladstone, then Chancellor of the Exchequer, about the use of his research into electrical phenomena, replied, so the story goes, with Franklin's counterquestion "What is the use of a newborn baby?", adding, "Well, sir, one day you might tax him". I do not think that I could, with any confidence, hold out hopes to a hard-pressed Minister of Finance that my work will one day help his exchequer —— in the way it has helped my own. Because there are no immediate practical benefits the immediate rewards of such work tend to be meagre. (Hans Adolf Krebs)

大約 100 年前，時任財政大臣格萊斯頓先生問麥可・法拉第，他的電現象研究有什麼用。據說，法拉第以富蘭克林的反問「新生兒有什麼用？」作答，還說「嗯，先生，有一天你可能徵他的稅。」我不認為自己能有任何信心，向一位捉襟見肘的財政部長提供希望，說我的工作將有一天幫助他的財源——就像它幫助過我自己一樣。由於沒有直接的實際益處，這類工作的直接回報往往是微薄的。（漢斯・阿道夫・克雷布斯）

To find the facts by hard and honest work, to evaluate them carefully and judiciously, and to make a final decision with courage and without prejudice —— if these principles guided our affairs throughout, the world would soon become a better place. (Hans Adolf Krebs)

以努力而誠實的工作發現事實，仔細而明智地評估它們，並勇敢而不帶偏見地做出最終決定——如果這些原則始終指導我們的事務，世界就會很快變得更好。（漢斯・阿道夫・克雷布斯）

The drive and urge to explore nature in all its facets is one of the most important functions of humanity. (Fritz Albert Lipmann)

全方位探索自然的強烈願望和迫切需求，是人類最重要的功能之一。（弗里茨・阿爾貝特・李普曼）

The decision to explore this particular reaction started me on a rather continuous journey into partly virgin territory to meet with some unexpected discoveries, but also to encounter quite a few nagging disappointments. (Fritz

1953 年

Albert Lipmann）

決定探索這一項特定反應之後，我開始了一段相當漫長的旅程，進入近乎處女地的區域而得到一些意外的發現，但也遭遇不少煩心的失望。（弗里茨‧阿爾貝特‧李普曼）

Altogether, in this area, a diversified picture is rapidly developing. There is good reason to hope that in the not too distant future, out of the fair confusion of the present, a clearer understanding will eventually evolve. A new level of complexity seems slowly to unravel and the gap between the biochemical and biological approach further narrows down. (Fritz Albert Lipmann)

總之，在這個領域，一幅多樣化的圖景正在迅速展現。有充分的理由期待，在不太遙遠的未來，從當前的一團混亂之中終將演化出更加清晰的理解。新程度上的複雜局面看來正逐漸瓦解，生物化學與生物學方法上的差異也進一步縮小。（弗里茨‧阿爾貝特‧李普曼）

To improve is to change; to be perfect is to change often. (Winston Leonard Spencer Churchill)

改善是改變，完美就是經常改變。（溫斯頓‧邱吉爾）

A pessimist sees the difficulty in every opportunity; an optimist sees the opportunity in every difficulty. (Winston Leonard Spencer Churchill)

悲觀主義者在每個機會中看到困難，樂觀主義者在每個困難中看到機會。（溫斯頓‧邱吉爾）

If you are going through hell, keep going. (Winston Leonard Spencer Churchill)

你如果正在走過地獄，就繼續走。（溫斯頓‧邱吉爾）

1951-1960 科學與人文的對話

To build may have to be the slow and laborious task of years. To destroy can be the thoughtless act of a single day. (Winston Leonard Spencer Churchill)

建設可能必須是多年緩慢而艱苦的任務。破壞可以是僅為一天的輕率行為。（溫斯頓‧邱吉爾）

We make a living by what we get, but we make a life by what we give. (Winston Leonard Spencer Churchill)

我們靠取得之物存活於世，但我們靠給予之物不枉此生。（溫斯頓‧邱吉爾）

We are happier in many ways when we are old than when we were young. (Winston Leonard Spencer Churchill)

年老時，我們在許多方面比年輕時更快樂。（溫斯頓‧邱吉爾）

When a thing is done, it's done. Don't look back. Look forward to your next objective. (George Catlett Marshall)

一事了結，即為了結。無須回顧。期待下一個目標。（喬治‧馬歇爾）

The one great element in continuing the success of an offensive is maintaining the momentum. (George Catlett Marshall)

持續成功進攻的一大要素是維持氣勢。（喬治‧馬歇爾）

What other people do shouldn't affect you —— we do things because of the kind of person we each want to be. (George Catlett Marshall)

別人做什麼不應影響你——我們行事是由於我們自己想成為什麼樣的人。（喬治‧馬歇爾）

1954 年

The human mind is conservative, and the scientist makes no exception from this rule. He will accept a new theory only if it stands the trial of many experimental tests. (Max Born)

人的思想是保守的，科學家也不例外。新理論只有經得起大量實驗測試的考驗，他才會接受。（馬克斯·玻恩）

When the work of a scientist is regarded by the Royal Swedish Academy of Science worth of the Nobel Prize, the highest honour open to a scholar, he will sense not only the deepest gratitude for this distinction but also a feeling of indebtedness to all those who have gone before and beside him. This feeling of all working together in the same direction is one of the most rewarding experiences of a scientist. (Max Born)

當一名科學家的工作被瑞典皇家科學院認定值得授予諾貝爾獎，為學者設立的最高榮譽，他會感到的，不僅是對這一項榮譽最深的謝意，還有對所有那些前輩和同儕的受惠之情。這種於相同方向共同努力的感覺，是科學家最可貴的體驗之一。（馬克斯·玻恩）

The work for which the Nobel Prize has been awarded to me is of a kind which has no immediate effect on human life and activity, but rather on human thinking. But indirectly it had a considerable influence not only in physics but in other fields of human endeavor. (Max Born)

我獲得諾貝爾獎的研究成果，對人類生活和活動沒有直接影響，而是作用於人類的思想。然而它不僅對於物理學、也對人類鑽研的其他領

域間接地具有可觀的影響。（馬克斯・玻恩）

I am now convinced that theoretical physics is actually philosophy. (Walther Bothe)

我現在確信，理論物理學實際上是哲學。（瓦爾特・博特）

The belief that there is only one truth, and that oneself is in possession of it, is the root of all evil in the world. (Walther Bothe)

相信自己擁有唯一的真理，是世界上一切邪惡的根源。（瓦爾特・博特）

If you want to have good ideas you must have many ideas. Most of them will be wrong and what you have to learn is which ones to throw away. (Linus Carl Pauling)

你如果想要有好的想法，就必須要有很多的想法。它們大多數都將是錯的，你需要學會的是把哪些拋棄。（萊納斯・鮑林）

You have to have a lot of ideas. First, if you want to make discoveries, it's a good thing to have good ideas. And second, you have to have a sort of sixth sense —— the result of judgment and experience —— which ideas are worth following up. I seem to have the first thing, a lot of ideas, and I also seem to have good judgment as to which are the bad ideas that I should just ignore, and the good ones, that I'd better follow up. (Linus Carl Pauling)

你必須有大量的想法。第一，如果你想有所發現，有好的想法是好事。第二，你必須有種第六感 —— 判斷力和經驗的結果 —— 哪些想法是值得跟進的。我似乎有大量的想法；我似乎也有良好的判斷力，關於哪些是壞的想法應該直接忽略，以及哪些是好的想法，最好跟進。（萊納斯・鮑林）

1954 年

I have always wanted to know as much as possible about the world. (Linus Carl Pauling)

我總是想盡可能多地了解世界。（萊納斯·鮑林）

Science cannot be stopped. Man will gather knowledge no matter what the consequences —— and we cannot predict what they will be. Science will go on —— whether we are pessimistic, or are optimistic, as I am I know that great, interesting, and valuable discoveries can be made and will be made. But I know also that still more interesting discoveries will be made that I have not the imagination to describe —— and I am awaiting them, full of curiosity and enthusiasm. (Linus Carl Pauling)

科學無法阻擋。人類將累積知識，不計後果 —— 而我們無法預知它們將是什麼。科學將繼續下去 —— 無論我們是悲觀的，還是樂觀的，我則確切知道，非凡的、有趣的、寶貴的發現可以被實現並將會實現。並且我也知道，還會有更有趣的發現，那是我的想像力所無法描述的 —— 而我滿懷好奇和熱情地等待它們。（萊納斯·鮑林）

We may, I believe, anticipate that the chemist of the future who is interested in the structure of proteins, nucleic acids, polysaccharides, and other complex substances with high molecular weight will come to rely upon a new structural chemistry, involving precise geometrical relationships among the atoms in the molecules and the rigorous application of the new structural principles, and that great progress will be made, through this technique, in the attack, by chemical methods, on the problems of biology and medicine. (Linus Carl Pauling)

我認為，我們不妨預期，對蛋白質、核酸、多醣和其他高分子量複雜物質的結構感興趣的未來化學家，將依靠一種新的結構化學，包括分子中原子之間精確的幾何關係和新的結構原理的嚴謹應用,透過這種技術,在以化學方法解決生物學和醫學難題時,將獲得巨大的進展。(萊納斯・鮑林)

I've been asked from time to time, "How does it happen that you have made so many discoveries? Are you smarter than other scientists?" And my answer has been that I am sure that I am not smarter than other scientists. I don't have any precise evaluation of my IQ, but to the extent that psychologists have said that my IQ is about 160, I recognize that there are one hundred thousand or more people in the United States that have IQS higher than that. So I have said that I think I think harder, think more than other people do, than other scientists. That is, for years, almost all of my thinking was about science and scientific problems that I was interested in. (Linus Carl Pauling)

我一直不時地問:「這是怎麼發生的?你做出了這麼多的發現,你比其他科學家聰明嗎?」而我的回答始終是,我確信自己並不比其他科學家聰明。我完全不清楚自己智商的確切評分,不過心理學家說過我的智商約為160,我知道在美國有10萬或更多人的智商更高。所以我說過,我認為,我思考得更努力,思考得比其他人、其他科學家更多。多年來,我幾乎所有的思考都是關於科學和我感興趣的科學問題。(萊納斯・鮑林)

When an old and distinguished person speaks to you, listen to him carefully and with respect —— but do not believe him. Never put your trust into anything but your own intellect. Your elder, no matter whether he has gray hair or has lost his hair, no matter whether he is a Nobel laureate —— may be wrong. The world progresses, year by year, century by century, as the members of the younger generation find out what was wrong among the things that

1954 年

their elders said. So you must always be skeptical —— always think for yourself. (Linus Carl Pauling)

年高德劭之人對你說話時，仔細聆聽，懷著敬意 —— 但不要相信。除了自己的智慧，一切勿信。年紀大於你的人，不管白髮還是脫髮，不管是否為諾貝爾獎得主 —— 都可能是錯的。年復一年，世紀復世紀，隨著年輕一代的成員發現長者言論中的錯誤，世界不斷進步。所以你必須總是持懷疑態度 —— 總是獨立思考。（萊納斯‧鮑林）

Satisfaction of one's curiosity is one of the greatest sources of happiness in life. (Linus Carl Pauling)

好奇心的滿足是人生最大的快樂泉源之一。（萊納斯‧鮑林）

I have been especially fortunate for about 50 years in having two memory banks available —— whenever I can't remember something I ask my wife, and thus I am able to draw on this auxiliary memory bank. Moreover, there is a second way in which I get ideas... I listen carefully to what my wife says, and in this way I often get a good idea. I recommend to... young people... that you make a permanent acquisition of an auxiliary memory bank that you can become familiar with and draw upon throughout your lives. (Linus Carl Pauling)

特別幸運的是，大約 50 年，我一直有兩個記憶庫可資使用 —— 每當想不起來什麼時，我就問妻子，於是得以啟用這個輔助記憶庫。此外，我還有第二條途逕獲得想法……我仔細傾聽妻子的話，從而常常得到好主意。我建議……年輕人……獲得永久的輔助記憶庫，可以畢生熟悉並運用之。（萊納斯‧鮑林）

I have something that I call my Golden Rule. It goes something like this: "Do unto others twenty-five percent better than you expect them to do unto you." (Linus Carl Pauling)

我有一個我稱為黃金法則的東西。它大致是這樣的:「對待別人比期望別人對待你的還要好幾分。」(萊納斯·鮑林)

We soon became friends, and thus I fell into the habit of going to the laboratory with him in the evening and watching him work. I became increasingly fascinated by the subject —— which manifestly gave him so much pleasure and about which he talked with such enthusiasm —— and so eventually decided to change the direction of my studies. (John Franklin Enders)

我們[45]很快就成了朋友,因而我養成了在晚上跟他去實驗室看他工作的習慣。我越來越著迷於這個課題——它顯然帶給他如此之大的快樂,他也如此熱情地談論它——於是最終決定改變我的研究方向。(約翰·富蘭克林·恩德斯)

A man of superlative energy. Literature, politics, history, and science —— all he discussed with spontaneity and without self-consciousness. Everything was illuminated by an apt allusion drawn from the most diverse sources, or by a witty tale. Voltaire seemed just around the corner, and Laurence Sterne upon the stair... Under such influences, the laboratory became much more than a place just to work and teach; it became a way of life. (John Franklin Enders)

一位擁有超高能量的人[46]。文學、政治、歷史和科學,他都自然隨性地討論。每件事的闡明都旁徵博引,來源極其多樣,或者以機智的故事說明。伏爾泰似乎就在轉角處,而勞倫斯·斯特恩[47]在樓梯上。……

---

[45] 哈佛大學細菌學與免疫學系的年輕教師休·沃德(Hugh Ward)和恩德斯。
[46] 指恩德斯在哈佛大學時的導師、微生物學家漢斯·津瑟(Hans Zinsser)。
[47] 勞倫斯·斯特恩,18世紀英國小說家,長於幽默。

1954年

在這樣的影響下，實驗室遠非僅為工作和教學的場地，它成了一種生活方式。（約翰·富蘭克林·恩德斯）

It has been a source of great satisfaction to us that our investigations on the poliomyelitis viruses have appeared to arouse a renewed and expanded interest in the adaption of the culture method to the analysis of many aspects of viral infections of both man and animals. Thus in Sweden as well as in many other countries new viruses are being revealed and new procedures for the study of those long recognized are being developed. These current observations emphasize the fact that broad fields for research still lie open. (Thomas Huckle Weller)

我們對脊髓灰質炎病毒的調查研究，似乎引起了人們對調整培養方法以分析人類和動物的病毒感染諸多方面的興趣，這使我們大為滿意。於是，在瑞典以及其他許多國家，新的病毒正在被發現，並且正在開發研究那些長期認識的病毒的新流程。當前這些觀察結果強調了一個事實：仍有廣泛的研究領域可供探索。（托馬斯·哈克爾·韋勒）

The significance of this award, however, we believe extends further than the recognition of our own observations on the propagation of the poliomyelitis viruses in tissue culture. Indirectly, it honors the many contributions of our predecessors which made our own investigations possible. For example, the discovery of the antibiotics previously recognized here, renders the tissue culture technique applicable in ways that were hitherto inconceivable. (Thomas Huckle Weller)

然而，我們認為，這個獎項的意義遠遠超過對於我們所做觀察——對於脊髓灰質炎病毒在組織培養中的傳播——的認可。間接地，它向我們前輩的許多貢獻致敬，他們的貢獻使我們自己的調查研究成為可能。

> 1951–1960 科學與人文的對話

例如，先前曾在此表彰的抗生素的發現，使得組織培養技術能夠以至今難以想像的方式應用。（托馬斯・哈克爾・韋勒）

The results of our research are not alone the product of our triple thought and effort. As nearly always in the undertaking of science many others who have worked with us have contributed of their minds and labor. (Frederick Chapman Robbins)

我們的研究成果，不單是我們三人的思想和努力的產物。在科學事業中幾乎一向如此，另有許多與我們共事的人，貢獻了自己的思想和勞動。（弗雷德里克・查普曼・羅賓斯）

All my life I've looked at words as though I were seeing them for the first time. (Ernest Miller Hemingway)

整整一生，我一直看著文字，彷彿第一次看到它們。（厄尼斯特・海明威）

A man can be destroyed but not defeated. (Ernest Hemingway)

人可以被摧毀，但無法被擊敗。（厄尼斯特・海明威）

Today is only one day in all the days that will ever be but what will happen in all the other days that ever come can depend on what you do today. (Ernest Miller Hemingwayy)

今天不過是所有總要存在的日子之一，但在將來所有其他日子裡會發生什麼，取決於你今天的行事。（厄尼斯特・海明威）

The world is a fine place and worth the fighting for and I hate very much to leave it. (Ernest Miller Hemingwayy)

世界是個美好的地方，值得為之奮鬥，我非常不想離開它。（厄尼斯特・海明威）

Courage is grace under pressure. (Ernest Hemingway)

勇敢即壓力之下的優雅。（厄尼斯特・海明威）

1955 年

I liked quantum mechanics very much. The subject was hard to understand but easy to apply to a large number of interesting problems. (Willis Eugene Lamb)

我非常喜歡量子力學。這個學科很難懂，但很容易應用於大量有趣的問題。（威利斯・蘭姆）

In fact, there really is not a new law of nature. It was all in the theory to begin with but nobody worked it out. (Willis Eugene Lamb)

事實上，真的不存在新的自然法則。一切都在理論上起步，只是無人完成。（威利斯・蘭姆）

Science is the greatest creative impulse of our time. It dominates the intellectual scene and forms our lives, not only in the material things which it has given us, but also in that it guides our spirit. (Polykarp Kusch)

科學是我們時代最偉大的創造動力。它主導著知識領域，並塑造我們的生活，不僅提供我們物質，同時引導我們的精神。（波利卡普・庫施）

Science shows us truth and beauty and fills each day with a fresh wonder of the exquisite order which governs our world. (Polykarp Kusch)

1951-1960 科學與人文的對話

科學向我們展示真與美，每一天都充滿了主宰世界的精細秩序的新奇蹟。（波利卡普‧庫施）

The knowledge and understanding of the world which science gives us and the magnificent opportunity which it extends to us to control and use the world for the extension of our pleasure in it has never been greater than it now is. (Polykarp Kusch)

科學帶給我們對世界的知識和理解，以及提供我們把握和利用世界以增加快樂的絕佳機會，從未比現在更宏大。（波利卡普‧庫施）

We live, I think, in the century of science and, perhaps, even in the century of physics. (Polykarp Kusch)

我認為，我們生活在科學的世紀，也許，甚至在物理學的世紀。（波利卡普‧庫施）

I have had the privilege and the thrill of following those researches that I've always wanted to do. I've always had the privilege of working on what I've wanted to work on. I have been accompanied in the various stages of these exploratory researches by a group of fine and loyal associates. I've also been fortunate throughout the years in the generous research support I've received from various sources. (Vincent du Vigneaud)

我始終很榮幸並驚喜於能夠持續參與自己想做的研究。我一直有幸從事想做的工作。在這些探索性研究的不同階段，我都有一群優秀而忠誠的同事為伴。多年來，我還幸運地得到來自各方面慷慨的研究支持。（文森特‧迪維尼奧）

Peace for mankind does not mean rest, but rather a feeling appearing to anyone in the evening after a day's well performed work. (Axel Hugo Theodor Theorell)

和平對於人們並不意味著休息,而是當任何人結束了一天的認真工作之後,傍晚時分所感受到的一種感覺。(胡戈·特奧雷爾)

For man is essentially alone, and one should pity him and love him and grieve with him. (Halldór Kiljan Laxness)

由於人本質上是孤獨的,人們應該同情他,愛他,和他一起悲傷。(赫爾多爾·拉克斯內斯)

1956 年

It has today occurred to me that an amplifier using semiconductors rather than vacuum is in principle possible. (William Bradford Shockley)

我在今天才想到,運用半導體而非真空的放大器,原則上是可能的。[48](威廉·肖克利)

Science is a field which grows continuously with ever expanding frontiers. Further, it is truly international in scope. Any particular advance has been preceded by the contributions of those from many lands who have set firm foundations for further developments. The Nobel awards should be regarded as giving recognition to this general scientific progress as well as to the individuals involved. Further, science is a collaborative effort. The combined

---

[48] 實驗筆記,1939 年 12 月 29 日。

results of several people working together is often much more effective than could be that of an individual scientist working alone. (John Bardeen)

科學是個持續成長的領域,邊界不斷擴展。此外,其範圍確實是國際的。任何特定的進展都離不開來自許多國家的人們先前的貢獻,他們為進一步發展打下了堅實的基礎。諾貝爾獎應當視為對這種普遍的科學進展以及相關個人的讚譽。此外,科學是合作的事業。與獨自工作的單一科學家相比,若干人一起工作的綜合結果往往有效得多。(約翰·巴丁)

You can't measure intelligence by IQ or any other single number. There are many different kinds of intelligence. (John Bardeen)

你不能以智商或其他任何單一的數字衡量智力。智力有許多不同種類。(約翰·巴丁)

I would like to start by emphasizing the importance of surfaces. It is at a surface where many of our most interesting and useful phenomena occur. We live for example on the surface of a planet. It is at a surface where the catalysis of chemical reactions occur. It is essentially at a surface of a plant that sunlight is converted to a sugar. In electronics, most if not all active circuit elements involve non-equilibrium phenomena occurring at surfaces. Much of biology is concerned with reactions at a surface. (Walter Houser Brattain)

首先我想強調表面的重要性。許多最有趣和有用的現象就出現在表面上。例如我們生活在一個星球的表面。化學反應的催化作用就發生於表面,陽光本質上是在植物的表面轉化為糖。在電子學中,幾乎所有的主動電路元件都涉及發生於表面的非平衡現象。生物學與大量的表面反應有關。(華特·布拉頓)

1956 年

Chemistry: that most excellent child of intellect and art. (Cyril Norman Hinshelwood)

化學：智力和藝術最出色的產物。（西里爾・欣謝爾伍德）

Nobody, I suppose, could devote many years to the study of chemical kinetics without being deeply conscious of the fascination of time and change: this is something that goes outside science into poetry; but science, subject to the rigid necessity of always seeking closer approximations to the truth, itself contains many poetical elements. (Cyril Norman Hinshelwood)

我想，沒有人能多年致力於化學動力學研究而不深刻意識到時間和變化的魅力：這是一種超乎科學而接近詩歌的東西；然而科學總是尋求更接近真理的嚴格必然性，本身就包含了許多詩意的元素。（西里爾・欣謝爾伍德）

Naturally, there are considerable obstacles in the way. The chemical process is the basic phenomenon which makes chemistry different from physics and makes the former a more complicated science. The development of the theory of a chemical process is also considerably more difficult than the development of the theory of chemical structure. (Nikolay Nikolaevich Semenov)

自然地，重重障礙不絕於途。化學過程是使化學有別於物理學的基本現象，使化學成為更加複雜的學科。化學過程理論的發展也比化學結構理論的發展困難得多。（尼古拉・謝苗諾夫）

Now, what of the future? Perhaps the only incontestable prophecy that can be made is that advances in methodology and advances in understanding will go hand in hand. (André Frédéric Cournand)

那麼，未來又將如何？也許，唯一無疑的預言是，方法論的進步和理解的進步將齊頭並進。（安德烈‧弗雷德里克‧考南德）

As progress is made, more results will pour in. Let us, then, beware of the danger of seeking security for our concepts in the accumulation of facts. As the poet has said: "Knowledge is proud that it has learned so much, Wisdom is humble that it knows no more." (André Frédéric Cournand)

隨著獲得的進展，更多的成果會源源而來。因而，讓我們謹防在事實的累積中為我們的觀念尋求安全感的危險。正如詩人[49]所說：「知識得意於所學眾多，智慧謙遜在所知有限。」（安德烈‧弗雷德里克‧考南德）

One may compare the art of healing with a work of art, which from different standpoints and under different lighting reveals ever new and surprising beauty. (Werner Forssmann)

我們可以將醫術與藝術品相比。位置和光線的變化展現出嶄新的、驚人的美。（沃納‧福斯曼）

I feel like a village parson who has just learned that he has been made bishop. (Werner Forssmann)

我感覺就像一個剛聽說自己被任命為主教的鄉村牧師。[50]（沃納‧福斯曼）

Our findings have been for the most part preliminary, revealing new problems more often than solving old ones. Of great value has been the interest which has been aroused and the excellent new work that has been stimulated in many laboratories and clinics in many countries. (Dickinson W. Richards)

---

[49] 指英國詩人威廉‧古柏（William Cowper）。
[50] 在得知榮獲 1956 年諾貝爾生理學或醫學獎時說。

1956 年

　　我們的發現大部分是初步的，揭示新問題的次數多於解決舊問題。其重要價值在於引起了人們的興趣，在許多國家的許多實驗室和診所中激發了許多出色的新工作。（迪金森‧伍德拉夫‧理查茲）

One must speak in such a way that although someone else, or many others, or an infinite number of people have said it before, it seems as though you said it first. (Juan Ramón Jiménez)

作家必須這樣表達，即儘管其他人，或別的許多人，或無數的人在此之前說過，但聽起來就像是你先說的。（胡安‧拉蒙‧希梅內斯）

No deep truth has ever been shouted. (Juan Ramón Jiménez)

深刻的真理從來不曾喊出來。（胡安‧拉蒙‧希梅內斯）

I do not cut my life up into days but my days into lives, each day, each hour, an entire life. (Juan Ramón Jiménez)

我不是把自己的生命分成幾天，而是把我的日子分成一段段的生命，每一天，每一小時，整個一生。（胡安‧拉蒙‧希梅內斯）

To live is nothing more than to come here to die, to be what we were before being born, but with apprenticeship, experience, knowledge of cause, and perhaps with will. (Juan Ramón Jiménez)

活著不過是來到現世等待死亡，回到出生之前的狀態，不過當然伴隨有見習、體驗、知識，也許還有意志。（胡安‧拉蒙‧希梅內斯）

| 1951-1960 科學與人文的對話

1957 年

The institution of the awarding of Nobel prizes started in the year 1901. In that same year another momentous event took place of great historical importance. It was, incidentally, to have a decisive influence on the course of my personal life and was to be instrumental in relation to my present participation in the Nobel festival of 1957. With your kind indulgence I shall take a few minutes to go a little bit into this matter.

In the latter half of the last century the impact of the expanding influence of Western culture and economic system brought about in China a severe conflict. The question was heatedly debated of how much Western culture should be brought into China. However, before a resolution was reached reasons gave way to emotions, and there arose in the eighteen nineties groups of people called I Ho Tuan in Chinese, or Boxers in English who claimed to be able to withstand in bare flesh attack of modern weapons. Their stupid and ignorant action against the Westerners in China brought in 1900 the armies of many European countries and of the U.S. into Peking. The incident is called the Boxer War and was characterized on both sides by barbarous killings and shameful lootings. In the final analysis, the incident is seen as originating from an emotional expression of the frustration and anger of the proud people of China who had been subject to ever increasing oppression from without and decadent corruption from within. It is also seen in history as settling, once and for all, the debate as to how much Western culture should be introduced into China.

The war ended in 1901 when a treaty was signed. Among other things the treaty stipulated that China was to pay the powers the sum of approximately 500 million ounces of silver, a staggering amount in those days. About ten years later, in a typically American gesture, the U.S. decided to return to China her share of the sum. The money was used to set up a Fund which financed a University, the Tsinghua University, and a fellowship program for students to study in the U.S. I was a direct beneficiary of both of these two projects. I grew up in the secluded and academically inclined atmosphere of the campus of this University where my father was a professor and enjoyed a tranquil childhood that was unfortunately denied most of the Chinese of my generation. I was later to receive an excellent first two years' graduate education in the same University and then again was able to pursue my studies in the U.S. on a fellowship from the aforementioned fund.

As I stand here today and tell you about these, I am heavy with an awareness of the fact that I am in more than one sense a product of both the Chinese and Western cultures, in harmony and in conflict. I should like to say that I am as proud of my Chinese heritage and background as I am devoted to modern science, a part of human civilization of Western origin, to which I have dedicated and I shall continue to dedicate my work. (Chen Ning Yang)

諾貝爾獎是 1901 年設立的。就在同年發生了另一件具有巨大歷史意義的重要事件。這個事件後來對我個人的人生道路附帶產生了決定性的影響，並對於我現在參加 1957 年諾貝爾盛會發揮了重要的作用。承蒙諸位惠允，我將花幾分鐘講一下這個事件。

上世紀後半葉，在西方日益擴大的文化和經濟體制影響的衝擊下，中國面臨一場激烈的論戰。爭論的焦點在於中國到底應該吸收多少西方文明。然而,爭論尚未得出結論,感情便代替了理智,在西元 1890 年代,義和團興起,英文叫做 Boxers,他們聲稱能以血肉之軀抵擋住現代武器的攻擊。他們採取了不理智和盲目的舉動反對在中國的西方人,並成為 1900 年歐洲多國和美國軍隊入侵北京的導火線。這就是義和團戰爭,一場野蠻殺戮和無恥掠奪的戰爭。歸根結柢,這個事件是由於在遭受到外部日益加深的壓迫和內部日趨衰落腐敗的情況下,自尊的中國人民無奈而憤怒情感的爆發所引起的。從歷史上來看,這一個事件也一勞永逸地平息了關於中國應該吸收多少西方文明的爭論。

那場戰爭於 1901 年結束,當時簽訂了一個條約。條約中有一款規定中國要向列強賠償共約 5 億盎司的白銀,這在當時是一筆驚人的數目。大約 10 年以後,作為典型的美國式的友善表示,美國決定把自己的那一份退還給中國,用這筆錢設立一個基金,由基金撥款籌建一所大學,就是清華大學,並且為去美國深造的學生提供獎學金。我是這兩項計畫的直接受益者。我父親擔任清華大學教授,我就生長在這個幽僻的、學術空氣濃厚的清華校園之中,愉快地度過了我寧靜的童年。這是絕大多數我這一代中國人不幸所不能享有的。後來在這同一所大學裡,我受到兩年極好的研究生教育,而後又得到上述基金提供的獎學金,去美國繼續深造。

今天,當我站在這裡和大家談這些事情的時候,我深深地意識到,廣義來說,我是既調和又牴觸的中、西方文化的產物。我願意說,我為自己的中國血統和背景而感到驕傲,同樣地,我為能致力於作為人類文明一部分的、源自於西方的現代科學而感到自豪。我已獻身於現代科學,並將竭誠工作,為之繼續奮鬥。(楊振寧)

1957 年

The scientific equations we seek are the poetry of nature. (Chen Ning Yang)

我們尋求的方程式其實就是自然的詩篇。（楊振寧）

If you can reduce many, many complicated phenomena to a few equations that's great beauty. What is poetry? Poetry is a condensation of thought. You write, in a few lines, very complicated thoughts. And when you do this well it becomes very beautiful poetry. It becomes powerful poetry. It becomes concentrated poetry and that is what we are after. And this is not a dream. It is a fact. Because we have already achieved some of these. By "we," I mean collectively, physicists, starting from Newton, Maxwell, Einstein and so and so forth. And along the way we continue to find that this is an achievable dream so that's why we are after this. (Chen Ning Yang)

如果能把許多許多複雜的現象簡化成幾個方程式，那就是非凡的美。詩是什麼？詩是思想的濃縮。以幾行字寫下非常複雜的思想。寫得好，它就成了非常美麗的詩。它成了強而有力的詩。它成了濃縮的詩。這就是我們所追求的。這不是夢。這是事實。因為我們已經實現了其中的一些。我說的「我們」，是統稱物理學家，從牛頓、馬克士威、愛因斯坦等人算起。在這個過程中，我們不斷發現這是可以實現的夢想，因此我們追求它。（楊振寧）

Nature seems to take advantage of the simple mathematical representations of the symmetry laws. When one pauses to consider the elegance and the beautiful perfection of the mathematical reasoning involved and contrast it with the complex and far-reaching physical consequences, a deep sense of respect for the power of the symmetry laws never fails to develop. (Chen Ning Yang)

1951-1960 科學與人文的對話

自然界似乎利用了對稱性定律的簡單數學表示。每當我們停下來思考其中涉及的數學推理的優雅和完美，並且將它與複雜而深遠的物理結果相比較時，不禁油然而生一種深深的對於對稱性定律的崇敬之感。（楊振寧）

I suggest that Chinese young students pay more attention to the development of their own interests. Meanwhile, if you ask me to give suggestions to American students, I would recommend that they pay less attention to some of their so-called interests and consider more the major developmental trends of society and science. Of course, there is also a suggestion for Chinese parents and teachers： please encourage and foster the interests of the young. (Chen Ning Yang)

我建議中國的年輕學生多關注自己興趣的發展。同時，如果你要我給予美國學生建議，我會建議少關注一些他們所謂的興趣，多考慮社會和科學的主要發展趨勢。當然，也有對於中國家長和教師的建議：請鼓勵和培養年輕人的興趣。（楊振寧）

Even for a graduate student it is important to develop one's own taste: what ideas, what types of questions, what types of approach to concentrate on, etc. Taste formation is influenced by many factors: native talent, family environment, early teachers, one's own temperament and luck. (Chen Ning Yang)

即便對於研究生，培養自己的品味也是重要的：哪些想法、哪些類型的問題、專注於哪些類型的方法等等。品味的形成受到許多因素的影響：天賦、家庭環境、早期教師、自身氣質和運氣等。（楊振寧）

I oftentimes thought that I was particularly lucky because I got the best of undergraduate education in China, and the best of graduate education at

Chicago. A graduate student who is still learning courses is not really taking a maximum advantage of a research university's offerings. He should already be finished with course-taking, as he would then be able to shape his own taste about what is a good subject for research work in the graduate school. So I was really extremely lucky. (Chen Ning Yang)

我常常想到,自己特別幸運,因為我在中國接受了最好的大學教育,又在芝加哥接受了最好的研究所教育。還在學習課程的研究生並沒有真正獲取研究型大學所提供的最大優勢。他應該已經修完了課程,這時才能形成自己的品味,以確定研究所的研究工作主題。所以我真的極其幸運。(楊振寧)

One of the most important choices any researcher makes is picking a significant topic to study. If you choose the right problem, you get important results that transform our perception of the underlying structure of the universe. If you don't choose the right problem, you may work very hard but only get an interesting result. (Chen Ning Yang)

任何研究人員做出的最重要的選擇之一,是選擇一個意義重大的課題做研究。如果選對了問題,你就得到重要的結果,從而改變我們對宇宙基礎結構的認知。如果沒選對問題,你就可能工作得非常艱苦,但只得到有趣的結果。(楊振寧)

There are many many smart people at the frontiers, and yet their performances eventually are quite different. One of the main differences is because there are people who happen to be working on the right field at the right time, and to know what is the right field at the right time and get at it early, you have to be in places where there is information going through, there is appreciation of the information. (Chen Ning Yang)

在科學前端領域有許許多多聰明的人,然而他們的表現最終截然不同。其主要差異之一在於有些人恰好於正確的時間在正確的領域工作,且知道何為正確時間的正確領域並及早著手,你必須處於資訊流通且能理解資訊的位置。(楊振寧)

We all have some sixth sense sometimes that something's right, and this is very important for any creative work in any field. I'm sure you would agree with this general description. But in physics and mathematics and, I think, in all the sciences, you have to substantiate this vague concept, and that requires the habit of going back and trying to examine all things and put things in order. I use the word compactify because in your rush to try to see something in the fog, you are likely to leave a lot of holes in your knowledge, and by re-examining them, you fill the holes. This constant practice of going back and forth, doing both, is a most essential thing. (Chen Ning Yang)

有時我們都有某種第六感,覺得某事是正確的,這對於任何領域的創造性工作都是非常重要的。我確信你會同意這種普遍說法。然而在物理學和數學,以至於我認為在所有的科學之中,你必須證實這個模糊的概念,這就需要養成回溯並細查、釐清所有事物的習慣。我使用「壓實」一詞,因為當你急於透過迷霧看出什麼時,很可能在所知中留下很多漏洞,而藉助複查,就填補了漏洞。這種反覆檢查的持續做法,回顧與探索並舉,是十分重要的。(楊振寧)

You go to a seminar and most of the time you don't quite understand what's going on. I told them you don't have to be afraid. I go there, I also don't understand quite what's going on, but that's not necessarily bad because you go there a second time you find that you learn more. I call this learning by osmosis. Learning by osmosis is a process which is frowned upon in China. The reason that the Chinese graduate students are less daring is because they don't want to get mixed up with something which they only half know. But in frontiers work it's always —— or research work —— it's always half knowing, half not knowing. (Chen Ning Yang)

你參加研討會，大多數時候都不太理解研討內容。我告訴人們無須生畏。我參加時，也不太理解研討內容，但這未必是壞事，因為再參加時就會發現自己學到的更多了。我把這種學習稱為滲透。在中國，滲透式學習是受到質疑的過程。中國的研究生之所以不那麼大膽，是因為他們不願涉足自己一知半解的領域。但在前端領域工作 —— 或者研究工作 —— 中，總是一半知道，一半不知。（楊振寧）

It shows me as a youngster who would periodically make up a table of what I should do every day, and then after two months blame myself for not having been able to stick to the schedules. This is probably not just my own experience. Probably many people do this. I come to the conclusion, thinking about this and reviewing my own life, that it's not useless, because it urges you on, at least for a few months, to do some regular things. Provided you do not let the guilty feeling overwhelm you, it's, not bad. The net result is positive. (Chen Ning Yang)

舊日記展示了年輕時的我，會定期為自己每天的任務做個表格，再於兩個月後自責未能遵守日程。這很可能不止是我個人的經歷。很可能許多人都這麼做。我思索這件事並回顧自己的生活，得出了結論：這種做法並非無用，因為它敦促你，至少幾個月，做些按部就班的事。如果

不讓罪惡感壓倒自己，那麼就不算壞事。最終結果是正面的。（楊振寧）

In 1956, all the leading researchers in our field were trying to solve the "θ-τ puzzle". At that time we felt like we were in a pitch-black room, and we knew there was a door somewhere, but we didn't know which direction to go. In a dark room, you don't know if you should go forward, backward, to the left or right, and that's the most frustrating thing, but again, I wouldn't say that was a painful experience. Sometimes, after thinking for a whole day, maybe I would decide to try right, and so I would fumble in that direction, but usually without any success, so I would think, maybe I should try left instead. Every researcher goes through this kind of experience. (Chen Ning Yang)

1956 年，我們[51]所在領域的首要研究者都在力圖解決「θ-τ 之謎」。那時候，我們覺得自己彷彿身在一個漆黑的房間裡，我們知道某處有扇門，但不知往哪個方向走。在黑暗的房間裡，不知道自己應該向前、向後、向左還是向右，這是最受挫的事情。不過再宣告一下，我不會說那是痛苦的經歷。有時候，經過一整天思考，也許我會決定嘗試向右，於是我會朝那個方向摸索，但是通常毫無成效，於是我會想，也許我應該轉而嘗試向左。每一個研究者都會體驗到這種經歷。（楊振寧）

Doing the kind of research that we do, "tired" is a word that never crosses our minds, because the subjects that interest us often have something fascinating about them. In other words, we are driven by our interests, so even if we don't always succeed, we never get tired. For some athletes, they need to consciously use their willpower to persevere through the training, but it's not the case with scientific research. Those who are engaged in scientific research

---

[51] 楊振寧和李政道。

often are greatly interested in what they do, and the interest itself is an enormous pull, so you don't get tired or confused. Of course, sometimes when you have an idea, you rack your brains, do some research and calculations, but end up not getting anywhere, you could feel a little frustrated, but I wouldn't say that's a painful process. (Chen Ning Yang)

在我們進行這樣的研究時,「累」這個字從來不曾出現在我們腦海中,因為使我們感興趣的課題經常具有某種迷人的性質。換言之,我們由自己的興趣驅動,所以即便並非總是成功,我們也完全不累。對於一些運動員來說,他們需要有意識地運用意志力來堅持訓練,科學研究卻不是這樣。從事科學研究的人經常對自己所做的事情有極大的興趣,而這個興趣本身就是巨大的吸引力,所以你不覺得累或困惑。當然,有時候當你有了一個想法,你絞盡腦汁做一些研究和計算,最終卻毫無進展,你可能會感到幾分受挫,但我不會說這是痛苦的過程。（楊振寧）

Revolutions in basic science always originate from a few individuals' efforts, never from large projects. Electromagnetism, Darwin's theory, fission, the semiconductor, the double helix, penicillin, all of these great revolutions in basic sciences have come from research by a few individuals with a small budget, never from big projects. (Chen Ning Yang)

基礎科學的變革總是源於少量人的努力,而非大項目。電磁學、達爾文理論、核裂變、半導體、雙螺旋、青黴素,所有這些基礎科學上的重大變革,都出自預算很小的幾個人,而非大項目。（楊振寧）

The common base of art and science is the creativity of the human race. What they pursue is the universality of the truth.

Arts such as poetry, painting and music, etc. arouse the existing emotions of the innermost consciousness of subconsciousness in a creative way. For instance, Li Bai (701-762 AD) wrote Ask the moon holding a cup of wine, in which he said：

How many times the moon comes in the sky?

I hope to ask her while I stop drinking.

...

People cannot see the moon of the ancient times,

But today's moon has lit the people of the ancient times.

The people of the ancient times and today have passed away like the river,

But the moon they have seen is always the same.

And 300 years later after Li, Su Shi (1037-1101) wrote Shuidiao Getou, in which he said：

When the moon will rise,

I ask the sky when I'm drinking,

...

Joys and sorrows, separations and reunions have always existed in human life,

And the moon is always shadowed, clear, full or half,

All this cannot be escaped by people from ancient times to now.

Wish brother good health,

Can enjoy the moonlight with me afar from thousand li.

> 1957 年

When reciting these poems, both the similarity and difference between the two poems excite readers. Though the times when Li Bai and Su Shi lived are completely different from today's society, the poems created hundreds of years ago, even thousands of years ago, can still inspire strong emotional resonance in the hearts of today's people. (Tsung-Dao Lee)

藝術和科學的共同基礎是人類的創造力，它們追求的目標都是真理的普遍性。

藝術，例如詩歌、繪畫、音樂等等，用創新的手法喚起每個人的意識或潛意識中深藏著的、已經存在的情感。如李白（701-762）在〈把酒問月〉中寫道：

青天有月來幾時？

我今停杯一問之。

……

今人不見古時月，

今月曾經照古人。

古人今人若流水，

共看明月皆如此。

而 300 年後，蘇軾（1037-1101）的〈水調歌頭〉寫道：

明月幾時有？

把酒問青天。

……

人有悲歡離合，

月有陰晴圓缺，

此事古難全。

但願人長久，

千里共嬋娟。

在吟誦這些詩的時候，它們的相似之點和不同之處同樣感動著讀者。儘管李白、蘇軾生活的時代和今天的社會已經完全不同了，但這些幾百年乃至一千年前的詩在今天人們的心中仍然能夠引發強烈的感情共鳴。（李政道）

Sciences such as astronomy, physics, chemistry, biology, etc., are the new correct abstraction of the phenomena of nature, and this abstraction is usually called natural laws. The more simply natural law is elaborated, the more widely it is applied, and the more profound science is. Though natural phenomenon exists independent of scientists, the abstraction and summary of it are man-made and are part of the crystallization of mankind's wisdom. This is the same as artistic creativity. (Tsung-Dao Lee)

科學，例如天文學、物理學、化學、生物學等等，對自然界的現象進行新的準確的抽象，這種抽象通常被稱為自然定律。定律的闡述越簡單、應用越廣泛，科學就越深刻。儘管自然現象不依賴於科學家而存在，但對自然現象的抽象和總結是一種人為的，並屬於人類智慧的結晶，這和藝術家的創造是一樣的。（李政道）

The universality sought by scientists is different from that of natural phenomena, it is man's abstraction and summary of nature and applicable to all natural phenomena. Its truthfulness is rooted in the outside world beyond scientists, with scientists and all mankind only an integrated part of it. The universality of truth sought by artist is also external, and located in all human beings without time and space limitations. Though the universality of science and that of art is not completely the same, there is a strong relation between them. (Tsung-Dao Lee)

科學家追求的普遍性不同於自然現象的普遍性，是人類對自然現象的抽象和總結，適用於所有的自然現象。它的真理性植根於科學家以外的外部世界，科學家和整個人類只是這個外部世界的一個組成部分。藝術家追求的普遍真理性也是外在的，植根於整個人類，沒有時間和空間的界限。儘管科學的普遍性和藝術的普遍性並不完全相同，但它們之間有著很強的關聯。（李政道）

The relationship of science and art is closely linked with the duality of wisdom and emotion. Both the aesthetic appreciation of great arts and the understanding of great scientific concepts demand wisdom. And the later sublimation of feelings can not be separated from emotion. Without the factor of emotion and its promotion, can our wisdom open new roads? Can emotion without wisdom achieve perfect results? Thus, science and art can not be cut apart, and both of them seek the universality of truth. The universality must be rooted in nature, and the exploration of nature is the greatest expression of mankind's creativity. In fact, science and art are like two sides of a coin. They are originated in the loftiest part of human creativity, and both of them seek depth, universality, eternity, and significance. (Tsung-Dao Lee)

科學和藝術的關係與智慧和情感的二元性密切相關，對藝術的美學鑑賞和對科學觀念的理解都需要智慧，隨後的感受昇華與情感又是分不開的。沒有情感的因素和促進，我們的智慧能夠開創新的道路嗎？而沒有智慧的情感能夠達到完美的意境嗎?所以,科學和藝術是不可分的,兩者都在尋求真理的普遍性。普遍性一定植根於自然,而對自然的探索則是人類創造性的最崇高的表現。事實上科學和藝術如一個硬幣的兩面,都源於人類活動最高尚的部分,都追求著深刻性、普遍性、永恆和富有意義。(李政道)

In art, be it poetry, painting, music… one creates something new to evoke a deep emotion that has been in existence in everyone's consciousness or subconscious. The more precious the feeling, the more intense the evocation, the more universal the response, the better is the art. (Tsung-Dao Lee)

藝術,例如詩歌、繪畫、音樂等等,用創新的手法喚起每個人的意識或潛意識中深藏著、已經存在的情感。情感越珍貴,回響越普遍,跨越時空、社會的範圍越廣泛,藝術就越優秀。(李政道)

The progress of science has always been the result of a close interplay between our concepts of the universe and our observations on nature. The former can only evolve out of the latter and yet the latter is also conditioned greatly by the former. Thus in our exploration of nature, the interplay between our concepts and our observations may sometimes lead to totally unexpected aspects among already familiar phenomena. (Tsung-Dao Lee)

科學的進步,一向都是我們的宇宙觀念和對自然的觀察二者密切影響的結果。前者只能從後者演化出來,而後者也受到前者極大的制約。因此,在對自然的探索中,我們的觀念和觀察之間的相互作用,有時可能在已經熟悉的現象中引向完全意外的形態。(李政道)

A scientific accomplishment is always the cumulative result of many people working in the same field or relative fields. (Tsung-Dao Lee)

> 1957 年

一項科學成就，總是在同一領域或相關領域工作的許多人的累積結果。（李政道）

Since the beginning of physics, symmetry considerations have provided us with an extremely powerful and useful tool in our effort to understand nature. Gradually they have become the backbone of our theoretical formulation of physical laws. (Tsung-Dao Lee)

自從物理學產生，對稱性的考慮對於我們理解自然的努力提供了一種極為強大而有用的工具。漸漸地，它們成了物理定律理論闡述的支柱。（李政道）

The secrets of the cell nucleus are at least as important as those of the atomic nucleus and their revelation may yet prove to be man's greatest triumph in the second half of the twentieth century. In this revelation, the organic chemist must play a major role and the outlook for the young research worker is as bright and full of promise as it has ever been in the past. (Alexander R. Todd)

細胞核的祕密至少與原子核的祕密同樣重要，它們帶來的啟發很可能會成為人類 20 世紀下半葉最偉大的勝利。在此啟發之中，有機化學家必須發揮重要作用，年輕研究人員的前景一如既往地光明，充滿了希望。（亞歷山大‧勞勃圖斯‧陶德）

Today the nucleotides occupy a prominent place in chemical, biochemical and biological research and new vistas are opening before us which may in a relatively short time lead to a far deeper understanding of the mechanisms of the living cell than seemed possible only a few years ago. (Alexander R. Todd)

1951-1960 科學與人文的對話

今天,核苷酸在化學、生物化學和生物的研究中占據了重要地位,新的前景正在我們面前漸次展開,使我們在相對短的時間裡比幾年前更深入地了解活細胞的機制。(亞歷山大‧勞勃圖斯‧陶德)

The future of pharmacodynamics is however so rich and promising, it still allows so many theoretical and practical possibilities, that I still have the hope of justifying, by my future work, not only the wonderful distinction paid to me today, but also the trust and friendship of my masters and colleagues whose work could not be separated from that which I now pursue with confidence, enthusiasm, and love. (Daniel Bovet)

不管怎樣,藥效學的未來如此豐富和充滿希望,依然容納如此眾多的理論與實務的可能性,以至我仍然期待,以未來的工作證明這一切都值得,不僅是今天賦予我的至高榮譽,還有主管與同事們的信任和情誼。我現在滿懷信心、熱情和熱愛所追求的事業,離不開他們的工作。(達尼埃爾‧博韋)

You will never be happy if you continue to search for what happiness consists of. You will never live if you are looking for the meaning of life. (Albert Camus)

一味探究幸福的本質你就永遠不會快樂。總是尋求生命的意義你就始終無法生活。(阿爾貝‧卡繆)

Whoever gives nothing has nothing. The greatest misfortune is not to be unloved, but not to love. (Albert Camus)

什麼都不付出的人將一無所有。最大的不幸並非不被愛,而是不付出愛。(阿爾貝‧卡繆)

I cannot think of anything more difficult than to say something which would be worthy of this impressive and, for me, memorable occasion, and of the ideals and purposes which inspired the Nobel Peace Award. (Lester Bowles Pearson)

要說出適合這個感人的、令我難忘的時刻的言詞，並配得上促成諾貝爾和平獎的理想和宗旨，我想不出還有什麼更難了。（萊斯特‧皮爾遜）

1958 年

Even so, we have not by a long way exhausted all the possibilities for their practical use. There can be no doubt that the usefulness of this radiation will in the future be rapidly extended. (Pavel Alekseyevich Cherenkov)

即便如此，我們還遠未窮盡其所有實際應用的可能性。無可置疑，這種輻射的豐富效用在未來將迅速擴展。（帕維爾‧阿列克謝耶維奇‧契忍可夫）

Creativity makes life valuable. Man is the sole creator; he stands out from the swarming masses of petty little folks. It doesn't matter what kind of creativity it is —— whether scientific or socio-political —— it's of equal value. (Igor Yevgenyevich Tamm)

創造力使生命有價值。人是唯一的創造者，他在大千世界芸芸眾生中脫穎而出。不管哪一種創造力 —— 無論科學的還是社會政治的 —— 都具有同等價值。（伊戈爾‧塔姆）

Many of the most important scientific problems can be solved only by a common effort of different sciences. It is therefore not at all accidental, that when a physicist reads the list of Nobelprize-winners in chemistry, he finds in it the names of a number of scientists, whom he regards as being unquestionably physicists, e. g. Joliot-Curie, Debye, McMillan. Perhaps some of the awards in physics may invoke a corresponding impression in a chemist. However, the dividing line between physics and biology is at present a rather sharp one. But a number of impressive recent achievements in biology make one believe that we are perhaps on the eve of an epoch of great discoveries in biology. I venture to express the opinion, that to achieve fundamental success in biology a very close working cooperation of all three sciences, representatives of which are honoured by Nobel prizes, will be indispensable. (Igor Yevgenyevich Tamm)

許多最重要的科學問題只能由不同學科的共同努力解決。因而完全不算意外，當一位物理學家在瀏覽諾貝爾化學獎得主名單時，他會在其中發現一些他認為無疑是物理學家的名字，例如約里奧－居禮、德拜、麥克米倫。也許有的物理學獎可能在化學家心中引起相應的印象。然而，物理學和生物學之間的分界線目前是相當清晰的。不過，生物學中最近的一些出色成就讓人相信，我們可能處於生物學偉大發現時代的前夕。這三種學科的代表都得到了諾貝爾獎的褒揚。我大膽提出，為了在生物學上獲得根本性成功，三大學科非常密切的合作，將是不可或缺的。（伊戈爾・塔姆）

When I was here 22 years ago I addressed the students of 1958 as "fellow students" because although I was 40 years old I still felt that I was one

1958 年

of them, and I still feel the same today. I and my colleagues here have been engaged in the pursuit of knowledge. We have been learning, are still learning and I hope will continue to learn.

I believe that we have been doing this not primarily to achieve riches or even honour, but rather because we were interested in the work, enjoyed doing it and felt very strongly that it was worthwhile.

Scientific research is one of the most exciting and rewarding of occupations. It is like a voyage of discovery into unknown lands, seeking not for new territory but for new knowledge. It should appeal to those with a good sense of adventure.

When I was young my Father used to tell me that the two most worthwhile pursuits in life were the pursuit of truth and of beauty and I believe that Alfred Nobel must have felt much the same when he gave these prizes for literature and the sciences. Through art and science in their broadest senses it is possible to make a permanent contribution towards the improvement and enrichment of human life and it is these pursuits that we students are engaged in.

So, fellow students, I would like to thank you for your part in these celebrations and for your words. (Frederick Sanger)

22 年前在此地，我稱 1958 年的學生們為「同學」，因為儘管年屆四十，我仍然覺得身為他們的一員，而今天我仍然覺得如此。我和這裡的同事們一直致力於對知識的追求。我們一直在學習，仍然在學習，而我希望繼續學習。

我認為，我們堅持這麼做主要不是為了獲得財富乃至榮譽，而是由於對這一項工作有興趣，喜歡做，並且非常強烈地感到值得。

科學研究是最令人激動並給予回報的事業之一。它就像一場探索之旅,進入未知的土地,尋找新的知識而非新的領土。它應該吸引富於冒險精神的人們。

我年輕的時候,父親常常對我說,人生最值得的兩種追求,是對真理和美的追求。我認為,阿佛烈·諾貝爾在為文學和科學頒發這些獎項時,感受必定大致相同。經由最廣泛意義上的藝術和科學,可能對人類生活的改善和豐富做出永久的貢獻,而我們所致力於的正是這些追求。

所以,同學們,為了你們對這些慶祝活動的參與和你們鼓勵的話語,我要向你們致謝。[52](弗雷德里克·桑格)

You too can win Nobel Prizes. Study diligently. Respect DNA. Don't smoke. Don't drink. Avoid women and politics. That's my formula. (George Wells Beadle)

你們也可以獲得諾貝爾獎。勤奮學習。尊重DNA。不抽菸。不喝酒。避女色而遠政治。這就是我的準則。(喬治·韋爾斯·比德爾)

Whatever inborn potentialities we have, we received from our parents. For what we have been able to do in developing and making use of these potentialities, we are grateful for our homes, for our teachers and fellow students, for our inspired and inspiring colleagues, for access to the knowledge and wisdom of those who preceded us, and for time and the best of laboratory facilities to develop our ideas. If we have been able to expose an additional bit of the mystery, beauty, and order that lie within each tiny cell of which every living creature is composed, we are profoundly thankful for the circumstances that have made it possible. It is in this spirit that we humbly accept this highest

---

[52] 這是桑格在諾貝爾獎宴會上的發言。

of all scientific honors. (Edward Lawrie Tatum)

無論任何與生俱來的潛力，我們都受之於父母。對於我們能夠開發和運用這些潛力，我們感激家庭，感激老師和同學，感激相互啟發的同事，感激前人知識和智慧的提供，也感激我們擁有時間和最好的實驗室設施而得以發展我們的想法。每一個生物都由微小的細胞組成。如果能揭示每一個細胞中更多一點的祕密、美與秩序，我們深深感謝使之成為可能的環境。正是本著這種精神，我們謙恭地接受這一項至高無上的科學榮譽。（愛德華・勞里・塔特姆）

I got my Nobel Prize for my lab work. (Joshua Lederberg)

我由於實驗室工作而獲得了諾貝爾獎。（約書亞・雷德伯格）

Literature is the art of discovering something extraordinary about ordinary people, and saying with ordinary words something extraordinary. (Boris Leonidovich Pasternak)

文學是發現平凡人的非凡之處，並以平凡話語表達非凡之事的藝術。（鮑里斯・巴斯特納克）

I don't like people who have never fallen or stumbled. Their virtue is lifeless and it isn't of much value. Life hasn't revealed its beauty to them. (Boris Leonidovich Pasternak)

我不喜歡從未摔倒或失足的人。他們的優點沒有活力，也沒多少價值。生活不曾向他們展示它的美。（鮑里斯・巴斯特納克）

The 1958 Nobel Peace Prize is not the end of a career, but a beginning, a fresh start, the continuation with renewed zeal, of all that has been done in the last ten years. The responsibility involved is enormous. (Georges Pire)

1951-1960 科學與人文的對話

1958年諾貝爾和平獎並非畢生事業的結束，而是一個開端，一個全新的起點，懷著新生的熱情延續過去十年的全部作為。其中包含的責任十分重大。（喬治·皮爾）

1959年

(After the flash of the atomic bomb test explosion) Fermi got up and dropped small pieces of paper… a simple experiment to measure the energy liberated by the explosion… When the front of the shock wave arrived (some seconds after the flash) the pieces of paper were displaced a few centimeters in the direction of propagation of the shock wave. From the distance of the source and from the displacement of the air due to the shock wave, he could calculate the energy of the explosion. This Fermi had done in advance having prepared himself a table of numbers, so that he could tell immediately the energy liberated from this crude but simple measurement… It is also typical that his answer closely approximated that of the elaborate official measurements. The latter, however, were available only after several days' study of the records, whereas Fermi had his within seconds. (Emilio Gino Segrè)

（原子彈試驗爆炸的閃光後）費米起身，撒下一些小紙屑。……一個測量爆炸所釋放能量的簡單實驗……當衝擊波的前端到達（閃光數秒後），紙屑隨之被推開若干公分。從爆炸源的距離，以及衝擊波導致的空氣位移，他計算得出爆炸的能量。費米事先已經準備了一個數字表格，從而能夠由此粗略而簡單的測量，馬上計算出釋放的能量。……同樣典

> 1959 年

型的是,他的答案非常接近精細的正式測量數值。然而,後者需要研究數日方才知曉,費米則在幾秒鐘內就得出來了。(埃米利奧・塞格雷)

The most striking impression was that of an overwhelming bright light. I had seen under similar conditions the explosion of a large amount —— 100 tons —— of normal explosives in the April test, and I was flabbergasted by the new spectacle. We saw the whole sky flash with unbelievable brightness in spite of the very dark glasses we wore. Our eyes were accommodated to darkness, and thus even if the sudden light had been only normal daylight it would have appeared to us much brighter than usual, but we know from measurements that the flash of the bomb was many times brighter than the sun. In a fraction of a second, at our distance, one received enough light to produce a sunburn. I was near Fermi at the time of the explosion, but I do not remember what we said, if anything. I believe that for a moment I thought the explosion might set fire to the atmosphere and thus finish the earth, even though I knew that this was not possible. (Emilio Gino Segrè)

最深刻的印象是一陣無比耀眼的強光。在 4 月的測試中,我見過大量——一百噸——普通炸藥爆炸的相似情景,然而新的場面使我大為震驚。儘管戴著顏色極深的墨鏡,我們看到整個天空都閃耀著令人難以置信的光芒。我們的眼睛適應了黑暗,所以,突如其來的光線即便只是一般的日光,對於我們,與平時相較,它也顯得過於明亮;然而由測量得知,原子彈的閃光比太陽明亮許多倍。在零點幾秒內,處於我們所在的距離,人所遭受的光照足以造成灼傷。爆炸之際,我在費米身旁,但不記得我們說了什麼。一時之間,我以為爆炸會點燃大氣層,從而毀掉地球,雖然心知這並不可能。(埃米利奧・塞格雷)

We Nobel laureates, although we work in widely diversified fields, share at least one thing in common: we spend a good part of our lives teaching and working with students and young people, the new generation on which the future depends. (Emilio Gino Segrè)

我們諾貝爾獎得主,雖然工作在廣泛多樣的領域,但具備至少一個共同點:一生中有相當一部分時間用於教學,以及與學生和年輕人一起工作,他們是決定未來的新一代。(埃米利奧·塞格雷)

The development of physics, like the development of any science, is a continuous one. Each new idea is dependent upon the ideas of the past. The whole structure of science gradually grows, but only as it is built upon a firm foundation of past research. Each generation of scientists stands upon the shoulders of those who have gone before. (Owen Chamberlain)

物理學的發展與所有學科的發展一樣,是個持續的過程。每種新觀念都有賴於以往的觀念。只有建立在以往研究的堅實基礎上,學科的整體結構才能逐漸成長。每一代科學家都站立於前人的肩頭。(歐文·張伯倫)

In a different way, each generation of scientists depends upon the previous generation for instruction and training. I was 21 years old when I came as a graduate student to the University of California in Berkeley. Within a short time I found myself working under Professor Emilio Segrè. Whenever there was a pause in the routine parts of our work, his agile mind produced intriguing questions and scientific puzzles to tease my intellect. A few years later, I worked under the late Professor Enrico Fermi, who was, I believe, the most intelligent man I have ever met. For a considerable period he devoted several hours per week to helping me with my research toward the doctor's degree.

1959 年

When I faltered, he found a method of circumventing the difficulty. Professor Segrè has taught me the value of asking the right question, for by asking the right question one may find a key to new knowledge. From Professor Fermi I have learned that even the simplest methods may give answers to difficult questions. (Owen Chamberlain)

每一代科學家都以不同的方式有賴於上一代的指導和訓練。21 歲時，我成為加州大學柏克萊分校的研究生。有一段不長的時間，我在埃米利奧·塞格雷教授手下工作。每當我們工作的常規部分有所停滯，他機敏的頭腦便提出吸引人的疑問和科學謎題，來激發我的智力。幾年後，我在已故的恩里科·費米教授手下工作，我相信，他是我所見過最聰明的人。在相當長的一段時間裡，他每週都拿出數小時幫助我進行博士學位的研究。當我躊躇不前，他找出一種繞過困難的方法。塞格雷教授教導我提出正確問題的價值，因為經由提出正確的問題，人們可能發現獲得新知的鑰匙。從費米教授那裡，我領會到即便是最簡單的方法，也可能對困難的問題提供解答。（歐文·張伯倫）

The late Alfred Nobel, through the medium of the Nobel prizes, has done much to dramatize this search for knowledge. In so doing, I am sure he has quickened the pace of scientific history. (Owen Chamberlain)

已故的阿佛烈·諾貝爾透過諾貝爾獎這項媒介，在相當程度上使這種對知識的探索引起了大眾的關注。我確信他這樣做加快了科學史的步伐。（歐文·張伯倫）

The reason why I keep some 38 years to the electrochemical researches with the dropping mercury electrode is its exquisite property as electrode material. (Jaroslav Heyrovsky)

1951-1960 科學與人文的對話

大約 38 年來，我一直從事滴汞電極的電化學研究，就是由於其作為電極材料的優異效能。（雅羅斯拉夫·海羅夫斯基）

At first, research needs more brains than means. (Severo Ochoa)

首先，研究需要更多的頭腦而非方法。（塞韋羅·奧喬亞）

Science is always worth it because its discoveries, sooner or later, are always applied. (Severo Ochoa)

科學總是值得的，因為或遲或早，其發現總是得以應用。（塞韋羅·奧喬亞）

A woman can change a man's life. (Severo Ochoa)

一個女人能夠改變一個男人的一生。[53]（塞韋羅·奧喬亞）

I told my three sons stories about germs more than fifty years ago as fanciful bedtime tales. (Arthur Kornberg)

50 多年前，作為奇異的睡前故事，我把關於細菌的事情講給三個兒子聽。（阿瑟·科恩伯格）

Poetry is the revelation of a feeling that the poet believes to be interior and personal which the reader recognizes as his own. (Salvatore Quasimodo)

詩歌是感情的揭示，詩人相信它是內心的、個人的，而讀者也認為是自己的。（誇齊莫多）

A poet clings to his own tradition and avoids internationalism. (Salvatore Quasimodo)

詩人堅持自己的傳統而避免國際化。（薩爾瓦托雷·夸西莫多）

---

[53] 奧喬亞與妻子相濡以沫 55 年。

In the age when the atom has been split, the moon encircled, diseases conquered, is disarmament so difficult a matter that it must remain a distant dream? (Philip J. Noel-Baker)

原子已被分割,月球已經被環繞,各種疾病也得以征服。在這個時代,裁軍還是如此困難,以致非得仍是遙遠的夢想嗎?(菲利普・諾埃爾—貝克)

1960 年

In their exploration of the submicroscopic world of atomic nuclei, physicists are like men groping in a dark cave with a flashlight that goes on for only an instant and each time lights only a tiny corner of the cave. (Donald Arthur Glaser)

在對於原子核的微觀世界的探索中,物理學家就像拿著手電筒在黑暗洞穴中摸索的人,每一次照射的片刻都只能照亮洞穴的一個小角落。(唐納德・格拉澤)

The advance of modern science is possible only because of the complete cooperation and collaboration of many scientists. We depend heavily not only on the insights and successes of our predecessors who have built the foundations on which we work, but also on the day-to-day exchanges of ideas and experimental results which are the product of scientific research. All of us feel quite strongly that we stand here to be honored mainly as representatives of the scientific community who share in this work. (Donald Arthur Glaser)

1951-1960 科學與人文的對話

現代科學的進步由於許多科學家的通力合作而成為可能。在相當程度上，我們不僅依賴前人的洞見和成就，他們造就了我們工作的基礎，也依賴作為科學研究產物的日常思想交流和實驗結果。我們所有人都強烈感受到，自己主要是代表參與了這項工作的科學界而站在這裡受獎。（唐納德・格拉澤）

My own field of research, high energy nuclear physics, is especially remote from the experience of ordinary daily life since it deals with experiments on objects much too small to see or perceive directly. Cooperative efforts are particularly essential in this field because very expensive and large machines must be used in the types of experiments which are currently the most fruitful. (Donald Arthur Glaser)

我自己的研究領域，高能核物理，與一般日常生活經驗相距甚遠，因為它涉及的實驗對象太小，無法直接看到或感知。在這一項領域，合作努力尤為重要，因為在目前最富於成果的實驗類型中，必須使用非常昂貴和大型的機器。（唐納德・格拉澤）

True, the initial ideas are in general those of an individual, but the establishment of the reality and truth is in general the work of more than one person. (Willard Frank Libby)

誠然，最初的想法一般都是出自個人，然而事實和真相的建立通常都不止是一個人的努力。（威拉得・利比）

And yet the Nobel Prizes, in singling out individuals, have done a great deal of good in pointing up to the world as a whole and setting forth clearly goals for achievement. (Willard Frank Libby)

> 1960 年

然而,諾貝爾獎在遴選個人的時候,已不遺餘力地強調作為整體的專業領域,並為成就設立了明確的目標。(威拉得·利比)

To advance science is highly honourable, and I believe the institution of the Nobel Prizes has done much to raise the prestige of scientific discovery. (Frank Macfarlane Burnet)

推動科學發展是非常光榮的,我相信諾貝爾獎的設立對於提高科學發現的聲望盡了極大的努力。(弗蘭克·麥克法蘭·伯內特)

The human mind treats a new idea the same way the body treats a strange protein; it rejects it. (Peter Brian Medawar)

人的頭腦對待新想法的方式與身體對待陌生蛋白質的方式相同,就是排斥它。(彼得·梅達沃)

Anyone who combines strong common sense with an ordinary degree of imaginativeness can become a creative scientist, and a happy one besides, in so far as happiness depends upon being able to develop to the limit of one's abilities. (Peter Brian Medawar)

任何將強而有力的常識與一般程度的豐富想像結合起來的人,都可以成為有創造力的科學家,以及幸福的人,因為幸福取決於能夠發展個人能力的極限。(彼得·梅達沃)

For a scientist must indeed be freely imaginative and yet skeptical, creative and yet a critic. There is a sense in which he must be free, but another in which his thought must be very precisely regimented; there is poetry in science, but also a lot of bookkeeping. (Peter Brian Medawar)

作為科學家,確實必須想像力飛揚而又有懷疑精神,創造性十足而

1951-1960 科學與人文的對話

又是個批評者。一方面他必須無拘無束,但另一方面他的思想必須絲絲入扣、中規中矩;科學中有詩,但也有很多帳簿。(彼得·梅達沃)

Scientific discovery, or the formulation of scientific theory, starts in with the unvarnished and unembroidered evidence of the senses. It starts with simple observation —— simple, unbiased, unprejudiced, naive, or innocent observation —— and out of this sensory evidence, embodied in the form of simple propositions or declarations of fact, generalizations will grow up and take shape, almost as if some process of crystallization or condensation were taking place. Out of a disorderly array of facts, an orderly theory, an orderly general statement, will somehow emerge. (Peter Brian Medawar)

科學發現,或科學理論的提出,是隨著質樸無華、不加修飾的感官見證開始的。它以簡單的觀察開始 —— 簡單的、公正的、無成見的、幼稚的或天真的觀察 —— 出自這種感知的見證,以簡單的命題或事實陳述的形式展現,逐漸形成概括,一如某種結晶或凝結發生的過程。從一系列無序的事實中,以某種方式呈現出一個有序的理論,一個有序的一般論述。(彼得·梅達沃)

Observation is the generative act in scientific discovery. For all its aberrations, the evidence of the senses is essentially to be relied upon —— provided we observe nature as a child does, without prejudices and preconceptions, but with that clear and candid vision which adults lose and scientists must strive to regain. (Peter Brian Medawar)

觀察是引起科學發現的行為。儘管存在各種偏差,感官的證據基本上是可靠的 —— 前提是像孩子一樣觀察自然,不帶偏頗與成見,而是

> 1960 年

採取成年人所失去的、而科學家必須努力重新獲得的那種明澈率真的視角。（彼得·梅達沃）

Today the world changes so quickly that in growing up we take leave not just of youth but of the world we were young in… Fear and resentment of what is new is really a lament for the memories of our childhood. (Peter Brian Medawar)

今天，世界變化如此迅速，在成長的過程中，我們不僅告別了青春，也告別了那時的世界。……對新事物的畏懼和怨恨，實際上是對童年記憶的深切惋惜。（彼得·梅達沃）

To be creative, scientists need libraries and laboratories and the company of other scientists; certainly a quiet and untroubled life is a help. A scientist's work is in no way deepened or made more cogent by privation, anxiety, distress, or emotional harassment. To be sure, the private lives of scientists may be strangely and even comically mixed up, but not in ways that have any special bearing on the nature and quality of their work. (Peter Brian Medawar)

科學家想要有所創造，就離不開圖書館、實驗室和同行們。當然，平靜安寧的生活也有助益。一位科學家的工作，絕不會由於貧困、憂慮、痛苦或心煩意亂而得以深入或更為服眾。誠然，科學家的私人生活也許一團糟，反常乃至可笑，然而這對他們工作的性質和品質，完全不至於產生特別的影響。（彼得·梅達沃）

There is nothing distinctively scientific about the hypothetico-deductive process. It is not even distinctively intellectual. It is merely a scientific context for a much more general stratagem that underlies almost all regulative processes or processes of continuous control, namely feedback, the control of performance by the consequences of the act performed. In the hypothetico-deductive scheme the inferences we draw from a hypothesis are, in a sense, its logical output. If they are true, the hypothesis need not be altered, but correction is obligatory if they are false. (Peter Brian Medawar)

假設推論的過程並無特別科學之處。它甚至不具有獨特的知識性。它不過是一種更普遍的策略的科學背景，這種策略支持幾乎所有調整過程或持續控制過程，也就是回饋，行動結果對行為的控制。在假設推論的過程中，我們從假設中得出的推斷，在某種意義上是它合乎邏輯的輸出。它們若是正確的，假設便無須更動；而它們若是錯誤的，修正就必不可免了。（彼得‧梅達沃）

It is a common failing —— and one that I have myself suffered from —— to fall in love with a hypothesis and to be unwilling to take no for an answer. A love affair with a pet hypothesis can waste years of precious time. There is very often no finally decisive yes, though quite often there can be a decisive no. (Peter Brian Medawar)

這是一種常見的失敗 —— 也是我自己所遭受的一種 —— 迷戀一個假設，不願意接受否定的答案。與鍾愛假設的纏綿足以浪費多年珍貴的時間。往往不存在最終決定性的肯定，儘管通常只有決定性的否定。（彼得‧梅達沃）

Twice in my life I have spent two weary and scientifically profitless years seeking evidence to corroborate dearly loved hypotheses that later proved to be groundless; times such as these are hard for scientists —— days of leaden gray skies bringing with them a miserable sense of oppression and inadequacy. (Peter Brian Medawar)

此生我曾兩度耗費兩年，在身心疲憊而科學上無益的歲月中尋求證據，以證實一些十分鍾愛的假設，它們後來被證實是站不住腳的。諸如此類的時候對於科學家是艱難的——天色鉛灰的日子，充滿痛苦的壓抑與匱乏之感。（彼得‧梅達沃）

I cannot give any scientist of any age better advice than this: the intensity of the conviction that a hypothesis is true has no bearing on whether it is true or not. (Peter Brian Medawar)

對任何年齡的所有科學家，我給不出比這更好的建議：認為一個假設正確，這種信念的強度與它是否正確無關。（彼得‧梅達沃）

In choosing topics for research and departments to enlist in, a young scientist must beware of following fashion. It is one thing to fall into step with a great concerted movement of thought such as molecular genetics or cellular immunology, but quite another merely to fall in with prevailing fashion for, say, some new histochemical procedure or technical gimmick. (Peter Brian Medawar)

年輕科學家在選擇研究主題和參與部門時，務必謹防趕時髦。與分子遺傳學或細胞免疫學等思想主流步調一致是一回事，僅與流行風氣一致則完全是另一回事，例如某種新的組織化學方法或技術噱頭。（彼得‧梅達沃）

Simultaneous discovery is utterly commonplace, and it was only the rarity of scientists, not the inherent improbability of the phenomenon, that made it remarkable in the past. Scientists on the same road may be expected to arrive at the same destination, often not far apart. (Peter Brian Medawar)

同時發現是最平常不過的。只是因為科學家的數量不多，而不是這

種現象本身的不可能，才使它在過去引人注目。走在同一條路上的科學家可能會抵達同一目的地，且往往相距不遠。（彼得・梅達沃）

You have… been told that science grows like an organism. You have been told that, if we today see further than our predecessors, it is only because we stand on their shoulders. But Nobel Prize Presentation is an occasion on which I should prefer to remember, not the giants upon whose shoulders we stood, but the friends with whom we stood arm in arm… colleagues in so much of my work. (Peter Brian Medawar)

你們……曾聽說過，科學如同有機體一般成長。你們曾聽說過，如果我們今天看得比前輩更遠，只是由於我們站在他們的肩膀上。然而，在諾貝爾獎頒獎典禮上，我更要記住的，不是我們站在他們肩頭的巨人，而是跟我們攜手並立的朋友們……我工作中的眾多同事們。（彼得・梅達沃）

It is… a sign of the times —— though our brothers of physics and chemistry may smile to hear me say so —— that biology is now a science in which theories can be devised: theories which lead to predictions and predictions which sometimes turn out to be correct. These facts confirm me in a belief I hold most passionately —— that biology is the heir of all the sciences. (Peter Brian Medawar)

這是……一個時代的符號 —— 儘管我們的物理學和化學兄弟可能一笑置之 —— 生物學現在是一門可以生成理論的科學：理論引發預測，預測有時被證明是正確的。這些事實使我極其強烈地堅信 —— 生物學是所有科學的繼承者。（彼得・梅達沃）

1960 年

In truth, every creation of the mind is first of all "poetic" in the proper sense of the word; and inasmuch as there exists an equivalence between the modes of sensibility and intellect, it is the same function that is exercised initially in the enterprises of the poet and the scientist. (Saint-John Perse)

事實上,心靈的每一項創造首先都是真正意義上的「詩意的」。由於在情感和理性的模式之間存在一種相同的要素,它是詩人和科學家的事業中最先運用的同樣功能。(聖瓊‧佩斯)

Poetry allies itself with beauty —— a supreme union —— but never uses it as its ultimate goal or sole nourishment. Refusing to divorce art from life, love from perception, it is action, it is passion, it is power, and always the innovation which extend borders. Love is its hearth-fire, insurrection its law; its place is everywhere, in anticipation. (Saint-John Perse)

詩使自己與美結合,成為絕配,然而不以之作為終極目標或唯一養分。拒絕將藝術與生活隔離,將愛與感知拆散,它是行動,是熱情,是力量,永遠是開疆拓土的創新。愛是它的爐火,叛逆是它的法則。它無所不在,先聲奪人。(聖瓊‧佩斯)

Learn from yesterday, live for today, hope for tomorrow. The important thing is not to stop questioning. (Albert John Lutuli)

學習昨天,過好今天,期待明天。重要的是不要停止提問。(艾伯特‧盧圖利)

You have to learn the rules of the game. And then you have to play better than anyone else. (Albert John Lutuli)

你必須學會遊戲規則。然後比別的人都做得好。(艾伯特‧盧圖利)

1951-1960 科學與人文的對話

1961–1970
革新與抗爭

1961 年

The Nobel Prize is given as a personal award but it also honors the field of research in which I have worked and it also honors my students and colleagues. (Robert Hofstadter)

諾貝爾獎是作為個人獎頒發的,但它也表彰我所從事的研究領域,也表彰我的學生和同事們。(羅伯特·霍夫施塔特)

Explain it! The most important thing is, that you are able to explain it! You will have exams, there you have to explain it. Eventually, you pass them, you get your diploma and you think, that's it! – No, the whole life is an exam, you'll have to write applications, you'll have to discuss with peers... So learn to explain it! You can train this by explaining to another student, a colleague. If they are not available, explain it to your mother —— or to your cat! (Rudolf Ludwig Mössbauer)

解釋它!最重要的是,你能夠解釋它!你會有一遍遍考試,那時你必須解釋它。終於,你通過了考試,拿到了文憑,你就想,萬事大吉!—— 沒有。整個人生都是一場考試。你得寫申請書,你得跟同行討論……所以學會解釋它吧！你可以透過向另一位學者、同事解釋來訓練這種能力。如果他們沒空，就向母親，或者家裡的貓解釋！（魯道夫・穆斯堡爾）

It's no trick to get the right answer when you have all the data. The real creative trick is to get the right answer when you have only half of the data in hand and half of it is wrong and you don't know which half is wrong. When you get the right answer under these circumstances, you are doing something creative. (Melvin Calvin)

當你掌握全部資料時，獲得正確答案並非難事。獲得正確答案的真正創造性技巧在於，當你手中只有一半資料，一半資料是錯誤的，而你不知道哪一半是錯的之時。在這些情況下獲得正確答案，你就在做創造性的事情。（梅爾文・卡爾文）

You have honoured my colleagues, my family and me, but mostly my comrades in science. I speak not only of those with whom I have had the pleasure to work directly —— but the many others who preceded us and surround us in our work. For each of us who appear to have had a successful experiment there are many to whom their own experiments seem barren and negative. But they contribute their strength to the structure within which we all build. (Melvin Calvin)

你們將榮譽給予了我的同事、家人和我，尤其是科學界夥伴。這不僅指我有幸直接共事的人們 —— 還有我們工作中的許多先行者與同行。相對於我們看起來實驗成功的人，有許多人的實驗似乎是沒有收穫和失敗的。然而他們為我們共同建立的框架做出了貢獻。（梅爾文・卡爾文）

1961 年

In one of my lectures many years ago I used the phrase "following the trail of light". The word "light" was not meant in its literal sense, but in the sense of following an intellectual concept or idea to where it might lead. (Melvin Calvin)

在多年前的一次演講中,我使用了「循著光的軌跡」這句話。其中「光」的意思並非字面所指,而是指遵循知識的概念或想法,前往其可能引領的地方。(梅爾文・卡爾文)

There is not a "pure" science. By this I mean that physics impinges on astronomy, on the one hand, and chemistry and biology on the other. And not only does each support neighbors, but derives sustenance from them. The same can be said of chemistry. Biology is, perhaps, the example par excellence today of an "impure" science. (Melvin Calvin)

「純」科學並不存在。我的意思是,一方面,物理學影響了天文學,另一方面,化學和生物學影響了物理學。它們不僅彼此提供支持,而且互相汲取養分。化學也是如此。也許,生物學是「不純」科學如今最出眾的例子。(梅爾文・卡爾文)

If we want to make a discovery, we have to take a risk, since everything new was discovered by accident or by the fact that somebody took a chance and went ahead when there wasn't 100 percent safety for the solution. (Georg von Békésy)

我們若想獲得發現,就必須冒險。因為所有新事物的發現都出於偶然,或者出於這一項事實:有人把握機會,在解決方法並非百分之百安全時勇往直前。(蓋歐格・馮・貝凱希)

1961-1970 革新與抗爭

Too much equipment can be, however, something that hampers scientific development. I had the feeling that if there is no equipment present, everybody is forced to simplify his ideas in such a way that the experiments become simple. If there is too much equipment available, he can attack any experiment immediately since all the difficulties will be overcome by putting more money in the equipment. In the long run, some of the equipment becomes so complicated that it is difficult to see how all the parts interact. (Georg von Békésy)

然而,過多的設備可能成為科學發展的阻礙。我有一種感覺:要是沒有現成設備,人人被迫簡化其想法,從而使實驗變得簡單。如果有過多的可用設備,他就可以立即著手任何實驗,因為所有的困難都將經由在設備上投入更多的金錢來克服。最終,一些設備變得如此複雜,以至難以看出各個部分如何相互作用。(蓋歐格・馮・貝凱希)

It is not the things that we have, but how we use them that is important. (Georg von Békésy)

重要的不是我們所擁有的東西,而是我們如何運用它們。(蓋歐格・馮・貝凱希)

A working day is always a celebration for me. (Ivo Andric)

對我來說,工作日永遠都是慶典。(伊沃・安德里奇)

Between the fear that something would happen and the hope that still it wouldn't, there is much more space than one thinks. On that narrow, hard, bare and dark space a lot of us spend their lives. (Ivo Andric)

在對某件事可能發生的恐懼和它仍有可能避免的希望之間,存在著比人們所設想的更大的空間。我們很多人就在這個狹窄、堅硬、貧瘠、黑暗的空間裡度過一生。(伊沃・安德里奇)

1961 年

Good friends are not good critics. (Ivo Andric)

好朋友不是好的批評者。（伊沃‧安德里奇）

Never measure the height of a mountain until you have reached the top. Then you will see how low it was. (Dag Hjalmar Agne Carl Hammarskjöld)

在登上山頂之前不要測量山高。到時候你就會看到它有多低了。（道格‧哈瑪紹）

Never look down to test the ground before taking your next step; only he who keeps his eye fixed on the far horizon will find the right road. (Dag Hjalmar Agne Carl Hammarskjöld)

在邁出下一步之前不要低頭探查地面，只有注視遠方地平線的人才能找到正確的道路。（道格‧哈瑪紹）

The more we do, the more we can do; the more busy we are, the more leisure we have. (Dag Hjalmar Agne Carl Hammarskjöld)

當我們做得越多，就能做得更多；越是忙碌，就越有空閒。（道格‧哈瑪紹）

The more faithfully you listen to the voices within you, the better you will hear what is sounding outside. (Dag Hjalmar Agne Carl Hammarskjöld)

當你越如實地傾聽內心的聲音，就會越清晰地聽到外界的聲音。（道格‧哈瑪紹）

If only I may grow: firmer, simpler, quieter, warmer. (Dag Hjalmar Agne Carl Hammarskjöld)

但願我能夠成長：更結實、更簡單、更沉靜、更熱心。（道格‧哈瑪紹）

Life only demands from you the strength that you possess. Only one feat is possible; not to run away. (Dag Hjalmar Agne Carl Hammarskjöld)

生活只要求你盡力而為。可能實現的壯舉只有一項：不要逃避。（道格‧哈瑪紹）

Time goes by, reputation increases, ability declines. (Dag Hjalmar Agne Carl Hammarskjöld)

時光流逝，聲譽漸長，能力漸衰。（道格‧哈瑪紹）

In the last analysis, it is our conception of death which decides our answers to all the questions that life puts to us. (Dag Hjalmar Agne Carl Hammarskjöld)

說到底，是我們對死亡的觀念決定了我們對生命所提出全部問題的回答。（道格‧哈瑪紹）

If even dying is to be made a social function, then, grant me the favor of sneaking out on tiptoe without disturbing the party. (Dag Hjalmar Agne Carl Hammarskjöld)

如果連死亡都被弄成社交場合，那麼，請允許我悄然離場而不打擾聚會。（道格‧哈瑪紹）

1962 年

A method is more important than a discovery, since the right method will lead to new and even more important discoveries. (Lev Davidovich Landau)

1962 年

方法比發現更重要，因為正確的方法將帶來新的甚至更重要的發現。（列夫・朗道）

This work contains many things which are new and interesting. Unfortunately, everything that is new is not interesting, and everything which is interesting, is not new. (Lev Davidovich Landau)

這一項工作包含許多新穎的、有趣的東西。遺憾的是，每種新穎的東西都不有趣，而每種有趣的東西，都不新穎。（列夫・朗道）

It is important to do everything with passion, it embellishes life enormously. (Lev Davidovich Landau)

懷著熱情去做每件事很重要，這極大地美化了生活。（列夫・朗道）

A discovery is like falling in love and reaching the top of a mountain after a hard climb all in one, an ecstasy not induced by drugs but by the revelation of a face of nature that no one has seen before and that often turns out to be more subtle and wonderful than anyone had imagined. (Max Ferdinand Perutz)

發現就像墜入愛河，又像經歷艱苦攀爬後抵達山頂，這種狂喜並非由藥物造成，而是由初顯真容的大自然所引發，那種面貌從來無人得見，且經常比任何人想像到的還要精美絕倫。（馬克斯・佩魯茨）

I distrust scientists who complain about others stealing their ideas —— I have always had to force new ideas down people's throats. (Max Ferdinand Perutz)

我懷疑抱怨別人竊取他們想法的科學家 —— 我總是不得不強迫人們接受新想法。（馬克斯・佩魯茨）

1961-1970 革新與抗爭

What is known for certain is dull. (Max Ferdinand Perutz)

確切了解的事情是枯燥無味的。（馬克斯・佩魯茨）

I rarely plan my research; it plans me. (Max Ferdinand Perutz)

我很少規劃我的研究，是它規劃我。（馬克斯・佩魯茨）

On hearing the news of being awarded a Nobel Prize, a friend who knows me only too well, sent me this laconic message: Blood, toil, sweat and tears always were a good mixture. (Max Ferdinand Perutz)

聽聞我獲得諾貝爾獎的消息，一個非常了解我的朋友送給我這句言簡意賅的話：熱血、辛勞、汗水和眼淚永遠是美好的結合。（馬克斯・佩魯茨）

Women's liberation could have not succeeded if science had not provided them with contraception and household technology. (Max Ferdinand Perutz)

假如科學不曾為女人提供避孕和家用科技，婦女解放就不可能成功。（馬克斯・佩魯茨）

When I looked at my four colleagues, it seemed to me that they looked solid enough, and I thought I could not be dreaming and that it must after all be true. (John Cowdery Kendrew)

看著四位同事，在我看來他們足夠實在了，我想自己不可能是在做夢，這確定無疑是真實的。（約翰・肯德魯）

My work has been altogether a team affair. I could, if I had the time, mention perhaps twenty names of those who have made essential contributions to a result which has won for me alone a share of the Prize. (John Cowdery Kendrew)

1962 年

我的工作完全是團隊合作的成果。如果有時間的話,我可以提出大約 20 個人的名字,他們對成果做出了不可或缺的貢獻,而這個成果為我個人贏得了諾貝爾獎。(約翰‧肯德魯)

Chance is the only source of true novelty. (Francis Harry Compton Crick)

機會是真正新奇事物的唯一來源。(法蘭西斯‧克立克)

Almost all aspects of life are engineered at the molecular level, and without understanding molecules we can only have a very sketchy understanding of life itself. (Francis Harry Compton Crick)

生命的幾乎所有方面都是在分子層面上安排的。如果不了解分子,我們對生命本身就只能有非常粗略的了解。(法蘭西斯‧克立克)

Dr. Crick thanks you for your letter but regrets that he is unable to accept your kind invitation to: send an autograph/help you in your project/provide a photograph/read your manuscript/cure your disease/ deliver a lecture/be interviewed/attend a conference/talk on the radio/act as chairman /appear on TV/ become an editor/speak after dinner/write a book/give a testimonial/accept an honorary degree. (Francis Harry Compton Crick)

克立克博士感謝你的來信,但很遺憾他不能接受你的盛情邀請而:簽名 / 為項目出力 / 提供照片 / 讀手稿 / 治病 / 講課 / 接受採訪 / 參加會議 / 於廣播中發言 / 擔任某主席 / 上電視 / 擔任編輯 / 餐後致辭 / 著書 / 寫推薦函 / 領受榮譽學位。(法蘭西斯‧克立克)

If you go into science, I think you better go in with a dream that maybe you, too, will get a Nobel Prize. It's not that I went in and I thought I was very bright and I was going to get one, but I'll confess, you know, I knew what it was. (James Dewey Watson)

1961-1970 革新與抗爭

你若進入科學領域,我認為你最好懷著你也可能獲得諾貝爾獎的夢想。這不是說我置身其中就自詡聰明非凡,就一定能獲獎,而是要坦承,你知道,我清楚它是什麼。(詹姆斯・杜威・華生)

(When asked by a student if he believes in any gods.) Oh, no. Absolutely not… The biggest advantage to believing in God is you don't have to understand anything, no physics, no biology. I wanted to understand. (James Dewey Watson)

(當一個學生問他是否信仰任何神)哦,不。絕對不……信仰上帝最大的好處是你無須了解任何東西,不懂物理學,不懂生物學。而我想了解。(詹姆斯・杜威・華生)

The general rule is if you're not prepared to make a mistake, you're not going to make much progress. (Maurice Hugh Frederick Wilkins)

一般而言,你要是不準備犯錯,就不會獲得大幅進步。(莫里斯・威爾金斯)

It is essential for genetic material to be able to make exact copies of itself; otherwise growth would produce disorder, life could not originate, and favourable forms would not be perpetuated by natural selection. (Maurice Hugh Frederick Wilkins)

對於遺傳物質,能夠精確地複製自身十分重要。否則,生長就會產生混亂,生命無法起源,有利的形式也無法透過自然選擇而延續。(莫里斯・威爾金斯)

Ideas are like rabbits. You get a couple and learn how to handle them, and pretty soon you have a dozen. (John Steinbeck)

想法就像兔子。當你得到幾隻並學會了怎麼對待牠們，很快你就有了一打。（約翰·史坦貝克）

It is true that we are weak and sick and ugly and quarrelsome but if that is all we ever were, we would millenniums ago have disappeared from the face of the earth. (John Steinbeck)

的確，我們是軟弱、病態、醜陋和爭吵的，然而，如果這就是我們的全部，幾千年前我們就會在地球上消失了。（約翰·史坦貝克）

No man really knows about other human beings. The best he can do is to suppose that they are like himself. (John Steinbeck)

沒有人真正了解其他人。他所能做的至多是假設他們與他自己相似。（約翰·史坦貝克）

The writer must believe that what he is doing is the most important thing in the world. And he must hold to this illusion even when he knows it is not true. (John Steinbeck)

作家必須相信，他所從事的乃是天下最重要的事情。即便知道這不是真的，他也必須堅持這種幻想。（約翰·史坦貝克）

1963 年

In science, it is not speed that is the most important. It is the dedication, the commitment, the interest and the will to know something and to understand it —— these are the things that come first. (Eugene Paul Wigner)

1961-1970 革新與抗爭

在科學中，最重要的不是速度。重要的是奉獻、承諾、興趣，以及認識和理解事物的意願——這些是首要的東西。（尤金‧維格納）

Physics is becoming so unbelievably complex that it is taking longer and longer to train a physicist. It is taking so long, in fact, to train a physicist to the place where he understands the nature of physical problems that he is already too old to solve them. (Eugene Paul Wigner)

物理學變得如此難以置信的複雜，以至於培養一名物理學家的時間越來越長。事實上，將一名物理學家培養到理解物理問題本質的程度時，他已經老得無法解決這些問題了。（尤金‧維格納）

The world is very complicated and it is clearly impossible for the human mind to understand it completely. Man has therefore devised an artifice which permits the complicated nature of the world to be blamed on something which is called accidental and thus permits him to abstract a domain in which simple laws can be found. (Eugene Paul Wigner)

世界非常複雜，人的心智顯然無法完全理解它。於是人發明了一種技巧，允許將世界的複雜本質歸咎於所謂偶然性，從而得以抽象出一個可以找到簡單規律的領域。（尤金‧維格納）

Mathematics began to seem too much like puzzle solving. Physics is puzzle solving, too, but of puzzles created by nature, not by the mind of man. (Maria Goeppert Mayer)

數學開始顯得過於類似解謎。物理學也是解謎，不過是由自然造成的謎，而非由人腦所創造的謎題。（瑪麗亞‧格佩特—梅耶）

When one considers all these questions as a whole——the problems of nuclear structure and nuclear forces, as well as the problems of elementary particles —— a verse by Rilke still seems to fairly describe the situation. In the early days of quantum mechanics my late teacher, Wilhelm Lenz, brought this verse to my attention. In it Rilke speaks of his feelings at the turn of the century in terms of a large book in which a page is slowly being turned over, he concludes:

Man fühlt den Glanz von einer neuen Seite,

auf der noch alles werden kann.

Die stillen Kräfte prüfen ihre Breite

und sehn einander dunkel an. (J. Hans D. Jensen)

當我們把所有這些問題作為整體來考慮——原子核結構和核力問題，以及基本粒子問題——里爾克的一首詩似乎仍然適合描述這種情形。在量子力學的發展初期，我已故的老師，威廉・冷次，給我看了這首詩。在詩中，里爾克以一本大書為喻，描述身處世紀之交的感受，書的一頁正在徐徐掀開。他如此作結：

你感到新一頁的光輝，

上面依舊會萬事皆備。

無聲的力量權衡自己

目光深沉地默然相對。（約翰內斯・延森）

My research path is like a hiking tour through a new country, with ever new and interesting vistas, on which one could frequently overlook a portion of the path to be travelled, but on which one never did know just where the journey was really headed. For decades, I never even remotely thought that my path would also include technological successes. (Karl Ziegler)

1961–1970 革新與抗爭

　　我的研究之路猶如穿越一片陌生區域遠足。新奇誘人的風景在望，旅行者經常會忽略了某段行經的路徑，而渾然不知旅程的真正走向。幾十年來，我絲毫未想到，自己的人生道路上也會包括技術上的成功。（卡爾·齊格勒）

　　Macromolecular chemistry is a relatively young science. (Giulio Natta)

　　高分子化學是一門相對年輕的科學。（居里奧·納塔）

　　I can explain my body and my brain, but there's something more. I can't explain my own existence —— what makes me a unique human being. (John Carew Eccles)

　　我能夠解釋我的身體和頭腦，然而這不是全部。我無法解釋自己的存在 —— 是什麼使我成為一個獨特的人。（約翰·卡魯·埃克爾斯）

　　If you ask me: "What would I do if I were to begin my life's work now?" I would reply: "I would start where I have left off." I do hope that some of you young students accept this great challenge of trying to understand man scientifically, and that you devote yourselves with passion and joy to your chosen work, as Alfred Nobel would so much have desired. (John Carew Eccles)

　　你們如果問我：假如現在要開始此生的工作，我會做什麼？我將回答：「我會從我未完成的地方開始。」衷心希望你們之中的一些年輕學生能接受科學地理解人類這一項巨大挑戰，並且懷著熱情和歡樂投身於所選擇的工作，就像阿佛烈·諾貝爾會殷切期待的一樣。（約翰·卡魯·埃克爾斯）

　　The zoologist is delighted by the differences between animals, whereas the physiologist would like all animals to work in fundamentally the same way. (Alan Lloyd Hodgkin)

動物學家由於動物之間的差異而高興,生理學家則希望所有的動物都以根本上相同的方式運作。(艾倫·勞埃德·霍奇金)

I am very conscious that there is no scientific explanation for the fact that we are conscious. (Andrew Fielding Huxley)

我深深意識到,對於我們具備意識這一項事實,沒有科學的解釋。(安德魯·赫胥黎)

Don't ask me who's influenced me. A lion is made up of all the lambs he's digested, and I've been reading all my life. (Giorgos Seferis)

別問我是誰影響了我。獅子是由他消化的所有羔羊構成的,我一生都在閱讀。(喬治·塞菲里斯)

1964 年

I woke up early in the morning and sat in the park. It was a beautiful day and the flowers were blooming. (Charles Hard Townes)

清晨我早早醒來,坐在公園裡。那是個美好的日子,鮮花盛開。[54](查爾斯·湯斯)

In many cases, people who win a Nobel prize, their work slows down after that because of the distractions. Yes, fame is rewarding, but it's a pity if it keeps you from doing the work you are good at. (Charles Hard Townes)

在很多情況下,得到諾貝爾獎的人由於受到外界干擾而使工作隨之

---

[54] 1951 年的那天,湯斯坐在公園長椅上,想出了後來引至雷射的理論。

1961-1970 革新與抗爭

放慢下來。沒錯,名聲是獎勵;然而倘若它阻礙你做擅長的工作,這就令人遺憾了。(查爾斯・湯斯)

As a student, I was interested in a variety of things: natural history and biology, swimming, newspaper editing, football band —— to name a few. My interest in physics won over eventually. I was fascinated by physics since my first course in the subject because of its beautifully logical structure. (Charles Hard Townes)

學生時代,我對各式各樣的事情都感興趣:自然史和生物、游泳、報紙編輯、足球隊 —— 只是稍加列舉。對物理學的興趣最終壓倒了一切。由於物理學優美的邏輯結構,從第一堂課我就被這個科目迷住了。(查爾斯・湯斯)

The pledge of success, I believe, was in the fruitful cooperation between young scientists and the main staff. The young researchers enjoyed everyone's confidence; it was equal respect both for very young investigators and our young professors. That, perhaps, was the main approach. (Nicolay Gennadi-yevich Basov)

我相信,成功的保證,在於年輕科學家和主要工作人員之間富有成效的合作。年輕研究人員享有每個人的信任,對於非常年輕的研究者和我們的年輕教授都應給予一樣的尊重。這大概是主要的方法。(尼古拉・巴索夫)

It is very important to have a good contact because you know that the science is so complicated and every scientist has a different approach to the same problem, and when you interact, you choose the best solution. (Aleksandr Mikhailovich Prokhorov)

1964 年

保持良好的連結是非常重要的。因為你知道,科學極其複雜,對於同樣的問題,每個科學家有不同的方法,你們互動時,就能選出最佳的解決方案。(亞歷山大・普羅霍羅夫)

There are two moments that are important. There's the moment when you know you can find out the answer and that's the period you are sleepless before you know what it is. When you've got it and know what it is, then you can rest easy. (Dorothy Crowfoot Hodgkin)

有兩個時刻是重要的。在某一時刻,你知道自己能夠找到答案,在知道它是什麼之前,你會徹夜難眠;當你得到了答案,知道它是什麼的時候,這時你便能夠安然入睡。(桃樂絲・霍奇金)

I was captured for life by chemistry and by crystals. (Dorothy Crowfoot Hodgkin)

我一生都被化學、被晶體迷住了。(桃樂絲・霍奇金)

I would not be among you to-night being awarded the 1964 Nobel Prize in Physiology or Medicine but for the mentors, colleagues and students who have guided and aided me throughout my scientific life. I wish I could name them all and tell you their contributions. More, however, than anyone else it was the late Rudolf Schoenheimer, a brilliant scholar and a man of infectious enthusiasm, who introduced me to the wonders of Biochemistry. Ever since, I have been happy to have chosen science as my career, and, to borrow a phrase of Jacques Barzun, have felt that "Science is, in the best and strictest sense, glorious entertainment". (Konrad Bloch)

要不是由於在我的科學生涯中指導和幫助過我的導師、同事和學生們,今晚我也不可能到此領受 1964 年諾貝爾生理學或醫學獎。但願可以

1961–1970 革新與抗爭

提到他們所有人的名字,對大家講述他們的貢獻。然而,尤其要說的是已故的魯道夫·舍恩海默,一位才華耀眼的學者和熱情洋溢的人,他引導我見識了生物化學的奇妙之處。從那時候起,我很高興地選擇了以科學為業,而且,借用雅克·巴爾贊的一句話,我始終覺得,「在最恰當、最準確的意義上,科學是輝煌的娛樂」。(康拉德·布洛赫)

The processes of life offer the most fascinating problems for a chemist. (Feodor Lynen)

對於化學家,生命過程提出了最令人著迷的問題。(費奧多爾·呂嫩)

Nature is always unpredictable, and the only way of tackling a biochemical problem is to do experiments. (Feodor Lynen)

大自然總是無法預知的,解決生物化學問題的唯一方法就是做實驗。(費奧多爾·呂嫩)

I am happy in my job, but I have never let it become an obsession. I have always taken the time to enjoy life. (Feodor Lynen)

我很喜歡我的工作,但我從未讓它變成一種痴迷。我總是花時間享受生活。(費奧多爾·呂嫩)

There is only one day left, always starting over: it is given to us at dawn and taken away from us at dusk. (Jean-Paul Sartre)

生命只剩下一天,總是重新開始:黎明時分它被賜給我們,在黃昏時分又被奪走。(尚一保羅·沙特)

A lost battle is a battle one thinks one has lost. (Jean-Paul Sartre)

失敗的戰鬥,指一個人認為自己已經失敗了的戰鬥。(尚一保羅·沙特)

1964 年

Life begins on the other side of despair. (Jean-Paul Sartre)

生活從絕望的另一面開始。（尚－保羅・沙特）

My thought is me: that is why I cannot stop thinking. I exist because I think I cannot keep from thinking. (Jean-Paul Sartre)

我的思想就是我：這就是我不能停止思考的原因。我之所以存在，是由於無法抑制思考。（尚－保羅・沙特）

It is not the same thing if I sign Jean-Paul Sartre or if I sign Jean-Paul Sartre, Nobel Prize winner. A writer must refuse to allow himself to be transformed into an institution, even if it takes place in the most honorable form. (Jean-Paul Sartre)

署名為尚－保羅・沙特，或者諾貝爾獎得主尚－保羅・沙特，這是不一樣的。作家必須拒絕讓自己被改造成一個機構，即便它採取了最榮耀的形式。[55]（尚－保羅・沙特）

If a man hasn't discovered something that he will die for, he isn't fit to live. (Martin Luther King Jr.)

人要是不曾發現值得自己為之而死的東西，他就不配活著。（馬丁・路德・金恩）

Nothing in the world is more dangerous than sincere ignorance and conscientious stupidity. (Martin Luther King Jr.)

世間危險之事，莫過於真誠的無知和認真的愚蠢。（馬丁・路德・金恩）

Injustice anywhere is a threat to justice everywhere. (Martin Luther King Jr.)

任何地方的不公正都是對所有地方公正的威脅。（馬丁・路德・金恩）

---

[55] 沙特宣告拒絕接受諾貝爾文學獎。

1961-1970 革新與抗爭

1965 年

When a theory is incompetent in part, it is a common procedure to rely on experiment for that part. (Sin-Itiro Tomonaga)

當一種理論部分地不適用時,通常的做法是依靠實驗來彌補該部分。(朝永振一郎)

The pressure for conformity is enormous. I have experienced it in editors' rejection of submitted papers, based on venomous criticism of anonymous referees. The replacement of impartial reviewing by censorship will be the death of science. (Julian Schwinger)

從眾的壓力是巨大的。在編輯們基於匿名審稿專家的惡評而退稿時,我體驗過這種情況。以審查制度取代公正評論將是科學的死亡。(朱利安‧施溫格)

The test of all knowledge is experiment. Experiment is the sole judge of scientific "truth." (Richard P. Feynman)

對一切知識的檢驗是實驗。實驗是科學「真理」的唯一評判者。(理查‧費曼)

It doesn't matter how beautiful your theory is, it doesn't matter how smart you are. If it doesn't agree with experiment, it's wrong. (Richard Feynman)

不管你的理論有多漂亮,不管你有多聰明。如果它與實驗不一致,它就是錯的。(理查‧費曼)

If you thought that science was certain —— well that is just an error on your part. (Richard P. Feynman)

1965 年

假如你以為科學是確定無疑的,這不過是你的誤解。(理查‧費曼)

We are trying to prove ourselves wrong as quickly as possible, because only in that way can we find progress. (Richard Feynman)

我們力求盡快證明自己是錯的,因為只有這樣我們才能獲得進展。(理查‧費曼)

Observation, reason, and experiment make up what we call the scientific method. (Richard P. Feynman)

觀察、推理和實驗構成了我們所說的科學方法。(理查‧費曼)

Science is a way to teach how something gets to be known, what is not known, to what extent things are known (for nothing is known absolutely), how to handle doubt and uncertainty, what the rules of evidence are, how to think about things so that judgments can be made, how to distinguish truth from fraud, and from show. (Richard P. Feynman)

科學是一種教導方式,它告訴人們,事物怎樣為人所知,什麼是未知的,對事物已知到什麼程度(因為沒有完全已知的事物),如何對待懷疑和不確定性,證據的規則是什麼,如何思考事物而得以做出判斷,如何去偽存真。(理查‧費曼)

But the real glory of science is that we can find a way of thinking such that the law is evident. (Richard P. Feynman)

然而科學真正的榮耀在於我們可以找到一種使定律變得明確的思考方式。(理查‧費曼)

If there is something very slightly wrong in our definition of the theories, then the full mathematical rigor may convert these errors into ridiculous conclusions. (Richard P. Feynman)

如果我們對這些理論的定義有微乎其微的差錯，充分的數學嚴謹性就可能把這些錯誤轉化為荒謬的結論。（理查・費曼）

We are at the very beginning of time for the human race. It is not unreasonable that we grapple with problems. But there are tens of thousands of years in the future. Our responsibility is to do what we can, learn what we can, improve the solutions, and pass them on. (Richard Feynman)

我們正處於人類時代的起點。我們致力於迎戰問題不無道理。但未來之漫長難以計數。我們的責任就是盡力而為，盡力而學，改進解決方法，並將它們傳遞下去。（理查・費曼）

Nature uses only the longest threads to weave her patterns, so that each small piece of her fabric reveals the organization of the entire tapestry. (Richard P. Feynman)

大自然只用最長的線編織圖案，於是每一小片織物都顯示了整幅織錦的組織。（理查・費曼）

You can know the name of that bird in all the languages of the world, but when you're finished, you'll know absolutely nothing whatever about the bird. You'll only know about humans in different places, and what they call the bird. So let's look at the bird and see what it's doing —— that's what counts. (I learned very early the difference between knowing the name of something and knowing something.) (Richard P. Feynman)

你可以知道這隻鳥在世界上所有語言中的名稱，但是當你知道以後，關於這隻鳥本身，你還是一無所知。你只會知道不同地方的人怎麼稱呼牠。所以，讓我們觀察這隻鳥，看看牠在做什麼—— 這才是重要

1965 年

的。（我很早就懂得了知道事物名稱和了解事物之間的差別。）（理查・費曼）

We have a habit in writing articles published in scientific journals to make the work as finished as possible, to cover up all the tracks, to not worry about the blind alleys or describe how you had the wrong idea first, and so on. So there isn't any place to publish, in a dignified manner, what you actually did in order to get to do the work. (Richard P. Feynman)

在撰寫發表於科學期刊的文章時，我們習慣盡可能使工作完善，掩蓋所有痕跡，略過死胡同，也不描述自己起初如何想法錯誤等等。於是，你為此項目所進行的實際工作，沒有任何場合得以莊重地公布。（理查・費曼）

If I could explain it to the average person, it wouldn't have been worth the Nobel Prize. (Richard P. Feynman)

假如我能對一般人解釋清楚得諾貝爾獎這件事，我就配不上它了。（理查・費曼）

I'm smart enough to know that I'm dumb. (Richard P. Feynman)

我聰明到足以知道自己很笨。（理查・費曼）

I believe that a scientist looking at nonscientific problems is just as dumb as the next guy. (Richard P. Feynman)

我相信，一個研究非科學問題的科學家跟其他人同樣愚蠢。（理查・費曼）

The structure known, but not yet accessible by synthesis, is to the chemist what the unclimbed mountain, the uncharted sea, the untilled field, the unreached planet, are to other men. The achievement of the objective in itself cannot but thrill all chemists, who even before they know the details of the journey can apprehend from their own experience the joys and elations, the disappointments and false hopes, the obstacles overcome, the frustrations subdued, which they experienced who traversed a road to the goal. The unique challenge which chemical synthesis provides for the creative imagination and the skilled hand ensures that it will endure as long as men write books, paint pictures, and fashion things which are beautiful, or practical, or both. (Robert Burns Woodward)

這種已知但還不能由合成取得的結構對於化學家而言，一如未攀登的山、未探明的海、未開墾的土地、未抵達的星球之於其他人。實現目標本身必然使所有化學家激動非常。甚至在了解征途的細節之前，他們就可以出於自身經驗領會到快樂和歡欣、失望和誤認的希望、克服的障礙、戰勝的挫折，那都是他們為了到達目的地而曾經歷過的。化學合成為創造性想像和靈巧的手所提供的獨特挑戰，確保它將持續不斷，只要人們仍著書、繪畫，製作美麗的、實用的，或兼而有之的物品。（勞勃・伯恩斯・伍華德）

Organic chemistry has literally placed a new nature beside the old. And not only for the delectation and information of its devotees; the whole face and manner of society has been altered by its products. We are clothed, ornamented and protected by forms of matter foreign to Nature; we travel and are propelled, in, on and by them. Their conquest of our powerful insect enemies, their capacity to modify the soil and control its microscopic flora, their ability to purify and protect our water, have increased the habitable surface of the

1965 年

earth and multiplied our food supply; and the dramatic advances in synthetic medicinal chemistry comfort and maintain us, and create unparalleled social opportunities (and problems). (Robert Burns Woodward)

在原有的自然基礎上，有機化學的確造就了新的自然。它不僅為研究者帶來喜悅和資訊，整個社會的面貌和執行都被它的產物所改變了。我們穿著它們，以不同於大自然的物質形態，我們遮蔽、裝飾和保護自己；我們搭乘它們，藉助它們的推進而旅行。它們征服了我們強大的昆蟲對手，它們改變土壤和控制其微生物群的能力、淨化和保護水的能力，擴大了地球的宜居表面，使我們的食物供應倍增；合成藥物化學的巨大進步帶給我們慰藉和維護，並創造了無與倫比的社會機會（以及問題）。（勞勃・伯恩斯・伍華德）

If I search for my personal achievement, it may be that I have led these men and women —— and perhaps in some measure all organic chemists —— to the higher ground of a greater appreciation of the power, and above all of the beauty of their science. (Robert Burns Woodward)

如果我尋找自己的個人成就，可能是我帶領這些男女 —— 或許某種程度上所有的有機化學家 —— 在更高的層次上對有機化學的力量，尤其是它的美獲得了更大的領會。（勞勃・伯恩斯・伍華德）

I have always been very fond of mathematics —— for one short period, I even toyed with the possibility of abandoning chemistry in its favour. I enjoyed immensely both its conceptual and formal beauties, and the precision and elegance of its relationships and transformations. Why then did I not succumb to its charms? … because by and large, mathematics lacks the sensuous elements which play so large a role in my attraction to chemistry. I love crystals, the beauty of their forms and formation; liquids, dormant, distilling, sloshing! The fumes, the odors —— good or bad, the rainbow of colors; the gleaming vessels of every size, shape and purpose. Much as I might think about chemistry, it would not exist for me without these physical, visual, tangible, sensuous things. (Robert Burns Woodward)

我一直都很喜歡數學 —— 有一陣子,我甚至多少想到為之放棄化學的可能。我極其欣賞它的概念與形式之美,以及它的關係與變換的精確和優雅。那麼,我為什麼沒有對它的魅力折腰呢?……因為整體而言,數學缺乏感官元素,它們在化學對我的吸引中發揮了極大的作用。我喜愛晶體,它們的形態和形成的美;液體,靜置,蒸餾,晃動!煙霧,氣味——或好或壞,顏色的彩虹;所有大大小小、形狀不同、用途各異的閃亮的器皿。儘管我可能心繫化學,但若沒有這些實實在在、看得見摸得著、令人愉悅的東西,化學對我來說就不會存在了。(勞勃・伯恩斯・伍華德)

It is well to remember that most arguments in favor of not trying an experiment are too flimsily based. (Robert Burns Woodward)

應該記住,大多數贊同不嘗試實驗的論點都很難站得住腳。(勞勃・伯恩斯・伍華德)

It is a very valuable asset to a chemist to be able to formulate his ideas, describe his experiments, and express his conclusions in clear, forceful English. Further, since thought necessarily involves the use of words, thinking is more powerful, and its conclusions are more valid, in the degree to which the thinker has a command of language. (Robert Burns Woodward)

能夠用清晰、有力的英語闡明自己的思想,描述自己的實驗,表達

> 1965 年

自己的結論,對化學家來說是非常寶貴的財富。而且,由於思考必然牽涉詞語的運用,思考者對語言的掌握程度越高,思考就越有力,結論就越有效。(勞勃‧伯恩斯‧伍華德)

One of the deepest functions of a living organisms is to look ahead... to produce future. (François Jacob)

生物最深層的功能之一就是展望未來……產生未來。(方斯華‧賈克柏)

For me, this world of questions and the provisional, this chase after an answer that was always put off to the next day, all that was euphoric. I lived in the future. (François Jacob)

對我來說,這個充滿疑問和臨時性事物的世界,這種對於總是拖到隔天的答案的追尋,全然是令人愉悅的。我活在未來。(方斯華‧賈克柏)

I had turned my anxiety into my profession. (François Jacob)

我把我的焦慮變成了我的職業。(方斯華‧賈克柏)

For very many years, a group of eminent researchers have devoted their activity to the study of viral order. My own work simply prolongs a long chain of discoveries and ideas. (André Lwoff)

許多年來,一群傑出的研究人員致力於病毒種類的研究。我本人的工作不過是延伸了一長串的發現和想法。(安德列‧利沃夫)

The researcher's art is first of all to find himself a good boss. (André Lwoff)

研究者的藝術,首先在於發現自己是個好老闆。(安德列‧利沃夫)

Chance alone is the source of every innovation, of all creation in the bio-

1961-1970 革新與抗爭

sphere. Pure chance, absolutely free, but blind, is at the very root of the stupendous edifice of evolution. (Jacques Monod)

在生物圈中,唯有偶然是每一項創新、全部創造的來源。純粹的偶然,絕對自由而又盲目的,正是演化的宏偉大廈的根基。(賈克・莫諾)

In my opinion, the true pioneers are those artists who make manifest in their works the new content, the determining characteristics of life in our time. (Mikhail Aleksandrovich Sholokhov)

我認為,真正的先驅者,是那些在作品中呈現當代生活的新內容和決定性特徵的藝術家。(米哈伊爾・蕭洛霍夫)

When swept out of its normal channel, life scatters into innumerable streams. It is difficult to foresee which it will take in its treacherous and winding course. Where to-day it flows in shallows, like a rivulet over sandbanks, so shallow that the shoals are visible, to-morrow it will flow richly and fully. (Mikhail Aleksandrovich Sholokhov)

一旦衝破尋常的河道,人生便散為無數的水流。變化多端,蜿蜒曲折,難以設想後來的流程。今天它淌在淺灘上,像一條漫過沙洲的小溪,淺到看得見水底,明天它又會湧流得浩浩蕩蕩。(米哈伊爾・蕭洛霍夫)

1966 年

In the course of the development of our research, we frequently had the satisfaction of seeing our predictions confirmed by experiments, but several times the experimental results were contrary to our predictions, thus creating problems whose solution led to advance that were as interesting as they were unexpected. (Alfred Kastler)

在研究的發展過程中，我們常常滿意於見到預測由實驗證實；不過有時候實驗結果卻與我們的預測相反，從而產生問題，而這些問題的解決帶來了出乎意料且有趣的進展。（阿爾弗雷德・卡斯特勒）

While it is never safe to affirm that the future of Physical Science has no marvels in store even more astonishing than those of the past, it seems probable that most of the grand underlying principles have been firmly established and that further advances are to be sought chiefly in the rigorous application of these principles to all the phenomena which come under our notice. (Robert S. Mulliken)

儘管永遠無法肯定地說物理科學的未來不會出現比過去更令人震驚的奇蹟，但似乎絕大多數的重大根本原理已經牢固地確立；而要尋求進一步發展，主要在於將這些原理嚴格運用於我們注意到的所有現象。（羅伯特・S・馬利肯）

May I ask one question, please, of the distinguished geneticists present in this gathering? Alan Hodgkin, my son-in-law, is here, who received a Nobel Prize in 1963. Can it be possible that my own Prize has been inherited through him? Between ourselves, I do hope not! (Peyton Rous)

在座的傑出遺傳學家們，我可以請教一個問題嗎？艾倫・霍奇金，我的女婿，也在場，他於 1963 年獲得了諾貝爾獎。我的獎有沒有可能是經由他而來的？在我們之間，我可希望不是！（裴頓・勞斯）

Nature can refuse to speak but she cannot give a wrong answer. (Charles Brenton Huggins)

1961-1970 革新與抗爭

大自然能夠閉口不言，但她不能給出錯誤的回答。（查爾斯·布蘭頓·哈金斯）

But perhaps the truth newly discovered is itself only temporary and when new discoveries are made these truths too will be abandoned. But one truth remains for ever, and that is the search for truth. (Shmuel Yosef Agnon)

然而，也許新發現的真理本身只是暫時的，新的發現一旦得出，這些真理也會被拋棄。但有一個真理永遠存在，這就是對真理的追尋。（山謬·約瑟夫·阿格農）

People's talk and the stories they tell have been engraved on my heart, and some of them have flown into my pen. (Shmuel Yosef Agnon)

人們的言談和他們講的故事已牢記於我心上，有些還飛入了我的筆下。[56]（山謬·約瑟夫·阿格農）

Not every man remembers the name of the cow which supplied him with each drop of milk he has drunk. (Shmuel Yosef Agnon)

並非每個人都記得為他提供每一滴牛奶的乳牛的名字。（山謬·約瑟夫·阿格農）

Thanks to the choice of the Swedish Academy, I am now in the midst of that ceremony. To me a fairy tale seems to have become reality. (Nelly Sachs)

多虧瑞典皇家科學院的選擇，現在我來到這個典禮。對於我來說，童話似乎變成了現實。（內莉·薩克斯）

---

[56] 與蒲松齡的話對照：喜人妄談鬼怪，耳聞筆錄，彙編成書。阿格農，1966 年諾貝爾文學獎得主。

1967 年

No one any longer pays attention to —— if I may call it —— the spirit of physics, the idea of discovery, the idea of understanding. I think it's difficult to make clear to the non-physicist the beauty of how it fits together, of how you can build a world picture, and the beauty that the laws of physics are immutable. (Hans Albrecht Bethe)

不再有人注意到 —— 如果我可以稱之為 —— 物理學的精神、發現的概念、理解的概念。它如何組合起來、你如何構成世界圖景之美，以及物理學規律永恆之美，我想，是很難對非物理學者解釋清楚的。（漢斯·貝特）

You have given me the Prize I believe for a lifetime of quiet work in physics rather than for any spectacular single contribution. I am very proud and very happy with this distinction. (Hans Albrecht Bethe)

我相信，你們授予我這個獎項，是由於我潛心鑽研物理學的一生，而非任何驚人的單一貢獻。我為這項殊榮而非常自豪，非常快樂。（漢斯·貝特）

You should look at all the experimental information at hand, not only the most relevant, and be prepared to make conjectures if that helps. (Hans Albrecht Bethe)

你應該檢視手中的所有實驗資料，而不僅是最相關的，而且要準備好做出推測，只要有所幫助。（漢斯·貝特）

1961-1970 革新與抗爭

Sometimes a scream is better than a thesis. (Manfred Eigen)

有的時候，一聲尖叫勝過一篇論文。（曼弗雷德‧艾根）

If you know before that you can develop a certain thing then okay you go ahead. It's important. It's important for industry that they do purposeful research and so, but if you really want to find something new, it can only come out of fundamental research and it often comes out at much later time it turns out to be. (Manfred Eigen)

如果事先清楚自己能夠開發出某種東西，你當然可以進行。這很重要。就產業而言，進行有目的的研究很重要，不過如果你真的想發現新東西，它只能出自於基礎研究，其結果也常常於很久以後才能看出新意。（曼弗雷德‧艾根）

Everything which is new has to come out of fundamental research otherwise it's not new. (Manfred Eigen)

任何新的東西均須來自於基礎研究，否則就不是新的。（曼弗雷德‧艾根）

In theory, there is no difference between theory and practice. But, in practice, there is. (Manfred Eigen)

理論上，理論和實務沒有區別。然而，在實務中，是有所區別的。（曼弗雷德‧艾根）

A theory can be proved by experiment; but no path leads from experiment to the birth of a theory. (Manfred Eigen)

理論可以由實驗證明，可是從實驗無路通往理論的產生。（曼弗雷德‧艾根）

> 1967 年

If I may speak of myself in retrospect, I must remember my father, who as a pharmacist at Cambridge in the years before the first world war inspired me with a love of chemistry. He helped and encouraged me to make a laboratory in which as a school boy I repeated some of the experiments of the early teachers, and more than once nearly came to grief. It was there that I conceived a love for the smells of chemistry, and experienced the excitement of chemical analysis. The nostalgia of those smells has never left me, and memories of those dear departed days are kindled again whenever I enter a truly chemical laboratory. In retrospect also, I think of those who have helped to keep my little flame alight, and to pass it now to those who follow. (Ronald George Wreyford Norrish)

如果可以回顧往事，我必定想起父親。第一次世界大戰之前的一些年裡，他作為劍橋的一名藥劑師，激發了我對化學的熱愛。他幫助和鼓勵我設立了一個實驗室。從小學到中學，我重複早年老師的一些實驗，也不止一次幾乎惹出禍來。就是在那裡，我萌生了對化學氣味的喜愛，體會到化學分析的興奮。我對這些氣味的懷念從未消失。每當進入真正的化學實驗室，那些美好往日的記憶就再度浮現。回想起來，我也想到那些曾幫助我的火苗燃燒不熄的人，現在我把它傳遞給那些後繼者。（羅納德·喬治·雷伊福特·諾里什）

To solve a problem is to create new problems, new knowledge immediately reveals new areas of ignorance, and the need for new experiments. (George Porter)

解決問題意味著產生新問題，新知識會立即揭示新的未知領域，以及對新實驗的需求。（喬治·波特）

1961–1970 革新與抗爭

It is a joyous occasion for a scientist when the subject which interests him most is recognised by the highest honour that the world can bestow. When the honour is given to that scientist personally the happiness is sweet indeed. (George Porter)

對於科學家,當他最感興趣的課題受到世界所能給予的最高榮譽的認可,這就是個快樂的時刻。當這一項榮譽被授予科學家個人時,幸福的確是甜蜜的。(喬治・波特)

Tonight I should like to thank all those who have shared my work and to acknowledge the debt that I owe to my wife whose encouragement to put research before all other things has been a great strength to me. (George Porter)

今晚,我要感謝所有分擔了我工作的人,並表達我對妻子的感激之情,她鼓勵我專注於研究而心無旁騖,這對於我是偉大的力量。(喬治・波特)

By these findings I was convinced that psychophysics could be translated into neurology but psychophysics was as strange a subject to neurologists as was neurology to psychophysicists and so the implications of this work fell between two chairs. Only the physiologists were understanding listeners. (Ragnar Granit)

透過這些發現,我確信心理物理學可以轉化為神經學;然而對於神經學家,心理物理學是個陌生的課題,就像神經學對於心理物理學家一樣,所以這項工作的意義處於兩種觀點之間。只有生理學家才是理解自如的聽眾。(拉格納・格拉尼特)

Fifty-fifty. (Ragnar Granit)

各占一半吧。[57](拉格納・格拉尼特)

---

[57] 格拉尼特(1900—1991)生於芬蘭,1941 年入瑞典籍。1967 年獲諾貝爾生理學或醫學獎。他

1967 年

One works in one's laboratory —— one's chaotic laboratory —— with students and colleagues, doing what one most wants to do —— then all this happens! It is overwhelming. (Haldan Keffer Hartline)

一個人在他的實驗室裡工作 —— 一個亂糟糟的實驗室 —— 跟學生和同事一起，做他最想做的事 —— 然後這一切就發生了！實在是突如其來。（霍爾登・凱弗・哈特蘭）

I am no linguist and know only two Swedish phrases —— the first is but a single word, internationally understood, and used wherever glasses are raised; the second I will use now: Tack så mycket. (Haldan Keffer Hartline)

我不是語言學家，只會說兩句瑞典話 —— 第一句只是一個詞，全世界都懂得，在哪裡舉杯時都用到；第二句我這就要用了：Tack så mycket.[58]（霍爾登・凱弗・哈特蘭）

The Nobel Prize is an honor unique in the world in having found its way into the hearts and minds of simple people everywhere. It casts a light of peace and reason upon us all; and for that I am especially grateful. (George Wald)

諾貝爾獎已經深入全球各地一般人的情感和思想，成為世界上獨一無二的榮譽。它以和平與理性的光芒照耀我們所有人，我為此而特別感激。（喬治・沃爾德）

And most singular of all, throughout the ages there has been no interruption in the constant creation. (Miguel Angel Asturias)

最不尋常的是，世世代代，持續的創造從無中斷。（米格爾・安赫爾・阿斯圖里亞斯）

獲獎後，對於其成就的來源乃至榮譽的歸屬應為芬蘭或瑞典，不免出現異議。格拉尼特於是頗有外交家風度地做出了判斷。

[58]「非常感謝。」

1961-1970 革新與抗爭

However life treats you, as time goes by you always get the feeling you've lost life in the very living of it. (Miguel Angel Asturias)

無論生活待你怎樣，隨著時間的流逝，你總是覺得自己就在活著的同時失去了生命。（米格爾·安赫爾·阿斯圖里亞斯）

I'm very poor; but I've got my work, my wife and my hut, and I don't think I'm to be pitied. (Miguel Angel Asturias)

我很窮；然而我有我的工作，我的妻子和我的小屋，我不認為自己需要憐憫。（米格爾·安赫爾·阿斯圖里亞斯）

Our best novels do not seem to have been written but spoken. There is verbal dynamics in the poetry enclosed in the very word itself and that is revealed first as sound and afterwards as concept. (Miguel Angel Asturias)

我們最好的小說似乎不是寫下來的，而是說出來的。詞彙本身內在的詩性具有話語的張力，它首先展現為聲音，然後才是所思所想。（米格爾·安赫爾·阿斯圖里亞斯）

1968 年

One indicator of Ernest Lawrence's influence is the fact that I am the eighth member of his laboratory staff to receive the highest award that can come to a scientist —— the Nobel Prize. (Luis Walter Alvarez)

關於歐內斯特·勞倫斯[59]影響力的展現之一為這個事實：在他的實

---

[59] 歐內斯特·勞倫斯，1939 年諾貝爾物理學獎得主。

1968 年

驗室成員中，我是第 8 位獲得科學家的最高榮譽——諾貝爾獎的人。（路易斯·阿爾瓦雷茨）

I'm convinced that a controlled disrespect for authority is essential to a scientist. (Luis Walter Alvarez)

我確信，對權威有節制的不尊重，對於科學家是不可或缺的。（路易斯·阿爾瓦雷茨）

There is no democracy in physics. We can't say that some second-rate guy has as much right to opinion as Fermi. (Luis Walter Alvarez)

物理學中沒有民主。我們不能說某個二流傢伙的發言權跟費米的一樣。（路易斯·阿爾瓦雷茨）

I have received the greatest honor in my life —— and the greatest surprise. Never did I dream that the Nobel Prize could be awarded for the reciprocal relations. (Lars Onsager)

我獲得了一生最大的榮譽——也是最大的驚喜。我從沒想到倒易關係能被授予諾貝爾獎[60]。（拉斯·昂薩格）

Never build your muscle and then go hunt for a problem. Build your muscle while solving the problem. That is the key to good research. (Lars Onsager)

切勿在鍛鍊好能力之後才去尋找問題。在解決問題的同時鍛鍊能力。這是做好研究的關鍵。（拉斯·昂薩格）

In these times of highly competitive research, few scientists have the satisfaction of carrying through a research problem that takes 9 years. Without

---

[60] 倒易關係，後來稱為昂薩格倒易關係，是線性不可逆過程熱力學的主要理論之一。

1961–1970 革新與抗爭

minimizing the pleasure of receiving awards and prizes, I think it is true that the greatest satisfaction for a scientist comes from carrying a major piece of research to a successful conclusion. (Robert W. Holley)

在研究處於高度競爭的這些時候,很少有科學家經由耗時 9 年的研究問題獲得滿足。並非淡化獲得獎項和榮耀的快樂,我認為,科學家最大的滿足的確來自成功地完成一項重大研究。(羅伯特・W・霍利)

Everything that human beings or living animals do is done by protein molecules. And therefore the kind of proteins that one has and therefore the ability one has is determined by the genes that one has. (Har Gobind Khorana)

人類或動物所做的一切都是由蛋白質分子完成的。因而一個人具有的蛋白質種類和一個人具有的能力,取決於其具有的基因。(哈爾・葛賓・科拉納)

The best kind of science is basically a lot of fun to do, it's fun to discover things and it's important to discover things. (Marshall W. Nirenberg)

最好的一種科學,基本上是從事時非常有趣的。有所發現很有趣,有所發現很重要。(馬歇爾・沃倫・尼倫伯格)

The best science may be to work on something where you don't know if it's going to work, to work on an idea that may be a really interesting idea and may be a very exciting idea and may lead to a lot of extraordinarily interesting things but whether it's going to work or not is up in the air, you don't know if it's going to work and you risk ruining your life by working on something like that if it doesn't happen to work, if it doesn't pan out and that's not good for science, I think that people should be given the opportunity to fail without it ruining their lives and people should be encouraged to explore and maybe to

1968 年

do risky projects in the hopes that maybe some of these projects are going to work. I think that's the best science. (Marshall W. Nirenberg)

最好的科學，可以是研究某件你不清楚它會不會有用的事物；是研究一個想法，可能是個確實有趣的想法，可能是個非常令人激動的想法，可能引起許多極其有趣的事情，但它會不會有用尚屬疑問，你不清楚它會不會成功，你以研究這樣的事而冒著毀掉自己生活之險，也許它偏偏沒用，也許它不成功而無益於科學。我認為，應當給予人們失敗而不毀掉其生活的機會，應當鼓勵人們探索，或許進行有風險的項目，期待它們有的也許會成功。我認為，這就是最好的科學。（馬歇爾·沃倫·尼倫伯格）

The continuity of the work has been the important stability in my life and the important driving force in my life. (Marshall W. Nirenberg)

工作的連續性一直是我生命中重要的穩定性，也是我生命中重要的驅動力。（馬歇爾·沃倫·尼倫伯格）

Our language is primarily for expressing human goodness and beauty. (Yasunari Kawabata)

我們的語言主要用於表達人之善與美。（川端康成）

Time flows in the same way for all human beings; every human being flows through time in a different way. (Yasunari Kawabata)

時間對於所有人都以同樣的方式流動，每個人都以不同的方式流經時間。（川端康成）

And as a child I was filled with passionate admiration for acts of civic courage I had seen performed by an elderly military doctor, who was a friend of my family. (René Cassin)

1961–1970 革新與抗爭

在我年幼時,有一位老軍醫,是我們家的朋友。目睹他展現公民勇氣的所作所為,我心中充滿了熱烈的欽佩。(勒內・卡森)

1969 年

We are driven by the usual insatiable curiosity of the scientist, and our work is a delightful game. (Murray Gell-Mann)

我們被科學家一貫的無盡好奇心驅使,而我們的工作就是一場愉快的遊戲。(默里・蓋爾曼)

As a theoretical physicist, I feel at once proud and humble at the thought of the illustrious figures that have preceded me here to receive the greatest of all honors in science, the Nobel prize. (Murray Gell-Mann)

想到那些傑出的人物,他們先於我在這裡獲得了科學的最高榮譽——諾貝爾獎,作為一名理論物理學家,我同時感到自豪和謙卑。(默里・蓋爾曼)

An acorn of hypothesis can become a tree of knowledge. (Derek H. R. Barton)

假設的橡實可以長成知識之樹。(德里克・巴頓)

The great things are happening in natural science today, they are more related to biology or to particle physics than to the real chemistry. (Odd Hassel)

在當今的自然科學界,重大事件接連出現。它們更多地關係到生物學或粒子物理學,而非真正的化學。(奧德・哈塞爾)

1969 年

If you're too sloppy, then you never get reproducible results, and then you never can draw any conclusions; but if you are just a little sloppy, then when you see something startling, you nail it down. So I called it the "Principle of Limited Sloppiness". (Max Delbrück)

你如果過於馬虎，那麼就永遠得不到可重現的結果，然後永遠得不出任何結論；然而如果只是稍許馬虎，那麼一旦見到令人驚奇的現象時，你就一查到底。所以我稱之為「有限馬虎原則」。（馬克斯‧德爾布呂克）

The progress of science is tremendously disorderly, and the motivations that lead to this progress are tremendously varied, and the reasons why scientists go into science, the personal motivations, are tremendously varied. I have said⋯ that science is a haven for freaks, that people go into science because they are misfits, and that it is a sheltered place where they can spin their own yarn and have recognition, be tolerated and happy, and have approval for it. (Max Delbrück)

科學的進步極其無序，導致進步的動機極其多樣，科學家進入科學領域的原因和個人的動機也極其多元。我說過⋯⋯科學是怪人的避風港，人們進入科學領域是由於有所不適應，而這裡是個庇護所，他們可以在此做自己的事，為人所知，獲得接納和快樂，並因而得到認同。（馬克斯‧德爾布呂克）

The scientist has in common with the artist only this: that he can find no better retreat from the world than his work and no stronger link with the world than his work. (Max Delbrück)

科學家與藝術家唯一的共同之處在於：他找不到比工作更好的遁世之處，也找不到比工作與世界更堅實的連繫。（馬克斯‧德爾布呂克）

1961-1970 革新與抗爭

The particular thing about science is to combine the dreams of obtaining power with a retreat from the world. Other people want to obtain power by going out into the world, but the scientist really wants to obtain power by retreating from the world. (Max Delbrück)

科學的特別之處,在於將獲得權力的夢想與出世相結合。其他人想由入世獲得權力,然而科學家實際上想由出世獲得權力。(馬克斯‧德爾布呂克)

The books of the great scientists are gathering dust on the shelves of learned libraries. (Max Delbrück)

偉大科學家的著作正在學術圖書館的書架上累積灰塵。(馬克斯‧德爾布呂克)

I can only point out a curious fact. Year after year the Nobel Awards bring a moment of happiness not only to the recipients, not only to colleagues and friends of the recipients, but even to strangers. (Alfred D. Hershey)

我只能指出一個奇異的事實。年復一年,諾貝爾獎不僅為獲獎者、獲獎者的同事和朋友,甚至為素不相識的人們帶來了快樂的時光。(阿弗雷德‧赫希)

Significant advances in science often have a peculiar quality: they contradict obvious, commonsense opinions. (Salvador E. Luria)

科學的重大進步往往具有一種特質:它們與顯而易見的、常識性的見解互相矛盾。(薩爾瓦多‧盧瑞亞)

Everyone knows that in research there are no final answers, only insights that allow one to formulate new questions. (Salvador E. Luria)

1969 年

人人皆知，在研究中沒有終極的答案，只有容許人們提出新問題的深刻見解。（薩爾瓦多·盧瑞亞）

The world of science may be the only existing participatory democracy. (Salvador E. Luria)

科學世界可能是僅有的參與式民主。（薩爾瓦多·盧瑞亞）

Ever tried. Ever failed. No matter. Try again. Fail again. Fail better. (Samuel Beckett)

試過了。失敗了。沒關係。再試試。再失敗。失敗得好一點。（薩繆爾·貝克特）

Birth was the death of him. (Samuel Beckett)

出生即為其死亡。（薩繆爾·貝克特）

What sky! What light! Ah in spite of all it is a blessed thing to be alive in such weather, and out of hospital. (Samuel Beckett)

怎樣的天空！怎樣的光明！啊，無論如何，在這樣的天氣活著，並離開醫院，真是一大幸福。（薩繆爾·貝克特）

Deep in the human nature, there is an almost irresistible tendency to concentrate physical and mental energy on attempts at solving problems that seem to be unsolvable. Indeed, for some kinds of active people, only the seemingly unsolvable problems can arouse their interest. (Ragnar Frisch)

在人性深處，有一種幾乎無法抗拒的傾向，即將身體和精神的能量集中，嘗試解決似乎無法解決的問題。的確，對於某些積極的人而言，只有看似無法解決的問題才能引起他們的興趣。（朗納·弗里施）

1961–1970 革新與抗爭

It has been bee-keeping and queen-rearing in which I have been engaged for 57 years, with emphasis on a genetic and statistical study with a view to improving the quality of the bee. If somebody asked me if I find this occupation pleasant and entertaining, I am not sure I could honestly say yes. It is more in the nature of an obsession which I shall never be able to get rid of. (Ragnar Frisch)

我從事養蜂及培育蜂后已經 57 年，專注於基因和統計研究，以期提高蜜蜂的品質。如果問我，是否覺得做這件事愉快有趣，我不確定自己能誠實地說是。它更像是一種我所無法擺脫的天生執念。（朗納・弗里施）

A beam of light takes about two million years to reach from us to the Andromeda nebula. But my thought covers this distance in a few seconds. Perhaps some day some intermediate form of body and mind may permit us to say that we actually can travel faster than light. (Ragnar Frisch)

一束光從我們到達仙女座星雲，需要大約 200 萬年。然而我的想法幾秒鐘就能跨越這段距離。也許有一天，某種身體和心靈的中間形式可以讓我們說，我們實際上可以比光的速度還快。（朗納・弗里施）

As a boundary science, econometrics is younger than the adjacent regions, which fact likewise has advantages and disadvantages. As a disadvantage, the lack of an established doctrine, and also the lack of established textbooks, can be felt; as an advantage is the fresh enthusiasm, with which its students work. (Jan Tinbergen)

作為一門邊界科學，計量經濟學比鄰近領域年輕。這一項事實也有利有弊。作為不利之處，缺乏既定的學說，也缺乏既定的教科書，是感

受得到的；作為有利之處，是研究者們懷著新鮮的熱情工作。（揚·廷貝亨）

For some queer and deplorable reason most human beings are more impressed by words than by figures, to the great disadvantage of mankind. (Jan Tinbergen)

由於某種奇怪的、可嘆的原因，大多數人對語言而非數字的印象更深刻。這對人類極為不利。（揚·廷貝亨）

1970 年

I have always believed that astrophysics should be the extrapolation of laboratory physics, that we must begin from the present universe and work our way backward to progressively more remote and uncertain epochs. (Hannes Olof Gösta Alfvén)

我始終認為，天體物理學應該是實驗室物理學的推論，我們必須從現在的宇宙開始，然後上溯至越來越遙遠和不確定的時代。（漢尼斯·阿爾文）

We should remember that there was once a discipline called natural philosophy. Unfortunately, this discipline seems not to exist today. It has been renamed science, but science of today is in danger of losing much of the natural philosophy aspect. (Hannes Olof Gösta Alfvén)

我們應該記得，曾經有一門學科叫做自然哲學。遺憾的是，這一門學科看來如今不復存在。它已被重新命名為科學，然而如今的科學，處

於嚴重缺失自然哲學特質的危險之中。（漢尼斯・阿爾文）

If humanity is to survive, we must go back to 25 centuries ago, to learn from the wisdom of Confucius. (Hannes Olof Gösta Alfvén)

人類要生存下去，就必須回到25個世紀以前，去汲取孔子的智慧。（漢尼斯・阿爾文）

In science, we often have predecessors much further back in time than we think a priori. (Louis Eugène Félix Néel)

在科學領域，先行者的年代往往比我們所設想的早得多。（路易・奈爾）

The prestige of the Nobel Prize is such that one is suddenly promoted to a new status. (Luis F. Leloir)

諾貝爾獎的聲望是這樣的：一個人突然被提升到新的地位。（路易・弗德里科・萊洛伊爾）

I might paraphrase Churchill and say: never have I received so much for so little. (Luis F. Leloir)

我不妨套用邱吉爾的話說：我從未付出這麼少而得到這麼多。[61]（路易・弗德里科・萊洛伊爾）

After all the honours that have been bestowed on us today, there is something great and even more sustaining that we may look forward to, namely when the fun and festivities are over, that we may try and return to our work. (Bernard Katz)

今天獲得了一切榮譽之後，我們期盼某種非凡的、甚至更持久的

---

[61] 指榮獲諾貝爾化學獎。

東西，也就是說，快樂和歡慶過後，我們將盡力回歸工作。（伯納德・卡茨）

There are few things as rewarding for a scientist as having young students starting their research work and finding that they have made an original observation. (Ulf von Euler)

看著年輕學者開始研究工作，並見到他們做出原創的觀察，對於科學家來說，沒有什麼比這更欣慰了。（烏爾夫・馮・奧伊勒）

This award comes at a time when our young and many of our most influential people believe that basic research is irrelevant or is put to evil uses. The selection of chemical neurotransmission for a Nobel Prize this year, makes our work highly visible to the general public and gives us an opportunity to show how misinformed and mistaken they are. I think we can easily demonstrate that although our work is of a fundamental nature, it also gives us insight in explaining such illnesses as mental depression, Parkinson's disease, hypertension and drug abuse. It can also lead the way to the treatment of these terrible afflictions. (Julius Axelrod)

這個獎項頒發之際，年輕人和許多極具影響力的人誤以為基礎研究無關緊要，或被用於有害的用途。今年的諾貝爾獎授予化學神經傳遞，使我們的工作得到了大眾的廣泛關注，並提供我們機會展示他們是如何受到誤導並誤解的。我想，我們能夠輕易證明，儘管我們的工作具有基礎性質，它也使我們能夠深入解釋諸如精神抑鬱、帕金森氏症、高血壓和藥物濫用等疾病。它還能提供治療這些可怕痛苦的方法。（朱利葉斯・阿克塞爾羅德）

1961-1970 革新與抗爭

There is nothing as exhilarating as an experiment that turns out the way you hoped it would. (Julius Axelrod)

實驗結果不出所料,沒有什麼比這更令人興奮了。(朱利葉斯・阿克塞爾羅德)

The meaning of existence was to preserve untarnished, undisturbed and undistorted the image of eternity which each person is born with – as far as is possible. Like a silver moon in a calm, still pond. (Aleksandr Isayevich Solzhenitsyn)

存在的意義,在於盡量保持未被玷汙、不受擾亂、沒有失真的永恆的意象,它與生俱來,人人如此。就像平靜的池塘裡銀色的月亮。(亞歷山大・索忍尼辛)

Call no day happy 'til it is done; call no man happy til he is dead. (Aleksandr Isayevich Solzhenitsy)

不要說哪一天快樂,直到它結束;不要說哪個人快樂,直到他死亡。(亞歷山大・索忍尼辛)

A man should build a house with his own hands before he calls himself an engineer. (Aleksandr Isayevich Solzhenitsy)

在自稱工程師之前,一個人應該親手蓋房子。[62](亞歷山大・索忍尼辛)

Hastiness and superficiality are the psychic diseases of the twentieth century, and more than anywhere else this disease is reflected in the press. (Aleksandr Isayevich Solzhenitsy)

---

[62] 對照:子曰:先行,其言從之。(先做,然後再在口頭上說。)

匆忙和膚淺是 20 世紀的精神疾病。這種病比其他任何地方都更甚地展現於媒體界。（亞歷山大・索忍尼辛）

When the Nobel Peace Prize Committee designated me the recipient of the 1970 award for my contribution to the "green revolution," they were in effect, I believe, selecting an individual to symbolize the vital role of agriculture and food production in a world that is hungry, both for bread and for peace. (Norman E. Borlaug)

由於我對「綠色革命」的貢獻，諾貝爾和平獎委員會指定我為 1970 年的獲獎者。我認為，他們這樣做時，實際上是在選擇一個人來象徵農業和糧食生產在一個麵包與和平都匱乏的世界上發揮的重要作用。（諾曼・布勞格）

The dream of any scholar has, for me, come true by virtue of this award. The Nobel Prizes are justly famous in the hard sciences, in literature, and for peace. (Paul A. Samuelson)

對我來說，任何學者的夢想都憑藉這個獎項而實現。諾貝爾獎在硬科學、文學與和平領域實至名歸。（保羅・薩繆森）

Funeral by funeral, theory advances. (Paul A. Samuelson)

葬禮接著葬禮，理論不斷發展。（保羅・薩繆森）

Economics is a choice between alternatives all the time. Those are the trade-offs. (Paul A. Samuelson)

經濟學即一直在選項之間進行的選擇。這就是權衡取捨。（保羅・薩繆森）

1961-1970 革新與抗爭

"There are no easy pickings." That would be a more accurate, less dramatic statement than "There's no such thing as a free lunch." (Paul A. Samuelson)

「沒有簡單的選擇。」這是一個比「沒有免費的午餐」更準確、更平實的說法。（保羅・薩繆森）

I think that it's more important for an economist to be wise and sophisticated in scientific method than it is for a physicist because with controlled laboratory experiments possible, they practically guide you; you couldn't go astray. Whereas in economics, by dogma and misunderstanding, you can go very sadly astray. (Paul A. Samuelson)

我認為，科學方法上的明智和成熟，對於經濟學家比對於物理學家更重要，因為在可受控的實驗室實驗中，科學方法實際指引你，你不會走錯路。然而在經濟學中，由於教條和誤解，你可能非常悲哀地誤入歧途。（保羅・薩繆森）

Economics is not an exact science. It's a combination of an art and elements of science. And that's almost the first and last lesson to be learned about economics: that in my judgment, we are not converging toward exactitude, but we're improving our data bases and our ways of reasoning about them. (Paul A. Samuelson)

經濟學不是一門精確的科學。它是藝術和科學元素的結合。這幾乎是經濟學最初的也是最後的經驗之談：在我看來，我們不是在日趨精確，而是在改進資料庫和關於它們的推論方法。（保羅・薩繆森）

Economics has never been a science —— and it is even less now than a few years ago. (Paul A. Samuelson)

1970 年

經濟學從來就不是一門科學 —— 甚至比幾年前還不是。（保羅·薩繆森）

I can't think of a president who has been overburdened by a knowledge of economics. (Paul A. Samuelson)

我想不出一位經濟知識過多的總統。（保羅·薩繆森）

What we know about the global financial crisis is that we don't know very much. (Paul A. Samuelson)

關於全球金融危機，我們所知道的是，我們所知不多。（保羅·薩繆森）

In this age of specialization, I sometimes think of myself as the last "generalist" in economics, with interests that range from mathematical economics down to current financial journalism. My real interests are research and teaching. (Paul A. Samuelson)

在這個專業化的時代，我有時認為自己是最後的經濟學「通才」，從數理經濟學直到當下的金融新聞都感興趣。我真正的興趣在於研究和教學。（保羅·薩繆森）

Investing should be dull. It shouldn't be exciting. (Paul A. Samuelson)

投資應該是枯燥乏味的。不應該是令人興奮的。（保羅·薩繆森）

Investing should be more like watching paint dry or watching grass grow. If you want excitement, take $800 and go to Las Vegas. (Paul A. Samuelson)

投資應該更像是看著油漆乾或看著草生長。想找刺激的話，你就帶著 800 美元去拉斯維加斯吧。（保羅·薩繆森）

It is not easy to get rich in Las Vegas, at Churchill Downs, or at the local Merrill Lynch office. (Paul A. Samuelson)

想在拉斯維加斯、邱吉爾唐斯或本地的美林營業部[63]發財，談何容易。（保羅·薩繆森）

My belief is that nothing that can be expressed by mathematics cannot be expressed by careful use of literary words.

我的信念是，能夠以數學表達的東西，文學語言的精心運用都無法表達。（保羅·薩繆森）

Time is our ultimate scarcity. Isaac Newton can give us more electricity, but he can't give us more than 24 hours of the day of time. And so we're constantly having to sacrifice alternate activities to get the one that pleases us most. (Paul A. Samuelson)

時間是我們最缺乏的東西。艾薩克·牛頓能夠給我們更多的電力，但不能給我們每天超過24小時的時間。所以，為了選擇最喜歡的活動，我們不得不時常犧牲另外一些。（保羅·薩繆森）

---

[63] 拉斯維加斯、邱吉爾唐斯、美林，分別為美國著名的賭城、賽馬場和證券公司。

1971–1980
理性與良知的碰撞

1971 年

My life-long love of physics started suddenly at the age of 15. I could not wait until I got to the university... I remember how fascinated I was by Abbe's theory of the microscope and by Gabriel Lippmann's method of colour photography, which played such a great part in my work, 30 years later. (Dennis Gabor)

我對物理學的畢生熱愛忽然發生於 15 歲。我迫不及待地想上大學。……我記得，阿貝的顯微鏡理論和加布里埃爾·李普曼的彩色攝影術使我何等入迷，30年後，它們在我的工作中發揮了巨大作用。（丹尼斯·蓋博）

The most important and urgent problems of the technology of today are no longer the satisfactions of the primary needs or of archetypal wishes, but the reparation of the evils and damages by the technology of yesterday. (Dennis Gabor)

當今科技最重要、最迫切的問題，不再是滿足原始需求或典型願望，而是彌補昨日技術所造成弊病與損害。（丹尼斯·蓋博）

1971-1980 理性與良知的碰撞

Till now man has been up against Nature; from now on he will be up against his own nature. (Dennis Gabor)

迄今為止，人一直在與自然抗爭；從現在起，他將要對抗自己的本性。（丹尼斯·蓋博）

It is very difficult to find appropriate words to say "thank you" for an honour like the Nobel Prize. It is the supreme honour that a scientist can receive. Some of the giants in physics and chemistry have received this prize. (Gerhard Herzberg)

對於諾貝爾獎這樣的榮譽，很難找到合適的詞語表達感謝。這是科學家所能得到的最高榮譽。物理學和化學領域的一些巨人曾獲得這個獎項。（格哈德·赫茨貝格）

The citation for the 1971 Nobel Prize in Chemistry reads, "for contribution to the knowledge of electronic structures and geometry of molecules, especially free radicals," and therefore implies that the Prize has been awarded for a long series of studies extending practically over my whole scientific life. (Gerhard Herzberg)

1971年諾貝爾化學獎的獲獎詞是「對電子結構和分子幾何學知識的貢獻，特別是自由基」，意味著這個獎項授予了我整個科學生涯中的一系列長期研究。（格哈德·赫茨貝格）

It is indeed an honour to me and a pleasure to receive this award. I believe we all realize the honour and pleasure that a scientist receives with this award.

I hadn't realized however how important this award is to others. A flood of telegrams and letters arrived after the announcement mostly from the USA but many from around the globe. These were positive and friendly letters,

1971 年

hopeful for medical research. What I liked especially was that many young people wrote me. One, eleven years old wanted to know the procedure for winning such a prize.

Now I mention this response for a reason. I am fully convinced that medical research can offer one a happy and productive life. And if one has a little viking spirit he can explore the world and people as no one else can do. The whole medical research area is wide open for exploration and I believe soon for productive application.

My experience with this award is that it does make me happy, but more importantly it stimulates many others including the young. We need much more medical research and this helps. (W. Sutherland, Jr.)

這個獎項讓我備感榮幸，很高興能得到它。相信我們都能體會一名科學家獲得此獎的榮幸和快樂。

然而我未曾意識到這個獎項對於其他人有多麼重要。消息公布後，電報和信件如潮湧來。大都來自美國，也有許多來自全球各地。它們都是積極、友好的，對醫學研究滿懷期待。我特別喜歡的是許多年輕人來信。有一個 11 歲的少年想要了解贏得這樣一個獎項的過程。

我現在提到這種回響是有原因的。我完全相信醫學研究可以為人提供快樂的、有所創造的一生。一個人如果有幾分冒險精神，他就能以其他人做不到的方式探索世界。整個醫學研究領域充滿廣闊的探索空間，我相信有效的應用也將很快如此。

這個獎項給我的體會是，它確實使我快樂，但更重要的是，它激勵了許多人，包括年輕一代。我們需要醫學研究，多多益善。（厄爾·威爾伯·薩瑟蘭）

1971-1980 理性與良知的碰撞

Someday, somewhere —— anywhere, unfailingly, you'll find yourself, and that, and only that, can be the happiest or bitterest hour of your life. (Pablo Neruda)

總有一天,在某一地 —— 不拘哪裡,確切無疑,你會發現自己,而這時,只是這時,才能成為你一生最快樂或最痛苦的時刻。(巴勃羅‧聶魯達)

Today is today, and yesterday is gone. There is no doubt. (Pablo Neruda)

今天是今天,昨天已經過去。毫無疑義。(巴勃羅‧聶魯達)

I want to do with you what spring does with cherry trees. (Pablo Neruda)

我想和你一起,做春天和櫻桃樹一起做的事。(巴勃羅‧聶魯達)

In one kiss, you'll know all I haven't said. (Pablo Neruda)

在一個吻中,你會知曉我未曾說出的一切。(巴勃羅‧聶魯達)

I do not feel like making loud appeals, for it is easy to demand moderation, reason and modesty of others. But this plea comes from the bottom of my heart: May all those who possess the power to wage war have the mastery of reason to maintain peace. (Willy Brandt)

我不想大聲呼籲,因為要求別人節制、理智和謹慎是很容易的。然而這個請求發自內心:願一切擁有發動戰爭力量的人都能掌握維持和平的理智。(威利‧勃蘭特)

It often takes more courage to change one's opinion than to keep it. (Willy Brandt)

改變自己的觀點而非堅持它,往往需要更多的勇氣。(威利‧勃蘭特)

If I am selling to you, I speak your language. If I am buying, dann müssen sie Deutsch sprechen. (Willy Brandt)

如果我要賣東西給你,我會使用你的語言。如果我要買,那你就必須說德語。(威利・勃蘭特)

When, over fifty years ago, I first became interested in economics —— as a discipline that provided the key to social structure and social problems —— it never crossed my mind that one day I might be the honored recipient of a Nobel Memorial Prize. (Simon Kuznets)

50多年前,我第一次對經濟學產生了興趣 —— 作為一門學科,它提供了社會結構和社會問題的關鍵 —— 當時我完全沒想到,有一天自己會成為諾貝爾經濟學獎光榮的得主。(西蒙・庫茲涅茨)

With the variety of fields within economics, broadly conceived and the increasing specialization of scholarly world, the award of a Nobel Memorial Prize honors not only the individual scholar but, implicitly, also a special field or a distinctive method. (Simon Kuznets)

隨著經濟學公認的領域多樣性和學術界的日益專業化,諾貝爾經濟學獎不僅是表揚個別的學者,也隱含了對於特殊領域或獨特方法的表彰。(西蒙・庫茲涅茨)

1972年

One can build from ordinary stone a humble house or the finest chateau. Either is constructed to enclose a space, to keep out the rain and the cold. They

1971-1980 理性與良知的碰撞

differ in the ambition and resources of their builder and the art by which he has achieved his end. A theory, built of ordinary materials, also may serve many a humble function. But when we enter and regard the relations in the space of ideas, we see columns of remarkable height and arches of daring breadth. (Leon Cooper)

一個人可以用普通的石頭建造一所簡陋的房子，或者最宏偉的城堡。兩者都是構築了一個蔽雨禦寒的封閉空間。它們的不同，在於建造者的抱負與資源，及其達成目標的技藝。一種由普通材料構成的理論，也可以發揮許多不起眼的功用。然而，當我們進入並觀察思想空間中的關係時，我們會看見非凡高大的豐碑和驚人寬闊的拱門。（利昂・庫珀）

The development of the theory of superconductivity was truly a collaborative effort, involving not only John Bardeen, Leon Cooper and myself, but also a host of outstanding scientists working over a period of half a century. As my colleagues will discuss, the theory opened up the field for many exciting new developments, both scientific and technological, many of which no doubt lie in the future. I feel highly honored to have played a role in this work and I deeply appreciate the honor you have bestowed on me in awarding us the Nobel prize. (John Robert Schrieffer)

超導現象理論的發展確實是合作的努力。不僅包括約翰・巴丁、利昂・庫珀和我本人，還有半個世紀以來一大批傑出科學家的努力工作。如我的同事們所要討論的，這一項理論開闢了新領域，迎接許多令人激動的進展，有科學的也有技術的，其中許多無疑屬於未來。我非常榮幸能在這項工作中發揮作用；也非常感謝諸位授予我們諾貝爾獎。（約翰・施里弗）

1972 年

Many prominent scientists —— including Darwin, Einstein, and Planck —— have considered the concept of God very seriously. What are your thoughts on the concept of God and on the existence of God? (Christian B. Anfinsen)

許多傑出的科學家——包括達爾文、愛因斯坦和普朗克——都非常認真地思考過上帝的概念。你對上帝的概念和上帝的存在有何看法？（克里斯蒂安·B·安芬森）

This ceremony and the intellectual aura associated with the Nobel Prizes have grown from the wisdom of a practical chemist who wrote a remarkable will. (Stanford Moore)

源自於一位立下非凡遺囑的應用化學家的智慧，成就了諾貝爾獎盛典及其智力光環。（斯坦福·摩爾）

In dedicating his estate to the honoring of endeavors that benefit mankind, Alfred Nobel expressed a lifelong concern that is even more timely in 1972 than it was in his lifetime. (Stanford Moore)

阿佛烈·諾貝爾將自己的遺產用於表彰造福人類的事業，表達了他畢生的關懷，在 1972 年甚至比他在世之際更適時。（斯坦福·摩爾）

I had majored in chemistry at college and decided to continue on at Harvard as a graduate student in that subject. This proved to be a rather unfortunate experience because my first graduate year was undistinguished, to say the very least. I was almost ready to abandon a career in science when it was suggested to me that I might enjoy biochemistry much more than straight organic chemistry. The next year, I transferred to the Department of Biochemistry, then headed by the late Hans Clarke at the College of Physicians and Surgeons, Columbia University in New York. The department at Columbia was an eye-opener for me. Professor Clarke had succeeded in surrounding himself with a fascinating and active faculty and an almost equally stimulating group of graduate students. From both of these I learned a tremendous amount in a short time. (William H. Stein)

我在大學主修化學,並決定在哈佛繼續就讀該領域的研究所。事實證明這是一段很不成功的經歷,因為在研究所的第一年可以說所獲無多。我幾乎準備放棄科學生涯了,這時有人指點,與純粹的有機化學相比,我也許更喜歡生物化學。第二年,我轉到紐約哥倫比亞大學內科與外科學院生物化學系,已故的漢斯・克拉克時任主任。哥大這個系使我眼界大開。克拉克教授成功地聚集了一群令人著迷的活躍教師,以及一群幾乎同樣使人興奮的研究生。短時間內,我從這兩群人身上學到了不計其數的東西。(威廉・霍華德・斯坦)

If our scientific description of the world is concerned with nature, our creativity reflects the ability of our brain to give rise to a second nature. (Gerald M. Edelman)

如果我們對世界的科學描述與自然界有關,我們的創造性就反映了人腦產生第二天性的能力。(傑拉爾德・埃德爾曼)

In the course of receiving the highest honor of my life, I had two thoughts about human community, both particularly moving to one. The first is of the selfless and spontaneous jubilation of people who are not scientists but who are glad of such occasions as these and the circumstances they celebrate. I have thought of what they must think and I suppose that, surrounded by painful and difficult news of struggle and darkness, they say: "Well, we must be

1972年

doing something right". In this way, the Nobel Foundation has made itself a part of the world community, and a part which is justly appreciated.

The second thought is that I am fortunate to have had the opportunity to know directly so many people in the world community of scientists, including people who have occupied this table before me. It is said that most of the scientists who ever existed are alive today. This extension of the community of researchers and the compression of time in our age are probably the reasons for my good fortune.

Science is imagination in the service of the verifiable truth and that service is indeed communal. It cannot be rigidly planned. Rather, it requires freedom and courage and the plural contributions of many different kinds of people who must maintain their individuality while giving to the group.

There is no more satisfying or fortunate way to belong to a community. Being here on this splendid occasion has reminded me more strongly than any event in my experience of this privilege for which I am truly grateful. (Gerald M. Edelman)

在獲得這一項此生最高榮譽的過程中，我對人類社會產生了兩點想法，它們都令人特別感動。第一是人們無私的、自發的歡欣鼓舞，他們不是科學家，然而為如此這般的時刻和慶祝場面而高興。我設想他們的心情，在充斥著掙扎和黑暗、痛苦與艱難的消息之中，他們說：「好吧，我們必須做正確的事。」於是，諾貝爾基金會使自己成為國際社會的一部分，備受讚賞的一部分。

第二個想法是，我很幸運有機會直接認識世界科學家界如此眾多的成員，包括使用過這個講臺的人們。據說先前的科學家大都依然在世。研究

1971-1980 理性與良知的碰撞

人員群體的擴大,以及我們這個時代的時間壓縮,很可能是我幸運的原因。

科學是服務於可驗證真理的想像力,這種服務無疑是公共的。它不能被生硬地規劃。相反地,它需要自由和勇氣,以及大量的各式各樣的人的多方面貢獻,他們必須在為群體付出的同時保持個性。

對於躋身一個群體,沒有比這更令人滿意或幸運的方式了。在這個輝煌的時刻處於此地,空前強烈地提醒我這種殊榮,對此我衷心感激。(傑拉爾德·埃德爾曼)

When I got the Nobel Prize I said to myself that it had made me neither smarter nor more stupid. (Heinrich Böll)

獲得諾貝爾獎時,我對自己說,它並沒有使我更聰明,也沒有使我更愚蠢。(海因里希·伯爾)

If you want to do something… get up and actually do it! (Heinrich Böll)

你如果想做什麼事……就起身實行吧!(海因里希·伯爾)

One ought to go too far, in order to know how far one can go. (Heinrich Böll)

一個人必須走得夠遠,才知道自己能走多遠。(海因里希·伯爾)

Economics comes in at the end; that I am sure is where we belong. Our science colleagues find permanent truths; economists, who deal with the daily actions of men and the consequences of these actions, can rarely hope to find the same permanency. (John R. Hicks)

經濟學終於加入了[64],我確信我們屬於這裡。研究科學的同事發現永恆的真理;經濟學家研究的是人們的日常行為和這些行為的後果,我

---

[64] 指諾貝爾獎增設經濟學獎項。

們很難得有希望發現同樣的永恆。（約翰・希克斯）

I have been reluctant to pronounce on larger issues of practical economics since I am convinced that one should not pronounce unless one knows the facts; and to keep abreast of changing facts on a world, or even on a nation scale, is more than can be done by one whose main concern is with principles. A mere familiarity with statistics that have been prepared and digested by others is not sufficient. (John R. Hicks)

我一直不願針對更大的應用經濟學問題發表意見，因為我深信，不了解事實就不應該發言；要隨時了解世界上或國家內不斷變化的事實，對於主要研究原理的人是很難做到的。僅僅熟悉由別人準備和分析的統計資料是不夠的。（約翰・希克斯）

Any purchase is one for the future. If you buy a refrigerator, you are making a commitment to the future so that you have food to eat for the next ten years. (Kenneth J. Arrow)

任何購買都是著眼於未來。如果你買了一臺冰箱，你就是對未來做出承諾：在接下來的十年裡有東西吃。（肯尼斯・阿羅）

1973 年

The most precious, creative and innovative period in your life is the 10-year period around the age of 32. Plan your career path to use this precious 10-year period wisely and effectively to produce your greatest achievement in your life. (Leo Esaki)

1971-1980 理性與良知的碰撞

你一生中最寶貴、最富於創造力和創新性的時期，是 32 歲上下的 10 年期間。規劃你的事業之路，明智而有效地運用這寶貴的 10 年，創造你一生最大的成就。（江崎玲於奈）

True, each of us has in his own way contributed a little to advance man's knowledge but Physics also advances through the conscientious and imaginative work of many people. Every new idea is tested and tried in many different laboratories throughout the world until the pertinent facts are crystallized and understood. (Leo Esaki)

確實，對於人類知識的發展，我們幾個獲獎者以各自的方式稍有貢獻，然而物理學也透過許多人盡心竭力和富於想像力的工作獲得了進步。在世界各地許多不同的實驗室裡，每個新想法都經歷了檢測和試驗，直到相關事實得以具體化並獲得理解。（江崎玲於奈）

There are just two things you can do to win a Nobel prize —— have a good idea and pursue it effectively. (Ivar Giaever)

想要贏得諾貝爾獎，你只須做兩件事 —— 想出一個好主意，以及有效地落實它。（伊瓦爾・賈埃弗）

You need to be curious, competitive, creative, stubborn, self-confident, skeptical, patient and be lucky to win a Nobel. (Ivar Giaever)

你需要好奇、爭勝、創新、固執、自信、懷疑、耐心以及幸運，從而贏得諾貝爾獎。（伊瓦爾・賈埃弗）

I read a book called The Tao of Physics by Fritjof Capra that pointed out the parallels between quantum physics and eastern mysticism. I started to feel there was more to reality than conventional science allowed for and some interesting ideas that it hadn't got round to investigating. (Brian David Josephson)

1973 年

我讀了弗裏肖夫·卡普拉寫的一本書，名為《物理學之道》。書中指出了量子物理學與東方神祕主義之間的相似之處。我開始覺得，現實中還有更多超越傳統科學所能理解的東西，還有一些有趣的想法還未被研究。（布萊恩·約瑟夫森）

Nature and the unexplored that remains hidden behind it and calls for veneration, has provided the chemist with an organ with over 100 different tones, on which he can compose and play music. (Ernst Otto Fischer)

大自然及其未被探索的部分，即藏而不露、需要敬重的部分，為化學家提供了一架音色極其豐富的風琴，任其用於作曲和演奏。（恩斯特·奧托·費雪）

It is an old English convention that experienced speakers always begin by saying "unaccustomed as I am to public speaking". In my case it is really true. (Geoffrey Wilkinson)

這是個久遠的英國慣例，有經驗的演講者總是以「我不習慣當眾演講」開場。就我而言，這完全是真的。（傑佛瑞·威爾金森）

These are problems whose solution is fully underway, and we may expect quite a few surprises. By this I do not mean that problems such as the perception of polarized light have been conclusively solved. On the contrary: A question answered usually raises new problems, and it would be presumptuous to assume that an end is ever achieved. (Karl von Frisch)

這是一些正在全面解決的問題，我們可以期待很多驚喜。然而這不等於說，對於偏振光的見解這一類問題已經徹底解決了。相反地，一個已解答的問題時常引發新的問題。若以為大功告成，這可謂自以為是。（卡爾·馮·弗里希）

1971–1980 理性與良知的碰撞

Nature has unlimited time in which to travel along tortuous paths to an unknown destination. The mind of man is too feeble to discern whence or whither the path runs and has to be content if it can discern only portions of the track, however small. (Karl von Frisch)

大自然具有無限的時間，沿著曲折的道路，前往未知的目的地。人的頭腦過於無力，難以釐清道路的來龍去脈。即便僅能釐清部分蹤跡，無論多小，都必須滿足。（卡爾·馮·弗里希）

If one is fortunate in finding capable students of whom many become permanent co-workers and friends, this is one of the most beautiful fruits of scientific work. (Karl von Frisch)

一個人如果幸運地發現了有才能的學生，其中許多人成為永久的同事和朋友，這是科學工作最美好的成果之一。（卡爾·馮·弗里希）

The bee's life is like a magic well: the more you draw from it, the more it fills with water. (Karl von Frisch)

蜜蜂的生活就像一口神奇的井：你從中汲取的越多，水就越充盈。（卡爾·馮·弗里希）

The ant is a collectively intelligent and individually stupid animal; man is the opposite. (Karl von Frisch)

螞蟻是一種集體智慧但個體愚笨的動物，人則相反。（卡爾·馮·弗里希）

It is a good morning exercise for a research scientist to discard a pet hypothesis every day before breakfast. It keeps him young. (Konrad Lorenz)

對於研究科學家來說，每天早餐前放棄一項心愛的假說是一種很好的晨間運動。這讓他保持年輕。（康拉德·洛倫茲）

Scientific truth is universal, because it is only discovered by the human brain and not made by it, as art is. (Konrad Lorenz)

科學真理是普遍存在的,因為它只能由人類的大腦發現,而非像藝術那樣由大腦創造。(康拉德·洛倫茲)

How thankful I should be to fate, if I could find but one path which, generations after me, might be trodden by fellow members of my species. And how infinitely grateful I should be, if, in my life's work, I could find one small "up-current" which might lift some other scientist to a point from which he could see a little further than I do. (Konrad Lorenz)

如果能找得到哪怕僅是一條路,可供後代的人類成員世代行走,我會何等感激命運啊。如果在此生的工作中,能找得到一小股「上升氣流」,托起其他科學家使之能比我看得稍遠一些,我會何等深為快慰啊。(康拉德·洛倫茲)

We are the highest achievement reached so far by the great constructors of evolution. We are their "latest" but certainly not their last word. The scientist must not regard anything as absolute, not even the laws of pure reason. He must remain aware of the great fact, discovered by Heraclitus, that nothing whatever really remains the same even for one moment, but that everything is perpetually changing. To regard man, the most ephemeral and rapidly evolving of all species, as the final and unsurpassable achievement of creation, especially at his present-day particularly dangerous and disagreeable stage of development, is certainly the most arrogant and dangerous of all untenable doctrines. If I thought of man as the final image of God, I should not know what to think of God. But when I consider that our ancestors, at a time fairly recent in relation to the earth's history, were perfectly ordinary apes, closely related to chimpanzees, I see a glimmer of hope. It does not require very great optimism to assume that from us human beings something better and higher may evolve. Far from seeing in man the irrevocable and unsurpassable image of God, I assert —— more modestly and, I believe, in greater awe of the creation and its infinite possibilities —— that the long-sought missing link between animals and the really humane being is ourselves! (Konrad Lorenz)

我們是偉大的演化力量迄今所獲得的最高成就。我們是它們「最新」但肯定不是最後的成果。科學家對任何事物都不能視為絕對，即便對純粹理性的法則都不能。他必須牢記赫拉克利特所發現的非凡事實，即沒有任何事物在任何一瞬間保持不變，而是一切都在永無休止地變化。人類是所有物種中最短暫、演化最迅速的。將其視為造物終極和不可超越的成就，尤其在其當今特別危險而可厭的發展階段，無疑是所有站不住腳的學說中最傲慢與危險的。如果把人設想為上帝的最終形象，我會不知道如何看待上帝。不過，想到我們的祖先，在與地球歷史相形之下頗為晚近的時候，就是與黑猩猩關係密切的普通類人猿，我看到了一線希望。我們人類可以演化出更好、更高的物種，這無需極度的樂觀。我不認為人類是上帝不可改變和不可超越的形象，我斷言 —— 更恰當地說，我認為，懷著對造物及其無限可能性的更大敬畏 —— 長期以來尋找的動物與真正人性之間缺失的環節，就是我們自己！（康拉德·洛倫茲）

As a boy, I had two small aquaria in our backyard in which I watched, each spring, the nest building and other fascinating behaviours of sticklebacks. (Nikolaas Tinbergen)

小時候，我在家裡後院有兩個小魚缸。每年春天，我都在其中觀察刺魚的築巢和其他有趣的行為。（尼古拉斯·廷貝亨）

1973 年

I was not much interested in school, and both at secondary school and at university, I only just scraped through, with as little effort as I judged possible without failing. (Nikolaas Tinbergen)

我對上學沒多大興趣，無論是中學或是大學都一樣。我只是勉強過關，盡可能少費力氣，但求及格。（尼古拉斯・廷貝亨）

Because he had nothing to hide, he did perhaps appear to have forfeited a little of his strength. But that is the irony of honesty. (Patrick White)

由於無可隱瞞，他確實似乎喪失了幾分力量。然而這對於誠實正直是反語[65]。（派屈克・懷特）

If you don't know where you are going, every road will get you nowhere. (Henry A. Kissinger)

你如果不知道自己要去哪裡，每條路都不會帶你到任何地方。（亨利・季辛吉）

Accept everything about yourself —— I mean everything. You are you and that is the beginning and the end —— no apologies, no regrets. (Henry A. Kissinger)

接受你自己的一切 —— 我說的是一切。你就是你，這是起點和終點 —— 沒有歉意，沒有遺憾。（亨利・季辛吉）

Moderation is a virtue only in those who are thought to have an alternative. (Henry A. Kissinger)

只有對於那些被認為擁有其他選擇的人而言，適度才是優點。（亨利・季辛吉）

---

[65] 反語，反話，正話反說。例如故意稱老實人為「傻子」。

1971-1980 理性與良知的碰撞

The nice thing about being a celebrity is that, if you bore people, they think it's their fault. (Henry A. Kissinger)

身為名人的好處在於,你如果令人生厭,他們會以為錯在自己。(亨利・季辛吉)

Power is the great aphrodisiac. (Henry A. Kissinger)

權力是最好的春藥。(亨利・季辛吉)

If he did not distort the truth, he would not be Mr. Kissinger. (Le Duc Tho)

他要是不歪曲事實,就不會是季辛格先生了。(黎德壽)

To my hosts on this festive occasion, I would like to say that as a small boy I used to hear fairy tales about beautiful far away lands, princesses and kings, splendid palaces on clear northern waters populated by white swans. Today one of these fairy tales came true; I am dining with the King and the Princesses in a golden hall, surrounded by the gracious ladies and gentlemen of their court. (Wassily Leontief)

在這個喜慶的場合,我想對主人說,小時候,我常聽童話故事,關於遙遠的美麗國度,那裡有公主和國王,清澈的北方水域上,華麗宮殿中住著白天鵝。今天,其中一個童話故事成真了。在金色的大廳裡,我跟國王和公主們一起用餐,周圍是宮廷中優雅的女士和先生們。(瓦西里・列昂季耶夫)

Among the many factors that have promoted economic change, I believe that technology or, rather, change in technology is the most prominent. (Wassily Leontief)

在推動經濟變革的諸多因素中，我認為技術，更確切說，技術變革，是最重要的。（瓦西里·列昂季耶夫）

So-called partial analysis cannot provide a sufficiently broad basis for fundamental understanding of the structure and operation of economic systems. (Wassily Leontief)

所謂的局部性分析，無法為根本理解經濟體系的結構和運作提供足夠廣泛的基礎。（瓦西里·列昂季耶夫）

1974 年

We must put our energies into solving the difficult problems, in many disciplines, which are involved in renewable sources —— on which both the developed and the developing countries must eventually depend. (Martin Ryle)

我們必須集中精力解決涉及可再生資源的諸多學科難題 —— 已開發國家和開發中國家最終都必須依靠可再生資源。（馬丁·賴爾）

We devise heart transplants, but do little for the 15 million who die annually of malnutrition and related diseases. Our cleverness has grown prodigiously —— but not our wisdom. (Martin Ryle)

我們發明了心臟移植，卻對每年因營養不良及相關疾病而死亡的1,500萬人無所作為。我們的聰明才智有了大幅成長 —— 可是智慧沒有。（馬丁·賴爾）

The world of man lies midway in scale between the inner space of atoms and particles, and the outer space of stars and galaxies. The exploration of

1971-1980 理性與良知的碰撞

both these regions stretches our imagination to its limits. (Antony Hewish)

原子和粒子的內層空間、恆星和星系的外層空間，人類的世界居於其間。對這兩個領域的探索將我們的想像力延展到極限。（安東尼・休伊什）

There is, I think, some special benefit for mankind in the realm of astrophysics. It is impossible to witness the interplay of galaxies without a sense of wonder, and looking back at Earth we see it in its true perspective, a planet of great beauty, an undivided sphere. Let us try and keep this image always in our view. (Antony Hewish)

我認為天體物理學領域能帶給人類一些特別的益處。目睹星系的相互影響，不可能不感到驚奇。回望地球，我們看到它真切的面目，一顆非凡美麗的行星，一個完整的球體。讓我們盡力將這幅美景永存心中。（安東尼・休伊什）

I believe scientists have a duty to share the excitement and pleasure of their work with the general public, and I enjoy the challenge of presenting difficult ideas in an understandable way. (Antony Hewish)

我相信科學家有義務與大眾分享他們工作的興奮和快樂，我也喜歡用簡單易懂的方式表達艱深思想的挑戰。（安東尼・休伊什）

Significant inventions are not mere accidents. The erroneous view that they are is widely held, and it is one that the scientific and technical community, unfortunately, has done little to dispel. Happenstance usually plays a part, to be sure, but there is much more to invention than the popular notion of a bolt out of the blue. Knowledge in depth and in breadth are virtual prerequisites. Unless the mind is thoroughly charge beforehand, the proverbial spark

1974 年

of genius, if it should manifest itself, probably will find nothing to ignite. (Paul J. Flory)

重大發明並非純粹意外。很多人錯誤地認定它們純屬意外,對於這種看法,遺憾的是,科學技術界沒有致力消除。的確,發明經常事出偶然;然而發揮作用的,遠遠不止於常人設想的晴天霹靂。 既深且廣的知識是本質上的先決條件。除非頭腦事先充足了電,否則眾所周知的天才火花,即便理當耀目一閃,恐怕也找不到任何東西點燃。(保羅‧弗洛里)

The Nobel Prizes have gained universal recognition as pre-eminent symbols of the importance and significance of intellectual achievement. They are much better known than the man who founded them. Yet, that wise but modest man, whose extraordinary vision and perception were obscured by a self-effacing manner, would not be offended, I believe, by the contrast between his own fame in the world of 1974 and that of his prizes. He founded them from the purest of motives, not as a means of memorializing himself. His will does not suggest, much less require, that the prizes bear his name; this was a decision of his executors, a well reasoned one to be sure. Alfred Nobel appears to have been motivated by the conviction that science and learning should be encouraged and more widely appreciated. (Paul J. Flory)

作為知識成就之重要性和意義的傑出象徵,諾貝爾獎已經獲得普遍認同。這個獎項比創立者更為人所知。創立者非凡的眼光和洞察力被謙遜的態度掩蓋。然而,我相信,這位睿智而謙遜的人,不會由於自己1974年[66]的世界名聲與其所創立獎項知名度的對比而不快。他創立這些獎項,是出於最純粹的動機,而非作為紀念他自己的方式。他的遺囑沒

---

[66] 弗洛里是這一年諾貝爾化學獎得主。

1971–1980 理性與良知的碰撞

有提示,更未要求獎項帶有他的名字;這是遺囑執行人的決定,當然是非常合理的決定。阿佛烈・諾貝爾顯然受到這般信念的激勵:科學和學識應該得到鼓勵和更廣泛的讚譽。(保羅・弗洛里)

Once Ptolemy and Plato, yesterday Newton, today Einstein, and tomorrow new faiths, new beliefs, and new dimensions. (Albert Claude)

曾經的托勒密和柏拉圖,昨天的牛頓,今天的愛因斯坦,明天的新信仰,新的信念,和新的維度。(阿爾伯特・克勞德)

No doubt, man will continue to weigh and to measure, watch himself grow, and his Universe around him and with him, according to the ever growing powers of his tools. For the resolving powers of our scientific instruments decide, at a given moment, of the size and the vision of our Universe, and of the image we then make of ourselves. (Albert Claude)

毫無疑問,依據人類的工具不斷增加的能力,人類將繼續計量,觀察自己以及周圍宇宙的成長。根據我們的科學儀器的解析能力,在特定時刻決定了我們宇宙的大小和視野,以及我們所構成的自我形象。(阿爾伯特・克勞德)

We have entered the cell, the Mansion of our birth, and started the inventory of our acquired wealth. (Albert Claude)

我們已經進入細胞,我們出生的宅第,並開始清點所獲得的財富。(阿爾伯特・克勞德)

Man, like other organisms, is so perfectly coordinated that he may easily forget, whether awake or asleep, that he is a colony of cells in action, and that it is the cells which achieve, through him, what he has the illusion of accomplishing himself. (Albert Claude)

1974 年

人，跟其他生物一樣，協調得如此完美，以至於可能容易忘記，無論醒著還是入睡，他都是一個活動的細胞群，正是這些細胞，透過他，成就了他實現自己的幻想。（阿爾伯特·克勞德）

When I went to the University, the medical school was the only place where one could hope to find the means to study life, its nature, its origins, and its ills. (Albert Claude)

我上大學的時候，想要找到方法研究生命，它的本質、起源，以及疾患，醫學院是唯一的處所。（阿爾伯特·克勞德）

I cannot look at a question and not try to find the answer, even if I don't know it. (Christian de Duve)

我無法看著問題而不尋求答案，即使我不知道答案。（克里斯蒂安·德·迪夫）

Once we stop learning and call ourselves learned, we become useless members of the scientific society. (Christian de Duve)

一旦停止學習，自詡博學，我們就淪為科學社會的無用成員了。（克里斯蒂安·德·迪夫）

Contrary to many of my fellow scientists, I was not initially attracted by a special field or problem. This turned out to be useful, because it left me free to allow whatever I discovered to dictate the next step of my research, without preconceived ideas. (Christian de Duve)

與許多科學家同行相反，我起初沒有被哪一個特別的領域或問題吸引。結果證明這是有益的，為自己留下自由，容許自己依據任何發現決定下一步研究，而無先入之見。（克里斯蒂安·德·迪夫）

1971-1980 理性與良知的碰撞

Whatever you have in mind, follow the facts. You may not discover what you were looking for. But what you discover may be more interesting than what you were looking for. (Christian de Duve)

不管你有什麼想法,遵循事實。你可能發現不了你在尋找的東西,但是你所發現的可能比所尋找的更有趣。(克里斯蒂安・德・迪夫)

Scientists are often described as persons who know a lot. This is not entirely wrong. To do good science, you must be trained in some discipline, like mathematics, physics, chemistry, or biology, sometimes in more than one. In addition, you must know what others have been doing in your field. But that is not enough. A "know-it-all" is no more a scientist than a collector of paintings is an artist. What counts is the generation of new knowledge or, better said, understanding. The true aim of science is to understand the world.

Not everyone, however, can be a Newton, Darwin, or Einstein. Most of us do not grapple with cosmic issues and have to be content with adding a little brick to the edifice. On a day-to-day basis, scientific research deals mostly with small problems. You are faced with some intriguing fact or observation that tickles your curiosity. Thinking about it, you let your imagination run, using all the available clues, all the bits of relevant knowledge you happen to have in store, trying to come up with some plausible explanation. This is the truly creative part of scientific activity, what it has in common with the arts. But it is only the first step. Then comes the hard job of confronting the hypothesis with facts. Does it fit with all observations? And, especially in the experimental sciences, how can you best test its validity? Not by trying to prove it right, incidentally, but by doing your best to prove it wrong —— and failing.

1974 年

This aspect of science is what makes it fun, like any other game of problem solving, like crosswords, chess, or conundrums of one sort or another. It has the same intellectual appeal, with the added benefit that it may tell you something about the world. What it tells, however, may become clear only after the fact.

This is another aspect of scientific research. Its results are unpredictable. Science explores the unknown and, therefore, cannot, by definition, foresee what it will discover, even less tell whether the discovery will be useful or profitable. This obvious fact is often overlooked by the politicians and administrators responsible for the funding of research. Because money is involved, they reason in terms of accountability and profitability. This is not only logically wrong; it amounts to ignoring the true value of science, namely its contribution to human culture. (Christian de Duve)

科學家經常被描述為知識淵博的人。這不無道理。要做好科學工作，你必須接受某種學科的訓練，比如數學、物理學、化學或生物學，有時不止一門。此外，你必須了解別人在你的領域的作為。但這還不夠。「萬事通」並不一定是科學家，正如繪畫收藏家不一定是藝術家一樣。重要的是新知識的生成，或者更準確地說，理解。科學的真正目的是理解世界。

然而，並不是每個人都能成為牛頓、達爾文或愛因斯坦。我們大多數人都不致力於宇宙問題，而只能滿足於為這座大廈新增一小塊磚。在日復一日的基礎上，科學研究多半處理小問題。你面對一些有趣的事實或現象，激起好奇心。你思索著，放縱想像力馳騁，運用著所有找得到的線索、所有偶然累積的零星相關知識，嘗試著得出一些似乎合理的解釋。這是科學活動真正創新的部分，是與藝術共同之處。然而這只是第

1971-1980 理性與良知的碰撞

一步。接著是以事實對照假設的艱苦工作。它符合所有的觀察結果嗎？而且，尤其在實驗科學中，你如何能夠最好地檢驗它的有效性？順便說一句，不是試圖證明它正確，而是由盡力證明它錯誤——然後失敗。

科學的這一面是使它有趣的地方，就像其他任何解題遊戲，如縱橫字謎、象棋或五花八門的難題。它具有同樣的知識吸引力，還有更多的益處，即可以告訴你關於世界的某種事情。不過，它所告知的，可能只在事實得到確認後才會變得清晰。

科學研究還有另一面。其結果是不可預知的。科學探索未知事物，因而，不言自明，無法預見它將發現什麼，更無法斷言其成果的用途或益處。這個顯而易見的事實，常常被負責研究經費的政治人物和行政人員所忽視。因為事關金錢，他們從責任和盈利的角度論證。這不僅在邏輯上是錯的，它相當於忽視科學的真正價值，也就是它對人類文化的貢獻。（克里斯蒂安・德・迪夫）

Although attracted by the humanities, I had chosen medicine as a career, seduced by the image of the "man in white" dispensing care and solace to the suffering. But science was lurking around the corner, in the form of an unpaid student assistantship in the laboratory of physiology. (Christian de Duve)

儘管受到人文科學吸引，我還是選擇了醫學作為畢生職業，憧憬於濟世救人的「白衣人」形象。然而科學潛藏在角落裡，以生理學實驗室無報酬助教的形式出現。（克里斯蒂安・德・迪夫）

What I was concerned with was life: what are the major features that are common to all living organisms that subtly define life. So I looked at the whole problem as a chemist, as a biochemist, and as a molecular biologist. (Christian de Duve)

1974 年

　　我所關心的是生命：所有生命有機體的主要特徵精細地定義了生命。所以我以一個化學家、一個生物化學家、一個分子生物學家的身分來看待整個問題。（克里斯蒂安・德・迪夫）

I have had the good fortune to live —— as an inside witness and, even, a modest participant —— at a time when our understanding of this wonder we call "life" has made its most revolutionary advances. (Christian de Duve)

　　我們對這個奇蹟（我們稱為「生命」）的了解獲得了極具革命性的進步。作為親身見證者，乃至於有限的參與者，我生活在這個時代，可謂三生有幸。（克里斯蒂安・德・迪夫）

The advantage of the analytical approach is that it is widely applicable, and it can provide a considerable amount of quantitative information even with a relatively poor resolving power. (Christian de Duve)

　　此分析方法的優點是廣泛適用，而且可以提供相當數量的定量信息，即使是相對較差的解決能力。（克里斯蒂安・德・迪夫）

For a scientist, it is a unique experience to live through a period in which his field of endeavour comes to bloom —— to be witness to those rare moments when the dawn of understanding finally descends upon what appeared to be confusion only a while ago —— to listen to the sound of darkness crumbling. (George E. Palade)

　　對於科學家，這是獨有的體驗，即親身經歷專攻的領域如花綻放的時期——當片刻之前尚呈混沌，而理解的黎明終於降臨之際，目睹那些罕見的時刻，聆聽黑暗崩潰的聲音。（喬治・埃米爾・帕拉德）

Cell Biology finally makes possible a century old dream: that of analysis of diseases, at the cellular level —— the first step towards their final control.

1971–1980 理性與良知的碰撞

We never truly touch or see these wonderful tiny devices that keep every cell and every being alive —— since they are far beyond what our senses can perceive unaided. But for us they are alive in our minds, close to our hearts, very much parts of the real world, just like the galaxies with their neutron stars and their pulsars are at the other end of the spectrum of dimensions of matter for our colleagues, the radio astronomers. (George E. Palade)

細胞生物學終於實現了百年來的夢想：在細胞層面分析疾病——這是最終控制疾病的第一步。我們從未真正接觸或看到這些保持每一個細胞和每一個生物生存的奇妙的微小裝置，因為它們遠非我們的感官所能獨力感知。不過對於我們而言，它們生存於我們的頭腦中，接近我們的內心，是現實世界的重要組成部分，正如對於我們的同事，無線電天文學家們，那些擁有中子星和脈衝星的星系處於物質維度範圍的另一端。（喬治·埃米爾·帕拉德）

Many men of science and poets have in their own manner, by various ways and means, and aided by others, sought unceasingly to create a more tolerable world for everyone. And this we should believe: that hope and volition can bring us closer to our ultimate goal: justice for all, injustice for no-one. (Eyvind Johnson)

許多科學家和詩人以各自的方式，經由各種方法和手段並在別人的幫助下，不斷地尋求為所有人創造一個更如意的世界。我們應該相信：希望和意志可以使我們更接近終極目標：人人享有正義，無一遭遇不公。（埃溫德·雍松）

A poet or prose narrator usually looks back on what he has achieved against a backdrop of the years that have passed, generally finding that some of these achievements are acceptable, while others are less so. (Eyvind Johnson)

　　每過幾年，詩人或散文作家往往回顧一下自己的收穫，通常會發現，有些成就可以接受，另一些則不盡如意。（埃溫德·雍松）

If you own two coppers, said Li-Ti on a journey,

buy one loaf of bread and one blossom.

The bread is there to fill you.

The blossom you buy is to tell you

that life is worth the living. (Harry Martinson)

如果你有兩個銅幣，李迪在途中說，

買一條麵包和一枝花。

麵包用來填飽你。

買的花用來告訴你

人生是值得的。（哈里·馬丁松）

Now we have fathomed what our space-ship is —— a tiny bubble in a glass of God. (Harry Martinson)

　　現在我們明白了我們的宇宙飛船是什麼 —— 上帝的玻璃杯中一個小小的氣泡。（哈里·馬丁松）

It is clear that it is not man who has created the universe —— whether you believe in God or in gods or deny any divine presence —— man cannot alter the laws that govern the universe without damaging it. (Seán MacBride)

　　很明顯，創造宇宙的不是人 —— 無論你相信上帝還是諸神，或者否認任何神靈的存在 —— 人類無法改變支配宇宙的法則而不破壞它。（肖恩·麥克布賴德）

1971–1980 理性與良知的碰撞

Had the Nobel Prize been established a thousand years ago, the first recipient of the Prize for Literature might well have been a Japanese woman. Also, had Japan taken part in the life of the international community several centuries earlier, Japanese recipients of the Physics, Chemistry, Biology and Economic Science Prizes might well have been numerous. At present, the Japanese recipients of Nobel Prizes, including myself, number only five. To me, it seems, this offers food for thought. (Eisaku Sato)

假如諾貝爾獎設立於一千年前,第一位文學獎得主或許是一位日本女性。而且,如果日本早幾個世紀參與國際社會生活,日本的物理、化學、生物和經濟科學獎的得主也許就為數眾多。目前,日本的諾貝爾獎得主,包括我本人,只有 5 位。在我看來,這值得深思。(佐藤榮作)

Japan is the only country in the world to have suffered the ravages of atomic bombing. (Eisaku Sato)

日本是世界上唯一遭受過原子彈轟炸毀壞的國家。(佐藤榮作)

We can widen our perspective. Everything can be studied. We are free to expand and perfect our knowledge about the world, only restricted by the number of scientists working and, of course, the degree of their diligence, brightness and their openness to fresh approaches. (Gunnar Myrdal)

我們可以拓寬自己的視野。一切都可以研究。我們自由地擴展和完善對世界的理解,只受限於從事研究的科學家的數量,當然,還有他們的勤奮程度、聰明和對新方法的開放態度。(貢納爾·默達爾)

In society, liberty for one may mean the suppression of liberty for others. (Gunnar Myrdal)

1974 年

在社會中，一個人所擁有的自由可能意味著對他人自由的壓制。（貢納爾‧默達爾）

One need not be a prophet to be aware of impending dangers. An accidental combination of experience and interest will often reveal events to one man under aspects which few yet see. (Friedrich August von Hayek)

人無須身為先知也能意識到迫近的危險。經驗與興趣的偶然結合，常會向一個人揭示一些鮮為人知之事的罕見面向。（弗里德利希‧海耶克）

It is always from a minority acting in ways different from what the majority would prescribe that the majority in the end learns to do better. (Friedrich August von Hayek)

總是少數人以異於多數人指定的方式行事，多數人最終才學會做得更好。（弗里德利希‧海耶克）

It is only because the majority opinion will always be opposed by some that our knowledge and understanding progress. In the process by which opinion is formed, it is very probable that, by the time any view becomes a majority view, it is no longer the best view: somebody will already have advanced beyond the point which the majority have reached. It is because we do not yet know which of the many competing new opinions will prove itself the best that we wait until it has gained sufficient support. (Friedrich August von Hayek)

由於多數人的意見總會受到一些人的反對，我們的知識和理解才得以進步。在意見形成的過程中，很可能當任何見解成為多數人的見解時，它就不再是最好的見解了：有的人會超越多數人的觀點。因為還不

1971-1980 理性與良知的碰撞

知道在眾多相左的新意見中,哪一種會證明自己最好,所以我們等待,直到它獲得足夠的支持。(弗里德利希・海耶克)

If the human intellect is allowed to impose a preconceived pattern on society, if our powers of reasoning are allowed to lay claim to a monopoly of creative effort... then we must not be surprised if society, as such, ceases to function as a creative force. (Friedrich August von Hayek)

如果人類的智慧被允許將一種先入為主的模式強加於社會,如果我們的推理能力被允許壟斷創造力……那麼,如果社會就此停止發揮創造性力量的作用,我們也不該驚訝。(弗里德利希・海耶克)

If most people are not willing to see the difficulty, this is mainly because, consciously or unconsciously, they assume that it will be they who will settle these questions for the others, and because they are convinced of their own capacity to do this. (Friedrich August von Hayek)

如果大多數人不願看到困難,這主要是因為他們有意或無意地認為自己將會為別人解決這些問題,因為他們對自己做此事的能力深信不疑。(弗里德利希・海耶克)

We shall not grow wiser before we learn that much that we have done was very foolish. (Friedrich August von Hayek)

在沒有理解到所做之事何等愚蠢不堪之前,我們是不會變得聰明一些的。(弗里德利希・海耶克)

I prefer true but imperfect knowledge, even if it leaves much undetermined and unpredictable, to a pretense of exact knowledge that is likely to be false. (Friedrich August von Hayek)

1974 年

與可能虛假的精確偽造知識相比,我更青睞真實但不完美的知識,即便它留有許多未定與莫測之處也罷。(弗里德利希·海耶克)

I must confess that if I had been consulted whether to establish a Nobel Prize in economics, I should have decidedly advised against it. (Friedrich August von Hayek)

關於是否設立諾貝爾經濟學獎,假如徵詢我的意見,我必須承認,我會堅決予以反對。(弗里德利希·海耶克)

The Nobel Prize confers on an individual an authority which in economics no man ought to possess. (Friedrich August von Hayek)

諾貝爾獎授予個人在經濟學方面無人應有的權威。(弗里德利希·海耶克)

Any man who is only an economist is unlikely to be a good one. (Friedrich August von Hayek)

任何僅僅是個經濟學家的人,都未必是好的經濟學家。(弗里德利希·海耶克)

The curious task of economics is to demonstrate to men how little they really know about what they imagine they can design. (Friedrich August von Hayek)

經濟學的奇特任務是向人們顯示,對於自以為能夠設計之物,他們的真正了解是何等微末。(弗里德利希·海耶克)

I have arrived at the conviction that the neglect by economists to discuss seriously what is really the crucial problem of our time is due to a certain timidity about soiling their hands by going from purely scientific questions into value questions. (Friedrich August von Hayek)

1971-1980 理性與良知的碰撞

我確信，經濟學家們之所以忽視認真地討論我們時代真正重要的關鍵問題，是因為他們害怕由純粹科學問題深入價值問題時沾染了自己的手。（弗里德利希・海耶克）

I do not think it is an exaggeration to say history is largely a history of inflation, usually inflations engineered by governments for the gain of governments. (Friedrich August von Hayek)

歷史大致上就是一部通貨膨脹史，這麼說我不認為誇張，通常是政府為了自身獲益而設計的通貨膨脹。（弗里德利希・海耶克）

And it's a necessity for journalists to pretend to be competent on every subject, some of which they really do not understand. They are under that necessity, I regret; I'm sorry for them. But to pretend to understand all the things you write about, and habitually to write about things you do not understand, is a very corrupting thing. (Friedrich August von Hayek)

記者有必要裝作事事在行，儘管有些事真的一竅不通。他們是迫不得已，我很遺憾。我為他們感到難過。但是，裝作懂得你所寫的一切，並習慣性地寫一些你所不懂的東西，是一件很墮落的事情。（弗里德利希・海耶克）

I was quite depressed two weeks ago when I spent an afternoon at Brentano's Bookshop in New York and was looking at the kind of books most people read. That seems to be hopeless; once you see that you lose all hope. (Friedrich August von Hayek)

兩個星期前，我在紐約的布倫塔諾書店待了一個下午。看著大多數人讀的那種書，我感覺很沮喪。這似乎是令人絕望的，一旦看見此景你將失去全部希望。（弗里德利希・海耶克）

1975 年

If it has been my good fortune to be in some sense a connecting link at one point in the development, that is but one among many evidences of the fruitfulness of the closest relations prevailing in the scientific world between those carrying on investigations under varying human conditions. (Aage Niels Bohr)

如果我有幸於發展過程中成為某種意義上的連接環節，這只不過是各種條件下從事諸多研究的人們所形成關係緊密的科學界其豐碩成果的眾多證明之一。（奧格·波耳）

It is clear that science progresses through the interplay of ideas, with contributions from so many different viewpoints and approaches. We have been singled out as individuals but our work has been part of a collective effort. We feel ourselves as representatives of a whole community imbued with a spirit of co-operation that has contributed so immeasurably not only to the progress of the work but also to make the whole adventure such a rich experience. (Ben Roy Mottelson)

顯而易見，科學透過思想的互動而進步，其中有來自眾多不同觀點和方法的貢獻。我們作為個人被挑選出來，但我們的工作始終是集體努力的一部分。我們覺得自己是一個充滿合作精神的整體的代表，這種精神不僅對於工作進展的貢獻無法估量，還使整個探險成為如此豐富的經歷。（本·莫特森）

In my schooling through high school, I excelled mainly in chemistry, physics and mathematics. (Leo James Rainwater)

1971–1980 理性與良知的碰撞

上中學的時候，我主要是化學、物理和數學學得好。（利奧‧雷恩沃特）

By combining chemical, biochemical and physical techniques, it has thus become possible to investigate the nature of enzymic catalysis in a novel manner, complementary to the other approaches which have developed over the same period. (John Warcup Cornforth)

將化學、生物化學和物理技術結合起來，就有可能以新的方式研究酶催化的性質，補充同時期發展的其他方法。（約翰‧康福思）

In a world where it is so easy to neglect, deny, corrupt and suppress the truth, the scientist may find his discipline severe. For him, truth is so seldom the sudden light that shows new order and beauty; more often, truth is the uncharted rock that sinks his ship in the dark. (John Warcup Cornforth)

在一個如此易於忽視、否認、敗壞和壓制真理的世界裡，科學家可能發現自己的學科局勢嚴峻。對於他，真理很難成為突然閃現的光芒，顯示新的秩序與美；更常見者為，真理是一塊地圖上未標示的礁石，在黑暗中撞沉他的船。（約翰‧康福思）

The way from Sarajevo to Stockholm is a long one and I am fully aware that I have been very lucky to arrive there. The journey could not have been made without the generous help of friends, colleagues, co-workers and also of innumerable earlier chemists "on whose shoulders we stand". (Vladimir Prelog)

從塞拉耶佛[67]到斯德哥爾摩的路程是漫長的。我充分意識到，自己到達這裡是極其幸運的。如果沒有朋友、同行、同事以及無數前輩化學

---

[67] 普雷洛格的出生地。

1975 年

家——「我們站在他們肩上」——的慷慨幫助，這段旅程不可能完成。（弗拉迪米爾·普雷洛格）

I have given lectures in more than 150 places, often several times. This in spite of the fact that I do not speak any language properly. I suspect that many people come to my lectures because they enjoy my strange accent and skill in managing without actually cheating. (Vladimir Prelog)

我曾在 150 多個地方進行演講，往往一回數次。儘管實際上我哪種語言都不精通。我認為，許多人來聽我的講課是由於欣賞我的古怪口音和直言不諱的說話方式。（弗拉迪米爾·普雷洛格）

No one has ever had an idea in a dress suit. (David Baltimore)

人們對於西裝革履沒有什麼想法。（戴維·巴爾的摩）

You must begin with an ideal and end with an ideal. (David Baltimore)

你必須以理想開始，以理想結束。（戴維·巴爾的摩）

What does gene A do? What does gene B do? What does it do in different contexts? What's its importance? We know the answer to that for a very small number of genes, the ones that made themselves evident many years ago. (David Baltimore)

基因 A 有什麼作用？基因 B 有什麼作用？它在不同的環境中有什麼作用？它的重要性是什麼？我們知道極少數基因的答案，多年前就已經明顯呈現的那些。（戴維·巴爾的摩）

I think I understand how much of an interrelationship there is between science and the rest of the world, and it gives me a sense of responsibility to try to help people understand what science is about, when it's doing well, and when it isn't doing well. (David Baltimore)

1971-1980 理性與良知的碰撞

我認為，我了解科學和世界其他方面的相互關係有多麼大。它給予我一種責任感，力圖幫助人們了解科學的性質，它什麼時候做得好，什麼時候做得不好。（戴維·巴爾的摩）

The study of biology is partly an exercise in natural esthetics. We derive much of our pleasure as biologists from the continuing realization of how economical, elegant and intelligent are the accidents of evolution that have been maintained by selection. (David Baltimore)

在一定程度上，生物學研究是自然美學的運用。我們作為生物學家，不斷理解到由選擇維持的演化事件有多麼高效、優雅和智慧，我們從中得到大量的樂趣。（戴維·巴爾的摩）

People keep e-mailing me to ask, "What is the meaning of life?" And they want me to e-mail them back quickly with an answer! (David Baltimore)

人們不斷寄電子郵件詢問我：「生命的意義是什麼？」而且希望我盡快回覆他們答案！（戴維·巴爾的摩）

People try to do better than other people. It's an incentive. (Renato Dulbecco)

人們試圖做得比別人更好。這是一種激勵。（羅納托·杜爾貝科）

I stress the relevance of my work for cancer research because I believe that science must be useful to man. (Renato Dulbecco)

我強調我的工作與癌症研究的關聯，因為我認為科學必須有益於人。（羅納托·杜爾貝科）

I always did as much as possible of the experimental work with my own hands, but in the later part of my research career this became progressively less feasible, both because the demand on my time increased and because the increasing technical sophistication and complexities of the experiments demanded a great deal of specialized skills. (Renato Dulbecco)

我總是盡可能多地親手做實驗工作。不過在我研究生涯的後期，這種做法越來越難以實行了，既由於對時間的需求增加，也由於實驗的技術難度與複雜性的增加需要大量的專門技能。（羅納托·杜爾貝科）

I know mortality exists, but I cannot do anything about it. So it does not make me anxious. (Renato Dulbecco)

我清楚死亡的存在，但對此無能為力。所以這並不使我焦慮。（羅納托·杜爾貝科）

Science is a communal effort —— what we have accomplished has rested on the achievements of others, and the future and practical significance of our work will also be determined by the achievements of others. (Howard Martin Temin)

科學是共同的努力 —— 我們的成就有賴於他人的成就，我們工作的未來和實際意義也將取決於他人的成就。（霍華德·馬丁·特明）

We realize how fortunate we have been to live in a country at a time and in a social class that has enabled us to realize our potential. We know that for many others this has not been possible. (Howard Martin Temin)

我們意識到自己有多麼幸運，能夠適逢其時地生活在這樣一個國家，處於這樣的社會階層中，從而能夠實現自身潛力。我們知道，對於其他許多人而言，這是不可能的。（霍華德·馬丁·特明）

Poetry does not live solely in books or in school anthologies. The poet does not know and often will never know his true receiver. (Eugenio Montale)

詩歌不僅僅存在於書籍或學院詩選之中。詩人不知道，而且通常永遠不知道自己真正的受眾。（埃烏傑尼奧‧蒙塔萊）

We regard as "scientific" a method based on deep analysis of facts, theories, and views, presupposing unprejudiced, unfearing open discussion and conclusions. The complexity and diversity of all the phenomena of modern life, the great possibilities and dangers linked with the scientific-technical revolution and with a number of social tendencies demand precisely such an approach, as has been acknowledged in a number of official statements. (Andrei Dmitrievich Sakharov)

我們認為「科學」的方法是基於對事實、理論和觀點的深入分析，以不帶偏見、不怕公開討論與結論為前提。正如許多官方聲明一向承認的，現代生活所有現象的複雜和多樣性，以及科學技術革命和許多社會趨勢相關的巨大可能和危險，都確切要求這種方式。（安德烈‧迪米崔維奇‧沙卡洛夫）

Profound insights arise only in debate, with a possibility of counterargument, only when there is a possibility of expressing not only correct ideas but also dubious ideas. (Andrei Dmitrievich Sakharov)

只有在容許反駁的爭論之中，只有在不僅容許表達正確想法也包容可疑想法的時候，才能產生深刻的見解。（安德烈‧迪米崔維奇‧沙卡洛夫）

I've always thought that the most powerful weapon in the world was the bomb and that's why I gave it to my people, but I've come to the conclusion that the most powerful weapon in the world is not the bomb but it's the truth. (Andrei Dmitrievich Sakharov)

1975 年

我一直認為世間最強大的武器是原子彈,所以我把它帶給我的人民;不過我得出了結論,世間最強大的武器不是原子彈,而是真理。(安德烈・迪米崔維奇・沙卡洛夫)

In our time mathematics has penetrated into economics so solidly, widely and variously, and the chosen theme is connected with such a variety of facts and problems that it brings us to cite the words of Kozma Prutkov which are very popular in our country: "One can not embrace the unembraceable". (Leonid Vitaliyevich Kantorovich)

在我們的時代,數學已經滲入了經濟學,如此堅實、廣泛而多方面,所選擇的主題與如此多樣的事實和問題相關,它使我們引用科茲馬・普魯特科夫廣為人知的話:「人不能擁抱無法擁抱之物。」(列昂尼德・坎托羅維奇)

We look upon economic theory as a sequence of conceptual models that seek to express in simplified form different aspects of an always more complicated reality. (Tjalling C. Koopmans)

我們把經濟理論視為一系列概念模型,它們尋求以簡化的形式表達一個總是更複雜的現實的不同方面。(佳林・庫普曼斯)

According to a frequently cited definition, economics is the study of "best use of scarce resources". The definition is incomplete. "Second best" use of resources, and outright wasteful uses, have equal claim to attention. They are the other side of the coin. (Tjalling C. Koopmans)

根據一個經常引用的定義,經濟學是對「稀缺資源最佳利用」的研究。這個定義是不完整的。對資源「次優」的利用,以及完全浪費的利用,都同樣值得關注。它們是硬幣的另一面。(佳林・庫普曼斯)

Econometrics may be defined as the quantitative analysis of actual economic phenomena based on the concurrent development of theory and observation, related by appropriate methods of inference. (Tjalling C. Koopmans)

計量經濟學可以定義為對基於理論與觀察並行發展的實際經濟現象的定量分析，用適當的推理方法加以連繫。（佳林・庫普曼斯）

1976年

Total failure isn't something I want to spend a lot of time envisioning. I'm pretty sure I'll recognize it if it comes. (Burton Richter)

徹底失敗不是我願意花很多時間預想的東西。我非常確定，它要是來了，我會認出它。（伯頓・里克特）

I got no thrill from solving an integral equation, but I did get a thrill from building an exotic piece of equipment that worked. (Burton Richter)

我無法從解開一個積分方程式中獲得刺激，但是建造一臺能正常運作的奇妙裝置確實令我感到興奮。（伯頓・里克特）

Modern science is fast-moving, and no laboratory can exist for long with a program based on old facilities. Innovation and renewal are required to keep a laboratory on the frontiers of science. (Burton Richter)

現代科學是快速發展的，沒有任何實驗室能夠以基於舊設施的項目長期存在。要保持實驗室處於科學前端，創新和更新不可或缺。（伯頓・里克特）

1976 年

If we don't fund the physical sciences, where will the Next Big Thing come from? (Burton Richter)

如果我們不資助物理科學，下一個大事件從何而來？（伯頓·里克特）

Politics is a lot tougher than physics. (Burton Richter)

政治比物理難得多。（伯頓·里克特）

The most important thing for a scientist is to find the right question to ask. (Samuel Chao Chung Ting)

作為一名科學家，最重要的是找到正確的問題加以探究。（丁肇中）

Human curiosity is the driving force behind basic research. (Samuel Chao Chung Ting)

人的好奇心是基礎研究背後的驅動力。（丁肇中）

If the universe came from a big bang there should be matter and antimatter equal amount at the beginning. Where is the universe made up of antimatter? There are many theories which says no, the antimatter universe does not exist. Actually the theory started in '67 by Andrei Sakharov. But in physics if you do not do the experiment, you will never know. (Samuel Chao Chung Ting)

如果宇宙來自大爆炸，起初就應該存在等量的物質和反物質。反物質構成的宇宙何在？有很多的理論說，不，反物質宇宙不存在。實際上，該理論是安德烈·迪米崔維奇·沙卡洛夫於 1967 年提出的。但在物理學中，你如果不做實驗，就永遠不會知道。（丁肇中）

What does pure research do to life on Earth? Well, many people ask me that. Let me give you a small example. About a hundred years ago at the frontier of research was the discovery of the X-ray and the discovery of the electron. At that time it was a pure curiosity. And then in the 30s they began to use the X-ray in the field of medicine. In 1920's the most frontier science was atomic physics. So called quantum mechanics. At that time it was also pure scientific research but now it's used in laser, in communication, super conductivity and can affect everybody's life. And the 40s and 50s the most advanced of science, the frontier was nuclear physics. Now, it's used in energy, defense, and in medicine. And so from discovery to application there's a time lapse. Typically 30 years or 40 years. But once it is used it really affects everyone's life. (Samuel Chao Chung Ting)

純粹的研究對現實生活有什麼影響？嗯，很多人問我這個問題。讓我為諸位舉個小例子。大約100年前，在研究的前端，有X射線的發現和電子的發現。當時這是純粹的好奇。然後在1930年代，他們開始在醫學領域使用X射線。在1920年代，最前端的科學是原子物理學，所謂的量子力學。當時它也是純粹的科學研究，但現在它用於雷射，用於通訊、超導電性，並且能夠影響每個人的生活。而1940年代和1950年代，最先進的科學，前端科學是核物理學。現在，它用於能源、國防，還用於醫學。所以從發現到應用有個時間差。典型者為30年或40年。然而一旦運用，就實實在在地影響到每個人的生活。（丁肇中）

If you scan through The New York Times in the last 100 years, very often a brilliant scientist will say, "Oh, we discovered this and now we've understood everything." only to turn out to be wrong. And so science is always progress. I think it's hard to say where or how it's going to end. (Samuel Chao Chung Ting)

1976 年

　如果瀏覽 100 年來的《紐約時報》，你會屢屢讀到某位傑出的科學家說，「哦，我們發現了這個，現在我們已經完全了解了。」結果卻是錯的。所以科學總是在進步。我認為很難說它將在哪裡或如何結束。（丁肇中）

　At the beginning, I really didn't speak any English. But since I was born in the University of Michigan hospital, I'm considered a citizen by birth and Michigan residence. So I got into the university. I don't know how I got in, because I speak hardly any English. At the first year, I studied mechanical engineering. After the first year, I had a conversation with my adviser, Robert White, very good engineer at that time. He took a look at my grade and said, you are no engineer. The problem was, at that time, there were no computers, so for every engineer, you have to do drawings. So for object, you have to look from the top, look from the side, look from the end, and I was no good. I couldn't even draw a line with equal thickness. And Professor White said, maybe you should study math and physics. Why don't you take math and physics at the same time? Why don't you begin to take some courses in graduate school. So in '56, when I first came in, I was 20 years old. I was the oldest in the class. And second semester, I began to take some graduate courses. And so I became the youngest. The university was really very nice to me. And the exempt me from taking English language, history, economics, allowed me to concentrate on math, concentrate on physics. So in '59, I got the Bachelor's degree in mathematics and physics. And in '62, end of '62, got my PhD degree. So from entering university to leaving was relatively around six years. So that is, at that time, considered fast. Particularly, when I started, I didn't hardly speak any English. After that, I realized, gee, I spent six years only in Michigan, maybe I should go to Europe. (Samuel Chao Chung Ting)

一開始，我真的不會說英語。可是由於出生在密西根大學醫院，我被認為是個土生土長的密西根人。我就進了密西根大學。我不知道自己是怎麼進去的，因為我幾乎不會說英語。第一年，我學習機械工程。第一年之後，我跟指導老師，羅伯特・懷特，談了一次話，他是當時的優秀工程師。他看了看我的成績說，你不是工程師的料。問題在於，那時候還沒有電腦，所以作為工程師，人人都得製圖。對於物體，你得從上方看，從側面看，從後面看，而我不擅長。我甚至畫不出一條粗細均勻的線。懷特教授說，也許你應該學習數學和物理。你怎麼不同時修習數學和物理？你應該開始選修一些研究所的課程。而 1956 年，剛入校時，我 20 歲，是班上年齡最大的。於是第二學期，我開始選修研究所課程。這樣一來我成了最年輕的。這一所大學實在是對我非常好。沒要求我學英語、歷史、經濟，使我得以專心攻讀數學，專心攻讀物理。於是 1959 年，我完成了數學和物理學的學士學位。1962 年，那年年底，拿到了博士學位。這樣，從入學到離校，算起來大約 6 年。這就是說，在當時被認為是很快的。尤其是，開始的時候，我幾乎不會說英語。在那之後，我意識到，嘿，我在密西根一待六年，也許應該到歐洲去了。（丁肇中）

Basic research is the driving force behind the development of new technology and industries. (Samuel Chao Chung Ting)

基礎研究是新的技術和產業發展的驅動力。（丁肇中）

There's two kind of physics. One is theoretical physics, one is experimental physics. Theoretical physics try to explain things. Experimental physics try to see whether the theory is right or wrong. (Samuel Chao Chung Ting)

1976 年

物理學有兩種。一種是理論物理學,一種是實驗物理學。理論物理學試圖解釋事物。實驗物理學試圖查明該理論是對還是錯。(丁肇中)

It's very dangerous for an experimentalist to have a preconceived idea. You must find out. Make sure your instrumentation is correct, your method is correct, and try to see what happened. (Samuel Chao Chung Ting)

對於實驗者來說,有先入為主的想法是非常危險的。你必須找出答案。確保你的儀器是正確的,方法是正確的,並試著看看發生了什麼。(丁肇中)

If you do an experiment and prove the theory is right you have learned nothing. It's when you do an experiment, prove the theory is wrong and you require a new theory, then you learn something. (Samuel Chao Chung Ting)

如果做一個實驗而證明了有關理論是正確的,你什麼都沒學到。當你做一個實驗,證明有關理論是錯誤的而你需要一種新的理論,這時你就學到東西了。(丁肇中)

I was a bit surprised. Because normally, the Nobel committee, from your discovery to when they give you a prize, they normally let you wait for 20 years or 30 years. And in my time, from the work to the awarded prize is only a little bit more than a year. (Samuel Chao Chung Ting)

我有點意外。因為通常,從你的發現到諾貝爾委員會給你獎項,他們通常讓你等 20 年或 30 年。而我這次,從所做的工作到授予獎勵只有一年多一點。(丁肇中)

I wanted to give the speech in Chinese. I want to give a message to the Chinese students. That's why I decided give the speech in Chinese. The United States ambassador to Sweden actually was not very pleased. That time, the relation with China was not perfect. So, the ambassador actually came to talk to me and said, "Well, you are American. Why do you give the speech in Chinese?" I said, "You know, I can speak whatever language I want." And the reason I give the speech in Chinese because I want to mention to the Chinese student in science that it's not only theoretical physics, theory that is important. To be able to do experiments, it's also very, very important. To be able to measure things, to measure experimental phenomenon, to study nature. It's very important. (Samuel Chao Chung Ting)

我要用中文發表演講。我要對中國的學生說一件事。這就是我決定用中文發表演講的原因。美國駐瑞典大使實際上不怎麼高興。那時候，與中國的關係並非完美。所以，大使實際上來找了我，說：「你看，你是美國人。怎麼用中文發表演講呢？」我說：「你知道的，我可以使用任何我想用的語言。」我之所以用中文發表演講，是由於要對學科學的中國學生提出，不僅理論物理學，理論是重要的。能夠做實驗，也非常、非常重要。能夠測量事物，測量實驗現象，研究自然。這非常重要。（丁肇中）

Having grown up in the old China, I would like to take this opportunity to emphasize to young students from developing nations the importance of experimental work. There is an ancient Chinese saying "He who labours with his mind rules over he who labours with his hand". This kind of backward idea is very harmful to youngsters from developing countries. Partly because of this type of concept, many students from these countries are inclined towards theoretical studies and avoid experimental work. In reality, a theory in natural science cannot be without experimental foundations; physics, in particular,

1976 年

comes from experimental work. I hope that awarding the Nobel Prize to me will awaken the interest of students from the developing nations so that they will realize the importance of experimental work. (Samuel Chao Chung Ting)

作為在舊中國長大的人，我願意借這個機會，向開發中國家的年輕學生強調實驗工作的重要性。有句古話：「勞心者治人，勞力者治於人。」這種落後的想法對開發中國家的年輕人是非常有害的。部分由於這種觀念，這些國家的許多學生傾向於理論研究而迴避實驗工作。實際上，自然科學理論不可能沒有實驗基礎；物理學尤其出自實驗工作。我希望，這次授予我諾貝爾獎，會喚起開發中國家學生的興趣，從而使他們理解到實驗工作的重要性。（丁肇中）

In physics, age and experience may or may not be the most important thing. And also, you really have to respect a student —— listen to what he has to say. (Samuel Chao Chung Ting)

在物理學科，年齡和經驗未必就是最重要的。而且，你真的必須尊重學生 —— 傾聽他要說的話。（丁肇中）

I developed a complete loyalty to the University of Michigan's football. And so in my six years at Michigan, I'm ashamed to say I did not go to all the classes. But I never missed a football game. (Samuel Chao Chung Ting)

我對密西根大學的美式足球隊產生了絕對的忠誠。於是，在校的 6 年裡，說起來不好意思，我沒有上所有該上的課。但我從來沒有錯過一場美式足球賽。（丁肇中）

We are tall only because we stand on the shoulders of others. (William Lipscomb)

1971-1980 理性與良知的碰撞

我們之所以高大，只是由於站在別人的肩膀上。（威廉·利普斯科姆）

For me, the creative process, first of all, requires a good nine hours of sleep a night. Second, it must not be pushed by the need to produce practical applications. (William N. Lipscomb)

就我而言，創意的過程，首先需要每晚 9 小時的良好睡眠。其次，不得受產生實際應用的需求所推動。（威廉·利普斯科姆）

I think the intuitive processes of discovery are the same, very much the same, in the arts as in the sciences. (William N. Lipscomb)

我認為，在藝術和科學領域，發現的直覺過程是一樣的，極其相似。（威廉·利普斯科姆）

I am inclined to make large intuitive jumps and then set about to test the conclusions. (William N. Lipscomb)

我傾向於做出大幅度的直覺跳躍，然後著手測試結論。（威廉·利普斯科姆）

When I was 11 years old, my mother bought me one of those chemistry sets, and I stayed with it. (William N. Lipscomb)

我 11 歲時，母親為我買了一套化學設備，我就離不開它了。（威廉·利普斯科姆）

There's a lot of music in my life, and I found it a very important part of my life. (William N. Lipscomb)

我的生活中有很多音樂，我覺得它是我生活非常重要的部分。（威廉·利普斯科姆）

1976 年

Sometimes I get too wound up in my chemistry, but if you play chamber music, it's impossible to think about chemistry. (William N. Lipscomb)

有時候我從事化學研究過於緊張,但你如果演奏室內樂,就不可能思考化學。(威廉・利普斯科姆)

My non-scientific interests are primarily in the out-of-doors. I have been a middle distance runner (very non-competitive) for many years and also play squash. We canoe on the many nearby lakes and rivers of Pennsylvania and New Jersey. I enjoy mountain walking and have hiked in many parts of the world on field trips. With several friends we own a farm in western Maryland which supplies beef for the local market. Shoveling manure for a day is an excellent counterbalance to intellectual work. (Baruch S. Blumberg)

我對科學以外的興趣主要在戶外。我是多年的中長跑運動員(非常不具競爭力),也打壁球。我們在賓夕法尼亞和紐澤西附近的許多湖泊和河流划船。我喜歡爬山,曾在世界許多地方徒步旅行。我們和幾個朋友在馬里蘭西部有個農場,為當地市場供應牛肉。鏟上一天牛糞對於腦力工作而言是極好的平衡。(巴魯克・塞繆爾・布隆伯格)

I started to read seriously before puberty. Books by Scandinavian authors, Henrik Ibsen and Sigrid Undset, were among the earlier works I read myself. I devoured enthusiastically three biographical works which must have had a profound effect on me: René Vallery-Radot's biography of his father-in-law, Louis Pasteur; Eve Curie's biography of her mother, Marie Curie; and Paul de Kruif's Microbe Hunters. I then stenciled the twelve names of microbiologists whom de Kruif had selected on the steps leading to my attic chemistry laboratory, where they remain today. At about this time, when I was about ten years

1971-1980 理性與良知的碰撞

old, I wrote an essay on why I planned to concentrate on chemistry, physics, and mathematics, rather than classical biology, in preparation for a career in medicine. Dr. Youden had succeeded in making it clear to me that education in mathematics, physics and chemistry was the basis for the biology of the future. (D. Carleton Gajdusek)

我在青春期以前就開始認真閱讀了。我早期獨自閱讀的書籍，包括斯堪地那維亞作家們，亨里克·易卜生和西格麗德·溫塞特的著作。我熱切地讀完3部傳記作品，它們必然對我產生了深遠的影響：勒內·瓦勒里－拉多所著岳父路易·巴斯德的傳記、伊芙·居禮所著母親瑪麗·居禮的傳記，和保羅·德·克魯夫所著《微生物獵人》。隨後，我把德·克魯夫選出的12位微生物學家的名字印在我閣樓化學實驗室的臺階上，它們至今還在。大約10歲左右，我寫了一篇文章，解釋自己打算專攻化學、物理和數學而非古典生物學，意在準備從醫。尤登博士成功地向我闡明了數學、物理和化學的教育是未來生物學的基礎。（丹尼爾·卡爾頓·蓋杜謝克）

My boyhood reading, first in Homer, Virgil, and Plutarch, on which we were nurtured by our Classicist-Romanticist Hungarian mother, led, upon the instigation of my poet brother, to my more thorough return to the classics as a young, too-ardent scientist-cum-physician, and to the modern literature of European authors and philosophers, which I had missed in my university days devoted too exclusively to mathematics and the sciences. This reading changed greatly my way of thinking. Particularly, I would have to credit Dostoevsky, Chekhov and Tolstoy; Montaigne, Baudelaire, Rimbaud, Valery and Gide; Shakespeare, Wordsworth, Yeats and Lawrence; Poe, Whitman and Melville;

1976 年

Ibsen; Goethe, Schiller, Kant, Nietzsche, Kafka and Mann; Saadi and Hafiz. (D. Carleton Gajdusek)

　　我的少年閱讀，受到我們既古典又浪漫的匈牙利籍母親的薰陶，最初浸淫於荷馬、維吉爾和普魯塔克。我的哥哥是詩人，在他的鼓勵下，我這個年輕、狂熱的科學家兼醫生，更徹底地回歸經典，拿起現代歐洲作家和哲學家的著作，我上大學時專注於數學和科學而錯過了它們。這種閱讀極大地改變了我的思考方式。尤其是，須歸功於杜斯妥耶夫斯基、契訶夫和托爾斯泰，蒙田、波特萊爾、韓波、瓦勒里和紀德，莎士比亞、華茲渥斯，葉慈和勞倫斯，坡、惠特曼和梅爾維爾，易卜生、歌德、席勒、康德、尼采、卡夫卡和曼，薩迪和哈菲茲。（丹尼爾‧卡爾頓‧蓋杜謝克）

　　All human accomplishment has the same origin, identically. Imagination is a force of nature. Is this not enough to make a person full of ecstasy? Imagination, imagination, imagination. It converts to actual. It sustains, it alters, it redeems! (Saul Bellow)

　　人類的全部成就同出一源，全無二致。想像力是自然的力量。這難道不足以令人滿心歡喜？想像力，想像力，想像力。它轉化為實際。它保持，它改變，它救贖！（索爾‧貝婁）

　　Silence is enriching. The more you keep your mouth shut, the more fertile you become. (Saul Bellow)

　　沉默是豐盛。你越是緘默，產能就越大。（索爾‧貝婁）

　　How quickly the visions of genius become the canned goods of the intellectuals! (Saul Bellow)

　　天才的遠見多麼快就成了知識界的罐頭食品！（索爾‧貝婁）

1971-1980 理性與良知的碰撞

In the greatest confusion there is still an open channel to the soul. It may be difficult to find because by midlife it is overgrown, and some of the wildest thickets that surround it grow out of what we describe as our education. But the channel is always there, and it is our business to keep it open, to have access to the deepest part of ourselves. (Saul Bellow)

在極端的混亂中，仍然有一條通往靈魂的開放路徑。它可能很難被找到，因為人到中年，路上雜草叢生，路旁一些最茂盛的野生灌木也掩蓋了我們所謂的教養。然而這個途徑總是在的，我們的任務就是保持它的開放，以便觸及自己的內心深處。（索爾‧貝婁）

When I received the news of the Nobel Peace Award, I could not believe it. I told my father, "I think they have the wrong name, Dad. Please, can you talk to this man on the phone? I'm busy cooking!" (Betty Williams)

得知諾貝爾和平獎的消息時，我簡直無法相信。我對父親說：「我想他們弄錯人名了，爸。可以請你和這位先生講電話嗎？我正在忙著做飯呢！」（貝蒂‧威廉斯）

The Nobel Peace Prize is not awarded for what one has done, but hopefully what one will do. (Betty Williams)

諾貝爾和平獎授予一個人，不是由於他所做的，而是由於希望他會做的。（貝蒂‧威廉斯）

We need radical thinking, creative ideas, and imagination. (Mairead Corrigan)

我們需要激進的思考、創造性的想法，以及想像力。（梅里德‧科里根‧麥奎爾）

1976 年

We can rejoice and celebrate today because we are living in a miraculous time. Everything is changing and everything is possible. (Mairead Corrigan)

今天我們可以歡樂和慶祝,因為我們生活在不可思議的時代。一切都在改變,一切皆有可能。(梅里德・科里根・麥奎爾)

It is really very, very nice for a week. It would corrupt you utterly if it lasted much longer. (Milton Friedman)

這真的是非常、非常美好的一個星期。它要是再持續下去,你就會忘乎所以了。[68] (彌爾頓・傅利曼)

There's no such thing as a free lunch. (Milton Friedman)

天下沒有免費的午餐。(彌爾頓・傅利曼)

The most important single central fact about a free market is that no exchange takes place unless both parties benefit. (Milton Friedman)

關於自由市場,最重要的唯一核心事實為,除非雙方均受益,就沒有交易發生。(彌爾頓・傅利曼)

Inflation is taxation without legislation. (Milton Friedman)

通貨膨脹是沒有立法的稅收。(彌爾頓・傅利曼)

I am favor of cutting taxes under any circumstances and for any excuse, for any reason, whenever it's possible. (Milton Friedman)

我贊成減稅,在任何情況下,以任何理由,任何原因,無論何時有可能。(彌爾頓・傅利曼)

Government should be a referee, not an active player. (Milton Friedman)

政府應該是個裁判,而非活躍的球員。(彌爾頓・傅利曼)

---

[68] 談及斯德哥爾摩的諾貝爾獎慶典。

1971-1980 理性與良知的碰撞

If you put the federal government in charge of the Sahara desert, in five years there'd be a shortage of sand. (Milton Friedman)

要是讓聯邦政府管理撒哈拉沙漠，5年就會出現沙子短缺。（彌爾頓‧傅利曼）

There are no politics that are as dirty as academic politics. (Milton Friedman)

沒有像學術政治一樣骯髒的政治了。（彌爾頓‧傅利曼）

1977 年

You never understand everything. When one understands everything, one has gone crazy. (Philip Warren Anderson)

你永遠不會無所不知。一旦無所不知，人就瘋了。（菲利普‧安德森）

All I can say to the younger theorists is: don't trust anyone over 45, except maybe me, and I'm not so sure about me. (Philip Warren Anderson)

對比較年輕的理論家們，我所能說的唯有：不要相信任何45歲以上的人，也許除了我以外，而我對自己也不太確定。（菲利普‧安德森）

The prize seemed to change my professional life very little. (Philip Warren Anderson)

這個獎項似乎絲毫未改變我的職業生涯。（菲利普‧安德森）

All scientific theories are provisional and may be changed, but... on the whole, they are accepted from Washington to Moscow because of their practical success. Where religion has opposed the findings of science, it has almost always had to retreat. (Nevill Francis Mott)

一切科學理論都是暫時的,都可能被改變,然而……整體而言,由於實務上的成功,它們得以被接受,從華盛頓到莫斯科。在反對科學發現之處,宗教幾乎總是不得不撤退。(內維爾·莫特)

One can still say that quantum mechanics is the key to understanding magnetism. When one enters the first room with this key there are unexpected rooms beyond, but it is always the master key that unlocks each door. (John Hasbrouck van Vleck)

人們仍然可以說,量子力學是理解磁力的關鍵。當一個人帶著這把鑰匙進入第一個房間時,遠處還有些意想不到的房間,但它始終是打開每扇門的萬能鑰匙。(約翰·范扶累克)

My work in this field of physical chemistry was always for me a specific pleasure, because the direct link with experimentation allows one to test the intuition of the theoretician. The successes we met provided the confidence which later was much needed in my confrontation with more abstract, complex problems. (Ilya Prigogine)

在物理化學領域工作對我而言一直是一種特殊的樂趣,因為與實驗的直接連結而得以檢驗理論家的直覺。我們所獲得的成功帶給我信心,在我後來面對更抽象、複雜的難題時,這是非常需要的。(伊利亞·普里高津)

The work of a theoretician is related in a direct way to his whole life. It takes, I believe, some amount of internal peace to find a path among all successive bifurcations. This peace I owe to my wife, Marina. (Ilya Prigogine)

理論家的工作與他的整個生活直接關聯。想要在所有不斷叢生的歧路中找出途徑，我認為，需要相當的內心寧靜。我的這份寧靜來自妻子瑪麗娜。（伊利亞‧普里高津）

Help people. I really wanted to be a physician … I knew all my efforts would be to help people. (Roger Guillemin)

幫助人們。我真的想成為一名醫生……我知道我的一切努力都是為了助人。[69]（羅歇‧吉耶曼）

During the Nobel Prize ceremony, there were representatives from the Nobel Foundation and the king and queen were there. The king gives you a book with your name on it with all the Nobel laureates and the medal, and when I sat down, I realized he had given me (co-recipient Andrew) Schally's book and he had given Schally my book. We nudged each other and chuckled. We were not about to switch books in front of 800 people and dignitaries. So we switched books privately. (Roger Guillemin)

在諾貝爾頒獎典禮上有諾貝爾基金會的代表，國王和王后也出席。國王發給你一本證書，上面有你的名字以及所有其他諾貝爾獎得主，並發給你獎章。回到座位上，我意識到他把（共同獲獎者）安德魯‧沙利的證書給了我，而把我的給了沙利。我們互相碰了碰，小聲笑起來。我們不打算當著 800 位出席者和貴賓的面交換。所以是私下交換的。（羅歇‧吉耶曼）

I believe that healthy competition stimulates the necessary elements to accelerate creativity. (Andrew V. Schally)

---

[69] 在被問及是否有自己的人生觀時，吉耶曼不假思索地答道。

1977 年

我相信，良性競爭可以激發加速創造力所需的必要元素。（安德魯·沙利）

If I mention now that I am Nobel Prize laureate, I do so in order to convince my sponsors; the job I do is serious, and it is necessary to enlist the trust of various organizations and institutions that may be helpful. But I do not live in the past. What counts most for me is the present and the future. (Andrew V. Schally)

如果我現在提到自己是諾貝爾獎得主，這樣做是為了說服贊助人：我所做的事情是嚴肅的，有必要爭取各種可能有幫助的組織機構的信任。但我並不活在過去。對於我最重要的是現在和未來。（安德魯·沙利）

You have to have curiosity and self-discipline, be a master of systematic work. I am not patient but I am disciplined. What also counts is to be at the right place at the right time. Like Napoleon. (Andrew V. Schally)

你得具備好奇心和自律性，成為系統工作的主宰。我沒有耐心，但是自律。重要的還有在適當的時間處於適當的地點。就像拿破崙。（安德魯·沙利）

Swimming as I already said is for me a must. Working so hard —— physically and mentally —— I need my rest. I need to be in good physical shape. When I come home after six o'clock, I am simply exhausted and probably, would not be able to answer a question about my address or telephone number. But after swimming for twenty minutes, I feel refreshed. (Andrew V. Schally)

如我曾說，游泳對於我是必須的。工作這麼辛苦 —— 身體上和精神上 —— 我需要休息。我需要保持良好的身體狀態。每當 6 點後到家，我

簡直精疲力竭，八成連自己的地址或電話號碼都說不上來。然而游過 20 分鐘，我便覺得神清氣爽。（安德魯·沙利）

Initially, new ideas are rejected. Later they become dogma if you're right. And if you're really lucky, you can publish your rejections as part of your Nobel presentation. (Rosalyn Yalow)

最初，新的觀念遭到拒絕。如果你是對的，它們後來就會變成信條。如果你真的很幸運，你可以把遭受拒絕的經歷作為你諾貝爾獎演說的一部分發表出來。（羅莎琳·薩斯曼·雅洛）

The Nobel Prize gives you an opportunity to make a fool of yourself in public. (Rosalyn Yalow)

諾貝爾獎給了你一個當眾調侃自己的機會。（羅莎琳·薩斯曼·雅洛）

The excitement of learning separates youth from old age. As long as you're learning, you're not old. (Rosalyn Yalow)

學習的興奮將老年人和年輕人區分開來。只要你在學習，你就不老。（羅莎琳·薩斯曼·雅洛）

The world cannot afford the loss of the talents of half its people if we are to solve the many problems which beset us. (Rosalyn Yalow)

要解決困擾我們的大量問題，世界就無法承擔喪失一半人的才能。[70]（羅莎琳·薩斯曼·雅洛）

I was born in a middle-class family, but I had the benefit of its eminently open and liberal outlook. My restless spirit led me to practise contradictory professions. I was a teacher of mercantile law, an employee in a railway com-

---

[70] 身為女科學家，雅洛為女性平等權利而大聲疾呼。

1977 年

pany, a financial journalist. From early youth this restlessness of which I have spoken lifted me to one particular delight: reading and, in time, writing. (Vicente Aleixandre)

我出生在一個中產階級家庭,但我得益於它非常開放和自由的思想。不安分的精神致使我從事相互矛盾的職業。我是商事法教師、鐵路公司職員、金融記者。從少年時代起,我的這種不安分使我產生了一項特別的愛好:讀書,漸漸地,還有寫作。(維森特・阿萊克桑德雷)

Hours of solitude, hours of creation, hours of meditation. Solitude and meditation gave me an awareness, a perspective which I have never lost: that of solidarity with the rest of mankind. Since that time I have always proclaimed that poetry is communication, in the exact sense of that word. (Vicente Aleixandre)

數小時的獨處、數小時的創作、數小時的冥想。獨處和冥想賦予我一種意識,一個我從未喪失的視角:與其他人類的緊密相聯。從那時起,我就一直宣稱詩歌即交流,這是這個詞的確切意義。(維森特・阿萊克桑德雷)

Poetry is a succession of questions which the poet constantly poses. Each poem, each book is a demand, a solicitation, an interrogation, and the answer is tacit, implicit, but also continuous, and the reader gives it to himself through his reading. It is an exquisite dialogue in which the poet questions and the reader silently gives his full answer. (Vicente Aleixandre)

詩歌是詩人不斷提出的一連串問題。每一首詩,每一本書都是一個要求、一次懇請、一次訊問,而回答是無言的、含蓄的,但也是連續的,讀者透過閱讀給予自己回答。這是一場精采的對話,在對話中,詩

1971–1980 理性與良知的碰撞

人提問而讀者無聲地給予充分的回答。（維森特・阿萊克桑德雷）

As mathematics had been my best subject at school, my parents proposed —— and I accepted —— studies at the University of Lund in mathematics, statistics, and economics. The choice of the latter subject is said to be due to the fact that at the age of five years, I was very fond of calculating the cost of the various cakes my mother used to bake. (Bertil Ohlin)

由於數學是我在學校裡學得最好的科目，父母建議我 —— 我也接受了 —— 到隆德大學攻讀數學、統計學和經濟學。對於最後這一科的選擇，據說是鑒於我 5 歲時的事實，當時我非常喜歡計算母親烘烤各種蛋糕的成本。（貝蒂爾・奧林）

The well-balanced economist is a normal human being with his warm heart on the Left, his practical work-a-day hand on the Right, and his clear and thoughtful head in the Centre. Nowhere today is this combination of a warm-hearted desire to improve the lot of mankind, of cool clear-headed analysis of the nature of the problems, and of realistic feasible action more needed than in the development of a decent and effective international economic order. (James E. Meade)

穩健的經濟學家與常人無異，熾熱的心屬於左派，務實的工作態度屬於右派，清醒深刻的頭腦屬於中間派。改善人類命運的熱切願望、對問題性質冷靜透徹的分析，以及現實可行的行動，如今，沒有哪裡比得上在適當而有效的國際經濟秩序的建立中，更需要這三者的組合了。（詹姆士・米德）

The frontiers of knowledge in the various fields of our subject are expanding at such a rate that, work as hard as one can, one finds oneself further and further away from an understanding of the whole. (James E. Meade)

在我們學科的各個領域，知識的邊界正在如此快速擴張，人們無論多麼努力，仍會發現自己距離理解整體越來越遠。（詹姆士・米德）

1978 年

In my young days scientific work was concentrated in universities and mainly done by a few professors. The material means were very modest. The spending of a few hundred roubles for apparatus was considered a great event. Towards the middle of our century the so called scientific-technical revolution took place. The social status of a scientist and his work took a new turn. Science became a productive force. Special scientific research institutions were organized, which possessed great material possibilities. Nowadays the money spent on a scientific apparatus might be as much as some hundred million dollars. (Pyotr Leonidovich Kapitsa)

在我年輕的時候，科學工作集中在大學裡，主要由少數教授從事。物質資源極其有限。花上幾百盧布買設備就被視為大事。到了本世紀中期，所謂科技革命發生了。科學家的社會地位及其工作出現新的轉變。科學成為生產力。特別的科學研究機構組織起來，擁有巨大的物質潛力。如今，花在一件科學設備上的款項也許高達數億美元。（彼得・列昂尼多維奇・卡皮察）

If you don't want to be replaced by a machine, don't try to act like one! (Arno Allan Penzias)

1971-1980 理性與良知的碰撞

你如果不想被機器所取代，就不要試圖表現得像一臺機器！（阿諾·彭齊亞斯）

Curiosity is a precious gift which comes so naturally to us that we sometimes fail to appreciate it. Children ask difficult questions. Why is it dark at night? Why do you smoke cigarettes? Why is that man lying on the sidewalk? Why does the car smoke when it's cold? We parents experience a feeling of relief when our children are finally old enough to go to school and learn to stop asking so many questions. (Arno Allan Penzias)

好奇心是一種寶貴的天賦，它對我們而言如此自然，以至我們有時未能欣賞它。孩子們會問一些難以解答的問題。為什麼晚上天是黑的？你為什麼抽菸？為什麼那個人躺在人行道上？為什麼天冷的時候汽車冒白煙？當孩子終於長大到可以上學，並學會不再問這麼多問題時，我們做父母的感到如釋重負。（阿諾·彭齊亞斯）

I hope that you have not learned that lesson too well in your schooling. I hope, instead, that you will encourage the spirit of free inquiry in yourselves, in the people around you, and in your institutions. Thus you can help build and maintain a society in which science, in all its forms, can flourish in the service of mankind. (Arno Allan Penzias)

我希望你們在學校裡功課別學得太好。我倒是希望，你們會在自己內心、在周圍的人和所處機構之中，鼓勵自由探究的精神。這樣，你們可以幫助建立和維護一個各種形式的科學都能蓬勃發展、為人類服務的社會。（阿諾·彭齊亞斯）

Change is rarely comfortable. (Arno Allan Penzias)

變化很少是舒適的。（阿諾·彭齊亞斯）

1978 年

I feel that I learned far more from my students than I could possibly have taught them. (Arno Allan Penzias)

我覺得，我從學生那裡學到的東西，遠比我有可能教給他們的多。（阿諾‧彭齊亞斯）

Cosmology is a science which has only a few observable facts to work with. (Robert Woodrow Wilson)

宇宙學是這樣一門科學，它只有少許可觀察的事實以供研究。（羅伯特‧伍德羅‧威爾遜）

Emile Zola described a work of art as a corner of nature seen through a temperament. The philosopher Karl Popper, the economist F. A. Hayek, and the art historian E. H. Gombrich have shown that the creative process in science and art consists of two main activities： an imaginative jumping forward to a new abstraction or simplified representation, followed by a critical looking back to see how nature appears in the light of the new vision. The imaginative leap forward is a hazardous, unreasonable activity. Reason can be used only when looking critically back. Moreover, in the experimental sciences, the scientific fraternity must test a new theory to destruction, if possible. Meanwhile, the originator of a theory may have a very lonely time, especially if his colleagues find his views of nature unfamiliar, and difficult to appreciate. The final outcome cannot be known, either to the originator of a new theory, or to his colleagues and critics, who are bent on falsifying it. Thus, the scientific innovator may feel all the more lonely and uncertain. On the other hand, faced with a new theory, the members of the scientific establishment are often more vulnerable than the lonely innovator. For, if the innovator should happen to be right, the ensuing upheaval of the established order may be very painful and uncongenial to those who have long committed themselves to develop and serve it. (Peter D. Mitchell)

埃米爾・左拉將藝術品描述為透過性情所見的自然的一個角落。哲學家卡爾・波普爾、經濟學家弗里德利希・海耶克和藝術史學家恩斯特・貢布里希則說明了，科學和藝術的創造過程由兩次重大行動構成：一次是富於想像的跳躍，以獲得新的抽象概念或簡化表現；接著是一次評判性的回顧，檢視新目光下的自然是何等模樣。富於想像的跳躍是冒險的、非理性的行動。理性只能在評判地回顧時運用。而且，在實驗科學中，科學組織必須對新理論進行推翻性的測試。此時，新理論的提出者也許經歷一段非常孤獨的時期，尤其是當同行發現他的自然觀是陌生又難以理解的之時。對於新理論的提出者，或其一心證偽的同行和評判者，最終結果都無從得知。於是，科學創新者也許感到更加孤獨和不確定。另一方面，面對新理論，科學機構成員往往比孤獨的創新者更易受傷。因為，如果創新者真的恰好正確，隨之而來的既有秩序的劇變可能非常痛苦，與那些長期致力於發展和服務它的人格格不入。（彼得・米切爾）

I would like to pay a most heartfelt tribute to my helpers and colleagues generally, and especially to those who were formerly my strongest critics, without whose altruistic and generous impulses, I feel sure that I would not be at this banquet today. (Peter D. Mitchell)

我要向我的助手和同事們表達最衷心的敬意，尤其對那些先前是我最強烈批評者的人，沒有他們無私而慷慨的推動，我確信自己不會出席今天這場諾貝爾獎宴會。（彼得・米切爾）

1978 年

Although a biologist, I must confess I do not understand how life came about.... I consider that life only starts at the level of a functional cell. The most primitive cells may require at least several hundred different specific biological macro-molecules. How such already quite complex structures may have come together, remains a mystery to me. (Werner Arber)

儘管身為生物學家,我必須承認自己並不了解生命是如何產生的。……我認為生命只是由功能細胞的層面開始。最原始的細胞可能需要至少幾百種不同的特定生物大分子。這些已經相當複雜的結構,是如何結合起來的,對於我始終是個謎。(沃納‧亞伯)

The future well-being of the human family depends on continuous creativity and new discovery. (Daniel Nathans)

人類大家庭未來的福祉取決於持續創造和新的發現。(丹尼爾‧那森斯)

Scientific knowledge is cumulative; each individual builds on the accomplishments of others. Recent dramatic advances in genetics, the science of heredity, represent a striking example of this process. (Daniel Nathans)

科學知識是累積的,每個人都以他人的成就為基礎而建樹。遺傳學,研究遺傳性的科學,其最近的突飛猛進,就是這個過程的顯著例子。(丹尼爾‧那森斯)

Getting the Nobel was a nice thing. I became nervous about how I should behave. I always looked up to Nobel Laureates but didn't feel like I was one of them. (Hamilton O. Smith)

獲得諾貝爾獎是件好事。我為應該如何自處而不安起來。我一向敬仰諾貝爾獎得主,但未曾想過作為他們中的一員。(漢彌爾頓‧史密斯)

1971-1980 理性與良知的碰撞

Every creator painfully experiences the chasm between his inner vision and its ultimate expression. (Isaac Bashevis Singer)

每個創造者都痛苦地體驗著內心所見與其最終表達之間的鴻溝。（以撒·巴什維斯·辛格）

Originality is not seen in single words or even in sentences. Originality is the sum total of a man's thinking or his writing. (Isaac Bashevis Singer)

創造性並不展現在單字乃至句子之中。創造性是一個人的思考或寫作的總和。（以撒·巴什維斯·辛格）

In any case, let's eat breakfast. (Isaac Bashevis Singer)

先把早餐吃了再說。[71]（以撒·巴什維斯·辛格）

Our knowledge is a little island in a great ocean of nonknowledge. (Isaac Bashevis Singer)

我們的知識是個小小的島，處於無知無識的汪洋大海之中。（以撒·巴什維斯·辛格）

If you keep on saying things are going to be bad, you have a good chance of being a prophet. (Isaac Bashevis Singer)

如果你不斷地說事情將要變糟，你很有可能成為先知。（以撒·巴什維斯·辛格）

Any life lost in war is the life of a human being, irrespective of whether it is an Arab or an Israeli. (Mohamed Anwar al-Sadat)

戰爭中喪失的任何生命都是人類的生命，無論它是阿拉伯人還是以色列人。（穆罕默德·艾爾·沙達特）

---

[71] 得知自己榮獲諾貝爾獎時，辛格對妻子這麼說。

1978年

Real success is success with self. It's not in having things, but in having mastery, having victory over self. (Mohamed Anwar al-Sadat)

真正的成功是自我的成功。不在於取得外物,而在於取得掌控,取得對自我的戰勝。(穆罕默德・艾爾・沙達特)

I can say, on the strength of my personal experience, that one should, in all circumstances, give free rein to the thirst for knowledge which is in every man. Even if you are brought down to the depths of humiliation, to the valley of the shadow of death —— open your eyes wide, and learn! (Menachem Begin)

基於個人經驗,我可以說,在任何情況下,一個人都應該對人皆有之的求知欲不加約束。即使被帶到屈辱的深淵、死亡陰影的山谷 —— 睜大你的眼睛,學習!(梅納罕・比金)

Peace is the beauty of life. It is sunshine. It is the smile of a child, the love of a mother, the joy of a father, the togetherness of a family. It is the advancement of man, the victory of a just cause, the triumph of truth. Peace is all of these and more and more. (Menachem Begin)

和平是生命之美。它是陽光。它是孩子的微笑,母親的愛,父親的快樂,家庭的團聚。它是人類的進步,正義事業的勝利,真理的凱旋。和平是這一切,逐日而增。(梅納罕・比金)

There will be no fraternal strife while the foe is at the gate. (Menachem Begin)

敵人上門之際,當無兄弟相爭。[72](梅納罕・比金)

---

[72] 對照:兄弟鬩於牆,外禦其侮。(《詩經》)

The world you perceive is drastically simplified model of the real world. (Herbert A. Simon)

你所感知的世界是真實世界的極度簡化模型。（司馬賀）

What information consumes is rather obvious: it consumes the attention of its recipients. Hence a wealth of information creates a poverty of attention, and a need to allocate that attention efficiently among the overabundance of information sources that might consume it. (Herbert A. Simon)

資訊所消耗之物很明顯：它消耗了接受者的注意力。因此，大量的資訊造成注意力不足，我們有必要在可能消耗它的過量資訊來源中有效地分配注意力。（司馬賀）

Forget about Nobel prizes; they aren't really very important. (Herbert A. Simon)

忘記諾貝爾獎。它們真的不是很重要。（司馬賀）

1979 年

Most of the progress in understanding how the universe works is made by people under 40, which is just as well, or we'd end up like the Kremlin run by people over 80. (Sheldon Lee Glashow)

在對於宇宙運作機制的了解中，大多數進步都是由 40 歲以下的人達成的。幸好如此，否則我們就會陷於停滯，一如由 80 歲以上的人執掌的克里姆林宮。（謝爾登·格拉肖）

1979 年

While my parents never had the time or money to secure university education themselves, they were adamant that their children should. In comfort and in love, we were taught the joys of knowledge and of work well done. I only regret that neither my mother nor my father could live to see the day I would accept the Nobel Prize. (Sheldon Lee Glashow)

雖然我的父母既無時間也無金錢保障自己的大學教育，但他們堅持認為子女應該得到。在舒適和愛中，我們學會了知識和完成工作的樂趣。我唯一遺憾的是，母親和父親都無法在有生之年，見到我接受諾貝爾獎的這一天。（謝爾登·格拉肖）

Tapestries are made by many artisans working together. The contributions of separate workers cannot be discerned in the completed work, and the loose and false threads have been covered over. So it is in our picture of particle physics. (Sheldon Lee Glashow)

掛毯是由許多工匠共同織成的。各個工匠的貢獻在成品中無法分辨，粗疏和錯誤的針腳已被掩蓋。這就是我們眼中的粒子物理學。（謝爾登·格拉肖）

This in effect is, the faith of all physicists; the deeper we seek, the more is our wonder excited, the more is the dazzlement for our gaze. (Abdus Salam)

實際上，這是所有物理學家的信念。我們探索得越深入，我們的驚奇就越強烈，我們的所見就越炫目。（阿卜杜勒·薩拉姆）

To be a good experimenter you must have patience towards things which are not always in your control. I think a theoretician has got to be patient too, but that is with something of his own creation, his own constructs, his own stupidities. (Abdus Salam)

1971-1980 理性與良知的碰撞

要成為優秀的實驗者，你必須對並不總是受你控制的事情有耐心。我想，理論家也必須有耐心，但那是針對他自己的創造、他自己的構思、他自己的愚笨而言。（阿卜杜勒‧薩拉姆）

Soon I knew the craft of experimental physics was beyond me —— it was the sublime quality of patience —— patience in accumulating data, patience with recalcitrant equipment —— which I sadly lacked. (Abdus Salam)

很快我就明白了，實驗物理學的技術超出了我的能力範圍 —— 它是一種崇高的耐心 —— 累積資料的耐心、對待不如意設備的耐心 —— 我可悲地缺乏這種能力。（阿卜杜勒‧薩拉姆）

From time immemorial, man has desired to comprehend the complexity of nature in terms of as few elementary concepts as possible. (Abdus Salam)

自遠古時代開始，人類就渴望依據盡可能少的基本概念理解自然的複雜性。（阿卜杜勒‧薩拉姆）

It seems that scientists are often attracted to beautiful theories in the way that insects are attracted to flowers —— not by logical deduction, but by something like a sense of smell. (Steven Weinberg)

科學家似乎經常被美麗的理論吸引，就像昆蟲被花朵吸引 —— 不是經由邏輯推理，而是經由一種嗅覺。（史蒂文‧溫伯格）

Like other theorists, I work with just pencil and paper, trying to make simple explanations of complicated phenomena. We leave it to the experimental physicists to decide whether our theories actually describe the real world. It was this opportunity to explain something about nature by noodling around with mathematical ideas that drew me into theoretical physics in the first place. (Steven Weinberg)

> 1979 年

跟別的理論家一樣，我只用筆和紙工作，試圖對複雜的現象做出簡明的解釋。我們由實驗物理學家認定我們的理論是否真實地描述現實世界。正是這種以思考數學觀念解釋自然現象的機會，使我當初投身於理論物理學。（史蒂文‧溫伯格）

Elementary particles are terribly boring, which is one reason why we're so interested in them. (Steven Weinberg)

基本粒子非常無聊，這是我們對它們如此深感興趣的原因之一。（史蒂文‧溫伯格）

I had just completed one semester at Crane Junior College when it was announced in 1933 that the school was to be closed for lack of funds. I then went to night school at the Lewis Institute, taking one or two courses, financing myself by working as a part-time shop clerk. (Herbert C. Brown)

我在克蘭專科學院剛上完一學期的課，1933 年，院方就宣布，由於資金不足，學院即將關閉。我隨後上了路易斯學院的夜校，學習一、兩門課程，當兼職店員為自己賺錢。（赫伯特‧布朗）

I went there and grew to know and love a fellow student, Sarah Baylen. Sarah had been the brightest student in chemistry at Crane prior to my arrival. She has described (Remembering HCB) how she initially "hated my guts." But since she could not beat me, she later decided to join me, to my everlasting delight. In 1934 Wright Junior College opened its doors. We went there and nine of us graduated in 1935 as the first graduating class. In my yearbook Sarah predicted that I would be a Nobel Laureate! (Herbert C. Brown)

我進入克蘭專科學院，認識並愛上了一個同學，莎拉‧貝倫。莎拉在我到來之前是學院的化學傑出人士。她曾經描述起初如何「討厭我的厚顏」。但由於未能使我知難而退，她後來下了決心跟我在一起。（見《回憶 HCB[73]》）這是我永遠的快樂。1934 年，萊特專科學院開始招生。我們進入學院，一共 9 位同學於 1935 年作為第一個畢業班畢業。在我的紀念冊上莎拉預言，我會成為諾貝爾獎得主！（赫伯特·布朗）

On my graduation, Sarah presented me with a gift —— a copy of Alfred Stock's book, The Hydrides of Boron and Silicon. This book interested me in the hydrides of boron and I undertook to study with Professor H. I. Schlesinger, then active in that area of research. (Herbert C. Brown)

當我畢業時，莎拉送給我一件禮物 —— 一本阿爾弗雷德·斯托克的著作，《硼和矽的氫化物》。這本書引起我對硼的氫化物的興趣，於是我師從赫爾曼·歐文·施勒辛格教授著手研究，後來就活躍在這個研究領域。（赫伯特·布朗）

I am an unusual example of a chemist who ended up in academic work because he could not find an industrial position. (Herbert C. Brown)

我是一個不尋常的例子，一個化學家由於找不到產業職位，結果從事了學術工作。（赫伯特·布朗）

Chemical research and mountaineering have much in common. If the goal or the summit is to be reached, both initiative and determination as well as perseverance are required. But after the hard work it is a great joy to be at the goal or the peak with its splendid panorama. However, especially in chemical research —— as far as new territory is concerned —— the results may sometimes be quite different: they may be disappointing or delightful. (Georg Wittig)

---

[73] HCB，即 Herbert C. Brown（赫伯特·C·布朗）。

> 1979 年

化學研究和登山運動有很多共同之處。欲達到目標或顛峰，就需要主動性和決心，以及毅力。然而在歷盡艱辛之後，達到目標或頂峰，滿眼風光壯麗，又是非凡的快樂。只是，尤其在化學研究上 —— 就新領域而言 —— 結果有時可能大不相同：也許令人失望，也許令人歡欣。（格奧爾格·威悌）

In high school my interests outside my academic work were debating, tennis, and to a lesser extent, acting. I became intensely interested in astronomy and devoured the popular works of astronomers such as Sir Arthur Eddington and Sir James Jeans, from which I learnt that a knowledge of mathematics and physics was essential to the pursuit of astronomy. This increased my fondness for those subjects. (Allan M. Cormack)

中學時我的課外興趣是辯論、網球，以及不那麼熱衷的表演。我對天文學產生了濃厚的興趣，貪婪地閱讀像亞瑟·愛丁頓爵士和詹姆士·金斯爵士這樣的天文學家的知名作品。我從中了解到數學和物理知識對於天文學追求不可或缺。這增加了我對這些科目的喜愛。（阿蘭·麥克萊德·科馬克）

Don't worry too much if you don't pass exams, so long as you feel you have understood the subject. It's amazing what you can get by the ability to reason things out by conventional methods, getting down to the basics of what is happening. (Godfrey N. Hounsfield)

只要覺得自己已經理解課程，考試不及格也無須過於擔憂。以常規方法推論問題，追本溯源，你能運用這種能力獲得的成果令人驚奇。（高弗雷·豪斯費爾德）

To hold the Sun in one's hands without being burned, to transmit it like

1971-1980 理性與良知的碰撞

a torch to those following, is a painful act but, I believe, a blessed one. We have need of it. One day the dogmas that hold men in chains will be dissolved before a consciousness so inundated with light that it will be one with the Sun, and it will arrive on those ideal shores of human dignity and liberty. (Odysseus Elytis)

把太陽擎在手上而不被灼傷，把它像火炬一樣傳遞給那些追隨者，這樣的行為是痛苦的，然而，我相信，也是幸福的。我們需要它。終有一天，把人們束縛在鎖鏈中的教條，將在一種意識面前消解，而這種意識如此輝煌，它將與太陽合一，它將照耀到人類尊嚴與自由的那些理想之岸。（奧季塞烏斯·伊利狄斯）

I am not speaking of the common and natural capacity of perceiving objects in all their detail, but of the power of the metaphor to only retain their essence, and to bring them to such a state of purity that their metaphysical significance appears like a revelation. (Odysseus Elytis)

我所說的，不是在所有細節中感知事物的普遍自然的能力，而是隱喻的力量，只保留它們的本質，並將它們提升到如此純淨的狀態，以至它們高度抽象的意義顯得猶如啟示。（奧季塞烏斯·伊利狄斯）

God doesn't require us to succeed; he only requires that you try. (Mother Teresa)

上帝沒要求我們成功。他只要求你們試一試。（德蕾莎修女）

Yesterday is gone. Tomorrow has not yet come. We have only today. Let us begin. (Mother Teresa)

昨天已經過去。明天尚未到來。我們只有今天。讓我們開始吧。（德蕾莎修女）

1979 年

Be faithful in small things because it is in them that your strength lies. (Mother Teresa)

在小事上要忠實,因為它是你的力量所在。(德蕾莎修女)

If you are humble nothing will touch you, neither praise nor disgrace, because you know what you are. (Mother Teresa)

你若謙卑即百事無礙,無論讚揚還是羞辱,因為你清楚自己為何等樣人。(德蕾莎修女)

You learn humility only by accepting humiliations. And you will meet humiliation through your life. The greatest humiliation is to know that you are nothing. (Mother Teresa)

只有接受羞辱才學得到謙卑。你將畢生遭遇羞辱。最大的羞辱是知道自己什麼都不是。(德蕾莎修女)

Never travel faster than your guardian angel can fly. (Mother Teresa)

行路永遠不要快於守護天使的飛翔。(德蕾莎修女)

I alone cannot change the world, but I can cast a stone across the waters to create many ripples. (Mother Teresa)

我一個人改變不了世界,但我可以向水面投一顆石子,激起層層漣漪。(德蕾莎修女)

Not all of us can do great things. But we can do small things with great love. (Mother Teresa)

並非所有人都能做大事。但我們可以懷著大愛做小事。(德蕾莎修女)

What we need is to love without getting tired. How does a lamp burn? Through the continuous input of small drops of oil. What are these drops of oil in our lamps? They are the small things of daily life: faithfulness, small words of kindness, a thought for others, our way of being silent, of looking, of speaking, and of acting. (Mother Teresa)

我們需要的是從無厭倦的愛。燈是怎麼燃燒的？透過涓滴燈油的持續輸入。我們的燈裡這些點點滴滴的燈油是什麼？它們是日常小事：忠誠，善意的片言隻語，為人著想，我們沉默的方式，觀察、說話和行事的方式。（德蕾莎修女）

It does not matter how much we give, but how much love we put into our giving. (Mother Teresa)

重要的不是我們付出多少，而是在付出中注入多少愛。（德蕾莎修女）

Love has no meaning if it isn't shared. Love has to be put into action. You have to love without expectation, to do something for love itself, not for what you may receive. If you expect something in return, then it isn't love, because true love is loving without conditions and expectations. (Mother Teresa)

如果愛不能分享就沒有意義。愛必須付諸行動。你必須不抱期待地愛，為了愛本身而行事，而非為了自己可能得到的東西。如果期待回報，那就不是愛，因為真正的愛是沒有條件和期待的愛。（德蕾莎修女）

We ourselves feel that what we are doing is just a drop in the ocean. But if that drop was not in the ocean, I think the ocean would be less because of that missing drop. I do not agree with the big way of doing things. (Mother Teresa)

我們自己覺得，我們在做的事不過是滄海涓滴。然而，如果這一滴水沒有流入大海，我認為大海會由於這一滴水的缺失而減少。我不認同做事轟轟烈烈。（德蕾莎修女）

1979 年

I want you to be concerned about your next-door neighbor. Do you know your next-door neighbor? (Mother Teresa)

我希望你關心鄰居。你認識鄰居嗎？（德蕾莎修女）

We shall never know all the good that a simple smile can do. (Mother Teresa)

我們永遠都不知道一個簡單的微笑能帶來多少好處。（德蕾莎修女）

Most of the people in the world are poor, so if we knew the economics of being poor, we would know much of the economics that really matters. Most of the world's poor people earn their living from agriculture, so if we knew the economics of agriculture, we would know much of the economics of being poor. (Theodore W. Schultz)

世界上大多數人都很窮，所以我們如果了解貧窮的經濟學，就會了解很多真正重要的經濟狀況。世界上大多數窮人依靠農業為生，所以我們如果了解農業的經濟學，就會了解貧窮的經濟學。（狄奧多·威廉·舒茲）

I have been asked: What do economists do? My reply is: When economists face disagreements, they appeal to a long-established, basic Law of Talk, which is, "The more intelligent people are, the more certain they are to disagree on matters of social principle and policy, and the more acute will be the disagreement." Herein lies the proof that economists are intelligent! (Theodore W. Schultz)

有人問我：經濟學家是做什麼的？我的回答是：經濟學家們面臨分歧時，會訴諸一種由來已久的、基本的談話法則，即：「人們越聰明，在社會原則和政策問題上就越必然意見分歧，且分歧就越尖銳。」這就證明了經濟學家是聰明人！（狄奧多·威廉·舒茲）

1971-1980 理性與良知的碰撞

Science affects all our ways of thinking about the world, both the physical world which, if I may make so bold, is easy to understand because it is regular and follows simple laws, and also the social world, which is more baffling and less predictable. (Arthur Lewis)

科學影響著我們對世界的所有思考方式，包括物理世界和社會世界。前者，我不妨大膽地說，是容易理解的，因為它有規律，遵循簡單的法則；後者則更令人困惑而難以預測。（威廉・阿瑟・路易斯）

We cannot give our students all that they expect, whether by way of the quality of their schooling or by way of the jobs that they were hoping to get. Student frustration is a worldwide phenomenon, pushing our societies into adjusting faster than they are used to. (Arthur Lewis)

我們無法給予學生他們所期待的一切，無論是教育的品質還是期待的職業。學生的挫折感是世界性現象，它推動著社會以更快的速度進行調整。（威廉・阿瑟・路易斯）

1980 年

I discovered through this high school physics class that I had a great love of analyzing data, any data —— the deviation of a pendulum period from a constant when the amplitude was too large, or the details of the approach to equilibrium in a calorimeter. While in high school, I read serious science books for youngsters: I especially liked the book by George Gamow, entitled One Two Three... Infinity: Facts and Speculations of Science. (James Watson Cronin)

1980 年

經由這一門高中物理課,我發現自己酷愛分析資料,任何資料——振幅過大時鐘擺的週期與常數的偏差,或者熱量計中接近平衡的細節。中學時期,我讀過一些嚴謹的青少年科學讀物,特別喜歡喬治·伽莫夫的那本《從一到無限大:科學中的事實和臆測》[74]。(詹姆斯·克羅寧)

When I ask myself, "Who are the happiest people on the planet?" my answer is, "those who can't wait to wake up in the morning to get back to what they were doing the day before.」 (James Watson Cronin)

當我問自己,「誰是這個星球上最幸福的人?」我的回答是:「那些等不及早上醒來回到前一天工作中去的人。」(詹姆斯·克羅寧)

On even the worst days, when nothing was working at the lab, I knew that at home I would find warmth, peace, companionship, and encouragement. As a consequence, the next day would surely be better. (James Watson Cronin)

即便在最糟糕的日子裡,當實驗室的研究毫無進展的時候,我知道在家裡會發現溫暖、安寧、陪伴和鼓勵。所以,第二天肯定會更好。(詹姆斯·克羅寧)

At any one time there is a natural tendency among physicists to believe that we already know the essential ingredients of a comprehensive theory. But each time a new frontier of observation is broached we inevitably discover new phenomena which force us to modify substantially our previous conceptions. I believe this process to be unending, that the delights and challenges of unexpected discovery will continue always. (Val Logsdon Fitch)

在任何時候,物理學家都會自然地傾向於相信我們已經知道了某一個綜合理論的基本要素。但每當開闢一個新的觀察領域,我們不免發現

---

[74] 此書有中譯本。

1971–1980 理性與良知的碰撞

新的現象,這就迫使我們對自己先前的觀念大加修改。我相信這個過程是無止境的,意外發現的快樂和挑戰將永遠持續下去。(瓦爾·菲奇)

It is highly improbable, a priori, to begin life on a cattle ranch and then appear in Stockholm to receive the Nobel Prize in physics. But it is much less improbable to me when I reflect on the good fortune I have had in the ambiance provided by my parents, my family, my teachers, colleagues and students. (Val Logsdon Fitch)

在牧場上出生長大,後來則現身於斯德哥爾摩接受諾貝爾物理學獎,推論起來,這太不可能了。然而當我回想起自己在父母、家庭、老師、同事和學生們提供的環境中所擁有的好運時,這件事就遠非多麼不可能了。(瓦爾·菲奇)

There is no greater joy than that of feeling oneself a creator. The triumph of life is expressed by creation. (Paul Berg)

沒有比感到自己是個創造者更大的快樂了。人生的歡欣是由創造表達的。(保羅·伯格)

With time, many of the facts I learned were forgotten but I never lost the excitement of discovery. (Paul Berg)

隨著時間流逝,學過的許多事實都遺忘了,但我從沒忘記發現的興奮。(保羅·伯格)

That work led to the emergence of the recombinant DNA technology thereby providing a major tool for analyzing mammalian gene structure and function and formed the basis for me receiving the 1980 Nobel Prize in Chemistry. (Paul Berg)

1980 年

這一項工作導致了重組 DNA 技術的出現,從而為分析哺乳動物的基因結構與功能提供了一種重要的工具,並為我獲得 1980 年諾貝爾化學獎奠定了基礎。(保羅·伯格)

One must think like a man of action, act like a man of thought. (Paul Berg)

人必須如行動家一般思考,如思想家一般行動。(保羅·伯格)

Looking back, I realize that nurturing curiosity and the instinct to seek solutions are perhaps the most important contributions education can make. (Paul Berg)

回顧之下,我意識到培養好奇心和尋求解決辦法的直覺,也許是教育所能做出的最重要的貢獻。(保羅·伯格)

Those who have worked with students and experienced the discomfort of their curiosity, the frustrations of their obstinacy and the exhilaration of their growth know first hand the magnitude of their contributions. (Paul Berg)

那些跟學生們一起工作過的人,體會過他們的好奇心引起的不適、他們的固執導致的挫折,還有他們的成長帶來的快慰,都真切了解自己的貢獻之大。(保羅·伯格)

The best project is one that asks a novel question. (Walter Gilbert)

最好的項目是提出新奇問題的那一個。(華特·吉爾伯特)

By asking a novel question that you don't know the answer to, you discover whether you can formulate a way of finding the answer, and you stretch your own mind, and very often you learn something new. (Walter Gilbert)

透過問自己一個不知道答案的新奇問題,你將發現自己是否能夠形

成找到答案的方法，並拓展自己的思路，而且通常你會學到新的東西。（華特‧吉爾伯特）

The virtues of science are skepticism and independence of thought. (Walter Gilbert)

科學的長處是懷疑精神和獨立思考。（華特‧吉爾伯特）

Early on, it's good to develop the ability to write. Learning to write is a useful exercise, even if what you're writing about is not that relevant. (Walter Gilbert)

儘早發展寫作能力是一件好事。學習寫作是一種有用的練習，即便所寫的東西沒多大意義。（華特‧吉爾伯特）

Training with Elvin Kabat was one of the significant experiences in my development as a scientist. Elvin Kabat is a hard task-master with rigorous standards and an absolute respect for the quantitative approach to science. He felt that if a phenomenon could not be quantitated, it did not deserve to be studied. He taught me Immunochemistry and basic Immunology, but more importantly, I learned the significance of experimental proof, the need for intellectual honesty and scientific integrity. (Baruj Benacerraf)

在我作為科學家的成長中，埃爾文‧卡巴特[75]的訓練是一段重要的經歷。埃爾文‧卡巴特對工作的要求非常嚴格，有著嚴謹的標準和對科學定量方法的絕對尊重。他認為，一種現象若不能量化，就不值得研究。他教我免疫化學和基礎免疫學，然而更重要的是，我了解了實驗證明的重要性、知識誠實和科學誠信的必要性。（巴茹‧貝納塞拉夫）

The way already trod is but a simple introduction. They are still many marvellous pages to be written. (Jean Dausset)

---

[75] 埃爾文‧卡巴特，著名生物醫學科學家，定量免疫化學創始人之一。

已經走過的路不過是簡單的序言。以下還有許多精采的篇章要寫。（讓・多塞）

Science is like a web, growing by interactions that reach out in time and, space. My own place in this web was made possible by strands from the past and the help of contemporaries. To them, my deep appreciation. (George D. Snell)

科學就像一張網，由於在時間以及空間中伸展的相互作用而成長。我本人在這一張網上的位置，離不開先賢的結網和今人的幫助。我向他們致以深深的謝意。（喬治・斯內爾）

Our species should have disappeared a long time ago, and it is still alive, incredibly resistant. That you and I happen to be part of it should be enough to give us pause for meditation. (Czeslaw Milosz)

我們這個物種理應早就消失了，而至今依然生存，頑強得難以置信。你我碰巧是其中的一部分，這足以讓我們停一停，好好思考。（切斯瓦夫・米沃什）

To believe you are magnificent. And gradually to discover that you are not magnificent. Enough labor for one human life. (Czeslaw Milosz)

相信自己很偉大。逐漸發現自己並不偉大。足以糾結一生。（切斯瓦夫・米沃什）

Nonviolence is absolute respect for each human being. (Adolfo Pérez Esquivel)

非暴力是對每一個人的絕對尊重。（阿道弗・佩雷斯・埃斯基維爾）

We cannot sow seeds with clenched fists. To sow we must open our hands. (Adolfo Pérez Esquivel)

我們無法握緊拳頭撒種。播種必須張開雙手。（阿道弗‧佩雷斯‧埃斯基維爾）

An early fascination with higher mathematics at the university level blossomed into speculative thinking that could provide a basis for dealing with economic issues. (Lawrence R. Klein)

早年對於大學高等數學的迷戀發展成理論性思考，為處理經濟問題提供基礎。（勞倫斯‧克萊因）

The completion of my undergraduate training at the University of California (Berkeley) provided just the needed touches of rigor at advanced levels in both economics and mathematics. (Lawrence R. Klein)

加州大學（柏克萊分校）的學士班訓練，賦予我進階程度的經濟學和數學不可或缺的嚴謹素養。（勞倫斯‧克萊因）

It came as a surprise to find that a professional society and journal (Econometrica) were flourishing, and I entered this area of study with great enthusiasm. (Lawrence R. Klein)

我驚奇地發現，一個專業的團體及期刊（《計量經濟學》）方興未艾，我於是懷著極大的熱情投身於這個研究領域。（勞倫斯‧克萊因）

1981–1990
全球視野與道德辯證

1981 年

I selected to specialize in the study of physics at the university, because I found this subject the most difficult and challenging. I was especially intrigued by the mathematical description of physical phenomena, such as the motion of matter and the direction of light waves. I was fascinated by reading about the lives of Marie Curie and Albert Einstein, who were famous scientists in my school days. At the university I considered myself not bright enough to specialize in theoretical physics, and I learned that laboratory work often involves setbacks and negative outcomes. The success in making some new observations is, however, very exciting, although it is usually achieved with one percent inspiration and ninety nine percent perspiration. (Nicolaas Bloembergen)

在大學裡我選擇專攻物理學，因為我發現這一科最難學、最富於挑戰性。我對物理現象的數學描述尤其著迷，比如物質的運動和光波的方向。我嗜讀瑪麗·居禮和阿爾伯特·愛因斯坦的傳記，他們是我學生時期著名的科學家。在大學裡，我認為自己不夠聰明，不能專攻理論物理；我還發現實驗室工作經常帶來挫折和否定的結果。然而，成功獲取一些

1981–1990 全球視野與道德辯證

新的觀察非常令人激動,儘管它通常是透過百分之一的靈感和百分之九十九的汗水實現的。(尼古拉斯·布隆伯根)

In retrospect my choice to become a physicist more than sixty-five years ago has been very rewarding. Perhaps the life sciences, geophysics and cosmology present even greater challenges at the present time. If you are curious enough, you should seriously consider further scientific training. New technologies have a profound influence on society in all countries, and they are all based on scientific principles. Every country will need further leaders with some familiarity of the scientific method. Perhaps you will be so intrigued by some questions posed by nature, that you will decide to remain a scientist. (Nicolaas Bloembergen)

回想起來,超過 65 年前我選擇成為物理學家是非常值得的。當前,生命科學、地球物理學和宇宙學也許提出了更大的挑戰。如果你足夠好奇,你應該認真考慮進一步的科學培訓。新技術對所有國家的社會都具有深遠的影響,它們都是以科學原理為基礎的。每一個國家都需要更多熟悉科學方法的領導者。也許你會對大自然提出的一些問題如此著迷,以至於決定持續做個科學家。(尼古拉斯·布隆伯根)

As was the case for Nobel's own invention of dynamite, the uses that are made of increased knowledge can serve both beneficial and potentially harmful ends. Increased knowledge clearly implies increased responsibility. (Nicolaas Bloembergen)

與諾貝爾本人發明炸藥的情形相同,對於知識成長的運用可能帶來好處,也可能帶來潛在的危害。知識的增加顯然意味著責任的增加。(尼古拉斯·布隆伯根)

1981 年

As a boy, I was always interested in scientific things, electrical, mechanical or astronomical, and read nearly everything that the library could provide on these subjects. (Arthur Leonard Schawlow)

少年時，我一直對科學上的事情感興趣，電子、機械或天文，我讀遍了圖書館能夠提供的這些方面幾乎所有書籍。（阿瑟·肖洛）

I do not have the patience with design details that an engineer must have. Physics has given me a chance to concentrate on concepts and methods, and I have enjoyed it greatly. (Arthur Leonard Schawlow)

工程師必須擁有設計細節方面的耐心，而我並不具備。物理學給了我專注於概念和方法的機會，我非常享受它。（阿瑟·肖洛）

To do successful research, you don't need to know everything, you just need to know one thing that isn't known. (Arthur Leonard Schawlow)

要做成功的研究，你無須知道所有的事情，只須知道一件未知的事情。（阿瑟·肖洛）

Anything worth doing is worth doing twice, the first time quick and dirty and the second time the best way you can. (Arthur Leonard Schawlow)

任何值得做的事都值得做兩次。第一次又快又粗糙，第二次力爭最好。（阿瑟·肖洛）

Working with Charles Townes was particularly stimulating. Not only was he the leader in research on microwave spectroscopy, but he was extraordinarily effective in getting the best from his students and colleagues. He would listen carefully to the confused beginnings of an idea, and join in developing whatever was worthwhile in it, without ever dominating the discussions. (Arthur Leonard Schawlow)

1981–1990 全球視野與道德辯證

與查爾斯・湯斯[76]共事尤其令人興奮。他不僅是微波光譜研究的領軍人物，還非常善於博採眾長，凝聚學生和同事的見解。他會仔細傾聽一個想法混亂的開端，參與開發其中任何有價值的東西，而從不主導討論。（阿瑟・肖洛）

I had no advance indication that I would be receiving it. The winner always comes as a surprise. (Kai M. Siegbahn)

得諾貝爾獎我事先並不知情。獲獎者總是出乎意料的。（凱・西格巴恩）

It's a decided advantage if you start discussing physics every day at breakfast. (Kai M. Siegbahn)

如果你家每天早餐時就在討論物理，這是一種決定性的優勢。[77]（凱・西格巴恩）

Japanese universities have a chair system that is a fixed hierarchy. This has its merits when trying to work as a laboratory on one theme. But if you want to do original work you must start young, and young people are limited by the chair system. Even if students cannot become assistant professors at an early age they should be encouraged to do original work. Industry is more likely to put its research effort into its daily business. It is very difficult for it to become involved in pure chemistry. There is a need to encourage long-range research, even if we don't know its goal and if its application is unknown. (Kenichi Fukui)

日本的大學有一種座次體系，即固定的層級。當試圖就一個主題作

---

[76] 查爾斯・湯斯，1964 年諾貝爾物理學獎得主。
[77] 西格巴恩的父親為 1924 年諾貝爾物理學獎得主。

1981 年

為一個實驗室工作時,這有其優點。但是你若想進行原創性工作,就必須從年輕時開始,而年輕人受制於座次體系。學生即便在年輕時當不上助理教授,也應該被鼓勵進行原創性工作。企業更有可能將其研究精力投入日常業務之中。它很難涉足純化學研究。我們有必要鼓勵長期研究,即使不清楚其目標何在,其應用亦屬未知。(福井謙一)

I must confess that, when I was writing the 1952 paper, I never imagined I would be coming to Stockholm to receive the Nobel Prize 30 years later. (Kenichi Fukui)

我必須承認,我在寫 1952 年那篇論文時,根本沒想到 30 年後自己會來斯德哥爾摩領諾貝爾獎。(福井謙一)

Chemists make molecules, by hard work, clever construction, and chance. They create, subject to some governing rules, something new, often something that has not been on Earth before. And then they study their creation, see its properties and relationships. They contemplate it. And they go on to make more molecules. I think the process is much like art. But there are differences. (Roald Hoffmann)

化學家經由辛苦的工作、巧妙的結構和偶然的機會製造分子。他們按照一些支配性規則,創造了新的東西,通常是地球上前未有的東西。然後他們研究自己的創造物,觀察其屬性和關係。他們冥思苦想。他們繼續創造更多的分子。我認為這個過程很像藝術。不過有所不同。(羅德·霍夫曼)

I love chemistry because it's sort of human in scale —— infinitely complex, but always tangible, always real. (Roald Hoffmann)

我鍾愛化學,因為它與人類有幾分相稱 —— 無限複雜,但總是具體的,總是真實的。(羅德·霍夫曼)

1981–1990 全球視野與道德辯證

We feel ourselves elevated because we identify ourselves with the powers of nature, ascribing their vast impact to ourselves, because our fantasy rests on the wings of the storm as we roar into the heights and wander into the depths of infinity. Thus we ourselves expand into a boundless natural power. (Roald Hoffmann)

我們感到自己提升了,因為我們認同自然的力量,把它們的巨大影響歸於自己,因為我們的幻想藉助於風暴的翅膀,上天入地於無限之中。於是,我們自己便擴展成無邊的自然力量。(羅德・霍夫曼)

The language of science is a language under stress. Words are being made to describe things that seem indescribable in words —— equations, chemical structures and so forth. Words do not, cannot mean all that they stand for, yet they are all we have to describe experience. By being a natural language under tension, the language of science is inherently poetic. There is metaphor aplenty in science. Emotions emerge shaped as states of matter and more interestingly, matter acts out what goes on in the soul. (Roald Hoffmann)

科學的語言是壓力下的語言。我們用詞句來描述似乎難以用詞句描述的事物 —— 方程式、化學結構等等。詞句並非也無法意味其所代表的一切,然而它們就是我們用來描述經驗的全部。科學語言是一種張力下的自然語言,天生就富有詩意。科學飽含隱喻。情感以物質的形態顯現,更有趣的是,物質表現出精神上發生的事情。(羅德・霍夫曼)

Music, perhaps better than any other art form, reflects our deep social-emotional nature. (Roald Hoffmann)

音樂,也許比其他任何藝術形式都真切地反映了我們深層的社會情感本質。(羅德・霍夫曼)

1981 年

There appear to be two modes of thinking, verbal and nonverbal, represented rather separately in left and right hemispheres respectively and that our education system, as well as science in general, tends to neglect the nonverbal form of intellect. What it comes down to is that modern society discriminates against the right hemisphere. (Roger W. Sperry)

似乎存在兩種思考模式,語言的和非語言的,分別在大腦左、右兩半球中分別地展現;而我們的教育系統,以及一般的科學,傾向於忽視非語言形式的智力。歸根究柢,現代社會歧視右半球。(羅傑‧斯佩里)

Can the brain understand the brain? Can it understand the mind? Is it a giant computer, or some other kind of giant machine, or something more? (David H. Hubel)

人腦能理解人腦嗎?它能理解心靈嗎?它是一臺巨大的電腦,還是其他某種巨大的機器,還是此外的什麼?(大衛‧休伯爾)

A colleague at Harvard sent me a note of congratulations with a quotation from Dante's Inferno which in translation reads "and turning our stern to the morning we made of our oars, wings for the mad flight." —— It states beautifully our dream as scientists, a dream only rarely realized. Perhaps it is more accurate to compare a scientist's life with the fate of Sisyphus, the shrewd and greedy king of Corinth, except that we feel blessed, not doomed, in our labors, —— and our greed is for discovery, not for power and wealth. Today, of course, the quotation from Dante seems most appropriate since we were literally winged to this beautiful city as a result of our labors. (Torsten N. Wiesel)

哈佛大學有一位同事寄來一封祝賀信,引用了但丁《地獄》篇的句子,翻譯為:「掉轉航向,背對晨光,我們把雙槳當成狂飛的翅膀。」[78]——它優美地講述了我們作為科學家的夢想,一個很少實現的夢想。比較一下科學家的生活與薛西弗斯,那個精明而貪心的科林斯國王的命運,也許更準確,除了我們在勞動之中感到幸福而非痛苦——我們的貪心是為了發現而非權力與財富。當然,如今引自但丁作品的話看來最合適,正是因為辛勤勞動的結果,我們乘著飛機來到這個美麗的城市,就像長了翅膀。(托斯坦·威澤爾)

I cannot become modest; too many things burn in me; the old solutions are falling apart; nothing has been done yet with the new ones. So I begin, everywhere at once, as if I had a century ahead of me. (Elias Canetti)

我做不到穩紮穩打,太多的想法在內心燃燒,舊的解決方案正在瓦解,新的方法還未見實效。所以我開始行動,同時從各個地方開始,彷彿我面前還有一個世紀。(伊利亞斯·卡內提)

One should not confuse the craving for life with endorsement of it. (Elias Canetti)

人不應該把對生命的渴望和對生命的認可混為一談。(伊利亞斯·卡內提)

I studied economics and made it my career for two reasons. The subject was and is intellectually fascinating and challenging, particularly to someone with taste and talent for theoretical reasoning and quantitative analysis. At the same time it offered the hope, as it still does, that improved understanding could better the lot of mankind. (James Tobin)

我學習經濟學並以之為事業有兩個原因。這個學科一直具有智力上的吸引力與挑戰性,尤其對於具備理論推理和定量分析興趣與才能的人

---

[78] 詩句所描述的是但丁一行知難犯險,闖入大洋的情景。

而言。與此同時，它帶來了希望，至今如此，即理解力的提升可以改善人類的命運。（詹姆士·托賓）

Many critics doubt that economics is either grown-up or science. Though economists have something to do for good or ill with the performance of economics, it makes little more sense thus to score the profession than to judge meteorology by the weather. (James Tobin)

許多批評家懷疑經濟學成熟與否，或是否科學。儘管經濟學家對經濟表現好壞發揮一定作用，但依此而評價此專業，就像根據天氣來評價氣象學一般毫無意義。（詹姆士·托賓）

I like teaching, and I do a lot of it. I never fail to learn, from the students themselves and from the discipline of presenting ideas clearly to them. A large and durable reward is the legion of friends of all ages. (James Tobin)

我喜歡教學，並且大量從事教學工作。從學生本身，從清晰地向他們表達想法的訓練中，我總是有所得益。一份龐大而持久的回報便是擁有各年齡層的朋友群。（詹姆士·托賓）

1982 年

The Nobel award occasions a unique celebration of the vision of science by the public at large. The prestige the prize confers today is largely due to the extraordinary diligence of the Nobel committees. (Kenneth G. Wilson)

諾貝爾獎是整體大眾對於科學願景的獨特慶祝。如今這個獎項賦予的聲望在相當程度上歸功於諾貝爾委員會的非凡努力。（肯尼斯·威爾森）

1981–1990 全球視野與道德辯證

Human curiosity, the urge to know, is a powerful force and is perhaps the best secret weapon of all in the struggle to unravel the workings of the natural world. (Aaron Klug)

人的好奇心，求知欲，是一股強大的力量，也許是所有人在探索自然界運作的奮鬥中最好的祕密武器。（阿龍·克盧格）

I am deeply conscious that though the Prize has been awarded to me, it is a Prize also to my field of the study of biological machinery. This field is not necessarily glamorous, nor does it often produce immediate results, but it seeks to increase our basic understanding of living processes. The work requires a moderately large investment in technological and theoretical developments and long periods of time to carry them out, without the pressure to achieve quick or short term results. This is, of course, in the gift of our fellow citizens and we very much appreciate the freedom to follow our instincts and to try to solve what we think can be solved. People often ask what is the use of it. In a world where there are pressing problems, why doesn't one devote one's efforts to the practical benefits of mankind. I need only recall the answer of the great Michael Faraday, when at a public lecture he was demonstrating the production of electricity. "Of what use is your invention, Mr. Faraday?" demanded an important lady. "Madam", he replied, "of what use is a new born child?" (Aaron Klug)

我深深意識到，這個獎項雖然是頒發給我，它也是授予我所從事的生物機械研究領域。這個領域未必魅力十足，也不常產生立竿見影的效果，但它尋求增加我們對生命過程的基本理解。這一項工作的技術和理論發展需要比較大的投資，完成它們也需要很長的時間，而免於達成快速或短期結果的壓力。當然，這取決於同胞們的慷慨。能夠自由地依從直覺，嘗試解決我們認為可以解決的問題，對此我們非常感激。人們常常問它的用途是什麼，在一個存在著各種緊迫問題的世界裡，一個人為什麼不致力於追求人類的實際利益。我只須重提偉大的麥可・法拉第的回答。在一次公開演講中，他演示著電流的產生，一位身分不凡的女士提問：「你的發明有什麼用，法拉第先生？」「夫人，」他答道，「一個新生的孩子有什麼用？」（阿龍・克盧格）

The traditional boundaries between various fields of science are rapidly disappearing and what is more important science does not know any national borders. The scientists of the world are forming an invisible network with a very free flow of scientific information —— a freedom accepted by the countries of the world irrespective of political systems or religions... Great care must be taken that the scientific network is utilized only for scientific purposes —— if it gets involved in political questions it loses its special status and utility as a nonpolitical force for development. (Sune K. Bergström)

不同科學領域之間的傳統界限正在迅速消失。更重要的是，科學不分國界。世界上的科學家正在形成一個無形的網路，擁有非常自由的科學資訊流動——被世界各國所接受的自由，無論政治制度或宗教。……必須極為注意的是，科學網路僅用於科學目的——如果捲入政治問題，它就失去了其作為非政治發展力量的特殊地位和效用。（伯格斯特龍）

The literature Nobel laureate of this year has said that an author can do anything as long as his readers believe him. A scientist cannot do anything that is not checked and rechecked by scientists of this network before it is accepted. (Sune K. Bergström)

1981-1990 全球視野與道德辯證

今年的諾貝爾文學獎得主曾說，只要讀者信任，作家什麼事都能做。在未經這個網路的科學家們反覆檢查而接受之前，一個科學家什麼事都不能做。（蘇恩・伯格斯特龍）

There are almost unlimited possibilities for making discoveries and to uncover the unknown. It is in the nature of the discovery that it can not be planned or programmed. On the contrary it consists of surprises and appears many times in the most unexpected places. However, the basis of the discovery is imagination, careful reasoning and experimentation where the use of knowledge created by those who came before is an important component. (Bengt I. Samuelsson)

發現和揭示未知事物的可能性幾乎是無限的。發現在本質上不能設計或規劃。相反地，它充滿驚奇，屢屢出現於最意想不到的處所。然而，發現的基礎是想像力、仔細的推論和實驗，對前人所創造知識的運用則是實驗的重要組成部分。（本特・薩穆埃爾松）

We are just in the beginning of gathering knowledge about man and his environment. We can hardly comprehend the enormous possibilities that are inherent in discovering the structure and function of nature from the inner space of particles and atoms to the cells of the human body as well as the outer space of stars and galaxies. To use the new knowledge in technical and medical developments to combat poverty and disease throughout the world is indeed a challenge. (Bengt I. Samuelsson)

我們才剛開始收集關於人類及其環境的知識。我們幾乎很難想像探索自然界結構與功能所包含的巨大可能性，從粒子和原子的內部空間到人體細胞，以及外太空的恆星和星系。運用技術與醫學發展方面的新知

1982 年

識在全世界對抗貧困和疾病實屬挑戰。（本特・薩穆埃爾松）

If we look back ten years at a time it is striking that the only consistent pattern is that we underestimate the rate of progress. In the biomedical sciences e.g. our knowledge about the structure and function of every cell in the human body is far greater today than ten years ago. The revolutionary findings of the new biology has swept through in all disciplines of biomedical research. And the increased knowledge and insight can be used to understand disease processes and to develop methods to combat disease and increase quality of life. (Bengt I. Samuelsson)

如果以 10 年為階段回顧過往，顯而易見，唯一不變的是我們低估了進步的速度。例如在生物醫學科學中，對人體各個細胞結構與功能的理解，如今比 10 年前遠遠進步得多。新生物學的革命性發現已經席捲生物醫學研究的所有學科。增加的知識和洞察可以用於了解疾病過程，開發對抗疾病和提高生活品質的方法。（本特・薩穆埃爾松）

And every time a significant discovery is being made one sets in motion a tremendous activity in laboratories and industrial enterprises throughout the world. It is like the ant who suddenly finds food and walks back to the anthill while sending out material called food attracting substance. The other ants follow the path immediately in order to benefit from the finding and continue to do so as long as the supply is rich. Then they switch to another source opened by another discovery. If we could understand the language of the ant we would probably hear the same excitement and exhilarating joy that one can hear in the laboratories when new knowledge is suddenly uncovered. (Bengt I. Samuelsson)

1981-1990 全球視野與道德辯證

每當有重大發現時，它就在全世界的實驗室和工業企業中引發重大行動。這就像螞蟻突然發現食物，於是走回蟻丘，同時釋出名為食物吸引物的物質。其他螞蟻會立即循路而去，以便從發現中獲益，只要供應充足，牠們就會繼續這樣做。然後他們轉向由另一項發現開關的另一個來源。假如我們聽得懂螞蟻的語言，很可能會聽到一片興奮歡欣，跟在實驗室裡突然發現新知識時所能聽到的一般無二。（本特·薩穆埃爾松）

It is sometimes said that the major discoveries have already been made and that there is nothing important left to find. This attitude is altogether too pessimistic. There are plenty of ideas and plenty of things left to discover. The trick is to find the right path from one to the other. (John R. Vane)

人們有時說，重大發現已經做出，沒有重要的東西等待被發掘了。這種態度實在過於悲觀。有大量的想法和大量的事物等待發現。要訣是要找到由此及彼的正確途徑。（約翰·范恩）

The medicines of today are based upon thousands of years of knowledge accumulated from folklore, serendipity and scientific discovery. The new medicines of tomorrow will be based on the discoveries that are being made now, arising from basic research in laboratories around the world. (John R. Vane)

今天的藥物是基於數千年來由民間傳說、意外發現和科學探索所累積的知識。未來的新藥將基於目前世界各地實驗室正在進行的基礎研究所帶來的新發現。（約翰·范恩）

Fundamental discoveries can and should be made in industry or academies, but to carry that knowledge forward and to develop a new drug to the market has to depend on the resources of industry. (John R. Vane)

基礎發現可以而且應該在企業或學術界中進行，然而要發展這種知

1982 年

識並針對市場開發新藥，就必須依靠企業資源。（約翰·范恩）

Ways have to be found to maintain university research untramelled by requirements of forecasting application or usefulness. (John R. Vane)

必須找到辦法確保大學研究不受制於預測用途或效益要求。（約翰·范恩）

What matters in life is not what happens to you but what you remember and how you remember it. (Gabriel García Márquez)

生活中重要的事不是發生在你身上的，而是你所記憶的和如何記憶的。（加布列·賈西亞·馬奎斯）

A man knows when he is growing old because he begins to look like his father. (Gabriel García Márquez)

一個人知道自己在變老了，因為他開始變得像他的父親。（加布列·賈西亞·馬奎斯）

No, not rich. I am a poor man with money, which is not the same thing. (Gabriel García Márquez)

不，不是富有。我是一個有錢的窮人，這是不一樣的。（加布列·賈西亞·馬奎斯）

I have, despite all disillusionment, never, never allowed myself to feel like giving up. This is my message today; it is not worthy of a human being to give up. (Alva Myrdal)

儘管幻想全部破滅，我從未、從未容許自己有放棄的想法。這就是我今天要說的話，人類不值得放棄。（阿爾瓦·默達爾）

Nobel was a genuine friend of peace. He even went so far as to believe that he had invented a tool of destruction, dynamite, which would make war so senseless that it would become impossible. He was wrong. (Alva Myrdal)

諾貝爾是和平的真正朋友。他甚至相信自己發明了一種毀滅工具，炸藥，它使戰爭變得如此毫無意義，而這是不可能發生的。他錯了。（阿爾瓦‧默達爾）

As so rightly stated by that eminent philosopher of history who was Arnold Toynbee "now we have something that could really extinguish life on our planet". Mankind has not found itself in a similar situation since the end of the palaeolithic age. (Alfonso García Robles)

正如那位傑出的歷史哲學家，阿諾德‧約瑟‧湯恩比非常正確地指出：「現在我們有了真正足以滅絕地球上生命的東西。」自舊石器時代結束以來，人類不曾遇到類似的情況。（阿方索‧加西亞‧羅夫萊斯）

Unlike the members of the physical and biological sciences, the economist is asked to explain his work in a manner that is interesting and convincing to a weary listener. Yet there is no reason to believe that the explanation of our economic and social world is inherently simpler than the explanation of our physical world. (George J. Stigler)

與物理和生物科學的研究者不同，經濟學家被要求採取既有趣味性又具說服力的方式，來向不耐煩的聽眾解釋自己的工作。然而沒有理由相信，對經濟和社會世界的解釋本質上比對物質世界的解釋更簡單。（喬治‧史蒂格勒）

The delicate and intricate pattern of competition and cooperation in the economic behavior of the hundreds of thousands of citizens of Stockholm offers a challenge to the economist that is perhaps as complex as the challenges of the physicist and the chemist. (George J. Stigler)

斯德哥爾摩千千萬萬公民的經濟行為中微妙而複雜的競爭與合作模式，為經濟學家帶來的挑戰恐怕跟物理學家和化學家所面對的同樣複雜。（喬治・史蒂格勒）

We economists are held responsible for the failures of economic policy. Each surge of inflation, each wave of unemployment is laid at our doors. The physicist is not blamed when a meteor hits the earth; the chemist is not held responsible for the misuse of poisons; and the medical sciences do not apologize for the common cold. (George J. Stigler)

我們經濟學家被認為對經濟政策的失敗負有責任。每一次通貨膨脹、每一波失業潮都歸咎於我們。流星撞擊地球時物理學家不受責備，化學家對毒藥濫用不擔責任，醫學科學也不為普通感冒道歉賠罪。（喬治・史蒂格勒）

1983 年

In some strange way, any new fact or insight that I may have found has not seemed to me as a "discovery" of mine, but rather something that had always been there and that I had chanced to pick up. (Subrahmanyan Chandrasekhar)

以某種奇怪的方式，我可能發現的任何新的事實或見解，在我看來都不算是我的「發現」，而是一直存在的東西，由我偶然得之。（蘇布拉馬尼安・錢德拉塞卡）

| 1981-1990 全球視野與道德辯證

I think one could say that a certain modesty toward understanding nature is a precondition to the continued pursuit of science. (Subrahmanyan Chandrasekhar)

我認為不妨說,對於了解自然保持一定的謙遜,是繼續追求科學的先決條件。(蘇布拉馬尼安·錢德拉塞卡)

You will note that my salutation includes my fellow students. Yes I am still a student. I even learned something from Professors Chandrasekhar and Taube two days ago. I came to Caltech as a new graduate student fifty years ago and I am now known as the oldest graduate student at Caltech. (William Alfred Fowler)

你們會注意到,我開頭提到的聽眾包括同學。沒錯,我還是個學生。就在兩天前我還從錢德拉塞卡和陶布教授那裡學到了一些東西。50年前,我作為新研究生進入加州理工學院,而現在我以加州理工學院年齡最大的研究生而知名。(威廉·福勒)

It is the great glory of the quest for human knowledge that, while making some small contribution to that quest, we can also continue to learn and to take pleasure in learning. Fellow students, there will be hard work and heart break in your futures but there will also be stimulating intellectual pleasure and joy. In less pompous language I call it fun. (William Alfred Fowler)

人類探求知識活動的偉大光榮之處在於,當我們為此尋求做出小小的貢獻同時,我們也可以繼續學習並享受學習之樂。同學們,你們將來會有艱苦的工作和傷心的經歷,但也會有令人興奮的智力上的快樂與歡欣。用不那麼浮華的語言來說,我稱之為樂趣。(威廉·福勒)

1983 年

My work is my life. For the first thirty years of my career I was an experimentalist. For the last twenty years I have been trying to analyze in the simplest possible theoretical way what I was doing in the laboratory and what others continue to do in laboratories around the world. For me it is still a source of amazement that we can duplicate in the laboratory in a small way what goes on in the sun and other stars. (William Alfred Fowler)

我的工作就是我的生活。在職業生涯的前 30 年裡，我是個實驗主義者。在過去 20 年裡，我一直在盡力以可能最簡單的理論方法，分析自己在實驗室裡正在做著的事，以及別人在世界各地的實驗室裡持續做的事。對我來說，可以在實驗室裡小規模地複製太陽和其他恆星上發生的事情，仍然使我驚訝。（威廉·福勒）

This joy of discovery is real, and it is one of our rewards. So too is the approval of our work by our peers. (Henry Taube)

探索的快樂是真實的，是我們所得回報之一。同行對我們的工作的認可也是如此。（亨利·陶布）

There is still so much beyond our understanding even in the simplest systems the chemist has cared to deal with. (Henry Taube)

即便在化學家用心研究的最簡單的系統中，仍然有太多的東西超出我們的理解。（亨利·陶布）

Science as an intellectual exercise enriches our culture, and is in itself ennobling. (Henry Taube)

科學作為一種智力鍛鍊，豐富了我們的文化，本身也令人尊崇。（亨利·陶布）

1981-1990 全球視野與道德辯證

I never thought of stopping, and I just hated sleeping. I can't imagine having a better life. (Barbara McClintock)

我從未想過停下來，我就是討厭睡覺。我無法想像有更好的生活。（芭芭拉・麥克林托克）

Novelists do not write as birds sing, by the push of nature. It is part of the job that there should be much routine and some daily stuff on the level of carpentry. (William Golding)

小說家並非像鳥兒歌唱一樣出於天性寫作。它是工作的一部分，有很多例行雜事和一些構思上的日常任務。（威廉・高汀）

Consider a man riding a bicycle. Whoever he is, we can say three things about him. We know he got on the bicycle and started to move. We know that at some point he will stop and get off. Most important of all, we know that if at any point between the beginning and the end of his journey he stops moving and does not get off the bicycle he will fall off it. That is a metaphor for the journey through life of any living thing, and I think of any society of living things. (William Golding)

想像一下一個騎腳踏車的人。不管他是何許人，關於他我們可以說三件事。我們知道他騎上腳踏車開始移動。我們知道在某個時刻他會停止並下車，最重要的是，我們知道，如果在騎行開始和結束之間的任何時刻停止移動而不下車，他就會跌倒。這是對任何生物生命歷程的隱喻，我想也是任何生物社會的隱喻。（威廉・高汀）

I'm lazy. But it's the lazy people who invented the wheel and the bicycle because they didn't like walking or carrying things. (Lech Walesa)

> 1983 年

我很懶。然而正是懶人發明了輪子和腳踏車,因為他們不喜歡步行或負重。(萊赫・華勒沙)

Obviously people want social calm, but if you do not let clever and ingenious people to participate, obviously there must be some dormant volcano that will erupt, sooner or later. (Lech Walesa)

顯然人們希望社會安寧,但若不讓聰明和有創意的人參與,必定有些休眠火山將要爆發,早晚而已。(萊赫・華勒沙薩)

I use many different gadgets connected with computers; I use PCs, laptops and a Palm Pilot. I also use the Internet to visit websites, especially within Polish-language Internet. I usually go to political discussion groups and sites —— of course, as I use my real name, people never believe that they are chatting with me! (Lech Walesa)

我使用許多與電腦相連的小器具,我使用個人電腦、筆記型電腦和掌上型電腦。我還使用網際網路訪問網站,尤其在波蘭語的網域。我經常前往政治論壇和網站——當然,在我使用本名時,人們從來不相信他們在跟我聊天!(萊赫・華勒沙)

Many Laureates before me must have been filled with wonder at the dazzling recognition they received in Stockholm for something that they enjoyed so much doing. The instant at which a scientist becomes certain that his problem is solved, the following days in which details are worked out and consequences unfold, even the preceding weeks or months of research are sources of unsurpassed, addictive intellectual pleasure. Magnificent rewards for that pleasure may indeed cause astonishment.

Yet a scientist knows that his motivations are often weakly related to the distant consequences of his work. The logical rigor, the generality, and the simplicity of his theories satisfy deep personal intellectual needs, and he frequently seeks them for their own sake. But here, as in Adam Smith's famous sentence, he seems to be "led by an invisible hand to promote an end which was no part of his intention," for his personal intellectual fulfilment contributes to promoting the social interest of the scientific community. The logical rigor of his theories provides a secure foundation to build upon; their generality makes them applicable to a broad class of problems; their simplicity makes them usable by a great number of research workers.

It was my great fortune to begin my research career at a time when economic theory was entering a phase of intensive mathematization, and when, as a result, the strength of that invisible hand became irresistible. (Gerard Debreu)

在我之前的許多獲獎者必定都對自己在斯德哥爾摩為自己熱衷的事物所獲得的巨大認可感到驚訝。科學家確信其問題得到解決的瞬間、隨後認定細節和呈現結果的日子，甚至此前進行研究的數週或數月，都是無以倫比、令人陶醉的智力樂趣的泉源。給予這種快樂如此豐厚的回報可能的確令人驚訝。

然而科學家知道，其動機往往與其工作的遙遠影響沒有太大關聯。其理論的邏輯嚴謹、普遍性和簡明易懂，滿足了深層的個人智力需求，而且他經常為了這些需求本身而尋求它們。然而在此處，就像亞當・史密斯的名言所說，他似乎「由一隻看不見的手引領，去實現一個並非他本意的結果」，因為他的個人智力滿足有助於促進科學界的社會利益。其理論的邏輯嚴謹提供了可靠的建構基礎，普遍性使它們適用於各式各樣的問題，簡明易懂使它們可以被大量的研究人員運用。

我非常幸運，在我開始自己的研究生涯時，經濟理論正在進入密集數學化的階段，於是那隻看不見的手的力量也因此變得不可抗拒。（傑拉德・德布魯）

1984 年

As a boy, I was deeply interested in scientific ideas, electrical and mechanical, and I read almost everything I could find on the subject. (Carlo Rubbia)

還在少年時，我對電子和機械方面的科學觀念就深感興趣，我閱讀找得到的幾乎任何此類讀物。（卡洛・魯比亞）

You have two alternatives. One: you can put your life on hold and wait for the phone to ring. Two: you run ahead as if your life depended on it. (Carlo Rubbia)

你有兩個選擇。一：不妨擱置生命，等待電話鈴響。第二：一意精進不止，猶如生命所繫。（卡洛・魯比亞）

I'm stubborn; I know what I want. I'll dedicate all my efforts to achieving it. (Carlo Rubbia)

我很固執。我知道自己想要什麼。我將盡自己所能達成它。（卡洛・魯比亞）

I don't believe I have special talents. I have persistence… After the first failure, second failure, third failure, I kept trying. (Carlo Rubbia)

我不相信自己有特別的才能。我有毅力。⋯⋯在第一次失敗、第二次失敗、第三次失敗之後，我仍繼續嘗試。（卡洛‧魯比亞）

I have to be where the best work can be done. (Carlo Rubbia)

我必須處於可以做出最好工作的地方。（卡洛‧魯比亞）

You people think it's hard to win a Nobel Prize, but it's easy. Trivial. Just put protons and antiprotons in a box, and shake them up, and then collect your prize. (Carlo Rubbia)

諸位以為得諾貝爾獎很難，其實很簡單。小事一樁。只要把質子和反質子放進盒子，搖一搖，就領獎吧。（卡洛‧魯比亞）

If I have at times been able to make original contributions in the accelerator field, I cannot help feeling that to a certain extent my slightly amateur approach in physics, combined with much practical experience, was an asset. (Simon van der Meer)

如果說我有時能在加速器領域做出原創性貢獻，我不禁覺得，一定程度上，我在物理學方面有些業餘的路數，加上大量實務經驗，是一大有利條件。（西蒙‧范德梅爾）

My father was a schoolteacher and my mother came from a teacher's family. Under these conditions it is not astonishing that learning was highly prized; in fact, my parents made sacrifices to be able to give their children a good education. (Simon van der Meer)

我的父親是位教師，母親來自教師家庭。在這樣的情況下，學習受

到高度重視並不令人驚訝。事實上,我的父母為了能夠為子女提供良好的教育而做出了各種犧牲。(西蒙·范德梅爾)

I have asked myself why am I here —— how did it happen —— and the answer is difficult. I recalled my first day in James A. Garfield high school some 50 years ago and remembered the words of our 20th president that we were all required to memorize and recite. He said, in part, that if one had "a clear head, a true heart and a strong arm" he could succeed in life. I did not have all those qualities, but took him to mean that if you were honest and worked hard you could accomplish your goals. I have tried to follow his advice, but I never dreamed that it would lead me to this place where I stand today. Clearly there was more; it required good teachers, a good place to work, good friends, a good family and a great amount of good luck. (Robert Bruce Merrifield)

我問過自己為什麼在這裡 —— 這是怎麼發生的 —— 要回答是很難的。我回憶起大約 50 年前在詹姆士·A·加菲爾德中學的第一天,想起了第 20 任校長要求我們都牢記和背誦的話。他說,在某種程度上,一個人如果有「清晰的頭腦、真誠的心和強壯的手臂」,就會在生活中獲得成功。我不具備所有這些特質,不過我理解他的意思是,你如果誠實並努力工作,就能實現自己的目標。我一直盡力遵循他的建議,但從未夢想它會把我帶到今天站立的這個位置。顯然有更多因素,需要好老師、好職場、好朋友、好家庭和大量的好運氣。(羅伯特·布魯斯·梅里菲爾德)

The Nobel Prize is a precious gift, and it is wonderful to receive this gift rather late in life: one does not then have to carry for a very long time the burden that this distinction imposes. (Niels K. Jerne)

諾貝爾獎是一份珍貴的禮物，在遲暮之年收到這份禮物非常美妙：這樣就無須長期承受這一項殊榮的負擔了。（尼爾斯・傑尼）

It seems a miracle that young children easily learn the language of any environment into which they were born. The generative approach to grammar, pioneered by Chomsky, argues that this is only explicable if certain deep, universal features of this competence are innate characteristics of the human brain. Biologically speaking, this hypothesis of an inheritable capability to learn any language means that it must somehow be encoded in the DNA of our chromosomes. Should this hypothesis one day be verified, then linguistics would become a branch of biology. (Niels K. Jerne)

幼兒能夠輕易學會出生所處任何環境的語言，這似乎是個奇蹟。諾姆・杭士基開創的生成式語法認為，只有這種能力的某些深層的、普遍的特徵是人腦的先天特徵，才可以解釋這一點。從生物學的角度來講，這種學習任何語言的能力具有可遺傳性的假設，意味著它必須以某種方式被編碼到我們染色體的 DNA 中。這種假設一旦真的證實，語言學就會成為生物學的分支了。（尼爾斯・傑尼）

We went down into the basement of the institute, which has no windows. I looked at the first two plates. I saw these halos. That was fantastic. I shouted. I kissed my wife, I was all happy. It was the best result I could think of. (Georges J.F. Köhler)

我們走進研究所的地下室，那裡沒有窗戶。我檢視了前兩個盤子。我見到這些光環。這簡直妙不可言。我叫了起來。我親吻我的妻子，我高興極了。這是我能想到的最好的結果。[79]（喬治・克勒）

---

[79] 這裡記述的是著名的製造單株抗體實驗於 1974 年底首次成功的情形。

1984 年

I have many ideas, but often they don't work. In discoveries, the most important thing is to do the experiment. (Georges J.F. Köhler)

我有許多想法，但常常行不通。在探索過程中，最重要的是做實驗。（喬治・克勒）

I learned what research was all about as a research student with Stoppani... Max Perutz, and... Fred Sanger... From them, I always received an unspoken message which in my imagination I translated as "Do good experiments, and don't worry about the rest." (César Milstein)

作為斯托帕尼……馬克斯・佩魯茨和……弗雷德里克・桑格的研究生，我體會到什麼才是研究。……從他們那裡，我總是收到一則無言的訊息，我思索著把它解釋為：「把實驗做好，不關心其餘。」（塞薩爾・米爾斯坦）

I believe that a culture is complete, mature, and capable of enduring and developing only if pathos has a place in it, if we understand pathos and can appreciate it —— and especially if we are capable of it. (Jaroslav Seifert)

我認為，只有當傷感在文化中有一席之地，只有當我們能夠理解傷感，能夠欣賞它 —— 尤其是當我們有能力傷感，這種文化才是完整的，成熟的，可以持續和發展。（雅羅斯拉夫・塞佛特）

Everything on earth has happened before,/nothing is new,/but woe to the lovers/who fail to discover a fresh blossom/in every future kiss. (Jaroslav Seifert)

世間萬事均曾發生，無一可稱全新，但如此戀人實在不幸，他們找不到鮮花，在每一個未來的吻中。（雅羅斯拉夫・塞佛特）

1981-1990 全球視野與道德辯證

In many ways, when you're a Nobel peace laureate, you have an obligation to humankind, to society. (Desmond Mpilo Tutu)

在許多方面，當你身為諾貝爾和平獎得主的時候，你對人類，對社會均負有責任。（戴斯蒙‧屠圖）

The minute you got the Nobel Peace Prize, things that I said yesterday, with nobody paying too much attention, I say the same things after I got it —— oh! It was quite crucial for people, and it helped our morale because apartheid did look invincible. (Desmond Mpilo Tutu)

一旦獲得諾貝爾和平獎，我昨天說的，沒人多麼在意的話，同樣的話我獲獎後再說——噢！它變得對人民十分重要了。它鼓舞我們的士氣，因為種族隔離的確顯得不可戰勝。（戴斯蒙‧屠圖）

I am not interested in picking up crumbs of compassion thrown from the table of someone who considers himself my master. I want the full menu of rights. (Desmond Mpilo Tutu)

我對於撿起自認為是我主人的人桌上扔下來的同情碎屑不感興趣。我想要整桌的權利大餐。（戴斯蒙‧屠圖）

Hope is being able to see that there is light despite all of the darkness. (Desmond Mpilo Tutu)

希望就是能夠看到有光，儘管一片黑暗。（戴斯蒙‧屠圖）

When we see the face of a child, we think of the future. We think of their dreams about what they might become, and what they might accomplish. (Desmond Mpilo Tutu)

看見孩子的臉時，我們想到未來。我們想到他們的夢想，關於他們

1984 年

會成為什麼人,成就什麼事。(戴斯蒙・屠圖)

Since the 18th of October I have been the prey to many emotions. First of all came surprise at having been selected for this high honour. Then came elation as the truth of it sank in. Then bewilderment at the Niagara of publicity that engulfed me. Then panic at the thought of producing a decent lecture in six weeks. Then exhilaration at the wonderful welcome I have received in Stockholm. Today, overshadowing them all is gratitude. (Richard Stone)

10月18日以來,我一直被眾多情感征服。首先就是由於已經入選這一項崇高榮譽而驚訝。然後在真實性確定無疑時歡欣。然後為淹沒於潮水般湧來的名聲而茫然。然後在六週之中每想到做一場像樣的演講便惶恐。然後因為在斯德哥爾摩受到美妙的歡迎而振奮。今天,使上述一切黯然失色的是感激。(理查・史東)

At Westminster, I was on the classical side: my father, who was a barrister, destined me for the law, and for this, a classical education was deemed indispensable. As a result, I learnt little mathematics beyond elementary arithmetic, algebra and geometry and was rather bored. I expect I could have had a more interesting education if I had shown more interest in what I was taught, but as a boy, my passion was model-building; not mathematical models but models of trains and boats, an activity in which my father was a skilled and enthusiastic collaborator. (Richard Stone)

在西敏寺,我所學偏於古典方面:我的父親,他是個律師,指定我從事法律,為此,古典教育被認為是不可或缺的。結果,除了初等算術、代數和幾何之外,我沒學到多少數學知識,而且相當厭煩。假如我當時對教給我的東西表現出多一些興趣,也許能得到更有趣的教育,然

1981-1990 全球視野與道德辯證

而作為一個少年，我所熱衷的是模型建造。不是數學模型，而是火車和輪船的模型。在這種活動中，我父親是個技術嫻熟而熱情的合作者。（理查・史東）

1985 年

The Nobel prize is unquestionably the most famous prize in the world, and very often, the prize is an object of prestige not only for a person but also for a research center, a country, or for a particular area of interest. (Klaus von Klitzing)

諾貝爾獎無疑是世界上最著名的獎項，而且十有八九，這個獎不僅是一個人的，也是一個研究中心、一個國家，或者一個特定關注領域的聲望所歸。（克勞斯・馮・克利青）

I believe that every Nobel Laureate has the feeling that this prize is really a gift – because nobody can or should work just for this prize. (Klaus von Klitzing)

我相信，每位諾貝爾獎得主都有此種感覺，即這個獎真的是份禮物，因為沒人能夠或者應當僅為這個獎工作。（克勞斯・馮・克利青）

As a scientist one has the chance to contribute to an extension of knowledge, which survives beyond one's life. (Klaus von Klitzing)

作為科學家，一個人有機會為知識的擴展做出貢獻，而知識的延續時間超過人的一生。（克勞斯・馮・克利青）

With the Internet we have today a worldwide network for communication and the dissemination of knowledge. As a scientist, I am optimistic for our future if we are able to avoid unacceptable gradients in living standards and improve worldwide the educational system in such a way that a manipulation of the public opinion can be avoided. Especially scientists will have an important responsibility since the fundamental laws in science are universal and the logical consequences leave no room for ideological interpretations. (Klaus von Klitzing)

如今,網際網路使我們有了一個交流和傳播知識的全球網路。作為科學家,我對未來感到樂觀,只要我們能夠避免無法接受的生活水準差別,並能夠以避免操縱民意的方式改善全世界的教育制度。尤其是科學家將肩負重要的責任,因為科學的基本規律是通用的,其邏輯結果不為意識形態的解釋留餘地。(克勞斯·馮·克利青)

Our journey to Stockholm began some 67 years ago when our parents, with unconscious wisdom, gave us a most precious gift, the freedom to grow as we wished, at our own pace, and in the direction of our own choosing. (Herbert A. Hauptman)

我們前往斯德哥爾摩的旅程始於大約 67 年前 [80],那時我們的父母以不假思索的睿智,給予了我們最可貴的天賦,即按照自己的意願,採取自己的步調,朝著自己選擇的方向成長的自由。(赫伯特·豪普特曼)

Our sole motivation was to overcome the challenge which this problem presented, and our satisfactions came from the progress we made. We were fortunate, indeed, that the implications for structural chemistry turned out to be so far reaching; we did not anticipate them. (Herbert A. Hauptman)

---

[80] 豪普特曼與同獲 1985 年諾貝爾化學獎的卡爾勒年齡相差 1 歲。

1981-1990 全球視野與道德辯證

　　我們唯一的動力就是克服這一個問題所帶來的挑戰，而我們的滿足來自於我們所獲得的進展。我們確實很幸運，結構化學的影響居然出乎意料地如此深遠。（赫伯特・豪普特曼）

　　We do new things. We don't do things that we've found out how to do. We just keep doing newer things. And at the present time we have some items going that we find to be extremely interesting, with great potential. (Jerome Karle)

　　我們做新的事情。我們不做已知如何做的事情。我們只是一直做更新的事情。目前有一些我們發現極為有趣、潛力龐大的項目在進行中。（傑爾姆・卡爾）

　　Joe and I were trained as physicians and we still perform clinical duties. Yet, we realized that the understanding of a complex problem such as atherosclerosis requires the tools of basic science. We are fortunate to live at a time when the methods of basic science are so powerful that they can be applied directly to clinical problems. Joe has mentioned the two attributes that are required – basic training and technical courage.

　　To apply tools of science, physicians must learn to think like scientists. They must acquire technical ability, taste in evaluating experiments, and a sense of creative adventure. Joe and I received such training at the National Institutes of Health —— Joe with Marshall Nirenberg, a Nobel laureate, and I with Earl Stadtman, a distinguished biochemist. Joe also studied with Arno Motulsky, a founder of medical genetics. We then joined a clinical department led by Donald Seldin that encouraged physicians to delve into the fundamental basis of disease.

1985 年

The second attribute is technical courage. The physician-scientist must be brave enough to adopt new methods. It is far too easy to learn one technique and then to repeat the same experiment over and over. In this fashion one can write many papers, receive large research grants, and remain solidly rooted in the middle of a scientific field. But the true innovator has the confidence to drop one set of experimental crutches and leap to another when he or she must move forward.

The two attributes, basic training and technical courage, are intimately related. Fundamental training gives the physician-scientist the technical courage to try new approaches. Strong departments of science must constitute the core of each medical school. The barriers that divide medicine from physiology must be broken down.

Joe and I are honored to accept the Nobel Prize in Medicine or Physiology. We hope that this award will be inspirational to young physicians who are trying to acquire the training and develop the boldness necessary to become creators and innovators in medical research. (Michael S. Brown)

喬[81]和我被訓練成醫生，我們仍在履行臨床職責。然而，我們意識到，理解諸如動脈粥狀硬化這樣的複雜問題，需要基礎科學的工具。我們幸運地生活在這樣一個時代，基礎科學的方法強大到可以直接應用於臨床難題。喬提到了所需的兩種特性——基本訓練和技術勇氣。

要應用科學工具，醫生必須學會跟科學家一樣思考。他們必須具備技術能力、評估實驗的能力，以及創造性冒險的能力。喬和我在國家衛生研究院接受了這樣的培訓——喬師從馬歇爾·沃倫·尼倫伯格，諾貝

---

[81] 喬，即約瑟夫·里歐納德·戈爾茨坦，與布朗同獲1985年諾貝爾生理學或醫學獎。

1981-1990 全球視野與道德辯證

爾獎得主;我師從厄爾・里斯・史塔特曼,著名生物化學家。喬還和醫學遺傳學建立者阿諾・莫圖斯基一起學習。隨後,我們加入了唐納德・塞爾丁領導的一個臨床部門,該部門鼓勵醫生深入研究疾病的根本基礎。

第二種特性是技術勇氣。醫生兼科學家必須有足夠的勇氣採用新的方法。學會一種技術,然後一再重複同樣的實驗,實在是太容易了。這樣做,一個人可以寫很多論文,得到大筆大筆的研究資助,並在一個科學領域中堅實地扎根。然而真正的創新者有信心拋開一副實驗枴杖,在必須前行時跳著去取另一副。

這兩種特性,基本訓練和技術勇氣,是密切相關的。基礎訓練給予醫生兼科學家嘗試新辦法的技術勇氣。強大的科學部門必須成為每一所醫學院的核心。將醫學與生理學分開的障礙必須打破。

喬和我很榮幸獲得諾貝爾生理學或醫學獎。我們希望,這個獎項能激勵那些努力獲得培訓並培養成為醫學研究創造者與創新者所需勇氣的年輕醫生。(麥可・斯圖亞特・布朗)

Of all the Prizes endowed by Alfred Nobel, only one has an ambiguous name —— the Prize for Physiology or Medicine. Nobel believed that physiology was an experimental science like physics and chemistry. On the other hand, medicine was an empirical art that would rarely merit a scientific prize. To the contrary, however, many of the advances in biology during the subsequent 85 years were made by people trained in medicine who were attempting to solve medical problems. (Joseph L. Goldstein)

在阿佛烈・諾貝爾贈予的所有獎項中,只有一種有個模糊的名稱 —— 生理學或醫學獎。諾貝爾認為生理學是一門實驗科學,猶如物理學和化學。另一方面,醫學是一門經驗技藝,可能很難適用於科學獎。

然而,出乎意料,在隨後的 85 年中,生物學上的許多進步,都是由一心解決醫學難題的醫學專業人士造就的。(約瑟夫・里歐納德・戈爾茨坦)

Michael Brown and I are grateful to the Swedish academic community for bestowing this honor on us. Some may think that we are too young for this award. But let me point out that we work as a team. If our efforts were only additive, our combined age would be 45 plus 44 or 89 years. But our efforts are more than additive: they are synergistic. They have a multiplying effect. Our true collaborative age is 45 times 44 or 1,980 years – surely old enough for a Nobel Prize. (Joseph L. Goldstein)

麥可・布朗和我感激瑞典學術界授予我們這一項榮譽。有些人認為,對於這個獎項,我們太年輕了。但是請允許我指出,我們兩人是作為一個團隊工作的。如果我們的努力只是疊加的,兩人的合併年齡就會是 45 加上 44 也就是 89 歲。然而我們的努力不僅是疊加的:它們是協同的。它們具有倍增效應。兩人真正的合作年齡是 45 乘以 44 也就是 1,980 歲——肯定大得足以獲得諾貝爾獎了。(約瑟夫・里歐納德・戈爾茨坦)

Life is not only full of sound and fury. It also has butterflies, flowers, art. (Claude Simon)

人生不僅充滿了喧譁與騷動[82]。它也有蝴蝶、花朵、藝術。(克洛德・西蒙)

From the instant I lifted that phone at 7 a.m. on October 15 our life has been miraculously transformed and we have lived in a state of elated drunkenness. In fact, ever since that instant, I have been trying to find a moment to sit

---

[82] 人生充滿喧譁與騷動,此說出自莎士比亞名劇《馬克白》(Macbeth):Life … is a tale told by an idiot, full of sound and fury, signifying nothing. (人生……如痴人說夢,充滿喧譁與騷動,意義則等同虛空。)

down and understand what has happened to us, but so far I have not succeeded. I am even surprised that I could ever manage to get dressed. And for this reason I have two important messages for future Nobel recipients: first, get dressed before you receive the fateful call, and second, get your Nobel lecture written even before you get dressed. (Franco Modigliani)

從我 10 月 15 日早上 7 點接電話之際，我們的生活就發生了奇蹟般的改變，我們生活在興高采烈的醉酒狀態之中。事實上，從那一刻起，我就一直在努力找時間坐下來，理解發生在我們身上的事情，然而至今尚未成功。我甚至驚訝於自己居然能穿戴整齊。有鑒於此，對於未來的諾貝爾獎得主，我謹提出兩條重要的忠告：第一，在你接到那個事關重大的電話之前就穿戴整齊；第二，甚至在穿戴整齊之前就把你的諾貝爾獎演講稿撰寫妥當。（法蘭科‧莫迪利安尼）

Economists agree about economics —— and that's a science —— and they disagree about economic policy because that's a value judgment... I've had profound disagreements on policy with the famous Milton Friedman. But, on economics, we agree. (Franco Modigliani)

經濟學家對經濟學看法一致 —— 這是一門科學 —— 他們在經濟政策上意見分歧，因為這是價值判斷。……關於政策，我跟名家彌爾頓‧傅利曼有過深刻的意見分歧。然而，關於經濟學，我們看法一致。（法蘭科‧莫迪利安尼）

1986 年

The light microscope opened the first gate to microcosm. The electron microscope opened the second gate to microcosm. What will we find opening the third gate? (Ernst Ruska)

光學顯微鏡打開了通往微觀世界的第一扇大門。電子顯微鏡打開了通往微觀世界的第二扇大門。打開第三扇門我們會發現什麼？（恩斯特·魯斯卡）

Most Laureates have been accompanied on their way to success by interested and diligent assistants who are not in the limelight today. Our sincere gratitude should therefore include these collaborators. (Ernst Ruska)

在大多數獲獎者的成功之路上，一直都由其充滿志趣、勤奮努力的助手相伴，而助手們今天並非眾人所矚目對象。因此，我們應該向這些合作者表達最真誠的感謝。（恩斯特·魯斯卡）

I realized that actually doing physics is much more enjoyable than just learning it. Maybe "doing it" is the right way of learning, at least as far as I am concerned. (Gerd Binnig)

我了解到，實際上從事物理比只是學習它更富於樂趣得多。也許「從事它」是正確的學習方式，至少在我看來如此。（格爾德·賓寧）

Science means constantly walking a tightrope between blind faith and curiosity; between expertise and creativity; between bias and openness; between experience and epiphany; between ambition and passion; and between arrogance and conviction —— in short, between an old today and a new tomorrow. (Heinrich Rohrer)

1981-1990 全球視野與道德辯證

> 科學意味著不斷地走鋼絲，在盲目信仰和好奇心之間，在專業知識和創造力之間，在偏見和開放性之間，在經驗和頓悟之間，在雄心和熱情之間，在傲慢與信念之間——簡而言之，在舊的今天和新的明天之間。（海因里希・羅雷爾）

Scientific fraud, plagiarism, and ghost writing are increasingly being reported in the news media, creating the impression that misconduct has become a widespread and omnipresent evil in scientific research. (Heinrich Rohrer)

科學詐騙、學術剽竊和代筆寫作越來越多地為新聞媒體所報導，於是造成這樣的印象：不當行為已成為科學研究中普遍出現、無所不在的邪惡。（海因里希・羅雷爾）

I like to tell my students that the neophyte student and the veteran researcher are very much alike in one important respect, namely both are confused most of the time. The difference is the neophyte is often upset about being confused, especially if they're a bright student, gone through high school and all, and have been patted on the head all the time for breezing through courses, and they find it's a different thing in college, especially when they start some research. They naturally think, "Well, there must be something wrong with me, or maybe the professor." Whereas the veteran researcher is very happy when he's confused because he realizes that unless you're confused and it's not perfectly clear already, then you're not going to learn anything new.

Furthermore, the researcher knows that in science you have a very special advantage over essentially all other human enterprises. I like to emphasize this because I think most people don't recognize it, namely what you're trying to find out in science, call it truth or understanding, waits patiently for you.

1986 年

It doesn't change. Contrast that with a chess game. You might make a great move, but whoops, your opponent makes a better one. So, in business, politics, sports, sadly war, people often make a very well-conceived, sensible move, but whoops, it's a little late or a little early and turns out to be a fiasco or a disaster instead of a triumph. In science you can get it wrong over and over again. It doesn't matter, if you find the right way, the right perspective and idea eventually. So I tell my students that to be a scientist is something like being a musician. A musician really needs to love music, devote a lot of effort into mastering their instrument, but in science you can play 99.9 percent of the notes wrong, get one right, and be justly applauded.

You should realize you probably will play 99.9 percent of the notes wrong, so you need this immunity to frustration that I mentioned already. You need to understand that you do have this advantage in science that is waiting in there for you. The Czech poet Jan Skacel who wrote a poem not about science but it could apply to science —— he said the poet really doesn't write a poem, it's already there, it's been there a long, long time, he merely finds it. (Dudley R. Herschbach)

我喜歡告訴學生，初學者和資深研究人員在一個重要方面非常相似，即二者大部分時間都感到困惑。不同的是，初學者經常由於困惑而煩惱，尤其是如果身為聰明學生，中學一路順風，輕易通過課業而一直得到讚許，進了大學卻發現遭遇不同，尤其是在開始從事研究時。他們自然會想：「嗯，我一定是出了什麼問題，或是教授有問題。」然而資深研究人員在感到困惑時會很高興，因為他了解，除非感到困惑加上研究還不夠清楚，否則你學不到任何新東西。

此外，研究人員知道，在科學中，與實質上所有其他人的行業相比，你擁有一種非常特別的優勢。我喜歡強調這一點，因為覺得大多數人都沒意識到它，就是說，你正努力在科學中發現的東西，稱之為真理或理解，也在耐心地等待你。它保持不變。與下棋做個類比。你可能走出一步了不起的好棋，但是，對手走出了更妙的一步。同樣，在商業、政治、體育，以及不幸在戰爭中，人們常常下了周密的、明智的一步棋，但是，它稍微晚了或早了一些，結果是一場慘敗或災難而非勝利。在科學中，你可以一再出錯。沒關係，只要你最終找到了正確的方法、正確的視角和思路。所以我告訴學生，當科學家好比作為音樂家。音樂家需要真正熱愛音樂，付出大量努力以掌握樂器；不過在科學中，你可以演奏錯 99.9% 的音符，只對了一個，而獲得應有的喝采。

你應該意識到自己很可能演奏錯 99.9% 的音符，所以需要對於我前已提及的挫折具備這種免疫力。你需要明白，在科學中，的確有這樣的優勢在那裡等著你。捷克詩人揚・斯卡塞爾寫了一首詩，不是關於科學的，但不妨用於科學——他說詩人真的不寫詩，它已經在那裡很長、很長時間了，他只是找到了它。（達德利・赫施巴赫）

I tell students sometimes, you may think from the textbooks and from all you read that "Gee, previous scientists had it easy, they just get all these lovely results. What's left for me to do?" And what you may not recognize is that you have a legacy of new tools, concepts as well as instruments, that open up new eyes literally, that you can use to see things your predecessors could not, and to think of doing probes that nobody thinks of until the technical feasibility of actually doing it is somewhere on the horizon, at least. (Dudley R. Herschbach)

1986 年

我有時跟學生說，你們可能經由教科書及各種讀物想到：「天哪，先前的科學家真輕鬆，他們就這樣獲得了一切美好的成果。我還能做什麼呢？」你們也許沒意識到自己繼承了一批新工具、儀器和觀念，它們提供了新的觀察方法，你們可以用於檢視各種事物，那是前輩無緣得見的；並且能夠展開實施技術可行性初現之前無人想過的各種探索。（達德利．赫施巴赫）

You don't need to be bright to be a scientist, you just need to be persistent as hell. (Dudley R. Herschbach)

成為科學家無須聰明，只須百折不撓。（達德利．赫施巴赫）

Think of a crowd at a baseball game. In ordinary chemistry, you have to deal with the whole crowd at once. You observe the general behavior of a crowd of molecules but want to know more about individual molecules. In effect, what we've done is eavesdrop on conversations between molecules, as if listening to a pair of people in that crowd. (Dudley R. Herschbach)

想像一群棒球比賽觀眾。在普通化學中，你得同時應付整個群體。你觀察一群分子的一般行為，但想更多地了解關於單一分子的資訊。實際上，我們所做的就是偷聽分子之間的對話，猶如聽人群中兩個人的交談。（達德利．赫施巴赫）

If I were to start again probably I will pay more attention to biological sciences even as a chemist. But it was interesting when I started out as a chemist many of my friends told me "Yuan, if you want to be a chemist you have to learn physics better otherwise you will not become a good chemist." So I studied lots of physics. And I entered areas called chemical physics. It's an inter discipline area. That certainly helped me develop other things. Now if the young people ask me I will see biology certainly given you excitement but you have to study chemistry better or physics better, otherwise you will not be able to go too far. (Yuan T. Lee)

假如重新開始,我會更多地關注生物科學,即便作為化學家。然而有意思的是,當我作為化學家起步時,很多朋友告訴我,「遠,你想當化學家的話,就得更認真地學習物理學,不然無法成為優秀的化學家。」所以我學了很多物理知識。我進入了稱作化學物理的領域。這是個跨學科的領域。這的確幫助我發展了其他東西。現在如果年輕人問我,我會認為生物學的確使你們興奮,不過你們得更認真地學習化學或者物理學,不然就沒辦法走得太遠。(李遠哲)

After I got my PhD people gave me a professorship and it went on and on and before I knew it I found myself to be 57 years old and I had spent 32 years in America. I decided to go back to help because Taiwan needed my help more than California. So I did go there. Taiwan is a small place with 23 million people —— a small island. According to physical law, if you push the acceleration is invert in proportion to the mass so Taiwan is relatively small. (Yuan T. Lee)

我拿到博士學位後,人們給了我一個教授職位。這樣年復一年,不知不覺我發現自己已經57歲,在美國待了32年。我決定回去幫忙,因為臺灣比加州更需要我的幫助。於是我真的去了。臺灣是一個人口2,300萬的小地方 —— 一個小島。根據物理定律,如果你推動,加速度與質量成反比,因此臺灣相對較小。(李遠哲)

I was a very shy person. Even if I see a lady my face become red. I was very shy. But after the prize I had to be in the limelight so often to give after dinner speeches and then gradually I got used to it. But I remember during the

1986 年

first three months I suffered so much so my wife said "Yuan, you enjoy so much working in the laboratory with students, why do you have to become an after dinner speaker? " And she suggested maybe we should return the prize to the Nobel Foundation and then you can go back to the laboratory. (Yuan T. Lee)

我是個非常害羞的人。甚至見到女士都會臉紅。我非常害羞。然而獲獎之後，我不得不經常在眾人矚目下發表餐後演講，於是漸漸地我也就習慣了。但我記得在前三個月裡，我是如此飽受折磨，以致妻子說：「遠，你是那麼樂於在實驗室裡跟學生們一起工作，為什麼非得當個餐後演講者？」她就建議：我們應當把獎還給諾貝爾基金會，然後你可以回到實驗室去。（李遠哲）

In the 1960s and 70s it certainly was a big brain drain. Many people went to America and stayed there. But now, during the last ten years, I asked many established scientists including the member of National Academy of Sciences, several of them returned during the last years to Taiwan. And so I would like to look at it this way: it's the brain circulation. Young people go out and they learn something and then they come back. (Yuan T. Lee)

在 1960 年代和 1970 年代，這無疑是巨大的人才流失。許多人去了美國並留在那裡。但是現在，在過去 10 年間，我問了很多卓有建樹的科學家，包括美國國家科學院院士，有幾位在過去幾年回到了臺灣。所以我想從這樣的角度來看它：它是人才的循環。年輕人出去學習一些東西，然後回來。（李遠哲）

You have to keep your body fit. In the laboratory we often work overnight or two days in a row in order to find something else so we don't sleep. Unless you have a strong body you won't be able to do it. (Yuan T. Lee)

1981-1990 全球視野與道德辯證

你必須保持身體健康。在實驗室裡，我們經常通宵工作或連續兩天工作以找到某種結果，否則無法睡覺。除非你有個強壯的身體，不然無法做到。（李遠哲）

Your Majesties, Your Royal Highnesses, Ladies and Gentlemen ⋯⋯ I know of no other place where Princes assemble to pay their respect to molecules.⋯ Because of you, our wives hesitate for just an instant before summoning us to do the dishes. (John C. Polanyi)

陛下、殿下、女士們、先生們⋯⋯據我所知，沒有其他地方像這裡一樣，有王子們聚集在一起向分子致敬。⋯⋯由於你們，我們的妻子在叫我們洗碗之前稍有躊躇。（約翰・查爾斯・波拉尼）

Authority in science exists to be questioned, since heresy is the spring from which new ideas flow. (John C. Polanyi)

在科學中，權威是存在以供質疑的，因為異端是新思想的泉源。（約翰・查爾斯・波拉尼）

Science never gives up searching for truth, since it never claims to have achieved it. It is civilizing because it puts truth ahead of all else including personal interests. (John C. Polanyi)

科學絕不放棄尋找真理，因為它從未聲稱已經獲得真理。科學推崇文明，因為它把真理置於其他一切之前，包括個人利益。（約翰・查爾斯・波拉尼）

When, as we must often do, we fear science, we really fear ourselves. Human dignity is better served by embracing knowledge. (John C. Polanyi)

當我們害怕科學時（就像我們經常做的一樣），我們實際上是害怕自己。擁抱知識才能更妥善地維護人的尊嚴。（約翰・查爾斯・波拉尼）

1986 年

My father was a tailor and my mother, a housewife. Though of limited education themselves, they instilled in me the values of intellectual achievement and the use of whatever talents I possessed. (Stanley Cohen)

我的父親是裁縫，母親是家庭主婦。儘管他們自身所受教育有限，他們漸漸教我懂得了知識成就的價值，以及善用我所擁有的才能。（斯坦利·科恩）

The process for awarding Nobel prizes is so complex that it cannot be corrupted. (Rita Levi-Montalcini)

諾貝爾獎評選的過程如此之複雜，不容許任何腐敗行為。（麗塔·列維－蒙塔爾奇尼）

I don't believe there would be any science at all without intuition. (Rita Levi-Montalcini)

我認為如果沒有直覺，就沒有任何科學。（麗塔·列維－蒙塔爾奇尼）

The phenomenon of creativity, we know, is closely related to the ability to yoke together separate, and even seemingly incompatible, matrices. (Wole Soyinka)

我們知道，創造力的奇蹟，與使不同的、甚至顯得對立的母體合作的能力密切相關。（渥雷·索因卡）

I love beauty. But I like the beauty accidentally, not dished up, served up on a platter. (Wole Soyinka)

我愛美好的事物。不過我喜歡美好偶然得之，而非盛在盤子裡端上來。（渥雷·索因卡）

You never know how much you need it until you're deprived of it. (Wole Soyinka)

1981-1990 全球視野與道德辯證

你永遠不知道自己有多需要它,直到它被剝奪。(渥雷・索因卡)

History teaches us to beware of the excitation of the liberated and the injustices that often accompany their righteous thirst for justice. (Wole Soyinka)

歷史教育我們,謹防被解放者的興奮和經常隨著他們對正義的正當渴望而來的非正義。(渥雷・索因卡)

Just as man cannot live without dreams, he cannot live without hope. If dreams reflect the past, hope summons the future. Does this mean that our future can be built on a rejection of the past? Surely such a choice is not necessary. The two are not incompatible. The opposite of the past is not the future but the absence of future; the opposite of the future is not the past but the absence of past. The loss of one is equivalent to the sacrifice of the other. (Elie Wiesel)

就像不能沒有夢想而活一樣,人不能沒有希望而活。如果說夢想反映過去,希望則召喚未來。這是否意味著我們的未來可以建立在拒絕過去的基礎上?這種選擇當然是不必要的。二者並非不相容。過去的對立面不是未來,而是未來的缺失;未來的對立面不是過去,而是過去的缺失。其中一個的失去等於另一個的犧牲。(艾利・魏瑟爾)

We must always take sides. Neutrality helps the oppressor, never the victim. Silence encourages the tormentor, never the tormented. (Elie Wiesel)

我們總得支持一方。中立幫助壓迫者,而非犧牲者。沉默鼓勵施暴者,而非受害人。(艾利・魏瑟爾)

It's easier to be conformist naturally; it's easier except for those who don't like conformism. (Elie Wiesel)

因循守舊當然比較簡單。對於那些不願墨守成規的人除外。（艾利・魏瑟爾）

I believe in God —— in spite of God! I believe in Mankind —— in spite of Mankind! I believe in the Future —— in spite of the Past! (Elie Wiesel)

我相信上帝，不管上帝怎樣！我相信人類，不管人類怎樣！我相信未來，不管過去怎樣！（艾利・魏瑟爾）

The opposite of love is not hate but indifference. (Elie Wiesel)

愛的對立面不是恨，而是冷漠。（艾利・魏瑟爾）

How would the US be different today if people coming off the boat were greeted with a welfare check instead of a shovel? (James M. Buchanan Jr.)

如果人們[83]下船時得到的是福利支票而非鏟子，今天的美國會有什麼不同？（詹姆士・麥基爾・布坎南）

Politicians and bureaucrats are no different from the rest of us. They will maximize their incentives just like everybody else. (James M. Buchanan Jr.)

政客和官僚與我們其他人並無不同。他們跟其他人都一樣，會最大化對自己的激勵。（詹姆士・麥基爾・布坎南）

If politicians get money to spend and don't have to be responsible for taxation, then of course that will bias their attitude toward more spending as opposed to cutting back on spending. (James M. Buchanan Jr.)

如果政客們有錢花，又無須為稅收負責，那麼當然會使其態度偏向增加支出而非削減支出。（詹姆士・麥基爾・布坎南）

People share a universal behavioural trait: if there are profits to be made,

---

[83] 指 17 世紀的歐洲殖民者。

the effort to get that money will attract investment. This is true in the private sector, the market sector, as well as the public sector. (James M. Buchanan Jr.)

人們具有共同的行為特徵:如果有利潤可賺,獲取這些錢的努力就會吸引投資。公共部門、私營部門和市場部門概莫能外。(詹姆士‧麥基爾‧布坎南)

1987年

My fascination in the natural sciences was roused while learning about chemistry rather than physics. The latter was taught in a more theoretical way, whereas in chemistry, the opportunity to conduct experiments on our own, sometimes even with unexpected results, was addressing my practical sense. (J. Georg Bednorz)

我對自然科學的著迷是在學習化學而非物理時引起的。後者以較為理論化的方式教學,而在化學課中有機會自己動手做實驗,有時甚至帶來意想不到的結果,總是帶給我踏實的感覺。(約翰尼斯‧比得諾茲)

I was working under the guidance of Hans Jörg Scheel, learning about different methods of crystal growth, materials characterization and solid state chemistry. I soon was impressed by the freedom even I as a student was given to work on my own, learning from mistakes and thus losing the fear of approaching new problems in my own way. (J. Georg Bednorz)

我在漢斯‧約爾格‧謝爾的指導下工作,了解晶體生長的不同方法、

1987 年

材料特性和固態化學。我很快便為這種自由所浸染，即使作為學生，我也被授權自主工作，從錯誤中學習，從而無懼於以自己的方式探究新問題。（約翰尼斯・比得諾茲）

Georg Bednorz and I work at the IBM Laboratory in Rüschlikon. Our friends Gerd Binnig and Heinrich Rohrer from the same Laboratory were honoured last year. From this fact, it is our opinion that strictly scientific considerations must have led the Royal Swedish Academy of Sciences to her decision. We thank very much for this decision and great honour! (K. Alexander Müller)

我和約翰尼斯・比得諾茲在位於呂施利孔的 IBM 實驗室工作。我們的朋友，來自同一個實驗室的格爾德・賓寧和海因里希・羅雷爾去年獲得了這一項榮譽。基於這一個事實，我們認為瑞典皇家科學院做出此決定必定是完全的科學考量。我們非常感謝這個決定和莫大的榮幸！（卡爾・米勒）

Any chemist reading this book can see, in some detail, how I have spent most of my mature life. They can become familiar with the quality of my mind and imagination. They can make judgements about my research abilities. They can tell how well I have documented my claims of experimental results. Any scientist can redo my experiments to see if they still work. (Donald J. Cram)

凡是閱讀這本書的化學家，都可以頗為詳細地了解我是如何度過大部分成年生活的。他們可以了解我的思想與想像力的品質。他們可以判斷我的研究能力。他們可以評價我對於實驗結果的陳述。任何科學家都可以重做我的實驗，看它們是否依然有效。（唐納德・克拉姆）

Science offers most exciting perspectives for the future generations. It promises a much more complete understanding of the universe, an always greater creative power of chemical sciences over the structure and transformations of the inanimate as well as of the living world, an increasing ability to take control over disease, aging and even over the evolution of the human species, a deeper penetration into the working of the brain, the nature of consciousness and the origin of thought.

First, I would like to say a few words about my own field of activity, chemistry, about what is making it so attractive to me. Indeed, chemistry plays a central role by its place in the natural sciences and in knowledge, as well as by its economic importance and omnipresence in our everyday lives. Being present everywhere, it tends to be forgotten and to go unnoticed. It does not advertise itself but, without it, those achievements we consider spectacular would not see the light of day : therapeutic exploits, feats in space, marvels of technology, and so forth. It contributes to meeting humanity's needs in food and medication, in clothing and shelter, in energy and raw materials, in transport and communications. It supplies materials for physics and industry, models and substrates for biology and medicine, properties and processes for science and technology.

In addition to the exploration of the molecules of life, chemistry seeks non-natural species, possessing a desired chemical or physical property. It opens wide the door to the creative imagination of the chemist at the meeting point of chemistry with biology and physics.

Like the artist, the chemist engraves into matter the products of creative imagination. The stone, the sounds and the words do not contain the works that the sculptor, the composer, the writer express from them. Similarly, the chemist creates original molecules, new materials and novel properties from the elements provided by nature.

The essence of chemistry is not only to discover but to invent and above all to create. The book of chemistry is not only to be read but to be written! The score of chemistry is not only to be played but to be composed! (Jean-Marie Lehn)

科學為後代提供了極其令人激動的前景。它承諾了對宇宙更加完整的理解，化學科學對生命及無生命世界的結構與轉變不斷增強的創造力，控制疾病、衰老甚至人類物種演化的能力，對人腦工作、意識本質和思想起源更加深入的探究。

首先，我想談談自己的活動領域，化學，以及它如此吸引我的特性。確實，化學以其在自然科學、知識體系中所占的地位，以及它在經濟上的重要性和我們日常生活中的無所不在，發揮著核心作用。它隨處可見，容易被遺忘和忽視。它不宣揚自己；但是，假如沒有它，那些壯觀的成就也就不會存在：醫療的偉業、太空的豐功、技術的奇蹟等等。它致力於滿足人類在食品和藥物、衣著和居住、能量和原物料、運輸和通訊等方面的需求。它為物理學和工業提供材料，為生物和醫學提供模型和基礎，為科學和技術提供特性和過程。

除了探索生命分子之外，化學還尋求具有期望的化學或物理特性的非天然物種。在化學與生物學和物理學的交會點上，它為化學家的創造性想像敞開了大門。

如同藝術家，化學家把創造性想像的產物雕刻於物質之中。石頭、聲音和文字本身並不包含雕刻家、作曲家和作家以之表現的作品。同樣地，化學家從自然界提供的元素中創造出新的分子、新的材料和新的特性。

1981–1990 全球視野與道德辯證

化學的真諦不僅是發現，而且是發明，尤其是創造。化學的書籍不僅要閱讀，而且要撰寫！化學的樂曲不僅是用來演奏，更是被用來譜寫！（尚－馬里・萊恩）

I envisaged to study philosophy at the University of Strasbourg, but being still undecided, I began with first year courses in physical, chemical and natural sciences (SPCN). During this year 1957/58, I was impressed by the coherent and rigorous structure of organic chemistry. I was particularly receptive to the experimental power of organic chemistry, which was able to convert at will, it seemed, complicated substances into one another following well defined rules and routes. I bought myself compounds and glassware and began performing laboratory practice experiments at my parents home. The seed was sown, so that when, the next year, I followed the stimulating lectures of a newly appointed young professor, Guy Ourisson, it became clear to me that I wanted to do research in organic chemistry. (Jean-Marie Lehn)

我本想在史特拉斯堡大學讀哲學，不過尚未決定，第一學年以物理、化學和自然科學這三大課程開始。在1957至1958年期間，有機化學連貫而嚴謹的結構帶給我深刻的印象。我尤其認同有機化學的實驗力量，看起來遵循明確的規則和途徑，能夠任意地將複雜的物質轉化成另一種。我為自己買了化合物和玻璃器皿，開始在父母家裡做實驗室的練習實驗。種子已經播下，於是，在第二年，聽了新任年輕教授居伊・歐里松令人激動的課，我明白了，自己是想從事有機化學研究。（尚－馬里・萊恩）

Chemistry is so insidious I would say that you often don't notice it. We are sitting here, and I think probably most of what we are wearing is chemistry. Most of the way in which … when we are sick what do we do? We use pharmaceuticals. What is pharmaceuticals? Molecules. Chemistry. So we meet chemistry all the time, all day long. It's hidden. You don't see it, in most cases. That's one of the problems. Chemistry is not in the forefront. But it's always there. People should realise that. (Jean-Marie Lehn)

化學是如此地深藏不露,你通常不會注意到它。我們坐在這裡,我想我們的穿戴,恐怕大都不離化學。大多數情況下……我們生病時怎麼做?我們用藥。藥物是什麼?分子。化學。所以我們隨時在接觸化學。它是隱匿的。在大多數情況下,你看不到它。這就是問題之一。化學並不處於最顯著的位置。但它始終存在。人們應當意識到這一點。(尚－馬里・萊恩)

Life is short. And the day is only 24 hours. That is the problem. We would like to have days with many many more hours and lifes much longer. So you have to select things. (Jean-Marie Lehn)

生命是短暫的,而每天只有24小時。這就是問題所在。我們希望每天有更多的時間,生命也更加長久。所以你得有所選擇。(尚－馬里・萊恩)

The future of science and of mankind lies in the hands of the coming generations. May they take up the challenge. Prometheus has conquered the fire and we cannot give it back. We have to walk, with enthusiasm, determination and a deep sense of responsibility, the way from the tree of knowledge to the control of destiny. (Jean-Marie Lehn)

科學和人類的未來掌握在後代手中。願他們接受挑戰。普羅米修斯已經征服了火,我們不能把它送回去。我們必須懷著熱情、決心和深切的責任感,從知識之樹走上掌握命運的道路。(尚－馬里・萊恩)

My excitement, which had been rising during this investigation, now reached its peak and ideas swarmed in my brain. One of my first actions was motivated by esthetics more than science. I derived great esthetic pleasure from the three-dimensional structure as portrayed in the computer-simulated model. What a simple, elegant and effective means for the trapping of hitherto recalcitrant alkali cations! I applied the epithet "crown" to the first member of this class of macrocyclic polyethers because its molecular model looked like one. (Charles J. Pedersen)

我的興奮感在這一項研究中持續高漲，現在到了頂點，頭腦中也擠滿了各種想法。我最初的行動之一，更多地是由美學而非科學引發的。電腦模擬模型中描繪的三維結構，使我獲得了極大的美感樂趣。這是多麼簡潔、優雅而又有效的捕獲頑固的鹼金屬陽離子的方式！我用「冠」一詞指稱這一類大環聚醚的首位成員，因為它的分子模型看來像是一頂王冠。（查爾斯‧佩德森）

It doesn't matter whether it is chemistry or immunology or neuroscience：I just do research on what I find interesting. (Susumu Tonegawa)

它是化學、免疫學還是神經科學並不重要：我只是研究自己有興趣的東西。（利根川進）

I became fascinated by the science of molecular biology. (Susumu Tonegawa)

我開始對分子生物學這一門科學著迷。（利根川進）

When I look back on my scientific career to-date, I am amazed at my good fortune. At every major turn, I met scientists who were not only at the very top in their own fields, but who also gave me insightful advice and generous help. (Susumu Tonegawa)

回顧迄今的科學生涯,我對自己的好運感到驚訝。在每一個重要轉捩點我都遇到了一些科學家,他們不僅在各自領域處於最頂端,還給了我深刻的建議和慷慨的幫助。(利根川進)

After all, it is hard to master both life and work equally well. So if you are bound to fake one of them, it had better be life. (Joseph Brodsky)

畢竟,生活與工作,要將它們掌握得同樣恰到好處,何其難也。因而,如果非得將就二者之一,那最好還是生活。(約瑟夫·亞歷山德羅維奇·布羅茨基)

There are worse crimes than burning books. One of them is not reading them. (Joseph Brodsky)

有些罪行甚於焚書。其中一項是不讀它們。(約瑟夫·亞歷山德羅維奇·布羅茨基)

By fighting for the impossible, one begins to make it possible. (Oscar Arias Sánchez)

透過為不可能之事而戰,一個人開始使它成為可能。(奧斯卡·阿里亞斯)

In an age of cynicism and greed, all just ideas are considered impractical. (Oscar Arias Sánchez)

在這個悲觀懷疑和貪得無厭的時代,所有公正合理的想法都被認為不切實際。(奧斯卡·阿里亞斯)

I like to build bridges... not walls. (Oscar Arias Sánchez)

我喜歡架橋……而非築牆。(奧斯卡·阿里亞斯)

There is a difference between the typical politician and the statesman. A typical politician is that person who tells people what people want to hear, while the statesman tells people what people need to know. (Oscar Arias Sánchez)

典型的政客與政治家之間是有區別的。典型的政客是那個說話投人民所好的人，而政治家告訴人民他們需要知道的事情。（奧斯卡‧阿里亞斯）

We live in the short run, and, in the short run, questions about employment, recession and inflation are still with us and still important. Unemployment rates in Europe used to be two or three points lower than in the U.S. Now they are two or three points higher. There are also big differences within Europe. Why is that? Many economists, including me, are trying to answer these questions. There is general agreement about some basic facts and their meaning, though not about all. But every year brings new evidence and some years bring new ideas. Some years even bring good new ideas. (Robert M. Solow)

人生短暫，而在這短暫的時期內，關於就業、衰退和通貨膨脹的問題依然纏著我們，而且依然重要。歐洲的失業率一向比美國的低百分之二或三，現在則高百分之二或三。歐洲之內也存在很大的差異。何以如此？許多經濟學家，包括我，都在試圖解答這些問題。對一些基本事實及其意義，人們有大致上的共識，儘管並非全部。但每年都會產生新證據，有些年帶來新想法。有些年甚至帶來好的新想法。（羅伯特‧索洛）

The study of long-run economic growth is not finished, and may never be finished. The reason has to do with an important difference between economics (along with other social science) and most natural science. As our societies and our technological possibilities evolve, in directions that no one can predict, many of the underlying cause-and-effect relations change too. So economics may have to rethink their basic ideas from time to time. (Robert M. Solow)

對於長期經濟成長的研究還沒結束,而且可能永遠不會結束。原因關係到經濟學(以及其他社會科學)跟大多數自然科學之間的重要區別。隨著社會和技術可能性的發展,在無人能夠預知的一些方向,許多潛在的因果關係也有變化。於是,經濟學可能必須時常重新思考基本概念。(羅伯特・索洛)

Seven weeks have gone by since it became known that I had won this Prize. During that time I have been asked how to solve the economic problems of the United States, Norway, Sweden, the Federal Republic of Germany, Israel, Spain, Portugal, Argentina, Brazil, Mexico, the Philippines, China, Japan, and Korea. It goes without saying that I know the answers to all those questions, but it would be unfair to tell you the answers so soon. (Robert M. Solow)

人們知道我獲得這個獎項已經七週。在此期間,我被問及如何解決美國、挪威、瑞典、德意志聯邦共和國、以色列、西班牙、葡萄牙、阿根廷、巴西、墨西哥、菲律賓、中國、日本和韓國等國的經濟問題。姑且不論我知道這一切問題的答案,然而這麼快就告訴你答案是不公平的。(羅伯特・索洛)

Economics was quantitative, precise and logical rather than merely ideological or rhetorical. I don't think that I ever believed that economics could be an exact science, like physics or even biology, but I still think that it is very important to observe carefully and think clearly and quantitatively about economics, and to give in as little as possible to prejudice and self-interest. It may be even more important in economics than in science because there is not much possibility of doing experiments, and because self-interest can be very strong. (Robert M. Solow)

經濟學是定量的、精確的、遵循邏輯的，而非僅為意識形態或修辭的。我不認為自己曾相信經濟學可以是一門精確的科學，就像物理學甚至生物學一樣；但我仍然認為，對經濟狀況的仔細觀察和清晰、定量的思考，以及盡可能抵制偏見與私利，是非常重要的。它在經濟學中可能比在科學中還重要，因為不太可能進行實驗，而且自身利益可能非常強大。（羅伯特・索洛）

No-one wants to spend their life working on a problem that is too hard to solve. For one thing, it is not easy to get promoted when you're doing that, but for another, you get your pleasures from academic work in economics by working on problems that you can just barely solve, that are hard, so you feel good if you have succeeded, but that are not so hard that you can't get anywhere. (Robert M. Solow)

沒有人願意終其一生鑽研一個太難解決的問題。一方面，你這麼做時不容易得到升等；另一方面，在經濟學學術工作中，你的快樂來自於你勉強能夠解決的問題，它很難，所以你成功了會感覺甚好，而即便一籌莫展也不是非常難受。（羅伯特・索洛）

I estimate that if I had neglected the students, I could have written 25 percent more scientific papers. The choice was easy to make and I do not regret it. (Robert M. Solow)

我估計，假如不好好帶學生，我能多寫出兩、三成的科學論文。這個選擇很容易做出，我也不後悔。（羅伯特・索洛）

1988 年

I realized that to be part of the group of scientists who were exploring the world, way down at the level of a billionth of a centimeter and out to 10 billion light years, was the most exciting life one could imagine. I discovered that scientists were like explorers, like Christopher Columbus or Vasco da Gama. In those times the oceans and continents of Africa and America were unknown mysteries. Today, the unknowns are in our own bodies, our own minds, and on a winter night we see the stars and galaxies. And today we have so many mysteries: how did galaxies form, what is the dark energy that pushes the whole Universe? And how do our minds work? There is still so much to learn! And scientists even get paid to do these things! (Leon M. Lederman)

我意識到，成為科學家團體的一員，以小至十億分之一公分、大到一百億光年的尺度探索世界，是一個人所能想像出最令人激動的生活。我發覺科學家就像探險家，像克里斯多福・哥倫布或瓦斯科・達伽馬。在那些時代，非洲和美洲的海洋和大陸是未知的奧祕。今天，未知事物在我們自己的身體裡，自己的頭腦中，在冬夜裡我們看到的滿天繁星和星系之上。今天我們面對如此眾多的謎團：星系是怎麼形成的，推動整個宇宙的暗能量是什麼？我們的頭腦如何運作？還有這麼多東西要學！而科學家甚至由於做這些事而得到報酬！（利昂・萊德曼）

1981-1990 全球視野與道德辯證

The best discoveries always seem to be made in the small hours of the morning when most people are asleep, when there are no disturbances and the mind becomes contemplative. You're out in a lonely spot somewhere, looking at the numbers on reams of paper spewing out of a computer. You look and look, and suddenly you see some numbers that aren't like the rest —— a spike in the data. You apply some statistical tests and look for errors, but no matter what you do, the spike's still there. It's real. You've found something. There's just no feeling like it in the world. (Leon M. Lederman)

最好的發現似乎總是在清晨的區區幾小時裡出現，此時大多數人尚在夢鄉，沒有干擾，頭腦進入沉思。你孑然獨處，檢視著湧出電腦的大量紙張上的數字。看著看著，突然看到一些異於其他的數字——數據的一個峰值。你運用一些統計測試尋找錯誤，然而無論做什麼，峰值仍然存在。這是真的。你發現了什麼東西。世界上簡直沒有一種感覺能與之相比。（利昂‧萊德曼）

If the basic idea is too complicated to fit on a T-shirt, it's probably wrong. (Leon M. Lederman)

基本想法如果過於複雜，不適合印在 T 恤上，它就很可能是錯的。（利昂‧萊德曼）

Part of being a scientist is compulsive dedication, the insistence on working without rest until you get what you're after. (Leon M. Lederman)

身為一名科學家的職責之一就是心甘情願地奉獻，廢寢忘食地工作，不達目的不罷休。（利昂‧萊德曼）

Scientists don't really ever grow up. I read, as a 10-or-so-year-old, a book for kids by Einstein. I think it was The Meaning of Relativity. It was exciting!

1988 年

Science was compared to a detective story, replete with clues, and the solution was the search for a coherent account of all the known events. Then I remember some very entrapping biographies: Crucibles, by Bernard Jaffe, was the story of chemistry told through the lives of great chemists; Microbe Hunters, by Paul de Kruif, did the same for biologists. Also, the novel Arrowsmith, by Sinclair Lewis, about a medical researcher. These books were a crucial component of getting hooked into science. (Leon M. Lederman)

科學家從未真正長大。在 10 歲左右，我讀到一本愛因斯坦寫的童書。我想就是《相對論的意義》。太令人興奮了！科學就像是偵探故事，線索重重，要解開謎團就得理出全部已知事件的來龍去脈。我還記得那時幾本引人入勝的傳記：伯納德・賈菲寫的《坩堝》，是透過偉大化學家們的生活講述的化學故事；保羅・德・克魯夫寫的《微生物獵人》，以同樣手法為生物學家們立傳。還有，辛克萊・路易斯寫的小說《阿羅史密斯》，描述一位醫學研究者。這些書籍是迷上科學的關鍵要素。（利昂・萊德曼）

We are honored for research which is today referred to as the "Two Neutrino Experiment". How does one make this research comprehensible to ordinary people? In fact "The Two Neutrinos" sounds like an Italian dance team. How can we have our colleagues in chemistry, medicine, and especially in literature share with us, not the cleverness of our research, but the beauty of the intellectual edifice, of which our experiment is but one brick? This is a dilemma and an anguish for all scientists because the public understanding of science is no longer a luxury of cultural engagement, but it is an essential requirement for survival in our increasingly technological age：In this context,

I believe this Nobel Ceremony with its awesome tradition and pomp has as one of its most important benefits; the public attention it draws to science and its practitioners. (Leon M. Lederman)

我們由於如今被稱作「兩種中微子實驗」的研究而獲此殊榮。如何使這項研究為普通人所能夠理解？實際上，「兩種中微子」聽起來就像個義大利舞蹈團。如何能讓我們的化學、醫學，尤其是文學領域的同事與我們分享，並非我們的研究之聰明才智，而是知識大廈之華美，而我們的實驗僅為其中一塊磚？這是所有科學家的困惑與苦惱，因為大眾對科學的理解不再是一種文化參與的奢侈品，而是在這個技術日益發達的時代生存的必需：由此而論，我認為這個具有驚人傳統和壯麗場面的諾貝爾頒獎典禮，其最重要的效益之一是它引起了大眾對科學及其從事者的關注。（利昂・萊德曼）

My children have often asked me why I never received a Nobel Prize. I used to tell them it was because the Nobel committee couldn't make up its mind which of my projects to recognize. (Leon M. Lederman)

我的孩子經常問我，怎麼從沒得過諾貝爾獎。我曾經對他們說，這是因為諾貝爾委員會無法決定該認可我的哪一個項目。（利昂・萊德曼）

Observation and measurement is the ultimate defining activity; the act of measurement itself forces a system to choose one of its various possibilities. (Leon M. Lederman)

觀察與測量是最終的決定性行動，測量行為本身迫使系統選擇其各種可能性之一。（利昂・萊德曼）

Physics is the science of observation, and probably no art is closer to the metier of the practitioner than is photography. How parallel are the tasks!

Blend respect for meticulous technique with inspiration in order to expose a small piece of the world. Explain through the eye and the mind how a thing subtle but of great wonder can be revealed... It all amounts to a glimpse of the world which is on the one hand abstract, ethereal and evocative of varieties of esthetic reactions. On the other hand there is for us physicists the faith in an underlying rationale of crystalline precision. (Leon M. Lederman)

物理學是觀察的科學,恐怕沒有什麼藝術比攝影更接近物理學研究者的行業了。任務多麼相似!把對精細技巧的崇奉跟靈感融合起來,以揭示一小片世界。透過眼睛與心靈,說明一種既深奧玄妙又大為驚人的事物如何能夠顯露。……這都屬於世界的一霎閃現,一方面是抽象的、優雅的,並能喚起各種美學反應;另一方面,在我們物理學家看來,其中包含著對澄明精確的根本原理的信念。(利昂・萊德曼)

Mathematics is much more than a language for dealing with the physical world. It is a source of models and abstractions which will enable us to obtain amazing new insights into the way in which nature operates. (Melvin Schwartz)

數學不僅僅是一種與物質世界對話的語言。它是模型和抽象的來源。關於大自然的執行方式,它會有助於我們獲得驚人的新見解。(梅爾文・施瓦茨)

The experience of trying to find a job as a twenty-year-old boy without connections was the most depressing I was ever to face. I tried to find any job in a chemical laboratory: I would present myself, fill out forms, and have the door closed hopelessly behind me. Finally through a benefactor of my older brother, I was accepted to wash chemical apparatus in a pharmaceutical laboratory, G. D. Searle and Co., at eighteen dollars a week. In the evenings I studied chemistry at the University of Chicago, the weekends I helped in the family store. (Jack Steinberger)

身為一個沒有任何關係的20歲年輕人,求職是我面對過最沮喪的經歷。我試著在化工廠找到任何工作:我要自我介紹、填寫表格,然後聽憑大門在身後毫無希望地關上。終於,透過一位照顧過我哥哥的人,我被一家製藥廠,希爾勒公司錄用,清洗化學器械,每週18美元。晚上我到芝加哥大學攻讀化學,週末則在家族商店打雜。(傑克·施泰因貝格爾)

The courses of Fermi were gems of simplicity and clarity and he made a great effort to help us become good physicists also outside the regular classroom work, by arranging evening discussions on a widespread series of topics, where he also showed us how to solve problems. Fellow students included Yang, Lee, Goldberger, Rosenbluth, Garwin, Chamberlain, Wolfenstein and Chew. There was a marvellous collaboration, and I feel I learned as much from these fellow students as from the professors. (Jack Steinberger)

費米的課程是質樸而透澈的珍品。為了把我們培養成優秀的物理學者,他做出了極大努力,且不限於常規課堂教學。他安排了一系列話題廣泛的晚間討論,並在其中示範如何解決難題。我的同學包括楊振寧、李政道、戈德伯格、羅森布盧特、加溫、張伯倫、沃芬斯坦和丘。這是一種不可思議的合作,我覺得向這些同學學到的東西,與向教授們學到的一樣多。(傑克·施泰因貝格爾)

I enjoyed being on my own, being by myself. I certainly played with other kids and interacted but I had no problems with being on my own and that is still so. I think I enjoyed the occasions most when I had a well-defined project and I could solve the problems by myself. (Johann Deisenhofer)

我喜歡只有我自己獨處的狀態。我當然會跟別的孩子玩耍和互動，但只有我自己也沒問題，至今如此。我想，我最享受的是有一個明確的項目並能夠自己解決問題的時刻。（約翰·戴森霍費爾）

The young people certainly want challenges. They would like to work in the forefront of science and we, the Laureates, try to convince them that work in biology is in fact in the forefront and it produces, even with simple experiments, often unexpected results opening new avenues for research. So to bring that forward there is so much to be discovered, in particular in biology, where we just have scratched the surface of an understanding of the biological phenomena. And on the other hand there are the methods available, an enormous development in methods that we have now available to study biological phenomena. So I would encourage them to study biology and work in biology. There's so much to be discovered. (Robert Huber)

年輕人當然喜歡挑戰。他們願意在科學的最前端工作，而我們，諾貝爾獎得主，試圖使他們相信從事生物學工作事實上就是處於前端，而且即使是簡單的實驗，也往往會產生意想不到的結果，為研究開闢新的途徑。要推動研究發展，有這麼多東西等待被發現，尤其是在生物學領域中，我們對於生物現象只有表面的理解。而另一方面，如今研究方法有了巨大發展，我們現在有許多方法可以用於研究生物現象。所以我要鼓勵他們研究生物學，從事生物學工作。有這麼多東西等待被發現。（羅伯特·胡貝爾）

1981-1990 全球視野與道德辯證

I had wonderful teachers in physics and in chemistry, inorganic and organic chemistry, so they were my heroes. (Robert Huber)

在物理、化學、無機和有機化學各學科，我都有非常好的老師，他們是我的英雄。（羅伯特・胡貝爾）

I can tell you what was very important for me as a student who had just finished his first exams and started to work on a scientific problem —— which looking back right now was a very minor problem, but at that time it was important —— it was a small molecule a Nobel Laureate was working on and a famous professor associated with him. I joined them as a diploma student, aged 22 or so. And I did a simple experiment and found that they were wrong, they made an error, an essential error, suggesting the molecular shape of this molecule incorrectly. And I could correct them, you see. This was great —— I, a nothing. All of this was then very friendly and they liked what I had done. But, for me, it convinced me that I could achieve something and it was very decisive for me to stay in science. (Robert Huber)

我可以告訴你們，對於初出校門的我來說，什麼是非常重要的。我剛完成首次考試，開始研究一個科學問題 —— 現在回頭看是個非常小的問題，但在當時很重要 —— 這是個小分子，一位諾貝爾獎得主正在研究，有一位著名的教授與之聯手。我作為大學畢業生加入團隊，年齡22歲左右。我做了一個簡單的實驗，發現他們錯了，他們犯了一個錯，一個根本性錯誤，不正確地呈現這個分子的分子形狀。你們看，我可以糾正他們。這太棒了 —— 我，一個無名小卒。這一切都是非常友善的，他們喜歡我所做的事。但是，對我來說，這件事使我確信自己可以有所作為，對於我留在科學界極具決定性。（羅伯特・胡貝爾）

1988 年

At age eleven, I became a member of the circulating library of my home town. From there on I was rarely seen outside but was reading two to four books per week, the subjects ranging from archaeology over ethnology and geography to zoology. Needless to say that I did not do much homework. (Hartmut Michel)

11 歲時，我成為本地流通圖書館的會員。從那以後，我很少出門，每週讀兩到四本書，主題涵蓋考古學到民族學和地理學乃至動物學。不用說，我沒做多少作業。（哈特穆特・米歇爾）

At school, my favorite subjects were history, biology, chemistry, and physics. Especially the teaching in physics was excellent. Most of my understanding of it I got at high school, not at the university. (Hartmut Michel)

在學校，我最喜歡的科目是歷史、生物、化學和物理。尤其以物理課最出色。我對物理學的了解大部分來自中學，而非大學。（哈特穆特・米歇爾）

Our brains seem to be organised to make random comparisons of the contents of our memories. Daydreaming allows the process to go into free fall. Suddenly, there is a new idea, born with intense excitement. We cannot organise this process but we can distort or even defeat it. (James W. Black)

頭腦似乎是有組織地對記憶的內容做隨機比較。白日夢允許這種過程自由降落。突然，一個新想法伴隨著強烈的興奮誕生。我們無法組織這個過程，但能夠扭曲甚至破壞它。（詹姆士・W・布拉克）

Our brains work best when doing focuses our thinking. (James W. Black)

我們的頭腦在全神貫注時工作得最好。（詹姆士・W・布拉克）

I learnt, for the first time, the joys of substituting hard, disciplined study for the indulgence of day-dreaming. (James W. Black)

以刻苦、規律的學習代替沉溺於白日夢，我第一次體會到其中的樂趣。[84]（詹姆士·W·布拉克）

There are certain things you may not seek directly. There's a kind of obliqueness necessary in life. An obvious one would be happiness. (James W. Black)

有些事情無須直接尋求。生活中有種必要的間接。明顯的例子就是幸福。（詹姆士·W·布拉克）

Entrenched attitudes can absorb reformist efforts like a punch bag. (James W. Black)

根深蒂固的態度會像拳擊沙袋一樣吞噬改革的努力。（詹姆士·W·布拉克）

I wish I had my beta-blockers handy. (James W. Black)

但願我的受體阻滯劑在手邊。[85]（詹姆士·W·布拉克）

The idea was to do research, find new avenues to conquer, new mountains to climb. (Gertrude B. Elion)

創意就是從事研究，尋找新的途徑去征服，新的山脈去攀登。（格特魯德·B·埃利恩）

I had fallen in love with a young man…, and we were planning to get married. And then he died of subacute bacterial endocarditis… Two years later with the advent of penicillin, he would have been saved. It reinforced in my mind the importance of scientific discovery… (Gertrude B. Elion)

---

[84] 布萊克在談及自己收穫豐富的大學學習時這麼說。
[85] 布萊克在得知自己獲得諾貝爾獎時這樣說。受體阻滯劑，指其所發現的治療心臟病藥物。

1988 年

我愛上了一個年輕人……我們正打算結婚。此時他死於亞急性細菌性心內膜炎。……兩年後，足以救他一命的青黴素問世。這在我心中強化了科學發現的重要性……（格特魯德·B·埃利恩）

I had no specific bent toward science until my grandfather died of stomach cancer. I decided that nobody should suffer that much. (Gertrude B. Elion)

我是到祖父死於胃癌時才對科學產生特別興趣。我決定不讓任何人遭受這麼多的痛苦。（格特魯德·B·埃利恩）

Maybe I was young and "cute" (after all, I was only twenty then), but I've learned over the years that when you put white lab coats on chemists, they all look alike! (Gertrude B. Elion)

也許我是年輕「漂亮」的（畢竟，那時我才 20 歲），只是這麼多年過去，我已經明白，把實驗室白袍罩到化學家身上後，他們看起來都一樣！[86]（格特魯德·B·埃利恩）

The Nobel Prize is fine, but the drugs I've developed are rewards in themselves. (Gertrude B. Elion)

諾貝爾獎很好，不過我開發的藥物本身就是獎勵。（格特魯德·B·埃利恩）

People ask me often whether the Nobel Prize was the thing you were aiming for all your life, and I say that would be crazy. Nobody would aim for a Nobel Prize because, if you didn't get it, your whole life would be wasted. What we were aiming at was getting people well, and the satisfaction of that is much greater than any prize you can get. (Gertrude B. Elion)

---

[86] 埃利恩回想往事時說，她曾經謀求一個實驗室職位遭拒，據說理由是顧慮到其體態魅力會分散男同事的注意力。

1981-1990 全球視野與道德辯證

人們經常問，諾貝爾獎是否為妳一生的追求。我說那就太瘋狂了。沒有人會追求諾貝爾獎，因為要是未能獲獎，一生就全部浪費了。我們所追求的是讓人們過得好，而這麼做的滿足感遠勝於所能得到的任何獎項。（格特魯德‧B‧埃利恩）

That was the turning point. It was as though the signal was there, "This is the disease you're going to have to work against." I never really stopped to think about anything else. (Gertrude B. Elion)

那就是轉捩點。就好像有一個信號在那裡：「這是妳將要對付的疾病。」我從未真正停下來想過其他事情。（格特魯德‧B‧埃利恩）

I think it's a very valuable thing for a doctor to learn how to do research, to learn how to approach research, something there isn't time to teach them in medical school. They don't really learn how to approach a problem, and yet diagnosis is a problem; and I think that year spent in research is extremely valuable to them. (Gertrude B. Elion)

我認為對醫生來說，學會如何從事研究、學會如何著手研究是非常有價值的，而醫學院沒有時間教他們這一課。他們沒有真正學會如何著手對付難題，而診斷就是難題。我認為那一年的研究對他們而言是極其寶貴的。（格特魯德‧B‧埃利恩）

Don't be afraid of hard work. Nothing worthwhile comes easily. Don't let others discourage you or tell you that you can't do it. In my day I was told women didn't go into chemistry. I saw no reason why we couldn't. (Gertrude B. Elion)

不要畏懼艱苦的工作。任何有價值的東西都不會輕易得到。不要讓別人勸阻你或對你說你做不到。當時也有人對我說女性不適合從事化學工作。我看不出為什麼我們不能。（格特魯德‧B‧埃利恩）

1988 年

When William Faulkner accepted the Nobel Prize in Literature in 1949, he spoke of the verities of the human heart —— love and honor, pity and pride, compassion and sacrifice. As a scientist, I should like to suggest three verities of the human mind —— curiosity, creativity, and the love of knowledge. (George H. Hitchings)

威廉‧福克納在 1949 年接受諾貝爾文學獎時，談到了人類心靈的真諦 —— 愛和榮譽、憐憫和驕傲、同情和犧牲。作為科學家，我願意提出人類心智的三種真諦 —— 好奇心、創造力和對知識的熱愛。（喬治‧H‧希欽斯）

Each scientific discovery is built upon its predecessors and we give thanks for the dedicated men and women who held tenaciously to their visions and for the legacy of their knowledge. (George H. Hitchings)

每一項科學發現都建立在先前的發現上。我們感謝那些執著於願景而一心奉獻的男女，感謝他們留給我們的寶貴知識。（喬治‧H‧希欽斯）

Forty years ago when we began our studies in nucleic acids, we certainly did not anticipate receiving such an award. We were inspired by basic questions concerning the biochemistry of cellular reproduction, and the search led us on a journey filled with new knowledge and exciting discoveries. That is the dream of every scientist. We have been further blessed with the privilege of seeing our work in the laboratory become medical therapies to combat diseases like malaria, leukemia, bacterial infections and gout. (George H. Hitchings)

40 年前著手研究核酸的時候，我們當然不曾預料得到這樣的殊榮。我們受到細胞繁殖生物化學一些基本問題的啟發，並被引領踏上充滿新鮮知識和驚人發現的旅程。這是每一位科學家的夢想。我們更有幸得以

看到，自己在實驗室的工作成為對抗瘧疾、白血病、細菌感染和痛風等等疾病的醫學療法。（喬治・H・希欽斯）

I thought they would never select an Eastern writer for the Nobel. I was surprised. (Naguib Mahfouz)

我曾以為他們永遠不會選擇一位東方作家獲得諾貝爾獎。我感到驚訝。（納吉布・馬哈福茲）

The Nobel Prize has given me, for the first time in my life, the feeling that my literature could be appreciated on an international level. (Naguib Mahfouz)

此生第一次，諾貝爾獎讓我感到我的文學作品可以在國際層面得到欣賞。（納吉布・馬哈福茲）

One effect that the Nobel Prize seems to have had is that more Arabic literary works have been translated into other languages. (Naguib Mahfouz)

諾貝爾獎似乎帶來的一種影響是，更多的阿拉伯文學作品被翻譯成其他語言。（納吉布・馬哈福茲）

Winning Nobel imposed on me a lifestyle to which I am not used and which I would not have preferred. (Naguib Mahfouz)

獲得諾貝爾獎帶給我一種我不習慣、原本也不情願的生活方式。（納吉布・馬哈福茲）

You can tell whether a man is clever by his answers. You can tell whether a man is wise by his questions. (Naguib Mahfouz)

判斷一個人是否聰明看他的回答。判斷一個人是否智慧看他的問題。（納吉布・馬哈福茲）

1988 年

We must take the world as it is and not as we would like it to be. (Maurice Allais)

我們必須接受世界的本來面目，而非我們想要的樣子。（莫里斯·阿萊）

My approach has never been to start from theories to arrive at facts, but on the contrary, to try to bring out from the facts the explanatory thread without which they appear incomprehensible and elude effective action. (Maurice Allais)

我的研究方法從來不是從理論出發以得出事實，而是相反，力求從事實中提取出解釋的線索。缺乏重要的線索，事實就顯得費解，有效行動也無從談起了。（莫里斯·阿萊）

At the beginning of my career, my desire to understand was associated with a profound desire to act, with the wish to influence opinion and policy; but, over the years, this motivation has come to be of secondary importance, far behind my desire to understand. (Maurice Allais)

在職業生涯初期，我對理解的渴望伴隨著濃厚的行動欲望，一心想影響輿論和政策；然而，多年之後，這種動機已經退為次要，遠不及我的理解欲了。（莫里斯·阿萊）

All science is based on models, and every scientific model comprises three distinct stages：statement of well-defined hypotheses; deduction of all the consequences of these hypotheses, and nothing but these consequences; confrontation of these consequences with observed data. (Maurice Allais)

一切科學均基於模型，每一個科學模型都包含三個明顯的階段：陳述明確的假設；推論出這些假設的全部後果，並且只討論這些後果；對照這些後果與觀測到的資料。（莫里斯·阿萊）

1981-1990 全球視野與道德辯證

1989 年

The award reminds the world that Physics is an experimental science and can still be successfully pursued in a university laboratory. Many scientists throughout the world are doing beautiful and accurate measurements. We believe that research of this nature will continue to make major contributions to the understanding of the fundamental laws of our universe. (Norman F. Ramsey)

諾貝爾獎提醒世界，物理學是一門實驗的科學，仍然可以在大學實驗室中順利進行。全世界許多科學家都在做著美妙而精確的測量。我們相信，這一類的研究將繼續為理解宇宙基本法則做出重大貢獻。（諾曼‧拉姆齊）

Well for a while I was in mathematics, which I enjoyed very much. But it was always, my basic interest was always there. I mean physical things have always interested me. I was curious and still am. (Norman F. Ramsey)

我一度很長時間沉浸於數學，我非常喜歡數學。不過我的基本興趣總是在物理學上。我是說物理學方面的東西總是讓我感興趣。我很好奇，至今如此。（諾曼‧拉姆齊）

When I learned, that you could make a living studying how nature operates, I knew that was what I wanted to do. (Norman F. Ramsey)

當我得知研究自然如何運作可以謀生時，我知道這就是自己所想做的。（諾曼‧拉姆齊）

I should like to cite a line from William Blake. "To see a world in a grain of sand…" and allude to a possible parallel to see worlds in an electron. (Hans G. Dehmelt)

我願引用威廉‧布萊克的一句詩,「一粒沙中看世界……」[87],以之比喻一種可能的對照,在一個電子中看大千世界。(漢斯‧德默爾特)

I grew up in Muenchen where my father has been a professor for pharmaceutic chemistry at the university. He had studied chemistry and medicine, having been a research student in Leipzig with Wilhelm Ostwald, the Nobel Laureate 1909. So I became familiar with the life of a scientist in a chemical laboratory quite early. (Wolfgang Paul)

我在慕尼黑大學長大,父親是這所大學的藥物化學教授。他學過化學和醫學,在萊比錫跟1909年諾貝爾獎得主威廉‧奧士華是研究所同學。所以我很早就熟悉科學家在化學實驗室裡的生活。(沃爾夫岡‧保羅)

At about the age of twelve, I received a book to read that explained some nuclear physics and also presented the ideas behind Mendeleev's Periodic Table. The book was sufficiently elementary so I could understand it. I cannot remember who gave it to me. Nevertheless, I found the book spellbinding and I was very excited by Mendeleev's ideas about the elements and how he managed to predict the existence of elements that had not been found at the time he wrote the volume. That, to me, was a lasting and clear example of the power of science and its beauty. (Sidney Altman)

大約12歲時,我得到了一本書。書中講解了一些核子物理學知識,還介紹了門得列夫元素週期表背後的想法。書的內容十分淺顯,所以我

---

[87] 原詩為:To see a world in a grain of sand and a heaven in a wild flower, hold infinite in the palm of your hand and eternity in an hour. (一粒沙中看世界,一朵野花裡見天堂。你的手掌托著無限,一小時也包含著永恆。)

看得懂。我不記得是誰給我的。然而,我發現這本書引人入勝。門得列夫關於元素的想法,以及他設法預測編制週期表時尚未發現其存在的元素的過程,都使我非常激動。對我來說,這是科學的力與美的永恆而明確的例子。(西德尼・奧爾特曼)

All the people who do well work very hard. Nobody who has a record of achievement has been lazy about it. (Sidney Altman)

所有表現出色的人都非常努力。任何有成就的人都並不懶惰。(西德尼・奧爾特曼)

We are privileged to have been afforded the opportunity to study Nature and to follow our own thoughts and inspirations in a time of relative tranquillity and in a land with a generous and forward-looking government. (Sidney Altman)

我們有幸在相對平靜的時代,在政府慷慨且有遠見的國家,得以擁有跟隨自己的思想和靈感研究大自然的機會。(西德尼・奧爾特曼)

The overall view of the human genome project has been one of great excitement and positive press, but there are people who have concerns that are quite reasonable, and they are frightened of things they don't understand. (Thomas R. Cech)

人類基因組計畫的整體情況一直非常令人激動並得到正面評價,但也有人懷著相當合理的擔憂,他們害怕自己不理解的事物。(托馬斯・切赫)

Because all of biology is connected, one can often make a breakthrough with an organism that exaggerates a particular phenomenon, and later explore the generality. (Thomas R. Cech)

> 1989 年

由於一切生物都是互相關聯的,人們通常可以經由放大特定現象的有機體獲得突破,再探索其普遍性。(托馬斯·切赫)

Tthere is value in having practising scientists as leaders of research institutions. (Thomas R. Cech)

讓從事實際研究的科學家擔任研究機構的領導者,這樣做是有價值的。(托馬斯·切赫)

It is a good thing for scientists to spend a little bit of their time either in the community or in schools or helping to train high school teachers. (Thomas R. Cech)

科學家將少許時間用於社區以及學校,或幫助培訓中學教師,誠屬好事。(托馬斯·切赫)

The popular mind imagines the scientist as a lonely genius. In reality, few of us are geniuses, and even fewer are lonely. (J. Michael Bishop)

在人們的普遍觀念中,科學家是孤獨的天才。事實上,我們很少有人是天才,孤獨的人就更少了。(麥可·畢曉普)

My life in science has been rich and rewarding. I have sacrificed very little. (J. Michael Bishop)

我的科學生涯始終是豐富且值得的。我幾乎不曾付出犧牲。(麥可·畢曉普)

If offered reincarnation, I would choose the career of a performing musician with exceptional talent, preferably, in a string quartet. One life-time as a scientist is enough —— great fun, but enough. I am a self-confessed book addict, an inveterate reader of virtually anything that comes to hand (with the notable exceptions of science fiction and crime novels). I enjoy writing and abhor the dreadful prose that afflicts much of the contemporary scientific literature. (J. Michael Bishop)

如果得以重生,我會選擇做一名才華洋溢的表演音樂家,弦樂四重奏成員就更好了。當科學家一輩子已足夠了——非常有趣,但足夠了。我自認是個書迷,一個嗜讀成癖的人,幾乎不放過到手的任何讀物(科幻作品和犯罪小說明顯例外)。我喜歡寫作,厭惡肆虐於當代許多科學文獻的枯燥乏味。(麥可・畢曉普)

Science is a rewarding, active process of discovery, not the passive absorption of what others had discovered. (Harold E. Varmus)

科學是充滿意義的、積極的發現過程,而非對他人發現的被動吸收。(哈羅德・瓦默斯)

I began doing serious work in a laboratory for the first time —— at the National Institutes of Health in Bethesda, Maryland —— at the relatively advanced age of twenty-eight. (I do not recommend such a protracted pathway into science for others, but it may be useful to remember that slow starts do sometimes occur and can still lead to satisfying results). (Harold E. Varmus)

我首次在實驗室裡進行學術研究——於馬里蘭州貝塞斯達的國家衛生研究院——是在年齡相對大的28歲。(我不推薦別人走如此拖沓的科學之路,但記住這一點或許有幫助:遲緩的起步的確並不罕見,然而仍可帶來令人欣慰的成果。)(哈羅德・瓦默斯)

Just after graduation in 1966, like many of my contemporaries, I applied for research training at the National Institutes of Health. Perhaps because his wife was a poet, Ira Pastan agreed to take me into his laboratory, despite my lack of scientific credentials. (Harold E. Varmus)

1966 年一畢業，跟許多同儕一樣，我申請了國家衛生研究院的研究培訓。也許由於其夫人是位詩人，艾拉·帕斯坦同意我進入他的實驗室，儘管我沒有科學文憑。（哈羅德·瓦默斯）

When high school students ask to spend their afternoons and weekends in my laboratory, I am amazed: I didn't develop that kind of enthusiasm for science until I was 28 years old. (Harold E. Varmus)

當中學生們要求在我的實驗室裡度過下午和週末時，我很驚訝：我是直到 28 歲才對科學產生這種熱情的。（哈羅德·瓦默斯）

I'm used to being surrounded by really smart 22-year-old students who have no problem saying that something I suggested is not a very good idea. (Harold E. Varmus)

我習慣了被十分聰明的 22 歲學生包圍，他們毫無顧慮地指出我的某一項意見不是太好。（哈羅德·瓦默斯）

Science can improve lives in ways that are elegant in design and moving in practice. (Harold E. Varmus)

科學能夠以構思優美雅致而富於行動力的方式改善生活。（哈羅德·瓦默斯）

My ideal summer day was reading on the porch. (Harold E. Varmus)

我理想的夏日是在門廊上看書。（哈羅德·瓦默斯）

Ideas? My head is full of them, one after the other, but they serve no purpose there. They must be put down on paper, one after the other. (Camilo José Cela)

想法嗎？我滿腦子都是，一個接一個，但它們在那裡毫無用處。它們必須被記錄在紙上，一個接一個。（卡米洛‧荷西‧塞拉）

The greatest reward is to know that one can speak and emit articulate sounds and utter words that describe things, events and emotions. (Camilo José Cela)

最大的回報是知道自己能夠說話，發出清晰的聲音，講述描摹事物、事件和情感的話語。（卡米洛‧荷西‧塞拉）

The field that I represent is perhaps one where recognition is particularly welcome and encouraging, and for this reason: We are not used to being thanked for what we do. If we warn against an economic set-back and get heard, the set-back may not materialize and we are called pessimists. On the other hand, if we stick to polite academic modesty and do not get heard, the set-back may come and we meet the usual verdict: Why did you not tell us! That is, heads you win, tails I lose. But for us there is only one conclusion that is tenable. We will continue to do our best. (Trygve Haavelmo)

我所代表的領域大概特別歡迎和鼓勵認可，原因在於：我們不習慣因我們所做的事情而得到感謝。如果我們警告經濟衰退並受到重視，衰退可能沒有出現，我們就會被稱為悲觀主義者。另一方面，如果我們信守斯文的學術謙遜並保持低調，衰退可能到來，我們則依舊被一口咬定：你們怎麼不告訴我們！這就叫正面你贏，反面我輸。然而就我們而言，只有一種結局可期。我們會繼續竭盡全力。（泰瑞夫‧哈維默）

1990 年

　　While I always had some interest in science, I developed a strong interest in physics when I was in high school as a result of reading a short book entitled Relativity, by Einstein. It opened a new vista for me and deepened my curiosity about the physical world. (Jerome I. Friedman)

　　我對科學一直保持著一定興趣，中學時則對物理學產生了濃厚的興趣，因為讀到愛因斯坦寫的小冊子《相對論》。它為我開啟一片新天地，加深了我對物質世界的好奇心。（傑爾姆・弗里德曼）

　　I had developed —— or had been born with —— an active curiosity and an intense interest in things mechanical, chemical and electrical and do not remember when I was not fascinated with them and devoted to their exploration. (Henry W. Kendall)

　　對於機械、化學和電這些方面的事物，我形成了 —— 或者天生有 —— 活躍的好奇心和強烈的興趣，我不記得有什麼時候不迷戀它們並致力於對它們的探索。（亨利・肯德爾）

　　Many people and governments share the mistaken belief that science, with new, ingenious devices and techniques, can rescue us from the troubles we face without our having to mend our ways and change our patterns of activity. This is not so. (Henry W. Kendall)

　　許多人以及政府都對科學懷有錯誤的信念，以為運用新型的、精巧的設備與技術，可以使我們擺脫面臨的各種麻煩，而無須修補行事方法和改變活動模式。事實並非如此。（亨利・肯德爾）

Although I read quite a bit and found mathematics easy, I was not an outstanding student. In high school I did reasonably well in mathematics and science thanks to some talented and dedicated teachers. (Richard E. Taylor)

我雖然讀了不少書,並且認為數學容易,卻不是個出眾的學生。中學時,多虧一些才華橫溢並敬業的老師,我的數學和科學學得相當好。(理查・愛德華・泰勒)

The quarks and the stars were here when you came, and they will be here when you go. They have no sense of humor so, if you want a world where more people smile, you will have to fix things yourselves. I am confident that you will try, and hopeful that you will succeed. (Richard E. Taylor)

當你來的時候夸克和星辰就在這裡,你走的時候它們也會在這裡。它們沒有幽默感,所以,你若想要一個更多人微笑的世界,你就得自己解決問題。我確信你會嘗試,也相信你會成功。(理查・愛德華・泰勒)

My special fascination has been to understand better the world of chemistry and its complexities. (Elias James Corey)

我一向特別著迷於更徹底地了解化學世界及其複雜性。(艾里亞斯・詹姆斯・科里)

Chemical synthesis is uniquely positioned at the heart of chemistry, the central science, and its impact on our lives and society is all pervasive. (Elias James Corey)

化學作為中心科學,化學合成位處於其獨特的核心地位,它對我們的生活和社會的影響無處不在。(艾里亞斯・詹姆斯・科里)

To a synthetic chemist, the complex molecules of nature are as beautiful

1990 年

as any of her other creations. The perception of that beauty depends on the understanding of chemical structures and their transformations, and, as with a treasured work of art, deepens as the subject is studied, perhaps even to a level approaching romance. (Elias James Corey)

在合成化學家看來，自然界的複雜分子與她的其他創造物同樣美麗。對這種美的感知取決於對化學結構及其轉變的了解，並且，就像對待珍貴的藝術品一樣，隨著課題研究而深入，也許甚至達到近乎浪漫的程度。（艾里亞斯‧詹姆斯‧科里）

Kidney transplants seem so routine now. But the first one was like Lindbergh's flight across the ocean. (Joseph E. Murray)

腎臟移植如今已變得十分常見。然而第一例猶如林白飛越大西洋。[88]（約瑟夫‧穆雷）

If you're going to worry about what people say, you're never going to make any progress. (Joseph E. Murray)

倘若顧慮輿論，進步毫無可能。（約瑟夫‧穆雷）

Let us continue to shorten the distance from the laboratory to the bedside. (Joseph E. Murray)

讓我們繼續縮短從實驗室到病床的距離。（約瑟夫‧穆雷）

You cannot stop the human mind from working. (Joseph E. Murray)

你無法阻止人的心智工作。（約瑟夫‧穆雷）

To the patient, any operation is momentous. (Joseph E. Murray)

---

[88] 穆雷於 1954 年成功實施了首例腎移植手術。查爾斯‧林白（Charles Lindbergh），1927 年獨自駕機飛越大西洋的美國飛行家。

> 對於患者，任何手術都是大手術。（約瑟夫·穆雷）

I still have a vivid memory of my excitement when I first saw a chart of the periodic table of elements. The order in the universe seemed miraculous. (Joseph E. Murray)

我仍然清晰記得初次見到元素週期表時的激動。宇宙中的秩序顯得不可思議。（約瑟夫·穆雷）

I had 48 years of surgery under my belt and I decided to just enjoy other aspects of my life. (Joseph E. Murray)

我做了48年的手術，我決定專心享受生活的其他方面。（約瑟夫·穆雷）[89]

My only wish would be to have 10 more lives to live on this planet. If that were possible, I'd spend one lifetime each in embryology, genetics, physics, astronomy and geology. The other lifetimes would be as a pianist, backwoodsman, tennis player, or writer for the National Geographic. (Joseph E. Murray)

我唯一的願望就是在這個星球上再活10次。如果這是可能的，我會在胚胎學、遺傳學、物理學、天文學和地質學上各用上一生。另外幾生則會用於當鋼琴家、邊遠地區居民、網球運動員，或者《國家地理》撰稿人。（約瑟夫·穆雷）

My high school class consisted of about 15 people. I was not an outstanding student even in this small group. I entered the University of Texas in Austin in 1937. In my first semester I made only B grades, but as time went

---

[89] 穆雷，著名外科醫生，1990年諾貝爾生理學或醫學獎得主。這是他退休時所說的話。他逝世於93歲高齡。

on and the courses became more difficult and challenging I began to enjoy the studies, mainly in chemistry and chemical engineering. (E. Donnall Thomas)

我的中學班級有大約 15 個人。即便在這一小群人中,我也不是個優秀生。我於 1937 年進入位於奧斯汀的德克薩斯大學。第一學期我只得了 B 級,然而隨著時間推移,課程變得更難、挑戰性更大,我開始享受學習,尤其是化學和化學工程課。(唐納爾·湯瑪斯)

During my undergraduate years at the end of the depression money was almost non-existent so I worked at a number of odd jobs. One of the jobs was waiting tables at a girls' dormitory. One January morning it snowed, a rare event in Texas. As I emerged from the girls' dormitory, an attractive young woman hit me in the face with a snow ball. I naturally had to catch her and avenge the insult to my male ego. Thus, I meet Dorothy Martin, the Dottie who has participated in all my endeavors up to the present time. (E. Donnall Thomas)

我讀大學時,時值大蕭條末期,我幾乎身無分文,所以做過一些稀奇古怪的零工。其中一份是在女生宿舍當服務生。一個 1 月的早晨,下雪了,這在德克薩斯很少見。當我從女生宿舍裡出來時,一個漂亮的年輕女孩投出的雪球打在我臉上。我當然得抓住她,找回男性的自尊。就這樣,我遇上了多蘿西·馬丁。多蒂[90]參與了我的所有事業,直到現在。(唐納爾·湯瑪斯)

Man does not speak because he thinks; he thinks because he speaks. Or rather, speaking is no different than thinking: to speak is to think. (Octavio Paz)

---

[90] 多蒂,多蘿西的暱稱。

1981–1990 全球視野與道德辯證

人並非為了思考而說話，而是為了說話而思考。或者更確切地說，說話與思考並無不同：說話就是思考。（奧克塔維奧·帕斯）

If what you have done yesterday still looks big to you, you haven't done much today. (Mikhail Sergeyevich Gorbachev)

如果昨天所做之事對於你仍顯重要，你今天就沒做多少事情。（米哈伊爾·戈巴契夫）

A society should never become like a pond with stagnant water, without movement. (Mikhail Sergeyevich Gorbachev)

社會不應變得猶如死水，陷於停滯。（米哈伊爾·戈巴契夫）

Sometimes we applied existing techniques; other times we developed new techniques. Some of these techniques have been more "successful" than others, success being measured here by acceptance in practice. (Harry M. Markowitz)

有的時候我們運用現有技術，有的時候我們開發新技術。其中一些技術比其他的更「成功」，而成功的衡量標準是實務中的接受程度。（哈利·馬可維茲）

I am sorry I cannot acknowledge all the people I have worked with over the last 38 years and describe what it was we accomplished. As each of these people know, I often considered work to be play, and derived great joy from our collaboration. (Harry M. Markowitz)

很抱歉，我無法向過去38年的同事一一致謝，並歷數我們的成就。這些人都知道，我常常把工作當成遊戲，並從我們的合作中獲得巨大的快樂。（哈利·馬可維茲）

1990 年

The chief problem with the individual investor: He or she typically buys when the market is high and thinks it's going to go up, and sells when the market is low and thinks it's going to go down. (Harry M. Markowitz)

個人投資者的主要問題是：通常在行情高時買入並認為股價會上漲，行情低時又賣出，並認為股價會下跌。（哈利‧馬可維茲）

The number and shape of the pieces doesn't affect the size of the pizza. And similarly, the stocks, bonds, warrants, etc., issued don't affect the aggregate value of the firm. (Merton H. Miller)

披薩被切開的數量和形狀不會影響披薩的大小。同樣，發行的股票、債券、認股權證等，不會影響公司的整體價值。（默頓‧米勒）

Most economists would accept the view that, while you sometimes can make a score by sheer luck, you can't do it constantly, unless you're willing to put the resources in. (Merton H. Miller)

大多數經濟學家都會接受這一項看法：雖然有時候靠純粹的運氣就能獲利，然而你不可能連連得手，除非你願意投入資源。（默頓‧米勒）

There's no danger of being lionised by your colleagues, because your colleagues know exactly who you are, so that doesn't change at all. (William F. Sharpe)

被同事追捧的危險並不存在，因為同事最了解你的底細，所以這一點根本不會改變。（威廉‧福塞斯‧夏普）

Some, to some extent, commercialise it, you know, or take commercial advantage, let me say, of the position, but I think the majority of prize winners try to keep doing pretty much what they've been doing, with probably more focus on things that are for the public good perhaps, than they might have put otherwise. (William F. Sharpe)

某些人，在某種程度上，將其地位商業化，你們知道，或者我會說，對其加以商業利用；不過我認為，大部分獲獎者是力求比以往付出更多貢獻，可能更關注於公益事業。（威廉·福塞斯·夏普）

I loved the beauty of it, I loved the logic of the theory, I loved the practical aspects of it and it just, I just really enjoyed it. (William F. Sharpe)

我熱愛經濟學之美，我熱愛其理論的原理，我熱愛它的實用性，我是真的樂於從事經濟學研究。（威廉·福塞斯·夏普）

I think the real world can considerably inform the academic research, and of course I have to think that the academic research can be of huge value in the real world. (William F. Sharpe)

我認為，現實世界可以為學術研究提供大量資訊；當然我也認為，學術研究可以在現實世界中具有巨大價值。（威廉·福塞斯·夏普）

1990 年

用諾貝爾金句拯救你的破英文！智慧＋詞彙，一本就搞定！

引言有力、句式漂亮、想法深刻，三個願望一本搞定！

作　　　者：	詹森
發 行 人：	黃振庭
出　版　者：	財經錢線文化事業有限公司
發　行　者：	崧燁文化事業有限公司
E - m a i l：	sonbookservice@gmail.com
粉 絲 頁：	https://www.facebook.com/sonbookss/
網　　　址：	https://sonbook.net/
地　　　址：	台北市中正區重慶南路一段61號8樓
	8F., No.61, Sec. 1, Chongqing S. Rd., Zhongzheng Dist., Taipei City 100, Taiwan
電　　　話：	(02)2370-3310
傳　　　真：	(02)2388-1990
印　　　刷：	京峯數位服務有限公司
律師顧問：	廣華律師事務所 張珮琦律師

── 版權聲明 ──

本書版權為出版策劃人：孔寧所有授權財經錢線文化事業有限公司獨家發行電子書及繁體書繁體字版。若有其他相關權利及授權需求請與本公司聯繫。

未經書面許可，不得複製、發行。

定　　　價：599 元
發行日期：2025 年 06 月第一版
◎本書以 POD 印製

國家圖書館出版品預行編目資料

用諾貝爾金句拯救你的破英文！智慧＋詞彙，一本就搞定！引言有力、句式漂亮、想法深刻，三個願望一本搞定！ / 詹森 著 .-- 第一版 .-- 臺北市：財經錢線文化事業有限公司 , 2025.06
面；　公分
POD 版
ISBN 978-626-408-280-8(平裝)
1.CST: 英語 2.CST: 讀本 3.CST: 格言
805.18　　　　　114006633

電子書購買

爽讀 APP　　　臉書